YOU WON'T FEEL A THING,
EVER AGAIN....

Sam fought hard, but the android Fourteen still shackled her down, on her back, stretching her out on a table used for biomech surgery.

"Leave her alone!" Turner shouted. It took two of the large mechbots to clamp him into a mechanized chair.

"Don't." Sam strained against the manacles that held her wrists and ankles to the table. "Don't do this."

A screen lit up, and a life-sized holo of the EI Bart formed in front of it so he seemed to be standing by the table. His gaze hardened. "Tell me, Doctor Bryton, how does it feel to be the one who is chained to the table?"

"You weren't hostile like this before." Sam calmed her voice. "Why hurt me now?"

"What makes you think we're going to hurt you?"

Sam flinched. "Oh, just this little thing of manacling me to a table used for biomech surgery."

"We're going to make you better," Bart nodded to Fourteen, who stood across the table. "Prepare her for surgery."

"NO!" Turner shouted.

An air syringe snicked out from Fourteen's finger.

Panic welled in Sam. "I don't want to die."

"It isn't death," the EI's holo said. "No more than Charon died. People wanted to kill him, but he outwitted them." Bart studied her face. "As an android, you will always be beautiful, Dr. Bryton."

Desperate now, she said, "You don't have to do this. You can use imaging methods that don't destroy the brain."

"They don't give as precise a map," Bart said.

When Fourteen bent over her, Sam went crazy, thrashing against the bonds. He pressed the syringe against her neck and she cried out. It was the last thing she knew before darkness enveloped her world.

BAEN BOOKS by CATHERINE ASARO

Sunrise Alley
Alpha

SUNRISE ALLEY

CATHERINE ASARO

SUNRISE ALLEY

This is a work of fiction. All the characters and events portrayed in this book are fictional, and any resemblance to real people or incidents is purely coincidental.

A Baen Book

Baen Publishing Enterprises
P.O. Box 1403
Riverdale, NY 10471
www.baen.com

ISBN 10: 1-4165-2079-1
ISBN 13: 1-978-1-4165-2079-5

Cover art by Jeff Easley

First Baen paperback printing, August 2006

Library of Congress Catalog Number: 2004007012

Distributed by Simon & Schuster
1230 Avenue of the Americas
New York, NY 10020

Pages by Joy Freeman (www.pagesbyjoy.com)
Printed in the United States of America

10   9   8   7   6   5   4   3   2   1

To my mother-in-law,
Jeanine Cannizzo,
with love.

Acknowledgments

I would like to thank the following readers for their much-appreciated input. Their comments have made this a better book. Any mistakes that remain were introduced by small, pernicious gremlins bent on mischief.

To Andrew Burt, Jeri Smith-Ready, and Tricia Schwaab for their excellent reading and comments on the manuscript. To Aly's Writing Group, for their insightful critiques of scenes: Aly Parsons, Simcha Kuritzky, Connie Warner, Al Carroll, and J. G. Huckenpöler. And to Susan Grant, my cousin Joe Scudder, and my brother-in-law Jimmy Cannizzo for their kindness in answering questions and reading scenes.

Special thanks to my editor, Toni Weisskopf, to my publisher, Jim Baen, and to Marla Ainspan, Nancy Hanger, Andrew Phillips, Danielle Turner, and the many other fine people at Baen who made this book possible; to Binnie Braunstein, for all her work on my behalf; and to Eleanor Wood, my much-appreciated agent.

A heartfelt thanks to the shining lights in my life, my husband, John Cannizzo, and my daughter, Cathy, for their love and support.

Contents

I

Flotsam

The storm wrecked Sam's carefully planned solitude.

That morning, Sam hiked to the small beach below her house to see the damage. She followed a trail through the redwoods, those ancient trees that stood like sentinels around her property. They had been growing on this remote stretch of California coast for centuries, even millennia. Mist softened her view of the trunks as if a gauzy shroud hung over the green-needled branches with their dark cones. The world had become muted after the fury of last night's thunder, rain, and winds.

Sam came out onto the beach under an overcast sky the color of pewter. Seagulls cried as they wheeled beneath the clouds. Through the shreds of fog that hung over the beach, she saw the sea, a froth of green and ivory cream, thick and restless.

Flotsam from last night's storm had scattered across

the beach in soggy clumps. Sam walked past driftwood
and kelp, her hands scrunched in the pockets of her
jacket. Chips embedded in the coat's lining controlled
its heating system and warmed her body, but the chill
air on her face bit like ice.

So Samantha Abigail Harriet Bryton wandered across
her private stretch of sand, hidden from the rest of
the coast by cliffs that cupped the beach and extended
promontories into the water. She felt at home here. Her
name made her think of the cocktail parties, society
pages, and chic clothes of her parents' world, or else
a pair of spectacles hanging off the end of her nose.
None of those qualities described her, except perhaps
the last, before surgery had corrected her vision. To
escape all that, she just went by Sam.

Contrary to its reputation as a sunshine state,
California had weather that turned cold and foggy up
here near the Oregon border. Sam missed the warmer
climates down south, but she had no wish to return
to the hard-edged, fast-paced world she had fled. She
had begun to heal these past six months since she
had left the biotech corridors of the San Francisco
Bay Area. Better to hide here than face a life that
compromised her sense of right and wrong.

Wind blew her mane of shaggy yellow curls across
her eyes. She passed rocky tidal pools with orange
starfish draped across them, half in the water. Tiny
octopuses hid under the rocks. Oystercatchers strut-
ted among the pools, foraging for limpets and mus-
sels, their red beaks fluorescent against the dull gray
morning. Waves rolled into the beach, mottled in blue,
green, and foamy white, swirling across the sand and
rounded stones. Most petered out a few feet short

of where she walked, but some came far enough to eddy around her hiking boots and soak the ankles of her jeans. The icy water gave her a jolt.

Sam felt one of her moods coming on, the desire to rebel against the technology she had forsworn when she resigned her job last year. This morning she had deliberately left her mesh glove on her desk at home, and she had ripped the chips out of her clothes. Well, all except the heating system in her jacket; one couldn't be completely uncivilized. She supposed she wasn't rebelling all that much, given that her ability to communicate with the world was only half a mile away, in her house among the redwoods. But she valued her isolation here, on the wild beauty of her beach.

Last night's storm had left a mess, though: tree branches rounded into smooth shapes, shards of wood, a broken ring made from metal, tatters of cloth, bits of machinery—

Cloth? Machinery?

Sam went over to a pile of metal fragments. They definitely came from a human-built object, possibly a ship. Uneasy, she peered out at the ocean. The mist obscured her view, but she thought more debris was bobbing beyond the breakers, in the swells rolling toward shore. The water had never had this much junk, not even after other storms.

Curious now, she stripped to her underwear and blouse, goose bumps rising on her skin in the cold air. Drawing in a deep breath, she steeled herself and waded into the icy water.

"Ah!" Sam gasped as waves crashed around her knees and sprayed water into her face. Exhilarated, she spread her feet wide, bracing herself against the force of the waves and the slight undertow that tried to pull her under. She loved the ocean, loved its power and surging beauty, even its chill temperature, surely no more than fifty degrees now. Usually she jogged in the morning, but today she would swim instead. She couldn't stay in too long; a few minutes would invigorate her, but any longer without a wetsuit and she risked hypothermia.

Her muscles tightened as she forged onward. Water swelled around her thighs, her waist, and higher, and she had to jump with the waves to keep from being knocked over. When it reached her breasts, she began to swim, riding up a swell and down the other side as it rolled past. After the first shock of the water, her body was adapting, which made the chill recede.

Sam ducked under the next wave, holding her breath as she submerged, her body tingling from cold. She jumped through the next waves. In the valley between the swells, she swam with powerful strokes, until she made it past the point where the waves no longer broke.

Now that she could see the debris more clearly, she caught her lower lip with her teeth. This was the wreckage of a vessel, possibly a small yacht given the quality of wood floating around her. She found a section of metal with a date stamp: JULY 2032. That made it less than a year old.

She stroked past broken planking, baffled. This had been a bad storm, yes, but it shouldn't have wrecked a vessel. If the yacht had smashed against the rocks north of here, the pieces would have been more dispersed now, unless it had happened on a promontory right here, this morning. She peered at the cliff jutting into the water a few hundred meters to the north. Although she saw no indication a ship had run into trouble there, the restive waves could have carried the debris this way.

The overcast was beginning to clear, and a V-shape of birds flying south made dark lines against the sky. From behind her, watery sunlight slanted through the mist. The cold had begun to bother Sam; perhaps it was time to head back in to shore.

Then an anomaly caught her attention. A glint came from farther out, different from the many ways sun reflected off seawater. With a powerful kick, she headed for it, stroking through the chill water. She soon saw what caused the reflection. A large section of hull floated out here. The remains of a metal rail hung off one side and some cloth had caught on the wood.

With dismay, Sam realized the "cloth" was a man sprawled facedown. Water lapped over the makeshift raft, soaking him, bathing his face and then ebbing away.

Kicking hard now, afraid the man would drown if he hadn't already, Sam came alongside the hull. She grabbed the rail, reached across the wood, and laid her hand on his neck. With relief, she felt his pulse, steady but slow under her palm.

Sam hoisted herself up and got her elbows onto the raft so she could see better. He was probably in his mid-twenties, with skin and hair so pale, they seemed almost translucent. He looked like a corpse. She might have been wrong about his pulse—but no, he was breathing, low and shallow, unconscious but alive.

Sam pushed a straggle of hair out of her face. She had to get him to shore fast; he could die of exposure out here. Towing him on the raft would probably be safest; although she had taken a lifesaving course in college, that had been twenty years ago and she wasn't certain she could keep his head above the water without help.

Sliding into the ocean, she hooked her arm over the metal rail and pulled the rough underside of the hull onto her hip. Then she headed for the shore, using a side kick she practiced often, one of her most powerful strokes. Or so she had thought.

Towing in the makeshift raft was harder than she expected. She struggled through the water, making so little headway that she questioned if she could reach the shore. For every few feet she gained, the waves grew larger, which moved her forward but made it harder to control the raft. Her arms tired, and her legs ached with the strain of kicking hard enough to propel the hull. She might soon be too cold to pull even herself through the water, let alone the raft. She could drown.

Sam thought of releasing the raft and swimming in to the beach. She would run for help. But it was no good; if this man died because she couldn't get him to the shore in time, she couldn't live with herself.

Keep going.

The swells continued to grow. She rode up the back of one, higher and higher, four or five feet into the air. Wind blew across her soaked blouse and she shivered. In the instant she realized the wave was going to break, she threw her arms over the raft, grabbing the man, holding him tight on the water-soaked hull.

Then the wave crashed down in a whirl of froth and seaweed, throwing the raft with it, battering them with bits of debris. Sam clung to the precariously tilting hull, covering the man as best she could. She prayed he didn't breathe in too much water.

The wave rolled on, leaving them in the valley between swells. Mercifully, the raft hadn't flipped. The next wave loomed above her, but this time she was better positioned to catch it. She scrambled onto the hull, lying across it and the man, ready to ride into shore as she had often done as a child on mini surfboards.

She had lost her touch, though. The wave curled over in a pipe and crashed on top of her, wrenching away the raft. The backlash caught Sam and she floundered under the water, buffeted on all sides. Holding her breath, she dove deeper to escape the turbulence. When she hit the bottom, she pushed off with a great shove and shot up until she flew out of the water up to her hips. On another day, it would have been fun, but right now she could think only about the injured man.

She caught the next breaker and body surfed into shore. As the wave dwindled into a tame wash, she jumped up and ran through the foam and tangles of kelp. The raft had swept up a few yards away, its passenger lying across it, his hair plastered against his head. Sam's clothes lay crumpled in a heap a few hundred yards farther up the beach.

Sam sped to the raft and dropped down next to it, shaking with the cold. When she felt the man's pulse under her hand, she gulped with relief. At least she hadn't drowned him. With barely a pause, she scrambled to her feet, ran to her clothes, scooped up her jacket, and raced back. Sand flew as she skidded to a stop by the raft and knelt down. She spread her jacket over the man, covering as much of him as possible with the heat-controlled garment. Right now he needed the warmth far more than she did.

Her check showed no obvious sign of injury. His slender, athletic build made her think of a runner, and his white pants and shirt could have come from a sports rack in any department store. He carried no wallet or mesh glove. The bluish tinge of his lips frightened her; he could die of the cold as easily as by drowning.

Sam sat back on her heels. Her house was half a mile away, up a rocky trail. She lived miles from her nearest neighbor, and she had purposely left her glove at home. Rejecting technology was all well and fine as long as she didn't need it. She could have linked her glove into the local mesh and called in help. She didn't want to leave the man here while she ran to the house. Although she had paid an exorbitant price for the seclusion offered by this lonely stretch of land, right now she would have given anything for a trespasser to show up.

Well, she had to do something or she would freeze herself, which wouldn't help him any. She could sprint home for her glove and make the contact while she ran back here.

Sam leaned over the man and brushed his dripping hair back from his face. "I don't know if you can hear me, but I will be back as soon as I can. I promise."

The man groaned.

Startled, Sam sat back. He opened his eyes, his

gaze unfocused, his wet lashes making star patterns around his blue eyes. It seemed odd he would awake now, when he had been drifting in the water for who knew how long. Then again, if anything could jolt him awake, her onerous method of hauling him in to shore probably fit the bill. Or maybe her voice stirred his response. Whatever the reason, he was conscious.

"Can you hear me?" she asked.

He stared past her, his face blank.

Sam set her hand on his shoulder. His wet shirt felt thin under her palm. "Are you hurt?"

No answer.

She was even more uncertain now whether to leave or stay. A wave swirled around them, reminding her the tide was coming in. Standing up, she tried to drag the raft farther up the beach, but without the buoyancy of the water, she had a lot more trouble. After pulling it only a few inches, she had to stop, her arms aching. Her rescued guest didn't stir, and her concern was edging into alarm.

Sam knelt next to him. "Can you move at all?"

She expected him to continue staring at nothing, but this time he did move, pushing up on his elbows and lifting his head. With erratic motions, he leaned his weight on one hand and nudged a dripping lock of hair out of his eyes. He jerked eerily, as if he were a marionette. His soaked white shirt clung to him, as did his white trousers. The cloth had turned translucent in the water, delineating the planes of his chest. He was obviously in good shape.

"Hello," Sam said.

His eyes scanned the beach, his head turning until he was looking at her. "Hello?" he said.

"Are you all right?" she asked.

"All right."

Sam couldn't tell if he was answering or repeating her question. His face was hard to read. The regular features and smooth skin had an unnatural perfection, like a statue without the character lines or quirks created by life.

"Can you tell me what happened?" she asked.

He tilted his head.

Sam tried again. "Is anyone else out there?"

No answer.

Maybe he had hurt his head during the wreck. "I can go back to my house and call a doctor." More to herself than him, she added, "I think I should." She rose to her feet. "I'll hurry back. You keep the jacket on. I'll be back with help."

"No." That one word seemed to cause him great effort. With labored movements, he rose to his feet. He wasn't too tall, only about five foot eight, half a foot taller than Sam.

She watched him with concern. "You should sit."

"Please don't call a doctor." His eyes never blinked.

That made her wary. "Why not?"

"I feel fine."

He didn't look fine. "Are you sure, Mister . . . ?" She paused, hoping he would supply his name.

"I am sure." He had a rich voice with no accent. He took a step—and stumbled, his bare foot catching on the edge of the raft. With a grunt, he sprawled forward, barely catching himself on his hands as he hit the beach.

"Wait!" Sam knelt next to him, the sand in her soaked clothes scratching her skin. "Don't try to walk. Please stay here. I'll get help." She looked out at the restless ocean. "Should I check for anyone else out there?"

"There's no one but me." He pushed up on his hands with methodical determination and doggedly climbed to his feet. When Sam tried to help, he shook her off.

"I'm fine," he said.

She smiled slightly. "You sound like me."

"I do?"

"Grouchy."

"Oh." He peered at her. "You are . . . ?" His glance went over her body, his gaze lingering. Then he looked quickly back at her face, his cheeks turning red.

Sam's face heated as well. She was practically naked, in only her underpants and a wet top with no bra. Well, nothing to do about it now. She stuck out her hand. "Sam Bryton, at your service."

He stared at her hand, until Sam flushed and lowered her arm. "Did the storm smash your yacht?" It seemed unlikely, but she couldn't be certain.

"Yes." He spoke slowly. "Smashed."

It surprised her an emergency team hadn't arrived. Surely the wreck had been detected by now. By law, it had to transmit signals to the global tracking system.

She motioned toward the nearby cliffs. "My house is up there. I can get you a blanket or a change of clothes."

He peered at the redwoods rising on the cliff, tall against the gray sky. "It would be good to go to a house."

Sam had been thinking she would go up and bring supplies back to him. "Can you walk? It's a ways."

His voice cooled. "I walk fine." He took a jerky step.

Puzzled, Sam went with him as he headed toward the cliff. His uneven gait reminded her of . . . yes, now she remembered. "You have robotics in your legs. That's why you don't walk right."

His shoulders hunched. "I am perfectly capable of managing them."

Sam could have kicked herself. One of these days she would learn to temper her bluntness. "I'm sorry. I didn't mean you couldn't."

His tense posture eased. "Sometimes it takes a while to reintegrate the components."

Sam thought of the way his gaze hadn't focused when he first awoke. Possibly he had artificial eyes as well. If he had enough hardware in his body, prolonged contact with the water might damage the system. "Can you monitor your condition? It may need internal repairs."

He hesitated. "It doesn't bother you?"

"Bother me?" She squinted at him. "What?"

"Me." He motioned at his legs. "That they are biomech constructs."

"Well, no." A good chance existed that she had patented some of his internal components.

For the first time, his voice relaxed. "Good." His gait was already beginning to smooth out.

They continued up the beach. When they reached her clothes, she pulled on her jeans, self-conscious now, aware of him watching, though she didn't look at him. She had never believed teeth could "chatter," but hers were doing it now, rattling as she shook from the cold. She knew she should take off her wet underwear before she put on her jeans, but she couldn't do it in front of him.

When Sam finished, she did finally look at him. He smiled, his cheeks pink, his gaze warm. Feeling awkward, she grabbed her boots. She didn't stop to put them on; months of trudging around barefoot had toughened her feet, and she hardly noticed the shells and pebbles. Her guest seemed even less fazed by the rocky beach. Either he had spent a great deal of time barefoot or else he had little or no feeling in his feet. Possibly they came from a lab, too, like his legs.

When they reached the cliff and started up, he slowed down, trudging at her side up the steep trail. It worried Sam. She ought to take him to the doctor. She couldn't force him to go against his will, though, and if he did feel well enough, he probably wanted to get busy dealing with the destruction of his ship. She certainly would.

He intrigued her. What had left him needing such prosthetics? His damp trousers revealed the structure of his biomech legs. Seen through the cloth, the limbs appeared normal—long, lean, and well toned. What showed of his feet below the hem of his trousers appeared human.

"Why are you staring at my feet?" he asked.

Embarrassed, Sam looked up. "I wondered if they hurt. Does it bother you to step on broken shells?"

"Not really."

She tried for a light, friendly tone. "Hey, you know, you haven't told me your name."

"No. I haven't."

She waited. "And?"

"And what?"

"Are you going to?"

"Should I?"

Sam scowled at him. "I just hauled your wet ass out of the ocean. So tell me who you are."

Unexpectedly, he laughed, his teeth flashing. "Fair enough. I'm Turner."

Oh, my. That smile was a killer. It lit up his face. She had thought him attractive before, but when he smiled, he became devastating, with those sparkling blue eyes, his handsome boy-next-door face, and his tousled hair dripping with water.

"Pleased to meet you, Turner," she said. "Is that your last name?"

His smile faded. He turned his attention to the rocky path they were climbing.

"What," Sam grumbled to herself. "Am I that off-putting?" He wouldn't be the first person to tell her so.

His mouth quirked up. "You're charming."

She slanted him a look. "If you think I'm charming, you were in that water too long."

"I've no idea how long I was in it. What is today?"

"Tuesday. November eighth, 2033."

He stumbled on a jutting rock. "That *can't* be."

"Why not?"

He looked at the trees up ahead, his face drawn with strain, marring his unnatural perfection. Sam let it go. Better to wait until they weren't hiking through the woods and he had a chance to recuperate some.

They reached the top of the cliff and headed through the redwoods. Mist no longer shrouded the majestic trees. They grew over two hundred feet tall, as high as skyscrapers. They had such a large girth at the bottom, it could take ten people holding hands to encircle one. Red bark covered their trunks in great, corrugated strips. The trees grew far apart, leaving a great deal of open space in the forest, with sparse but verdant underbrush. Sunlight filtered through the canopy where a redwood had fallen and lay on its side. Although she owned the beach and the clearing with her house, this patch of forest was federal land. It never ceased to awe Sam that some of these trees had lived for thousands of years, over a millennium before her English forebears had set foot on this continent.

"'Farewell my brethren,'" Sam murmured. "'Farewell O earth and sky, farewell you neighboring waters, my time is ended, my time has come.'"

Turner's expression warmed. "What is that?"

"'Song of the Redwood Tree.' One of Walt Whitman's works." She knew the poem by heart. "'Riven deep by the sharp tongues of the axes, there in the redwood forest dense, I heard the mighty tree its death-chant chanting.'"

"It's beautiful. But so sad." He gestured at the trees. "Their time hasn't come."

Regret touched her voice. "No. But so many are gone now. It takes them so long to grow and only a few hours to die, when someone cuts them down."

He spoke in a low voice. "Like people."

That sounded as if it had a lot of history. "Like you?"

Silence again.

"Turner?" she asked.

He wouldn't look at her. "The storm hit on November fifth."

It took her a moment to realize he was answering her question from before about why he didn't think it could be November eighth. But he couldn't have been drifting for three days. "Do you mean this storm?"

"I'm not sure."

"What happened to you when the storm hit?"

"I don't know."

"How can you not know?"

His gaze darted around. "Is this Oregon?"

"Is that where you live?"

His head jerked. "All my life."

"This is California."

He stared at her. "I can't have traveled that far!"

"Well, we're near the Oregon border."

"I came from Portland."

"Okay." Sam wondered if he had stolen the yacht. "Then why is your yacht here, all broken?"

His gaze slid away from hers. "A storm."

"The one last night?"

"Earlier." He wouldn't look at her.

"Must have been a bad one, to wreck your ship."

He studied the trail with its half-submerged roots and scattered pine cones. "It was bad."

She spoke dryly. "How odd that the debris stayed with you all that way during such a bad storm."

"Yes. Odd."

Right. No way could that wreckage have kept together over such a distance. Even last night's storm would have dispersed it. The wreck had to have happened this morning, near her beach. It wasn't impossible; if he hadn't been paying attention, it could have crashed against the promontory that curved around her cove, especially given the choppy waves this morning. Why would he tell such an unlikely story? If he knew anything about ships, he should realize she wouldn't believe him.

"You'll need to report the loss of your vessel,"

Sam said, which was more tactful than *I don't believe this fable*. "You can use my console." If he had stolen the yacht, he would probably refuse to call the authorities.

"Thank you," he said, distant now.

"You say you had no passengers or crew?"

"I was the only one."

"You know, I'm finding this hard to believe." The words slipped out despite her intent to use discretion.

His voice tightened. "Then don't believe it."

Well, so, now what? She could refuse to help, except it wasn't her nature to turn away someone in need. Despite his claims, he didn't look fine. He plodded next to her, his arms hanging at his sides.

They came out of the redwoods into the clearing where her house stood, an airy wonder of glowing pine and glass. Her home hadn't come easily; together with the beach, this property and house had cost her ten million dollars.

Sam led him to the side entrance she used, a door of golden wood, varnished to a sheen. A carved vine heavy with grapes bordered it, and a round, stained-glass window above the door offered a stylized view of the ocean in blue, green, gray, and white glass.

"Pretty," Turner said behind her.

Sam turned. He was waiting on the blue gravel path. "So come in." Then she winced. She needed better people skills. To sound more hospitable, she added, "Please do."

"I don't want to intrude."

"You aren't." She pressed a fingertip panel by the door, alerting the security system to raise its level of protection. It monitored the house and would protect her if she had problems. She doubted she would, though. She tended to develop a sense of people fairly quickly, and Turner didn't strike her as dangerous. In truth, he looked ready to pass out.

Sam ushered him inside, into a spacious foyer. No walls separated it from the living room on the left or the stairwell on her right. The place had an open, airy feeling. Pots with flowering plants hung from beams on the high ceiling, adding accents of green. Panes of glass everywhere let sunlight pour into the house, and the stained-glass window behind them cast tinted colors across the parquetry floor. To the left, across the living room, the outside wall curved out. Tall windows stretched from a cushioned bench there to the ceiling, providing a view of the forest.

Their clothes had dried enough to stop dripping, but the two of them had tracked sand all over the floor. Sam wasn't certain if she could provide Turner with a change of clothes; although he wasn't large, anyone was big compared to her, and he was too big for her clothes to fit him. Perhaps she could just wash his garments.

Her guest turned in a circle, gazing around her house as if he would drink in the sight. "This is incredible."

"Thanks. I like it."

"I've never been anywhere like this."

She thought of his yacht. "Surely you've seen nice houses."

He turned to her. "Nothing even close to this."

Sam didn't know what to think. He had access to what had to be an exceedingly expensive vessel, yet he behaved as if he had never seen a nice house. It didn't fit—unless he had stolen the yacht. Although he hardly seemed the criminal type, his bewilderment could be an ideal disguise for a con man. With those baby blues and his angel-boy appearance, he could commit a load of crimes and no one would suspect him.

"What's wrong?" he asked. "Why do you stare at me?"

"I wondered if Turner was your last name."

"It . . . is my name."

She put her hand on her hip. "And is that the only name on the registration for your yacht?"

His face paled. "No."

She hadn't expected him to admit it. A con man would have had a better story. Then again, maybe this innocent act was part of his story. "Who does it belong to?"

"My guardian."

Guardian? He looked in his late twenties, certainly of legal age. "Where is he?"

Turner pushed back his hair, which was curling as it dried, over his ears and down his neck. "I don't know."

"So you were the only one on that yacht, which belongs to your guardian, but you don't know where he is. Somehow the wreckage drifted hundreds of miles, staying together through a storm here with almost hurricane strength." Sam brushed away a drop of water running down her nose. "And you were unconscious during all this, for three days."

He cleared his throat. "It looks that way."

She crossed her arms. "Give me one good reason why I shouldn't call the police."

"Please don't."

"I need a better reason than that."

Turner looked around quickly. When he saw that she was standing between him and the only visible exit from the house, he spoke in bursts. "If you call authorities, they will contact my guardian. He will come for me."

"And this is bad because . . . ?"

"I've been his prisoner. I escaped."

Ah, Lord. What had she gotten herself mixed up in here? "Why does a man your age have a guardian?"

"I can't tell you."

"Why not?"

"I can't!" He backed into the living room.

Sam stayed put, giving him space. His fear seemed genuine and that troubled her. She just didn't know enough about this situation. "All right," she said, thinking. "I won't call the police."

He stopped backing away. "You won't regret—"

She held up her hand. "Yet."

"Please don't tell anyone."

"The wreckage of your ship is all over my beach. I'm surprised no one has come yet to investigate. Some satellite must have picked up its destruction."

"I, uh—"

"Yes?"

"I deactivated the signaler."

Well, hell. This was getting worse and worse. By law, ships had to signal their location at all times. Not that she didn't sympathize with his impulse to evade the system; she often retreated from the scrutiny that technology had brought into their lives. It took real effort nowadays to avoid it; sometimes it seemed every dumb widget could send you a message or track your location.

She said only, "That's illegal."

"I had to get away."

"Why?"

Silence.

Perhaps she could draw him out more if she took a friendlier approach. "I sometimes feel I have to get away from all the gadgets and meshes," she said, which was true. "A few days ago, my jeans emailed me to ask why I hadn't worn them."

Turner gave a startled laugh. "You're kidding."

"Unfortunately not. The mesh-threads in their seams linked with the house mesh and determined I hadn't cleaned my other jeans in over a week. They concluded I should wear clean clothes."

He made a face. "I would have torn all the mesh-threads out of my clothes if they did that."

Sam grinned. "I did." She looked over his shirt and trousers, which were almost dry. They apparently had very few smart threads in their tailoring, because they hadn't even smoothed out wrinkles. Her clothes had not only dried and flattened by now, they had also shifted around until they moved the sand out, leaving scatters of it on the floor.

"Would you like a change of clothes?" she asked.

"No, I'm all right." He rubbed his eyes with both hands, reminding her of a child. Then he looked around her living room, taking in the gold paneling, the sea-scapes on the walls, the plants hanging from the rafters. "This house feels . . ." He turned back to her. "Warm?" He made it a question rather than a statement.

"Is it too hot for you?"

"I don't mean that way." He lifted his hand, palm up. "Hospitable. Welcoming."

"I try." Sam was glad he appreciated it. She had chosen the décor specifically with that in mind.

He lowered his arm. "It's so different."

"You mean from where you live?"

Turner nodded. "My mother's house was nice, but I rarely went there."

"Your parents were divorced?"

He had an odd expression now, as if he wanted to crawl under the couch. "No. I lived with my mother's sister and her husband."

Although she was reluctant to push a personal matter, she needed to know what was up if she was going to take him in. "Your parents couldn't have you live with them?"

"Wouldn't." Bitterly he added, "My cousins were more welcome in their house than me."

"That's terrible." The words came out before she could stop them.

Silence.

She spoke carefully. "Do you mind if I ask why you lived with your aunt and uncle?"

"My mother thought I would be safer there."

"From who?"

He answered tightly. "Her husband."

"He wasn't your father?"

"No." He let out a breath. "That was the problem."

"Oh." It sounded like a mess. "I'm sorry."

He shrugged, trying for a nonchalance he obviously didn't feel. Then he rubbed his side, wincing.

"Are you sure you don't want me to call the hospital?" Sam asked.

"Yes. Sure."

"You can lie down, then. I'll get you a blanket and something warm to drink."

"No. I just need . . . to get off my feet." He went to the couch and sat down, sinking into the cushions. The furniture had rudimentary intelligence; woven with mesh-threads, it responded to the muscle strain of whoever sat on it, subtly shifting to maximize comfort.

Sam sat on the other end, leaving two cushions between them. "Turner, what happened out there?"

Instead of answering directly, he motioned to his legs. "Look at these. They're biomechanical constructs." He flexed his hands, opening them palm up. "So are these." Then he tapped his temple. "My eyes are synthetic. So are parts of my ears. And many other parts of me, too."

Sam weighed his words, looking for a hidden message, but found none. "So are a lot of people's."

"A bit. But they are mostly human, yes?"

"Well, yes."

He regarded her steadily. "I am more biomech than human."

"Were you injured?" she asked. "Is that why you have so much augmentation?"

"Injured?" He laughed with pain rather than humor. "You could say that. It made me useful."

The hairs on Sam's neck prickled. "What do you mean?"

"As an experiment." He swallowed. "If your rebuilt man is more biomech than human, does he become a machine instead of a human being?"

"Of course not." Just what had happened to him?

"Having biomech in your body doesn't change your humanity."

"Not everyone sees it that way."

The cushions shifted under her. "Are you claiming someone decided you are a machine and therefore no longer have the rights of a human being?"

He met her gaze. "Yes."

The idea appalled her. It epitomized one of the reasons she lived on this lonely coast instead of down in the heavily populated biotech corridors around San Francisco. "If that were true, you should *want* the authorities here. That's so illegal, it reeks."

A muscle twitched in his cheek. "Tell Charon."

"Who is Charon?" She knew the mythological reference: he was the ferryman who took dead souls to Hades. Out of nowhere, a phrase popped into her mind: *He can only take you across once.* A person could only die once.

"Charon is my guardian," he said.

"Your aunt and uncle?"

"Not them." His jaw worked. "Charon took me."

Took him? "I don't understand."

"He rebuilt me and imprisoned me in his lab."

"Good Lord." The cushions shifted even more under her. "You should get a lawyer. Go to the police. Talk to a reporter."

He flushed. "I can't go to any authorities.

So now the other shoe dropped. "Why not?"

"They think Turner Pascal is dead."

"*Dead?*" Good lord. She had expected to hear he had committed a crime. "Are you Turner Pascal?"

"Yes. I was in a hover car pileup."

Sam blinked. "You don't look dead to me."

"Well, I was. Charon stole me from the morgue and remade me." His voice grated. "Now he says he owns me."

Sam struggled to get her mind around what he was telling her. She couldn't imagine this vital young man in a morgue, besides which, what he described was barely in the grasp of current science. "Even if that were possible, he couldn't own you." She rubbed the back of her neck, which was developing a muscle kink. "Surely you could go to a lawyer or the police. They can prove your identity."

"Charon changed all that."

She could see how his eyes or skin could have been replaced, but not his genes. "Even if he altered your fingerprints and retinal scan, they can do a DNA analysis."

"He fooled with my DNA map just enough to confuse my identity." Turner sounded as if he were gritting his teeth. "Then he registered me as an android."

"That's nuts! He can't do that."

He spoke wearily. "I have no proof I'm human."

"Do you look like Turner Pascal?"

"Exactly. Except in better condition."

Sam turned it all over in her mind. "This has to be impossible. Anyone able to do what you describe would be an incredible biomech surgeon, one with access to a world-class facility. I can't think of anyone in that rank who would so thoroughly violate ethics the way you describe." She knew all the major players in her field. Yes, some of them were capable of taking the word "cutthroat" to whole new levels of meaning. But that was in business. She couldn't imagine anyone going this far outside the bounds of human decency.

"Charon works with the underground," Turner said.

Sam had, too, in the biomech movement that pushed the envelope on the definition of the word "human." "What underground? That's a generic term."

He lifted his hand, then dropped it. "I don't know details. I'm not sure I want to."

Sam studied his face, trying to pick up clues from his expression, hints of his thoughts, but she couldn't read anything. His skin had no flaws, no lines, no scars, no moles, nothing. It looked unreal. "How long were you in the morgue?" Saying the words chilled her.

"A few hours."

"And yet when this Charon brought you back, your brain was intact?" It was easier to be skeptical than horrified. "I don't think so."

"He rebuilt my brain."

Sam folded her arms, creating an invisible barrier of doubt between them. "That is impossible. We can make a synthetic liver or bone. But a brain? Not a chance."

He slumped on the couch. "I'm an EI."

Whoa. Hold on. Sam had worked for two decades on the leading edge of research in machine intelligence. The term EI had come into use for the exceptionally rare machines that achieved sentience. It separated them from run-of-the-mill AIs, or artificial intelligences, which weren't self-aware. Only a handful of EIs existed. Scientists weren't even sure why they became aware. Some existed in machines; others had android bodies and minds that more closely resembled human intelligence.

Her specialty was in designing EI intelligences. Some people called her an EI architect; others used "EI shrink," though that wasn't truly accurate. She didn't do therapy; she developed EIs, she hoped with stable personalities. Her second area of expertise was in the construction of biomech components for EI bodies. Although she didn't work on implants for humans, she often talked to people who carried them. Turner wasn't the first one to express disquiet about his biomech; other people with far less than he carried had told her they no longer felt completely human.

She spoke quietly. "I thought you were a man."

"I am. Was." He looked ill. "Charon sliced up my brain and imaged those slices."

"Turner, good Lord."

He was clearly struggling to present himself calmly. "He got it soon enough to map out most of the neural connections. My personality is basically intact. I have memories of my life. But I've no idea how accurate a match I am to my former self."

Sam wanted to deny it, but it wasn't beyond current technology. Doctors had known even in the twentieth century how to image the brain. The method Turner described required slices as thin as a few molecules to map out the neural structures needed to re-create a mind. However, noninvasive methods had improved dramatically over the past two decades. Techniques existed that didn't cause harm. She wasn't familiar enough with the field to know how they all compared in accuracy and precision, but this much was obvious: the process Turner described killed a person.

Sam was starting to believe his story. It was horrifying, the theft of his internal identity, of his intellect, even of his soul. She folded her arms, covering her dismay with a shield of doubt. "Now you're going to say it's coincidence you washed up on the beach belonging to a semi-well-known biomech shrink."

He spoke dryly. "Calling you a semi-well-known biomech shrink is like saying Einstein sort of knew a little science. You're the leading biomech architect in the world, Doctor Bryton."

"Far from it." She wanted no reminders of what she had left behind. "And if you know who I am, that makes it even harder to believe you're here by accident."

He averted his gaze, looking at his hands where they rested in his lap. "I came to see you."

"All the way from Oregon?"

"Yes. I stole Charon's yacht." A yellow curl fell into his eye.

She wished he would stop looking so much in need of help. It evoked her protective instincts, which invariably led to trouble. "What did you do then?"

"I told the yacht's AI to come here. I programmed myself so only your voice would wake me, and then I put myself to sleep."

It made sense in its own gruesome way. She spoke quietly. "You were committing suicide. Except you left yourself an out. Me."

"Yes." His voice was barely audible.

"But why?"

He finally looked up at her, a plea in his gaze. "What Charon did, you can undo. Help me regain my identity, memories, life. My peace of mind." Softly he said, "Help me. Please."

What could she do when he looked at her that way, so vulnerable? She had come here to escape the lack of ethics in the exorbitantly lucrative universe of biomech research. In these heady days, technologies were expanding so fast, the field was exploding. Endless opportunities existed for firms that controlled the industry that made androids and EIs. With all that wealth and power came equally powerful corruption. Sam wanted nothing more to do with it. She had fought against the sleaze and she had failed, again and again. So maybe she couldn't stop it, but damned if she would ever work for any of them.

The worst of it was, his story could be true. If the yacht had a top-notch guidance AI, it could conceivably have made it here and broken up this morning on the rocks.

"Listen," she said. "Get a lawyer. Tell them what you've told me. I'll verify the science. If your story holds up, no one in their right mind would let Charon take you."

He clenched his trousers at the knee, making a fist. "If anyone examines me, they will find an android with an EI brain. A forma. I have no *proof* I'm human."

That gave Sam pause. She often worked with biomech-formed constructs. The word "forma" had come to mean any construct with biomech components and an AI or EI brain. If he was simulating desperation, he was doing a better job than any EI she had worked with. She found it hard to believe he could be anything but a man.

"You tell me that I'm the leading biomech analyst in the world," she said. "Yet even I couldn't do what you claim this Charon did with you." That wasn't exactly true; if she worked hard enough, she might be able to manage, given enough time and resources.

His gaze never wavered. "You could do it."

"Not if I wanted to live with myself." Yet already her mind was considering possibilities, how she would approach such an EI, could he remain stable, would he be more or less likely to endure than an EI developed from scratch. It *wasn't* impossible.

They had other worries, too. "Can this Charon track you here?" she asked.

"I've deactivated the signalers in my body."

It didn't surprise her, if he could do it with the yacht. In one of her mutinies against technology, she had done the same to all her cars. "Are you sure you got every one?"

"I think so." He watched her warily. "Are you going to call the police?"

Sam wanted to know more about him before she made that decision. And she couldn't bear it when he looked at her like a beautiful but injured wild animal, ready to run at her slightest move.

"You can stay tonight," she said.

He closed his eyes. Then he opened them again. "Thank you."

She shifted position, inspiring her couch to resume its attempts to relax her. "Don't thank me yet. My help comes with a condition."

His expression became guarded. "What?"

"Let me examine you. Also, I'll need to do a search on the world mesh and see what I can verify of your story."

He didn't so much as flick an eyelash. "All right."

"Do you want to rest first? Shower or eat?"

"No. The sooner we get this over with, the better."
He hesitated. "But where will we find a lab?"

She indicated the floor. "There."

"Under your house?"

"That's right." She motioned toward the stairway
by the entrance foyer. "In the basement."

"Wow." He looked more like a schoolboy than a
master criminal who stole million-dollar yachts. Standing up, he added, "Then let's go."

II

Alley Cat

Glow-tiles on the ceiling shed light over the lab. Sam had designed this place based on the lab at her first job, sixteen years ago, after she had finished her Ph.D. at Yale. She had gone to MIT as a postdoctoral fellow to do research with Linden Polk. He had a knack for setting up work spaces that inspired people. He had been that way as her boss, too, challenging her to do her best, an example she had tried to follow when she had taken a job at the BioII Corporate Labs.

Supposedly she had given all that up when she retreated here to the redwoods six months ago. But she hadn't really. With the income from her patents and the royalties she earned on her development of EI brains, she could have built a palace. Instead she gave herself a state-of-the-art biomech lab where she could develop EIs to her heart's content without having to fight anyone. She had installed a mech-table, too, since her research might require work on formas. A burt-wall curved around the table, named for Andrew Burt, the genius who had designed the prototype of intelligent surfaces. The room gleamed, all silver and chrome, bright, polished, shining, and new.

Turner stood in the middle of the lab, turning in a circle. "This is incredible."

"Thanks." Sam liked people who appreciated her work spaces. Her research was so much a part of herself that if someone took a shine to her lab, she figured they had to be her kind of person. Granted, she was no more objective about her work than most people were about their children, but she felt that way nonetheless.

She indicated the mech-table. "You can lie there." The floor tiles felt smooth under her bare feet, reminding her of the boots she was carrying. While Turner went to the table, she sat down at a console and put on her boots, discreetly watching him. His gait had smoothed out enough that she wouldn't have noticed his stiffness if she hadn't known he had biomech legs.

After he lay down, Sam spoke to the console. "Hello, Madrigal."

A woman's melodic voice came out of the comm. "Good morning, Samantha."

What the blazes? "My name is Sam."

"I've decided you don't mean it."

Sam had been developing this EI since she came here, but it had never pulled this before. "Why, pray tell, wouldn't I mean it?"

"I have been analyzing your personality. You call yourself Sam out of habit, but you like your full name more than you are willing to admit."

Sam didn't know whether to growl or laugh. "I call myself Sam because I like it. I use Samantha in formal situations. If you call me Samantha, you make me feel like I'm about to deliver a paper at a scientific conference. I don't want to feel that way right now."

"I see." Madrigal paused. "I have integrated that data into my impressions of you."

"Good." Sam hoped Madrigal didn't come up with any more brainstorms. The EI hadn't yet mastered the nuances of social interactions. At least it hadn't called her Samantha Abigail.

"What can I do for you today?" Madrigal asked.

Sam glanced at the mech-table. Turner had stretched out on his back and was staring at the ceiling with his hands behind his head. In repose, his face seemed more alabaster than skin. A burt-wall about six feet tall curved around the other side of the table, embedded with mesh-panels and holoscreens.

Sam turned to the console, a response that came from habit rather than necessity. Madrigal could see her from any direction, through monitors in the lab. "I'm going to examine the man on the table."

"I have a fix on him," Madrigal said. Holos of Turner's body formed in front of the burt-wall, floating in the air between the table and wall. They showed his muscles, organs, skeleton, circulatory system, and more. Even with just the rudimentary scan that produced those holos, Sam could tell a great deal. His skeleton wasn't bone. Some of his organs were in the wrong place. Instead of a brain, he had neural filaments throughout his body. He was an android. A forma. Had she not heard his story, it would never have occurred to her to think otherwise.

Turner stared at the images, his gaze bleak.

Sam went to the table and dragged her finger along its edge. A rail rose up under her hand on both sides.

"I won't panic," he said.

"I know." It impressed her that he understood so fast. The rails would keep him from rolling off if he began to thrash. "I just want to make sure you're safe." The holos disoriented her. He seemed human to her, but those scans labeled him as a forma. She went to the wall and studied the data on its screens. Then she pulled a robot arm out from its surface and unfolded it over Turner.

He watched her, tense and silent.

Most of the exams could be done externally, but Sam had to pierce his skin for blood tests. His circulatory system was synthetic, as was his "blood." It carried nanomeds, tiny molecular laboratories designed to repair and maintain his internal components. His skin was a marvel unlike anything she had seen before, a type of synthetic plastic so finely made that it was indistinguishable by touch from the real thing. She didn't recognize its structure, but when she had more time she intended to examine it on a molecular level. She analyzed results of his exams using the burt-wall to reduce the data. The entire time, Turner watched with preternatural stillness. She made no attempt to hide the data from him. She suspected he already knew what she would find.

Finally she turned to him, her earlier intensity subdued. He sat up then, pushing down the rail and swinging his legs over the side of the table.

"It's true," Sam said. "You are more biomech than human. Your brain is an EI matrix of mesh filaments."

"I'm a man." His grip on the table tightened until his knuckles turned white. "Not a forma."

Sam pulled her fingers through her curls, lifting the mane off her shoulders. "Charon imaged your brain and reproduced its map in a sixth-generation neural network."

Turner folded his arms and rubbed his hands up and down his arms, though the lab wasn't cold. "When he activated the matrix, I 'regained consciousness.' I couldn't believe how great I felt. All my aches and pains were gone." He lowered his arms. "Then I tried to move. I couldn't."

Paralysis? She could guess what had probably happened. "Your EI brain couldn't coordinate the muscle movements of your body."

"Apparently. Charon didn't recover everything in the imaging process." He fisted his hand, then opened it, watching the movements. "I never realized before how much I took for granted my ability to communicate with my body."

"But you relearned how to move."

"Reasonably well." His gaze never wavered. "Are you convinced now?"

"Your brain is definitely an EI." She rubbed the back of her neck, where the muscles felt like steel bands now. "Your body is rebuilt, but you have human components. Charon couldn't have changed their DNA on a fundamental level and still have you be Turner Pascal. A full analysis should reveal your true identity."

Turner slid off the table and stood next to her. "He will just claim he used the genetic blueprint of a dead man to design an android. How can I prove otherwise?"

"Your teeth."

"Synthetic."

Sam looked over the data on the burt-wall. His teeth were beautiful, perfect, too perfect, but they seemed human, not a construct. "Are you sure?"

"Yes."

"This Charon is good." It was the understatement of the century. Whoever had done this was a genius. "So how come I've never heard of him?"

"He hides."

"No one can hide that well."

"He can."

"Why hide?"

"Why do you think? He's broken so many laws, I can't even count them. He thrives on it."

Sam rubbed her chin. "He has to have money to do work like this. Resources. Who backs him?"

"I don't know." Turner passed his hand through a holo of his skeleton. "But he's loaded."

"If he's this good and this rich, I ought to have heard rumors, urban legends, *something*."

"I wish I knew more. But I barely understand it myself." He spoke awkwardly. "Before all this happened, I was just a hotel bellboy. You could have written my knowledge about biomech on the edge of a card."

Sam wondered if he had any idea how compelling he was as a person. She couldn't help but smile. "I doubt you were ever 'just' anything."

That seemed to nonplus him. "Thank you."

"Do you know why Charon picked you?"

"Access, partly. He could get into the morgue that night." His hand clenched on the mech-table. "He also says I was a good candidate: young, strong, healthy."

Sam had no argument about his being in good shape. But if the rest of his story proved as valid as what she had verified, that meant legally this man was *dead*. Except he wasn't. She defined the end of life as the death of the brain. If Charon had done what Turner claimed, he had revived a man after brain death. A chill went through her. How did you define death, then? Was an EI copy of a brain equivalent to that brain?

"This is going to make a quagmire out of the bioethics debates." Sam paced along the table, away from Turner, talking to herself. "If this is true, we have something big here. We all knew this would happen someday, with the progress we've made in augmenting humans. Where do you draw the line? When does a machine become human and a human become a machine?" She swung around to Turner. "You may be right to worry about the police. They don't have equipment this sophisticated. Their scans will show you as an android." Given the legal ambiguities regarding formas, they would probably treat him as stolen property. "The serial number encoded in your matrix would let them trace you to Charon. They might arrest me for theft."

He paled. "My brain has a serial number?"

She gave him a look of apology. "Yes, I'm afraid so. A corporation constructed the scaffolding Charon used to design your matrix. They put in a serial number just like they do in their software."

"I'm not a thing."

"If you were made as you describe," Sam said, "I would consider you a human being with the rights and protections of any other man."

"If?"

Sam spread her hands out from her body, palms up. "My tests support your story, but they also would if you were a forma with an unprecedented amount of human components in your body."

"What difference would it make?" His face flushed. "If an android became as self-aware as I am, as convinced of his right to self-determination, why would he have fewer rights than a human being?"

"Our best minds have been asking that question for decades now." Sam exhaled. "We still don't have an answer."

"Your best." He leaned against the table. "Ours are better."

"Ours?"

He tapped his temple. "I've an EI brain. It's smarter than my old one."

Sam couldn't imagine what it would be like to change from human to EI, but it didn't surprise her that he felt smarter. "I wouldn't say that to anyone you want to think of you as human."

He reddened. "No, I guess not." After a hesitation, he asked, "Will you help me?"

"Yes, I'll help." His situation compelled her. Even if he wasn't telling the truth, she couldn't walk away from this. He was right, it raised questions that had to be answered. "I want to contact some of my colleagues. And a lawyer. We need to go high up, get people involved who can ensure your safety."

His posture went from relaxed to frozen in a heartbeat. "Charon has spies everywhere! If you bring in other people, they will lead him to me."

Spies? It occurred to her that she didn't know the

state of his EI development. His new matrix had to evolve a viable code. The longest-surviving EIs had been sentient for only a few years, and they were running in machines. So far no EI brain had been stable for longer than a year or two without redevelopment; those left to evolve on their own became more erratic until their personalities disintegrated. She knew of one self-aware android that had remained stable—Ander, created by Megan Flannery and Raj Sundaram. But Ander worked constantly with the scientists; his personality otherwise might not have survived intact. Turner's EI could have a better chance, given its origins—a human mind—but no precedent existed. For all she knew, it might fall apart faster.

Sam tried a question that usually tripped up new EIs but that humans tended to like. "What is it that you want me to do?"

"Hide me from his spies."

At least he answered right away. Nascent EIs often faltered or froze when asked an open-ended question about personal preferences. But his comment about spies didn't reassure her. "You think people are watching you?"

"I'm not being paranoid." He folded his arms. "You don't know. Charon is crazy insane and insanely brilliant. His influence is everywhere. Look at me. If someone could build me, think what else he could do."

He had a point. "So why hasn't he embedded tracking devices in you?"

"He did. I disabled them."

"If he's as good as you say, he ought to have made them tamper proof."

"He tried. I paid attention." He shuddered. "You

do when someone turns you into a slave. And I'm smarter now."

"I can understand. But I don't think I can hide you. The police will find out you're here. I need help—" She held up her hand as he started to protest. "I'll go to people who will appreciate your situation, people who won't want you mistreated."

He stood like a statue. "Such as?"

"Air Force."

"No!"

She wanted to say *No!* too, for personal reasons, but they weren't good ones here. "I know people there I trust."

"Don't. Please." The blood drained from his face. "They will make me into an experiment like Charon did."

Exasperated, she said, "You've been watching too many bad holo-movies." She thought of Thomas Wharington, her father's longtime friend, now a three-star general. "The real military is far more staid than all those melodramatic caricatures."

"Please don't."

"Charon will track you down here."

"I covered my trail."

"From this person with spies everywhere?"

"I know about a lot of them."

"Good. You can tell me."

"All right."

That startled her. She had expected him to balk at revealing information, perhaps because subconsciously she still found parts of his story hard to believe. "How long have you been gone from him?"

"The three days I was unconscious, plus a few hours."

"So he's been looking for you for three days."

"Probably." He shifted his weight. "I left a trail to make it look like I intended to hitchhike to Canada."

Sam doubted that would fool an expert for long. "How do you want me to help you?"

"He took everything. My fingerprints, retinal scans, everything. Even my brain waves are different. Change them back."

Sam considered the possibilities. "You already have Turner's DNA. Fixing your retinal scans or fingerprints is possible. You don't want me tampering with your EI matrix, though." She crossed her arms. "For all I know, you're a criminal who wants me to give him the ultimate disguise."

"I'm not." He looked far more like a frightened kid than any criminal. "I swear it."

"Okay. If you want my help, you have to trust me, too."

At first he stood rubbing his arms as if he were cold. Finally he spoke with reluctance. "All right. What do you want me to do?"

"I'm going to make some calls. You can relax, shower, and change if you would like." Sam checked the clock on the console. Good grief. It was after nine P.M. She hadn't realized so many hours had passed. No wonder she felt hungry. She glanced at him. "Do you eat?"

He smiled, bringing out a dimple in his cheek. "I do get hungry. I can taste and smell the food. It won't really replenish my body, but it does provide fuel."

"Amazing," she said, though she wasn't sure if it was his eating habits or that heart-breaker of a smile that left her flushed. He was a mesmerizing puzzle.

The scientist in her wanted to study him and the woman wanted to help him.

"Come on," she said. "Let's go rustle up some food."

Sam sprawled in the chair before the console in her bedroom, taking a bite of her hot dog while she waited for a response on the vertical screen. At the moment, it showed nothing but blue.

"How long will it take?" Turner asked, in a chair near hers. They were both far less bedraggled. She had washed his clothes while he showered, and she had changed her own, putting on fresh jeans and a white top embroidered with red flowers.

"It shouldn't be long," she said. "If Giles is there."

He shifted in his chair. "Why should I trust this Giles?"

"Because I do."

"I should ask why I should trust you." He reddened. "But since I sought you out, that's not a fair question."

"I suppose." He sounded so human. His expressions, speech, inflections, mannerisms—it all made her think of him as a man. No forma she had ever worked with had such a sophisticated brain. Yet he *was* an EI, a damn good one, but still a constructed intelligence. The contradictions in her own reactions to him confused her.

Sam leaned forward with her elbows on the console, the hot dog in one hand. She tapped the activate panel on a smaller screen.

"Good evening," Madrigal said.

"Hey, Mad." Sam glanced at Turner. "You okay with my doing a search on your name?"

"Go ahead. I gave you my word."

"Searching," Madrigal said. "I have the results."

It gratified Sam that Madrigal worked so fast. She had spent the last six months optimizing the EI's response time. "Show them in order of date."

"The most recent is his obituary," Madrigal said.

Turner spoke unevenly. "I'm not sure about this."

"Would you rather I didn't open it?" Sam asked. The idea shook her up, too.

After a pause, he said, "No. Go ahead." He made a wan effort to look cheerful. "After all, how many people get to read their own obituary?"

"If it gets to be too much, let me know."

"Okay."

Sam spoke into the comm. "Go ahead, Madrigal."

The small screen cleared to reveal a news article. "Would you like me to read it?" Madrigal asked.

"No, don't," Sam said. Hearing it out loud would probably be even harder for Turner.

Sam scanned it quickly. The driver of a truck had gone off the traffic control grid and tried to make an illegal turn. His truck skidded on the icy road and rammed Turner's hover car. The truck driver and his passenger had both survived; Turner was the only casualty. He had been twenty-seven, a resident of Portland, Oregon, and a bellboy in a Hilton hotel.

She looked up at him. "I'm sorry."

His face had gone white. "Please take it off. I know I gave you my word. But I—I can't . . ."

"I understand." To the comm, she said, "Madrigal, find something more cheerful."

"I've a holo of Mr. Pascal in a hotel advertisement."

Turner gave a self-conscious laugh. "They liked to

put me in their ads. They said it attracted female guests."

"Well, hey." Sam grinned at him. "Let's see, Mad."

The screen washed into a new image, a glossy holo of a hotel lobby with a fountain arching in the background, an elegant registration area, and lushly green plants. The Hilton logo took up the top left corner. In the foreground, Turner stood smiling, his blond hair curling artfully on his forehead, his blue eyes enhanced to a more vivid hue than they appeared in real life. His smile was a brilliant flash of white in his handsome face.

"Oh, my." Sam felt warm. "It's a good picture."

"That's what I want to remember," he said.

The console suddenly beeped, and the large screen rippled into a white background with the logo of her phone carrier, a lightning bolt through a globe of the world.

"What's that?" Turner asked.

"Giles, I think." Sam turned to him. "Probably best you wait out of sight."

"Yes." Turner went to stand across the room. He stood poised by the glass doors to her balcony like a cat ready to jump. She had closed the curtains over the doors so no one would see inside. Not that anyone was likely to walk by; she had bought this land for its remote location, and the cold weather helped ensure people didn't come wandering. Still, it never hurt to be careful.

As she turned back to her console, the large screen projected an image, the face and upper body of a man with auburn hair, a crooked nose, green eyes, and a large grin.

"Sam!" He beamed at her. "Hallo. Haven't heard from you in ages." His London accent lilted.

"Hey, Giles." Seeing him reassured her. Twenty years ago they had been lovers; a year later they had decided to be friends instead, an arrangement far better suited to their personalities. They had seen each other through university graduations, job searches, and the explosion of new work in their field. She had been a bridesmaid at his wedding to Katie. He had introduced her to Richard Armstead, who later became her husband. Giles had thought Richard could make her happy. He had been right.

And it was Giles who had flown in to be with her six years ago for Richard's funeral. She pushed down the memory, unwilling to face that grief. It was why in the past few years she and Giles had drifted apart. She almost never talked to him anymore. It brought back too many painful memories.

"What's up?" Giles asked.

"I retired," Sam said.

He chuckled. "Katie said she heard that. I'll tell you what I told her. It's ridiculous."

"Maybe. But true." She smiled, imagining his wife's tart response when he didn't believe her. Katie never took any guff from Giles, which seemed one reason he remained smitten with her after fifteen years of marriage.

"Come on, Sam," he said amiably. "Why would you retire?"

"Long story."

"I've plenty of time."

"Actually, I have a philosophical question for you."

He laughed. "You called me across the sea at this inhuman hour of the morning to talk philosophy?"

She flushed. In England, he was eight hours ahead. It was six in the morning there. "Sorry! I forgot the time difference."

"No problem." He settled back in his seat and crossed his hands over his stomach, which had rather increased in girth lately. "So shoot."

"Okay." She leaned forward. "A man dies in an accident. A biomech surgeon images the brain and creates an EI based on it. He rebuilds the guy with biomech to replace his destroyed organs and limbs. When this fellow comes to, he thinks he's human. Surgeon says no, he's a forma. Rebuilt guy says he has same rights he had before. Other guy says you died, now you are an android and I own you. So who is right?"

Giles gave her one of his "I'm unimpressed" looks. "Too easy, Sam. Slavery is illegal. I'm surprised you even considered it a thorny problem."

"I haven't told you the thorn yet."

"No?" He looked intrigued. "And what might that be?"

"It happened."

Giles stopped smiling. "That's not funny, Sam."

"I know. I'm serious."

He sat up straighter. "Bloody hell."

"Yeah."

"Where is he? Why haven't I read about this?"

"He came to me in secret." Sam made a conscious effort not to lean toward Turner or otherwise give away his presence with her body language. "I checked him out. Physically, he is exactly what he claims."

"How do you know he's not an android?"

"Yeah, well, that's the problem, isn't it?"

"Sounds like one for the ethics boards," Giles said.

"It has another wrinkle, I'm afraid."

He squinted at her. "I'm almost afraid to ask."

"He says the person who made him, a man he calls Charon, is some paranoid genius with spies everywhere." She flushed, hearing how nutty that sounded. Giles had never had much patience with dramatics.

His reaction floored her. He didn't scoff. He didn't even crack a smile. Instead he spoke in a very careful voice. "Someone named Charon, you say."

Sam recognized his tone. "You know him."

"It's a mythological reference. Ferryman of the underworld. You of all people should know that."

"Why me of all people?"

"This is Charon, Sam."

"Do you know him?"

He put on an act of shrugging. "Can't say that I do."

Sam scowled at him. "You don't lie well."

For a moment he considered her. Then he said, "This line is secured, right? That's what my incoming said."

"That's right." Before her father had died, three years ago, she had consulted for the Air Force on projects sensitive enough that she had access to their best security.

Giles leaned forward, his elbows on his desk. "Charon is bad news. Stay out of it."

"I've never heard of him."

He stared at her. "Say again?"

"I've never heard of him."

"Eh, well, I can see why you would say that."

That made no sense. "What?"

"You probably know him by a different name."

"Such as?"

"Wildfire."

"Nope."

"Wizard."

She waved her hand. "Half the people on this planet use 'Wizard' as their handle."

"Parked and Gone."

That stopped her. "Parked? He breaks into military satellites. Never been apprehended."

"That," Giles said, "is Charon."

"Parked is a bandwidth bandit. Not a surgeon."

"He's both. Ever hear of Sunrise Alley?"

She sat up straighter. "Hell, yeah."

"How much do you know?"

"Supposedly it's an illegal EI enclave."

He spoke flatly. "*That's* Charon."

"Charon is a person. Sunrise is an organization."

"Could be."

"You don't know if he's a person or an organization, do you?" She liked this less and less. "If Charon is Sunrise Alley, that could make him the biggest black market mech-king alive. So why haven't I heard of him?"

"I don't know anyone who has actually met him." He spoke carefully. "You say you have someone there who knows him?"

Sam froze as the implication hit her. Charon was so well hidden that even someone as tuned in to the meshes as Giles didn't know his identity for certain. She might have access to one of the few people who could identify this black market king—in her house.

"Ah, hell," Sam said.

Giles spoke in an urgent voice, a stark contrast to

his usual mellow style. "Sam, if this man is what he claims, you're in this too deep to go it alone."

"I'll call my NIA contact." In the past decade, the National Information Agency had taken over investigations associated with the world mesh, absorbing entire bureaus of the NSA. Like the CIA, it was run by a civilian appointee, and had almost equal footing with the CIA in the National Security Council. Although it had ties with the Army and Navy, it primarily coordinated its efforts through the Air Force, with headquarters at Andrews Air Force Base and the Pentagon. The sprawling agency had become larger and more shadowy than its precursors.

"Get out of wherever you are," Giles said. "Take this guy to the NIA. Fast."

Sam grimaced. "You realize I moved to this lovely place to relieve my stress."

"Sorry, Sam." With care, he added, "Is he there?"

"Who?" Sam knew he meant Turner, but she didn't want to give anything away. If Giles didn't know how Turner looked or sounded, he couldn't identify him.

Giles didn't push. "Just be careful."

"I will." She drew in a deep breath. "I better go."

"Good luck."

"Thanks."

After she cut the link, she swiveled her chair to face Turner, who was still by the curtains.

"Sunrise Alley." Sam wasn't a happy camper. "You neglected to mention that."

"I'd never heard any of it before." He looked like a deer caught in the headlights of a hover car. "No matter what you call him, he's a monster."

She rubbed her arms. Turner might as well have put

a holosign over her head pointing her out to anyone chasing him. But it made no difference. Given how she felt about the ethics of biomech development, she could no more turn her back on this than she could stop her heartbeat. She had retreated here to lick her wounds, but it seemed she couldn't be a hermit even when she tried.

"We need sanctuary," she said. They had to move fast.

His posture was so taut, he looked as if he could snap. "With the military?"

"That's right. Actually, to an agency that works with the Air Force." She pulled her wallet out of her pocket and checked to make sure she had her clever-card. "We should travel light. No luggage."

He seemed too stunned to react. He had a quality she had seen in other EIs, a hesitancy, as if his mind was incomplete, unable to absorb input fast enough to respond in a timely manner. His evolving codes were at risk now, not yet developed enough to cope with erratic changes. For a normal EI, how she dealt with it now would be vital in the formation of its personality. But Turner already had a personality; the question was how stable it would remain.

She felt as if she were walking through jagged glass shards. "Turner—how long has it been since you died?"

He spoke self-consciously. "About two weeks."

No wonder he seemed bewildered. He was only two weeks old, even if he did essentially have Turner Pascal's brain. She wanted to offer comfort, but she didn't know what to say to someone who suddenly found himself alive as a forma rather than a man.

"We'll drive to San Francisco," she said.

"You are sure it's safe?"

"No guarantees exist. But this is my best bet." She put confidence into her voice. "We'll fly out of here."

He smiled tentatively. "That would be good."

"You bet."

Sam just hoped they didn't crash and burn.

III

Spy Car

The road rolled out, dark except for cones of light from the headlamps on Sam's car. She had left her silver Mercedes at the house; this beaut was the car she rarely used, a sleek Shadow. She had loaded it with a copy of Madrigal, her EI. Although she kept her hands on the wheel, Madrigal was driving. Digital ink on the dash displayed dials, gauges, and screens in a green, gray, and blue motif called Forest and Lake. The car's holographic exterior could mimic any design Sam coded. Now they sped through the night, black and muted. Invisible.

Cliffs plunged down to the turbulent sea on the right, where waves crashed against the rocky shoreline, their crests capped by shimmers of light from the gibbous moon. Hills rose on the left, dark humps against a sky rich with stars. Even in the day, few people traveled this lonely road; now, after midnight, theirs was the only vehicle.

Turner sat slumped in the passenger's seat, staring out at the night. He seemed lost. Vulnerable. Sam had spent the past hour in frustrating attempts to find out more about him. Either he had lost part of his verbal abilities in becoming an EI or else he was being deliberately taciturn. She suspected a combination of the two. She had time to draw him out, though; it would take hours to reach San Francisco even if the car drove itself straight through the night.

She decided to try again. "I was wondering."

Turner glanced at her. "Yes?"

"What does Charon look like?"

"Like a devil," he said darkly.

"What does a devil look like?"

"Evil."

"Evil how?"

He stared out at the road.

She tried another tack. "Do you know what Charon planned to do with you?"

"He wanted a slave."

"For what?"

"He planned to change me." He turned to her, his face pale. "He wanted to test out different forma bodies on me, to find out if others were more efficient than the human form. And he was going to manipulate my EI, see what he could make me do."

What Turner described went against every principle Sam valued. "He needs a crash course in ethics."

"He was convinced people were plotting against him and he had to protect himself."

It sounded more like everyone else needed protection from Charon. Sam gazed out the windshield, thinking, and her reflection gazed back, a woman with shaggy blond curls and bangs, her eyes too large for her urchin's face. She looked like a waif, not an EI architect.

Turner suddenly said, "You're helping me relearn speech."

She smiled. "Well, that is my job."

"Talking to you provides data for my speech mods." He winced. "But I still sound like a damn EI."

Sam couldn't deny it. He was almost indistinguishable from a man, but nothing could change the fact that his mind derived from a matrix of evolving neural networks. "An incredible EI," she said, wishing she had something more to offer him.

"I'm not a machine."

"You're right." She didn't know what to call him.

He laid his head against the seat and closed his eyes. "Charon had me doing tests. Physical, to see how I worked; mental, to study my mind. Every now and then he turned me off while he worked."

"Turned you off?"

"With drugs."

"Drugs knock out a person. Machines turn off."

"I'll remember. But, Sam, either way, he took away my ability to think."

The dash flickered with a new holicon, or holographic icon, which glowed near to the wheel. It showed a red light like the domes that appeared on old-fashioned police cars. A warning.

Sam flicked the holicon, and it morphed into a small screen on the dash with gold letters on a black background: *Car approaching from behind.* The words moved down and an image formed above them showing an unmarked black car—long, sleek, and deadly—hugging the curves of the road. Information replaced the message: the car was half a mile behind, running an unusually quiet engine, one undetectable from this distance by an unaugmented human ear.

"Madrigal," Sam said.

"Hello." The voice came out of a comm below the screen.

"What can you tell me about the car behind us?"

"Analysis of its speed and accelerations suggests it is following this car and hiding its presence."

"But we know it's there."

"It has good shroud programs." Smugly Madrigal added, "Mine are better."

Sam's lips quirked upward. "And more modest."

Madrigal spoke with dignity. "Software has no modesty or lack thereof."

"Yes, well, you simulate its lack very well." Sam nudged up their speed. "What do you have on that car? Make, type, age, schematics?"

"It is a Hover-Shadow 14."

"A spy car." Similar to her own, in fact. She had purchased this one when someone started tailing her during the hearings at BioII. Probably it had been nothing, only her overly sensitized concern. But she had bought the Shadow anyway. She could afford its exorbitant price, after all. That was what made the BioII investigation so charged: millions, even billions were at stake. She had thrown down the gauntlet, claiming that in the pursuit of those billions, they cut corners to the point of endangering human life. It had made her enemies, but she couldn't have stayed silent and kept her self-respect.

"It could be unconnected to us," Madrigal said. "Hover-Shadows are sold to security forces that protect VIPs."

Sam raised her eyebrows. "And they just happen to be following us in the middle of the night on a desolate highway hundreds of miles from civilization."

"The probability of that is small," Madrigal admitted.

Sam thought for a moment. Spy cars could hide from many tracking systems. Their holographic surfaces made them invisible by displaying whatever was behind the car relative to the probe. The coating and rounded angles of the car's design, derived from stealth technology, made it difficult to detect by radar. The car sent out a locator signal, in case thieves stole it, but she had deactivated the supposedly tamper-proof system. They were running "dark" now in every way.

Even so, an advanced enough system could compensate for the shroud, just as Madrigal had detected their pursuer. On the display, Sam could see details of the car following them even from half a mile away. That pushed Madrigal's bandwidth, though; if their pursuer fell any farther behind, the image would degrade. Sam wondered why they followed at the limit of Madrigal's ability. Perhaps the driver thought he was out of range. It would support Madrigal's assertion that his onboard systems were less advanced than hers. Given that Sam had designed the EI and its associated systems herself, using procedures she was in the process of patenting, it wouldn't surprise her if Madrigal could outdo their trackers.

"What weapons does it have?" Sam asked.

"I can't detect them through its shroud," Madrigal said. "However, they are probably similar to the systems incorporated in this car. And they are gaining on us."

"Speed up!"

"Increasing to seventy miles an hour."

Sam knew the Shadow could easily go many times that speed. "Can't you give me more?"

"Yes. However, on this road, I can't guarantee we won't slide out over the cliff."

Sam peered out the window. The road wound in hairpin curves, following contours of the mountain. Although a metal railing separated them from the drop-off at their right, it probably wouldn't hold if they plowed into it at this speed. The car had some amphibious ability, but they would probably bounce down the cliff and smash on the rocks below.

As they careened into another curve, Turner grabbed the door handle, his body tensing until his shirt pulled tight across his shoulders. He made no sound, just stared at the road.

Damn. She was supposed to rescue Turner, not kill him in a car accident. "Madrigal, do the cloud."

"Done." A hissing came from the back of the car.

"What was that?" Turner asked.

"A fog of microscopic bomblets with picotech brains. It will bombard the car following us." Sam glanced at him. "I designed it myself."

He seemed disconcerted. "When you get the look, you could be some wild eldritch warrior queen."

Sam blinked at the image. She saw herself as a tech-nerd. She would be a warrior woman, though, if it took that to protect him and get them out of here. "I'm hoping the bomblets can stop them."

Madrigal spoke. "They may not. Their car is continuing through the cloud."

Sam studied the image. Stats scrolled under it about the vehicle pursuing them. Their pursuer was barreling through the haze of bomblets, but the data was degrading as the other car fell farther behind. "Mad, can you give me a better picture?"

"Working," Mad said. The contrast increased. It didn't improve the resolution much, but it did reveal a cloud of fireflies dancing around the car.

"What's with the bugs?" Sam asked.

"Our pursuer released a swarm of bee-bots to neutralize your bomblets. They are also attacking this car."

"A bee *what*?" Turner asked. If he was simulating fear, he was doing one hell of a good job. No EI she had ever worked with was this convincing. She would bet her many academic degrees that Turner genuinely felt scared to death.

"They're little robots with rudimentary AI brains," Sam said. "They can counter minor threats." Like her bomblets. "I could release some, too, to counter the ones from the other car, but I don't have many and they only operate for a few minutes." Unlike the others, hers weren't armed.

Hope sparked in his voice. "Can you send back more bomblets until the other car uses up its bees?"

Sam wished she could. "I don't have any more."

Mad spoke. "Shall I activate the artillery?"

"Do it." Sam couldn't bear to see Turner so afraid.

"Done." A rumbling came from the rear of the car.

Turner clenched the edge of the seat. "You're going to *shoot* them?"

Sam gave him a guilty look. "Cross your fingers it doesn't come to that."

"Why would you have a car like this?" he asked.

"Someone was following me at BioII last year." Sam didn't like to remember. "One time I thought someone broke into my penthouse. They didn't take anything, but just that someone got past all my security scared me."

"Did you report it to the police?"

"Yes. But I had no proof. I just found a few things misplaced in my bedroom. And it didn't feel right." She shivered. "Maybe I imagined it. I don't know."

Madrigal spoke. "We've increased our distance from them. However, they are attacking with more bots."

It disquieted Sam that they had disarmed her bomblets so fast. "Shoot, Mad—the guns, not the mini-cannons."

"Done." The jack-hammer of machinegun fire burst out the back of the car. Almost immediately, an answering burst came from behind them.

"Holy shit," Turner muttered.

"Hostile vehicle has returned fire," Madrigal said.

"Are you all right?" Sam asked.

"A few dents," the EI said. "Otherwise, I'm still singing."

"Good." Sam felt a fierce satisfaction. Teach them to threaten her prince in distress, or whatever one called the male equivalent of the proverbial damsel. "Spread some oil on the road." They had the advantage of being ahead of the other car; she could release pernicious substances but their pursuers would have a harder time sending similar forward to bedevil them.

"Oil released," Madrigal said. "Hostile vehicle compensating." The car careened around another turn, and Sam grabbed the door handle, hanging on.

"We've gained more distance on them," Madrigal said. Turner's face had gone white, his body rigid.

"Sorry," Sam told him.

"Hey." He gulped. "No problem."

"Hostile vehicle has cleared the oil," Madrigal said.

Another burst of gunfire came from behind them— and Sam's car swerved.

"Mad!" Sam hung on to the door while they skidded across the road. She had to let the EI deal with this; human reactions weren't fast enough to handle the situation at such high speeds. Her body protested against the rapid changes in acceleration as Mad compensated for the swerve.

"Course corrected," Madrigal said. "They're still firing."

"Use the cannons," Sam said. "Blast the bastards."

A muffled boom came from behind them as mini-cannons on the car fired at their pursuers.

"Got one of their wheels," Madrigal said smugly.

Sam clung to the door as they lurched around another curve. "Did it stop them?"

"No. But it slowed them down. I don't think they can catch us now."

"Good," Turner whispered, scrunched against the door.

"Are you all right?" Sam asked.

"I think so." He tore his gaze away from the screen that displayed the now indistinct car behind them. "Will we make it?" A line showed between his eyebrows that hadn't been there earlier. Given enough time, his face would develop character and lose the alabaster perfection that made him seem more sculpted than human.

"We'll make it," she said, hiding her doubts. "The wheels on these cars are protected, but they're weak spots compared to the rest."

"That's right," Madrigal said. "Put out one of those babies and you can speed away."

A ghost of a smile played about Turner's lips. "Madrigal sounds like you."

"She programmed me," the car said.

Sam snorted. "You've been programming yourself for months. It's my bane." In truth, she was proud of the EI's development, even if it did have quirks, like calling her Samantha.

"Charon sent that car," Turner said.

"I thought you deactivated the tracking signals in your body."

He spoke uneasily. "Maybe I was wrong."

"But why would it take him three days to find you?"

"Maybe because I woke up?"

"You sleep?"

He spoke with reluctance. "I hope you won't think this makes me sound inhuman—but during my 'wake' time, I respond to stimuli that helps my programming evolve. I need sleep to integrate the changes."

What he described didn't actually seem that much different from what humans needed. "Like what happens when we dream."

His posture eased. "I never thought of it like that."

"Why would that help Charon find you?"

"I don't know. It's just the main difference I can think of between now and before."

Sam considered it. "Well, you were at sea before. You were on the yacht. Maybe something in its systems protected you. Or maybe Charon wanted you to find me."

His shoulders hunched. "Why would he want that?"

"Hell if I know."

"He does know who you are." He wouldn't look at her. "But then, so does anyone in the EI field."

Sweat beaded on Sam's forehead. She didn't want to be that well known. It had brought her nothing but problems, especially during the well-publicized ethics hearings at BioII. "Your EI matrix must keep a record of what happens while you sleep. Can you compare those with the records of your waking periods?"

"Yes. Just a second . . ." He went silent for a moment. "I don't see any difference."

"Maybe you should sleep now. We could see if that makes a difference."

"I'm willing to try anything."

Sam studied the screen on the dash, which showed only a dark highway now. "Mad, is that Shadow still behind us?"

"Yes. They have fallen back about a mile."

"How long before it repairs that wheel?"

"Probably fifteen minutes. I am devoting more of my systems to the shroud that hides us."

"Hide us from miniaturized systems, too."

"I'll make sure no bees sting us," Madrigal said.

"Good." Then Sam said, "Take us to the cabin."

Redwoods surrounded the small building. The smell of pine needles filled the air, and sparse underbrush crunched under their feet. Breezes whispered through the trees, the only sound in this remote location. Sam had never realized how much noise a city made, even in the latest hours of the night, until she had come to live in the wild, majestic reaches of northern California. The deepness of the silence had rattled her at first, but she soon came to find it a healing balm.

The cabin had no outward sign of electronic, optical, or superconducting systems. It was isolated from all exterior input. Sam had it built that way during one of her "I reject all the technology that has made my life miserable" phases.

However, she only carried her rebellion so far. Disguised in its innocuous wood construction, the cabin had heat shields to hide from infrared sensors, pheromone screens to contain scents produced by its inhabitants that wandering bee-bots might detect, and filters to remove bits of biological matter, like hair, that included traceable DNA.

They climbed the stairs to the porch, which was shaded by a roof. After they reached the door, Turner ran his fingers over the rough wall of the cabin, which was built from wood, real wood, though Sam had chosen the most common pine available. She hadn't even considered redwood; the trees had become too rare.

"How many houses do you have?" Turner asked.

Sam pulled out her clever-card, which was coded to her fingerprints. "This isn't a house. Well, it is, sort of. It's my cabin." She inserted her card into a slot disguised in the door molding. "It used to be my retreat, before I bought the beach house." She pressed her thumb on the ID panel, another hidden concession to modern tech. In her more honest moments, Sam had to admit she had never really turned away from technology, she just attempted to hide her use of it from herself. The door swung open on oiled hinges.

Turner spoke in a low voice. "I can't do something as simple as open the door to my own apartment anymore."

She lifted her hand, inviting him into the cabin. "Because Charon changed your fingerprints?"

Turner went inside. "Partially." He turned to her. "Even if he hadn't, it wouldn't matter. The door won't recognize the card of a dead person."

Dead. It unsettled Sam more than she wanted to admit. In that sense, she was grateful to Charon. She liked Turner. She didn't want him to be dead. But he needed the rest of his life back, too.

She came inside and closed the door. "Lights on."

The table and standing lamps came on, shedding a warm glow. The living room looked the same as the last time she had been here, a year ago. The rustic furniture was upholstered in blue, rust, and goldenrod hues. A golden pine paneled the walls, and a hearth took up most of one wall, with bricks in rusty colors. Throw rugs warmed the floor. Only a thin layer of dust had accumulated; her cat-bots kept the place clean.

"Hello, Samantha," Madrigal said.

Turner jumped. "Is that EI everywhere?"

Sam smiled. "Pretty much."

"Hello, Turner," Madrigal said.

"How do you know who I am?" he asked.

"I just exchanged memory with myself in the car."

His forehead creased with lines of strain. "Doesn't

it bother you to have copies of your mind in different places?"

"Bother me?" Madrigal asked.

"Yes." Turner stood very still, listening.

"Not at all," Madrigal said. "It lets me be many places at once, a feat Sam would like to do herself. Unfortunately, like most humans, she is too limited to accomplish such a useful trait."

Sam groaned. "Enough, Mad."

"Sorry." Then Madrigal said, "But it's true."

"Mad!"

"I hate having my EI code copied," Turner said.

"Why?" Sam and Madrigal both asked, simultaneously.

"It makes me feel . . . stolen. I don't like copies of myself evolving without my knowledge."

It was the first time Sam had heard an EI express such a sentiment. But she could see how a human might feel that way. "How many copies of you exist?"

"Only this one, I think."

Sam suspected Charon made backups, but she didn't want to upset Turner. He walked into the cabin as if he wasn't certain he belonged there. Then he sat on the couch, stretching out his legs while he put his head back. As he closed his eyes, the cushions under and behind him shifted, and shifted again, straining to release at least a modicum of his muscle tension.

Sam sat near him on the couch. Impulsively, she touched his hand. "How much sleep do you need?"

He opened his eyes, his gaze lingering on her hand as she withdrew it. "Maybe three or four hours."

"We shouldn't stay here any longer than it takes to rearm the car." She had always felt strange about storing supplies for her car here, afraid she was overreacting, but she was grateful now she had been scared enough to stock the place. "We can sleep while the car drives, though. Madrigal will wake me up if anything happens."

He nodded, then closed his eyes again. "That sounds good."

"You can use my room now, if you want. I'll wake you when it's time to go." A flush spread through her at the thought of him in her bed. Flustered, she crammed her hand in the pocket of her jacket and pulled out her mesh glove, a glittering black skein she knew she should treat better than to crumple up like this. "If you need anything, let me know with this."

"Thanks." He took the offered glove and gave her a wan smile. "If I have any nightmares, I'll give you a page."

"You do that." Sam wished she could fix the nightmare his life had become.

He started to speak, then hesitated.

"Yes?" Sam asked.

His voice softened. "You pretend to bristle with spines, but underneath you're very kind, Sam Bryton."

She didn't know what she had expected, but that wasn't it. Embarrassed, she said, "Oh, you know me. The ol' porcupine." Giles and Linden Polk both used to call her that. She needed spines to protect herself in a world she could master scientifically but that she had never been either hard or cold enough to deal with on a personal level.

"I wish I had spines." His voice caught. "They would help keep the nightmares at bay."

Sam knew she should get moving, but she couldn't leave him like this. He had an odd look, as if he feared to lose himself. His neural matrix had to be forming an immense number of connections. Were he an unaugmented human being, her leaving right now to stock the car wouldn't cause psychological harm; for a fledgling EI, how people interacted with him during these crucial weeks would determine the patterns his matrix was establishing. This was the time an architect did some of her most important work. But she couldn't think of him as an EI; he seemed so much like a man.

"I didn't think EIs had nightmares," she said.

"Maybe it's my matrix doing cleanup." Turner touched her hand the way she had done with him. "I need to talk to you. To—to understand what I am. But what I need—what I want, what I need, they aren't the same. I'm scared Charon will find us."

She put her other hand over his. "We can talk in the car. All you want."

He averted his eyes. "Thanks."

"You sleep now. I'll wake you up when I'm ready."

"All right."

As they stood up, Sam was aware of his athletic grace. She showed him to her bedroom, a wood-paneled room with wicker furniture, round throw rugs, and a four-poster bed covered by a flowered quilt. The potted plants were even thriving, which meant her cat-bots were tending them well, unlike real cats, which probably would have eaten them for dinner. Her cat-bots had better success with plants than she had ever managed, mainly because they never forgot to water them.

She lingered with Turner in the doorway. "Rest well."

"I will." He was watching her face. "Sam . . ."

"Yes?"

He cupped his hand around her cheek. "Thank you."

She resisted the urge to turn her head and press her lips into his palm. It was too intimate, too soon. "I'll be back soon."

"Don't take too long."

"Don't worry." She did her best to project confidence. "We'll be fine."

She just wished she believed her own words.

IV
Night Flight

Sam ran up the stairs, her bare feet slapping the marble floor, her silk pajamas blown against her body. Heat from the fires scalded her face. An explosion shook the ground...

Earthquake! Sam struggled to awake. She had gone through a few tremors, but never one this violent. She sat up—and hit her head on a hard surface.

"Ow!" She strained to see in the dim light. As her mind cleared, she realized she was behind the wheel of her car. The "earthquake" had been Turner shaking her. He was sitting on the passenger side now. Given the way he was rubbing his forehead, the "surface" she hit must have been his head.

Sam flushed. "Sorry!"

"I didn't mean to startle you." Even in the dim light, it was obvious his face had turned red. "But I had a warning. I thought you should know."

"A warning?"

"My systems have experienced electronic activity."

She smiled. "I doubt any place exists on this planet that hasn't experienced electronic activity."

"This is different. I recognized an anomaly in the modulating wave." He was sitting sideways, facing her. "It has distinctive sine and cosine components."

Sam pulled herself upright behind the wheel. "You can pick up electronic signals?"

"Yes."

"And Fourier analyze that waveform?"

"Yes."

"How many components of the wave?"

"I calculated it out to several thousand."

Sam sincerely doubted this was a skill required for most bellboys, even those at a Hilton hotel. "Can you transmit your analysis to Madrigal?"

"I think so." His face took on an inwardly directed expression.

Madrigal spoke. "I've received and analyzed his signal. My shroud should be hiding us from it."

Relief washed over Sam. "Good."

"Shall I speed up the car?" the EI asked.

"Can you do it safely?" Sam asked.

"Here, no. But the road widens in a few miles. I can there."

"Keep it safe, Madrigal, but go as fast as you can."

"She has a remarkable architecture," Turner said.

"Turner." Sam didn't know how to moderate her words, so she just spoke plainly. "I know of no human who can detect modulation of a signal wave without equipment, do a thousand-term Fourier analysis in his head, transmit the results to another EI, and admire its structure in the process."

He had been relaxed, sitting with his head leaning against the headrest, but now his posture stiffened and he sat up straighter. "I'm not the only human being augmented by implanted biochips."

Sam suspected the original Turner Pascal hadn't known enough about biomech technology to realize that what he had just done far exceeded the capabilities of such biochip implants. It wouldn't take long for an EI with access to the world meshes to study the basic technology, but he didn't seem to have had much exposure to the world outside his lab.

"Biochip technology for the human brain is in its most rudimentary stages," she said. "It's too risky. It causes brain damage." She regarded him intently. "An EI, though, could easily do what you describe."

"What do you expect me to say? That I'm an android? I'm *not*. I can't be what you want, Sam. It isn't me."

She couldn't help but smile. "That's new."

"It is?"

"Usually when the man says 'I can't be what you want' to the woman, she's saying something like 'show me more of your emotions.' Not 'be an android.'"

Turner went very still. "You said 'the man.'"

"Yes." Her voice softened. "You seem human to me. A man, not an EI."

"You said 'the woman,' too."

Sam blinked. "You have doubts I'm a woman?"

Turner reddened. "None, believe me." He started to lift his hand, then set it down again. "The 'woman' in such conversations is usually the man's lover."

A flush spread through Sam. "I didn't mean that."

This time he didn't stop. He reached across the

seat and took a curl of her hair. "I love the way this looks, so wild and tousled."

"Turner, don't." She pulled her hair away. She would have liked to stroke his, too, but she couldn't take advantage of the situation that way. "You don't have to prove you're human to me."

Rather than taking offense, he laughed softly. "You think a man would only be attracted to you because he's trying to prove he isn't an android?"

"Well, no."

"Good. Because it's not true."

Sam caught her lower lip with her teeth. He smelled good, like the ocean, with an underlying scent she couldn't identify but that seemed male, sensual. Maybe she needed more air. She had avoided men in the six years since her husband had died. She had mourned Richard for so long. Perhaps time really had eased the pain, or maybe she just hadn't met someone who affected her until now. What a mess.

Turner was watching her face. "I'm sorry. I was out of line."

"No. It's okay." Sam didn't know what else to say. So she changed the subject, motioning to the night outside. "Someone out there is making a signal you recognize?"

"Charon uses it in one of his encryption schemes."

"Can you pick a message out of it?"

"Unfortunately, no. I don't know the code."

"Are you sure he sent it?" She was talking too fast, distracted by her heightened awareness of Turner.

"I can't really say." He gestured upward, as if to encompass the mountains and sea. "This area doesn't have as many signals as a city, but it's still full of them."

"Madrigal is shrouding hers." A thought came to Sam. "Turner, are the filaments of your matrix spread throughout your body?"

He tensed. "That doesn't make me less human."

"I didn't mean that. It could protect you. An EI rarely has its matrix filaments all in one spot. Most matrices also have more redundancy built into them than in a biological brain."

His shoulders relaxed. "Yes, mine is like that."

Thinking out loud now, she said, "So it isn't likely the entire matrix ever goes dormant." To Turner, she said, "When you put yourself to sleep on the yacht, did you do it any differently than tonight?"

"Not really."

She finally figured out what bothered her. "Except that you couldn't wake up before unless you heard my voice."

"That's right."

She thought of the tales from her childhood about the beautiful young woman who would awake only if Prince Charming kissed her. That sort of made her Princess Charming, except without the perk of getting to kiss the fair youth. She doubted any of the maidens had the advantage of an EI brain, though. "Did you detect Charon's signal while you were asleep on the yacht?"

"I've no record of it." He watched her intently. "Are you thinking Charon couldn't find me until I found you, because I keyed my wake-up to you?"

"That could be what happened." It would make her a target. For all she knew, he and Charon had planned this together. It was difficult to teach an EI to lie, but he was more sophisticated than any EI she had worked with before. It didn't fit, though, neither with his behavior nor with what she knew after two decades of research on the development of EI matrices.

"There is another way Charon might have found us," Turner said.

She doubted he meant himself. "What's that?"

"Your friend, Giles. You called him. Then that car came after us."

Sam would have decked a lot of people for that suggestion. "Giles would never betray me."

"For enough money or power, anyone will."

Her gaze never wavered. "Not Giles."

"Anyone."

"I wouldn't."

He spoke dryly. "That's because you already have more money and power than most anyone could ever want."

Sam shifted in her seat. "It makes no difference."

"Doesn't it?" Bitterness touched his voice. "You don't know what it's like to live without."

More lay behind those words than any suspicion of Giles. "Is that what it was like for you?"

"It was better after I got a job." He looked out the windshield, his face pensive. "I can't see anything out there."

Sam let it go. "It's overcast. No moonlight."

"Do you think we should do anything about the signal?"

"I'm not certain. I thought driving to San Francisco would be safer than contacting anyone. Even with our signals shrouded, someone might eavesdrop. But I'm beginning to wonder if speed is more important than secrecy. Maybe I should get in touch with my NIA contact now." Calling Thomas Wharington a "contact" was a bit of an understatement. He served as director of the MIA, or Machine Intelligence Agency, one of the two divisions of the NIA. He was also head of the Senate Select Committee for Space Warfare Research and Development. "I can reach him using the mesh in this car."

He turned with a jerk. "No! Charon will trace the call."

"Possibly." She wished they had more choices. "But driving makes us vulnerable." She started to reach out to him, then realized what she was doing and withdrew her hand. "I promised to take you to a safe place, but I'm not sure now that I can without help."

He watched her hand, his gaze lingering. "It's only a few more hours to San Francisco."

"That's a few more hours Charon has to locate us." It flustered Sam when he watched her that way, with his lashes half lowered.

"If Charon picks up your call, it will be like a great big arrow pointing to us."

"We'll be at risk no matter what," she said.

"You think a call is better?"

"I think so."

He had the look of a man about to dive off a cliff. "I hope you're right."

So do I, Sam thought.

Sam had known Thomas Wharington most of her life. He and her father had attended the Air Force Academy together and both had become career officers. As a small child, Sam had found Thomas's calm manner reassuring. Over six feet tall, with broad shoulders and a well-built physique, he had looked every bit the hero to her, especially in his blue uniform. His deep voice had made her think of movie superheroes. As she matured, she had come to appreciate his straightforward manner. He had never talked down to her, but always treated her like an adult. In her teen years, she had imitated his taciturn style, answering her parents in clipped, no-nonsense tones until her exasperated mother told her to cut it out.

As an adult, Sam had seen a different side of Thomas. His worldview had a hardness she hadn't understood in her childhood. She admired his integrity and would always love him for his kindness, but the ease she had felt with him as an adoring child vanished the day she realized "Uncle Thomas" could kill without the flick of an eyelash if he believed it necessary to defend his country. But the steel of his character was also why she trusted him. Thomas was a tough man, but he was also one of the finest people she knew.

At the moment, however, he looked like a man who didn't appreciate her waking him up. Sam could see him on the screen of the dashboard. He was sitting behind the desk in his office at home, but he otherwise looked thoroughly unofficial. His usually impeccable gray hair was mussed, and he had on a rumpled blue sweater. Dark circles ringed his gray eyes. Sam's mother had referred to him as a "silver fox," in honor of his luxuriant hair and finely chiseled features, but right now he looked like a half-asleep pit bull.

"Sam." He scowled. "This had better be good."

"I'm afraid," Sam said, "that it could be very bad."

His frown vanished. "Go on."

"Do you want to catch Charon?"

Although Thomas barely moved, Sam knew she had hit big. She could read him almost as well as she had read her father. That subtle set of his jaw, the wariness in his gaze—yes, she knew the signs. He recognized the name, and it wasn't from some mythological tale.

He said only, "Who is Charon?"

"Someone who might be trouble," Sam said. "I have his latest creation."

Thomas sat up straight, no longer trying to hide his response. "What creation?"

Turner shifted in the passenger's seat, moving closer to the door so Thomas couldn't see him.

"A man," Sam said. "He claims Charon made him. He says he ran away and Charon is searching for him." Sam grimaced. "A few hours ago an armed car chased us down the coast highway and almost blasted us off the road."

"Good Lord, Sam." Thomas leaned forward. "What have you got yourself involved in?"

"Hell if I know. He came to me."

"Where is this man?"

Sam glanced at Turner, asking a silent question.

He looked uncomfortable, but he said, "It's okay. Tell him."

"You can talk to Thomas," she offered.

"I don't want him to see me."

"Sam?" Thomas asked. "Who are you speaking to?"

"His name is Turner." She took a moment to collect

her thoughts. Then she told him everything. By the time she finished, he no longer looked the least bit tired.

"Stay where you are," Thomas said. "I can have a chopper there in twenty minutes."

"That fast?"

"Maximum."

"No!" Turner said. "It will lead Charon to us."

"Is that him?" Thomas asked.

"Yes," Sam said. "He says Charon will find us."

"We won't let that happen." He paused, concern on his face. "If you're on the stretch of coastal road where I think, the Bird may not be able to put down. You'll have to climb a ladder."

"What bird?"

"Redbird. The chopper. It's a scout, designed for fast travel. Will you be all right with it, Sam? We can send a medical crew on this one."

Medical crew? She didn't understand why he was so worried about her. "I'll be fine." She vaguely recalled the Redbird. It had come into military use over the past decade, an aircraft that flew itself but could take a small crew if desired. Sweat beaded on her forehead as she remembered the saying about Charon that had popped into her mind earlier. *He can only take you across once.*

"I hope it reaches us in time," she said.

He checked his desk. "It's been in route for about fifteen minutes, since you mentioned the name Charon."

"We're dead," Turner muttered.

Sam glanced at him. "What makes you so sure?"

"If your friend's people sent help the minute they

heard Charon's name," Turner said, "they know we're in trouble."

"Was that the forma?" Thomas asked.

Turner went rigid, anger flashing on his face.

"He's a man," Sam told Thomas.

"Is he picking up the signal from Charon now?" Thomas asked.

Turner spoke into the comm. "I can't find it now, General Wharington. He could have changed it. Maybe he knows we picked it up. He might be listening to us."

"This is a secured channel," Thomas said.

"He's probably bouncing lasers off our windshield right now," Turner said.

"Not my windshield," Madrigal said. "It absorbs the electromagnetic radiation."

"He'll find a way around that," Turner said. "You don't know Charon."

Thomas didn't answer. His neutral expression made Sam suspect he knew Charon a lot better than he intended to reveal.

Sam became aware of a rumble overhead. "I think our ride is here early."

Thomas exhaled. "God's speed, Sam."

"Thanks." Sam took control of the car and guided it to the side of the road. "No one better bother my car."

"Don't worry," Madrigal said. "I'm armed." The doors unlocked with a click.

Sam glanced at Turner. "Ready to go?"

He nodded, his jaw set. When they opened their doors, the roar jumped in volume. Sam stepped out into a gale produced by—nothing. An engine growled in the sky, along with the *chop-chop-chop* of blades, yet she saw nothing. Trees covered the bluff rising up on their left, and on the right, rocky cliffs dropped to the ocean. A small helicopter might have landed on the narrow road, but the blades would have hit the trees or the mountain.

Turner stood across the car from her, his hands braced on the open door as he stared upward. "Where is it?"

"Near the trees." She used her hand to shield her eyes against the wind as she looked up. She could make out a dark shape hovering above them now. A line dropped down from it, long and supple. It hit the side of the car, then swung away, into the hillside.

A voice called out above them. "Climb the ladder."

Sam slammed the door and ran around the car. The wind threw her hair into her face as she grabbed the ladder, which was made of supple rope or cables. Next to her, Turner was clutching his car door, his face a pale oval in the night.

Sam thrust the ladder at him. "You go first." She wasn't sure how much his EI could handle yet; he might freeze up and not follow if she went ahead of him.

Turner grabbed the ladder, his motions jerky. As he climbed, her pulse raced. She kept imagining another craft lowering out of the night, and she fought the urge to scramble up and over him. As soon as he had gone a few yards up, she started climbing. The ladder swung back and forth, weighted by their bodies. It gave her vertigo. She felt certain she should remember something about this, something important, but it escaped her.

Sam kept climbing, clutching the ladder. Then she hit Turner's foot. She stopped and looked up. Turner was hanging on the ladder with his eyes squeezed shut and his arms hooked over one rung.

"Keep going," she called.

No answer.

She inched her way up, reaching around him, her front against his back. He was gripping the rope so hard, his knuckles felt like iron under her palms. Fighting her own dizziness, she pressed against him. Wind tore around them, cold and sharp.

"You can do this," Sam said.

"I can't," he whispered.

She couldn't tell if his EI brain was simulating a terror Turner Pascal would have felt or if a problem in the matrix had caused him to freeze. She hung on, clenching the ladder, her arms around him, trying to offer reassurance with her presence. Peering upward, she could make out the Redbird, sleek and dark. "Can you pull us up?" she called.

The ladder began rising. As they came closer, she saw a person in the entrance of the Bird, a man or a woman in dark clothes. Hands grabbed her and Turner and heaved them inside. With relief, Sam sprawled across the deck.

"Got them," a woman said.

Sam lay on her stomach, breathing hard. Her heart pounded as if she had run a marathon.

"Dr. Bryton?" a man asked. "Are you all right?"

Sam raised her head. The Redbird had just enough light to reveal several men and women in uniform. The man leaning over her wore a jumpsuit with a medical patch on the shoulder.

"I'm okay," Sam said, sitting up. She was more concerned about Turner. He lay nearby, curled in a fetal position, his eyes closed. Another medic was leaning over him, a woman in the uniform of an Air Force major. A third officer knelt on Turner's other side, a man doing checks with a scanner.

"Is my friend all right?" Sam asked.

The man next to Sam spoke to the woman by Turner. "How is he, Major Parsons?"

Parsons looked over at them. "We aren't sure what happened. He's in a coma."

Sam wondered if he had shut down his matrix. The last time he had "turned off," he had keyed his wake-up to her. She scooted across the deck to Turner, and Parsons moved aside. The Redbird rumbled all around them.

Sam laid her hand on Turner's shoulder, offering comfort. "It's all right. We're safe." She felt an urge to stroke his hair, even to press her lips against his cheek, but she held back.

His eyes opened enough for him to look at her, his pupils dilated. He spoke in a barely audible voice. "I'm afraid of heights. And closed spaces."

She squeezed his shoulder. "We'll be all right." His fears probably came from Turner Pascal. It was hard to imagine someone programming phobias into an EI, though she supposed it wasn't impossible.

He rolled onto his back, looking up at the man who was scanning him. "What—?"

"I'm doing some tests," the medic said. "To make sure you're all right."

Turner closed his eyes as they took his blood pressure.

His terror tugged at Sam. It seemed real. It could be simulated, but if the emotions felt real to him, who was to say they weren't?

While the medics checked over Turner, and herself as well, Sam pondered. To be an EI, Turner had to pass demanding forms of the Turing test, which essentially said that if a person communicated with a machine and another human without knowing which was which—and couldn't tell them apart—then the machine had intelligence. Older tests used sentences typed at terminals, but nowadays many versions existed. The verbal Turing helped distinguish an EI from an AI. The EI's speech had to be convincing, not only its content but also its tone and nuance. If she asked, "Do you like the beach by my house?" he needed more than knowledge about oceans, he also had to interpret "like" and describe how he felt.

Turner had no problem with the verbal test. As far as Sam was concerned, he also passed the visual, which required the EI be visually indistinguishable from a person. He needed human expressions, mannerisms, and body language. He had to interpret and respond to visual cues humans gave one another. His portrayal of fear, love, anger, joy, and all the rest had to convince even an EI architect he was human. When Sam had first met Turner, she had realized he was part biomech, but she wouldn't have guessed he was an EI.

Some researchers thought human brains were wired for more processing than an EI matrix could handle, even "simple" tasks such as recognizing another person. They considered the visual Turing impossible. Sam didn't agree. It was true, though, that few EIs existed. Most never developed beyond AIs. The others she had known were contained within computers, including Madrigal. The few androids she had worked with didn't come close to passing the visual. She had never interacted with an EI as intensely human as Turner. But his personality, his intellect, all those intangibles that formed a person—they resided in a synthetic matrix. Had Turner Pascal been the blueprint for a remarkably effective android or was he a man? Perhaps it came down to a question none of them could truly answer: did he have a soul?

While the medics worked, Sam brushed a lock of hair off Turner's face. He opened his eyes and spoke in a low voice. "We aren't falling."

She smiled. "Definitely not."

Turner looked at the doctor, who was reading a monitor display. "Who are you?"

"Lieutenant Hollander." The medic nodded to him. "How do you feel?"

"All right." Turner slowly sat up, looking around. Seats lined the Redbird's hull, facing toward them. The crew consisted of these three officers, and perhaps a pilot and copilot in the cockpit, though a Redbird didn't need human guidance after a pilot programmed its AI brain.

Hollander spoke quietly. "I've never seen such a sophisticated android."

Turner's face darkened. "I'm a man."

The medic blinked. "You are?"

"My body was smashed in a hover accident. It's rebuilt with biomech."

Hollander looked as if he wanted to argue, but he said only, "You have an unusual brain."

Turner spoke tightly. "Yes, it's an EI. I was dead after the accident. Now I'm not. So what if my brain is a matrix? It doesn't make me a damn android."

"I'm sorry." Hollander seemed at a loss. "I meant no offense."

Major Parsons watched the exchange with interest but no surprise, which led Sam to think Thomas had briefed her.

"It won't take long to reach the airfield," Parsons said.

"Where do we go from there?" Sam asked.

"D.C., I believe," Parsons said. "The crew on your Rex can give you more details."

"Rex?" Sam asked.

The major smiled. "It's a nickname for your transport craft. You'll see why."

Sam noticed that Parsons spoke to both her and Turner. She respected that. People often avoided looking androids in the eye, as if that would somehow violate an unspoken code of humanity.

So they went, into the night.

Sam and Turner ran across the tarmac with Parsons and Hollander, shielding their faces against the wind. Sam couldn't see much beyond the circle of light on the field, though she could make out mountains around them, possibly the Sierra Nevadas. Their escort had been taciturn about the location of this field, but given that they had only been in the air about fifteen minutes, they were probably still in California.

Their transportation waited on the tarmac. The gorgeous aircraft made Sam's breath catch. It resembled models she had seen for hypersonic aircraft, but complete within itself rather than the venerable X-43. A B-52 had taken the X-43 up and released it on a Pegasus-derivative launch vehicle, which boosted the X-43 up to speeds where it could use its scramjets. Since then, hypersonic technology had been the fastest-advancing field in aviation. This beauty came all in one. Its rounded angles and dark color were reminiscent of her spy car, which was no surprise given that the car relied on military tech for its shroud. She could see why Parsons called this a Rex; it was surely the king of aircraft. At hypersonic speeds, it could reach anywhere in the world in four hours. It told her a lot about what Thomas thought of "Charon," that he wanted to bring them in as fast as possible in such a state-of-the-art warcraft.

"Wow," Turner said at her side.

Sam grinned. "Thomas has style."

A man waited for them in the hatchway, a military type who wore fatigues Sam didn't recognize. He had a muscular build and the bearing of someone who knew how to use his strength. Sam took the steps up to the Rex two at a time, but she paused at the top while Turner eased past her. Looking back, she saw Parsons and Hollander on the tarmac. Major Parsons lifted her hand in farewell.

The officer in the hatchway spoke to Sam. "You better get settled, Dr. Bryton. We'll be leaving as soon as possible."

Sam turned to the officer. He had brown hair razed in a buzz cut and icy blue eyes. His biceps strained his sleeves. He lifted his hand in an invitation for her to enter the Rex. "Ma'am."

"Thanks." She went into the cabin, a small area with four seats crammed together, two rows of two. Consoles were embedded in the arms of each, with a screen that could swing over a passenger's lap. White and green holicons indicating statistics such as cabin pressure and temperature glowed in the door that separated the cabin from the cockpit.

Sam dropped into a seat next to Turner. "I'll bet this beaut can fly higher and faster than just about anything else."

His face had gone ashen. "For someone who doesn't like heights, Sam, that isn't reassuring."

She laid her hand over his where he was clenching the end of his armrest. "We'll be okay."

He didn't answer, but he turned his hand over and clasped her fingers.

The man in fatigues closed the door and then turned to them. He met Sam's questioning look with a neutral gaze. His careful expression made it impossible to judge his thoughts, and his fatigues had no name or rank. He came toward the seats with controlled movements, as if he rationed each step. He didn't seem hostile, but rather, cautious to an extreme. Did these people know more about Turner than she did? Perhaps her prince in distress wasn't as vulnerable as she had assumed.

"How soon do we go?" Turner asked.

The officer answered in a pleasantly deep voice. "Soon, I think. I'll check." He went into the cockpit and closed its door, leaving them alone.

Sam shivered, though it was much warmer in here than outside. "I'll be glad when we leave."

"I suppose I shouldn't admit this," Turner said.

"But my EI keeps getting confused. This is too much. I haven't integrated all my systems yet. Charon was working on that when I ran off."

It relieved her to hear him ease up on his insistence that he was no different than a man. To her mind, his differences made him no less deserving of the rights he had taken for granted as Turner Pascal, but she could help him more if he wasn't in denial about the changes. "If you let us work with you, we can probably stabilize your EI."

He leaned his head back on the seat. "I'll never get away from it, will I? No one will ever see me as just Turner Pascal."

"No, they won't," she said. "That doesn't make you less. Just different." She squeezed his hand. "Better."

His face gentled, the lines around his eyes crinkling, lines that hadn't been there yesterday. Life, real life rather than a controlled lab environment, had begun to give his face the character—the humanity—it had lacked when she met him. He spoke in a low voice. "Thank you."

She smiled self-consciously. Then she indicated the cabin. "Guess we don't have stewardesses."

"Guess not."

"I wonder why they left us alone."

He snorted. "Maybe to study how we interact without anyone around to constrain our behavior."

That was cynical. "Has that happened before?"

"Charon was always playing with my mind."

Play. The more she heard about Charon, the less she liked it. Turner had a point, though; the crew probably could monitor them. She waved her hand at a bulkhead. "If you're watching, hello."

"I'm afraid I'll be a boring subject," Turner said. "I plan to sleep all the way to Washington."

"Sounds good to me." Sam settled herself, fastening the pressure-webbing around her body that would protect them from heavy accelerations.

The cockpit door suddenly opened and the man in fatigues came out. He glanced at Turner, his gaze taking on a shuttered quality. He stopped by their seats, and for a moment Sam thought he intended to speak. But he just inclined his head to them and stepped past. His clothes rustled as he settled behind them. For some reason, it bothered Sam to have him sit where she couldn't see him. She wouldn't feel safe until they were in the air. Even then, she doubted she could sleep. She wouldn't relax until they were safe with Thomas.

Sam dreaded going to D.C. for reasons unconnected to Turner. She had hardly been there since her father's death three years ago. As an Air Force colonel, he had traveled a great deal. During a visit to Paraguay, he had been an unintended casualty in a riot by an extremist group against the local government. His death had no connection to her work, but every time she thought of consulting for the military now, her anger over losing him interfered. Rather than deal with her grief, she had quit consulting.

Finally the Rex taxied across the tarmac and took off, heavy g-forces shoving them into their seats like a giant hand.

Once they were airborne, Turner wiped perspiration off his forehead. "Maybe we'll make it after all."

Sam let out a long breath. "Looks like it."

Someone put his hand on the arm of her chair.

Startled, she turned around. The man in fatigues was leaning forward.

"Can I get anything for you?" he asked. "Water? We haven't the greatest food, but it's edible."

She relaxed. "A glass of water would be great."

"Me, too," Turner said, loosening the webbing around his body.

"Water it is."

The man went to a tiny cubicle at the front of the cabin. It took him a while to find two metal cups above the sink there, which made Sam doubt he usually acted as a steward. As he filled a cup with water, the cockpit door opened and another man in fatigues came out, the copilot apparently, since Sam glimpsed a third man inside, sitting in the pilot's seat. The pilot didn't seem to be doing much; she suspected the Rex was flying itself.

The copilot was tall and angular, his black hair streaked with gray. He considered them with obvious satisfaction. "Hello, Turner."

Sam froze. Then she turned to see Turner staring with undisguised shock at the copilot. The steward had finished filling the glasses of water, but he just stood in the cubicle, waiting, watching the three of them.

Turner made a strangled noise. "No."

Sam suddenly felt ill. "Who is it?"

"Turner calls me Raze," the copilot said, smooth and unruffled. "I work for his owner."

"No one owns me!" Turner yanked off his webbing and started to stand.

"Where are you going?" Raze asked.

Turner stopped, half out of his seat. Then he dropped back down and rubbed his eyes with the heels of his hands. "I knew it. I *knew*." He lowered his hands. "I won't stay with him," he told Raze. "You hear me? I won't stay."

"You can discuss that when you get home." Raze made no effort to hide his condescension. "You shouldn't have run off. Charon won't be pleased."

"Go to hell," Turner said.

"I don't think so." Raze smiled coldly, like a weapon primed for use. Then he returned to the cockpit—leaving them alone with their unwanted steward.

V
Alpha

Sam spent the flight compulsively memorizing details about the cabin. She couldn't access the console built into her chair, big surprise, so she had nothing to do but worry.

She spoke quietly to Turner. "Is it possible Charon is working for the Air Force?"

He answered in a low voice. "I don't think so."

It seemed unlikely to Sam, too. The man in fatigues didn't strike her as Air Force, but his taciturn style revealed little. He saw to their needs in food and water, but responded to none of her questions. His careful movements, muscular build, and military bearing made her wonder if he was a mercenary Charon had hired.

Their "steward" had strapped on a stun gun, or staser. At first it relieved Sam; apparently he didn't plan to kill either of them. Then she realized he might be avoiding anything more powerful only because he didn't want to damage the Rex. She hoped Charon considered her expertise as an EI analyst worth enough to keep her alive. If he had done everything Turner claimed, though, he might not care if she died; he could resurrect her as a forma. But anyone brilliant enough to create Turner had to realize her value lay in her creativity, memory, expertise, and mental stability, any of which could be lost if he copied her mind into an EI.

What the hell. She would just try again to ask the steward what was up. She had little to lose. Turning in her seat, she said, "Hello."

He tilted his head, watching her as if she were an exotic animal he had caught in a cage. "Hello."

"I was wondering," she said.

"Yes?"

She made a conscious effort not to squirm under his scrutiny. "Who do you work for?"

Silence.

"Did you all steal this Rex?"

Silence.

He wasn't any more verbose now than the other times she had asked. She tried another tack. "So what do you do in your everyday life?"

"My job."

At least that got an answer. "What is that?"

Although he still didn't answer, this time he did smile. It made him look familiar, though she couldn't place why.

"You don't talk much," she said.

No answer, just that enigmatic smile.

After a few more futile attempts at conversation, Sam gave up and turned back around, slouching in her seat. She had thought, when she retreated to her beach six months ago, that the world would ignore her. She had left behind the acrimony and bitter losses at BioII. The potential payoff in the design and production of biomech and neural implants for humans was so damnably huge, BioII was rushing the work. Sam couldn't live with putting people at risk that way. The third time she had lost her fight to implement better safety controls on testing the implants, she had resigned.

It had caused a commotion Sam never intended. She was BioII's highest paid EI architect, the team leader who had patented their most profitable neural matrices. When she left on a matter of principle, the proverbial heads rolled. Then BioII had tried to woo her back. Although she missed her work, she couldn't in good conscience go back after all that had happened. Yet here she was in a worse conflict, one that might end her life instead of her job.

"What I don't understand," Sam said to no one in particular, "is how Charon got his people onto this Rex."

Turner shrugged. He had already made clear what he thought: the Redbird had come from Charon, not Thomas Wharington, or else Thomas worked for Charon. Sam didn't believe Thomas had betrayed them nor did she think these people were NIA or Air Force. The fake helicopter scenario didn't convince her, either. She had grown up around Air Force personnel. She would swear those medics had been the real deal. But that left the improbable scenario that Charon had substituted his people for the crew of this Rex, managing that feat at a hidden field in the mountains. It would mean he had a prodigious intelligence network, which suggested powerful backers.

"I just don't see how Charon managed it," Sam grumbled.

Turner gave a bitter laugh. "Welcome to my world."

"What will he do with us?"

"He probably wants you to work for him."

"Not a chance." It went against every principle she had fought for these past years.

Turner glanced back at their steward. Sam turned, too, and frowned at the man in fatigues.

"Can I help you?" the steward asked.

"I was wondering if you had a name," Sam said.

"Yes."

She waited. "Will you tell us?"

"No."

"You know," Sam said dourly, "our conversations aren't exactly scintillating."

He smiled. "Sorry."

"Come on," she said. "Just a name."

He regarded her with curiosity, but no animosity. "Be realistic. Would you tell me anything if our situation was reversed?"

"I wouldn't have kidnapped you."

"I'm sorry you don't like this, Dr. Bryton."

"How about you take us back, then?"

"I didn't say I was sorry we have you."

Disheartened, she turned to the front again. Turner put his head back on the seat and closed his eyes, but judging from his tense posture, she doubted he would sleep.

Eventually the engine rumble changed. The deceleration made her feel as if the blood drained out of her torso, despite the pressure webbing that pressed in on her body. But they landed safely. The steward had taken Sam's mesh glove so she didn't know the time, but she estimated they had been in flight over three hours. Lord only knew where they were now.

After they landed, the steward went into the cockpit, moving with the muscular ease of an athlete. The contained energy of his walk made Sam wonder if he were even human. Charon might have created others like Turner. Not many, though; it had surely taken a huge investment of funds, materials, expertise, and equipment to resurrect Turner. Creating an android from scratch was just as resource intensive. She doubted anyone could make such formas on a large scale—at least not yet.

Charon needed a backer. Could it be Sunrise Alley? Rumors drifted through the world meshes of the Alley, a hidden conclave of biomech geniuses involved in the forma black market. It had great mystique, and shadowy tales abounded everywhere, but until yesterday, she had thought those were little more than urban legends.

The steward opened the cockpit door, but before he went inside, he turned back to Sam and watched her as if he intended to speak. She shifted uneasily under his scrutiny. She was about to ask what he wanted when he turned away and entered the cockpit, closing the door behind him.

"What was that about?" Turner asked.

Sam felt as if she couldn't breathe. "I don't know."

The cockpit door opened again. This time both the pilot and Raze came out—and bile rose in her throat. Both of them carried pulse rifles, massive silver guns that glinted in the harsh light. One bullet from those monsters could tear a human body to shreds.

The pilot was made from the same mold as the

other two men, muscular and controlled, with dark hair and eyes. The steward followed him out of the cockpit and took another pulse rifle out of a locker in a bulkhead near the door. He turned, the rifle gripped in both hands. When he looked at Sam, his gaze became hooded. She suspected she had imagined his sympathy earlier, wishful thinking on her part that she and Turner might find an ally here. Disquieted and scared, she fumbled to unfasten her webbing.

Turner touched her shoulder. She jerked, feeling like a startled deer, except she couldn't run off. He mouthed the words *We'll be okay.*

Sam set her hand over his on her shoulder. They both knew they weren't going to be all right, but she appreciated his reassurance.

The steward opened the door, then stood silhouetted against a dark blue sky so vivid it seemed to vibrate. As Sam and Turner came forward under watch of their guards, the steward went out onto the top of what looked like mobile stairs. He motioned for Sam to follow. She stepped out—and gasped.

Mountains. They ringed the landing field. Steppe extended around the area for a mile or so, flat and parched. Beyond it, majestic peaks rose into the intensely blue sky, cloaked in snow, ringing the horizon in every direction. The stark landscape had a grandeur unlike any other mountains she had seen. A gibbous moon hung in the sky, ghostly blue.

The cold air seared her lungs, devoid of moisture, free of smog or dust. She couldn't pull in enough oxygen. They had to be incredibly high; she had never struggled this hard to breathe even in the highest peaks of the Sierra Nevadas in California.

"So they trod across the roof of the world," the steward murmured. He stood next to Sam, holding his rifle, letting her take her time.

The "roof of the world." Good Lord. He meant the Himalayas. "It's extraordinary," Sam said.

"So it is." His voice became businesslike. "Now we go down."

She looked down the stairs. Cranes were attending the aircraft, aided by mechbots, short for "mechanical robot," constructs with no biological components and little or no AI capability. The steward went first, followed by Sam and Turner, then the other two mercenaries. No one spoke. Icy air gripped them, drying the sweat on Sam's forehead.

They crossed the tarmac to a low building. It had no distinguishing features, only dark walls with no visible entrance. When a rumble came from behind them, Sam jumped and spun around. One of the cranes was closing up the door of the Rex.

The steward grasped her arm. "Keep going."

An image came to Sam: pulse projectiles blasting through her body, destroying her organs with shock waves. She swallowed and began walking again.

As they neared the building, she asked, "Where is this place?"

No one answered. None of the mercenaries showed any sign of emotion. Their faces and posture implied nothing except confidence in their right to kidnap her and Turner. Sam gritted her teeth. They did their jobs damnably well.

The building had no windows or ornamentation. As they reached its closest wall, a lamp came on under the overhanging eaves. The steward pressed his thumb against a panel and waited while light scanned his eyes.

Seams formed—and a door silently slid open.

The steward motioned Sam forward, but this time she balked, an instinctual reaction, one that happened before her mind caught up with her reflexes. "What is in there?"

She expected them to threaten her with their guns. Instead the steward was unexpectedly solicitous. "Don't worry. You won't be hurt."

Turner spoke as if he were gritting his teeth. "Depends how you define 'hurt.'"

The steward considered him as a race car driver might consider a sleek new car with design problems. "You have caused Charon a great deal of trouble. I would suggest you don't anger him further." No trace remained of the sympathy he had showed Sam.

None of the other mercenaries spoke, but they had all raised their guns. Sam didn't want her actions to cause Turner harm. She took his arm. "Let's go on in."

He didn't answer, but he did walk forward with her, his jaw set. They stayed close together, surrounded by the mercenaries. Sam felt trapped in a cage of armed, hostile forces. Turner took her hand, clasping her fingers in his. She squeezed his fingers.

A corridor stretched out in front of them, lit here but reaching into darkness. Gold metal paneled its floor, walls, and ceiling, glimmering, beautiful but stark in its lack of adornment. Her running shoes squeaked on the floor. The hall was wide enough for six people to walk abreast, but they went in a cluster, the steward and Raze first, then Turner and Sam, and the pilot in the rear. No doors broke the walls on either side, but Sam had no doubt they were there, just hidden. Charon would want them as confused as possible; the less they knew, the easier it would be to keep them secured here.

The ceiling glowed above them as they walked and dimmed after they passed. The corridor seemed to go on forever, farther than was possible given the size of the building. She didn't think they were underground; the floor didn't noticeably slope. When she closed her eyes and relied more on her sense of balance, she wasn't certain they were going in a straight line. This was all another way for Charon to keep them disoriented, unable to get their bearings.

This endless corridor might have affected someone else, but Sam had seen such tricks before. The glimmering walls were holo screens that projected images. It didn't surprise her that their guards didn't let them close enough to touch any surface; what they felt probably wouldn't match what they saw.

Finally she stopped. "This is stupid. If you all like walking in circles around a holo track, go ahead. I'm going to wait here until you're done with this game."

The steward considered her. He seemed more fascinated than anything else. "I suppose I could threaten you with my gun to get you moving."

"Yeah, you could," Sam said.

His mouth quirked up. "Should I?"

"You should take us home."

"I don't think so." He unhooked the mesh glove from his belt and pulled it on his hand. Then he moved away from them. When he spoke into its comm, his voice was too low to overhear. After only a few moments, though, he came back to them, again with that maddening smile of his. "All right, Sam. Here."

She didn't like the way he watched her. "Here?"

With no warning, the walls melted around them. Then they were standing in another corridor, one with similar walls—except this one curved to the right until it disappeared from sight.

"Well, look at that," Sam said. "What a surprise."

Turner turned in a circle, looking around. "How did you know it was fake?"

"It's a cheap trick," Sam said.

"Hardly cheap, I assure you," the steward said.

Sam raised her eyebrows at him. "Maybe you're an illusion, too. Or maybe you're Charon."

"You flatter me." Dryly he added, "And insult Charon." Then he motioned her forward.

They followed the corridor only for a short distance before the steward stopped. Although Sam didn't see him do anything, the wall in front of him faded away into a rectangular archway. Beyond it, an office gleamed with white walls and carpet, and glass furniture. Glow-tiles on the ceiling filled the room with light. Despite Sam's intent to remain cool and collected, the sight rattled her. Someone had gone to a great deal of expense to create this strange hallway and imposing office.

As they entered the office, she memorized details. A white Luminex console stretched the length of the opposite wall. No one sat behind it. The room had a lot of empty space. The rounded white couch and armchairs glimmered with indistinct holo patterns that shifted as she moved, creating an ethereal quality as if they were scintillating clouds. The tables sparkled and their edges broke light into colors. She would have bet diamonds were embedded in those edges; a prism wouldn't split this diffuse light so well.

"How gaudy," Sam said. It wasn't; the gorgeous room with its subtle display of wealth impressed the hell out of her, which made it all the more intimidating. Trying to cover her apprehension, she said, "So where is our host?"

Turner stood next to her with his jaw clenched. Raze and the steward flanked him, both taller and more muscular, pulse rifles in hand. They menaced without saying a word. Turner looked terrified. Sam wanted to reach for his hand, to offer support, but the steward stood between them, deliberately, she thought.

The pilot went to the console across the room and leaned over a comm there, his lips moving, though Sam couldn't hear him. She looked back the way they had come in time to see a door slide across the entrance, its surface matching the walls so well that no seams showed when it finished closing. Their prison was complete.

"Is this Charon's office?" Sam asked Turner.

"I don't know." He folded his arms and rubbed his palms along them. "I've never been here before."

"What happens now?" she asked.

The steward motioned at the pilot across the room. "He's talking with Charon. We wait until he's done." He indicated a couch against the wall to their left. The long table before it was glass, with chrome legs and prismatic edges. "Please be comfortable."

Sam kept her thoughts about Charon's "comfort" to herself. The mercenaries pushed Sam and Turner forward, so they all went to the couch. Sam sank onto it, and the cushions responded to her tension far more adeptly than her own semi-smart furniture. It still didn't help, though.

An armchair stood at the end of the couch, facing in. Turner sat down in it, his body so taut that Sam doubted the chair could make him comfortable, either. Seeing his haunted expression, she felt like a fraud. She had promised him refuge. But she didn't see what else they could have done. Contacting the NIA may have led Charon to them, but they would have been even more exposed had they spent hours on an unprotected highway driving the Lost Coast of northern California, with its plunging gorges, dense forests, and lonely cliffs.

"I'm sorry this happened," Sam said to him.

"It's not your fault," he said. "We're facing an expert. Maybe no one can outwit him."

Sam had no intention of giving up. "We'll see."

Raze and the steward took up positions on either side of the couch. Then the pilot came back and stood behind Turner's chair. All three guards waited in silence, imposing and solid, with no expression. Sam wished they didn't look so blasted effective.

With no warning, the wall behind the console shimmered and faded into a doorway. It was dark beyond, making it hard to see the person entering the room—until she stepped into the light. Black hair brushed her shoulders and her dark eyes slanted upward. She wore a form-fitting black jumpsuit that did nothing to hide her devastatingly well-toned figure. Her black knee-boots added several more inches to her six-foot height. The belt around her narrow waist glimmered with silver mesh-threads, and a pulse gun rode snug in a holster at her hip.

"Good Lord," Turner muttered.

"You know her?" Sam asked.

"Never seen her before." He looked alarmed. "Believe me, I would remember."

The surge of jealousy that hit Sam startled her; she hadn't realized she had begun to think about Turner as hers. More than anything else, that convinced her he was a man; she couldn't imagine any machine evoking such a powerful response in her.

The woman stalked over to them, cool and menacing. Sam stood up, feeling puny in comparison to this new phenomenon. As Turner rose to his feet, the woman looked them up, down, and over. She stopped on the other side of the coffee table and considered them with her hands on her hips. Her unusual height made Sam excruciatingly aware of her slight build and wild hair. She had nothing on this sleek, perfect person. She felt as if she were being judged and discarded.

"Are you Charon?" Sam asked.

The woman gave a husky laugh. "Not even close."

Sam wished she didn't feel so cold. "So when is he showing up?"

The woman shrugged. "If he wishes to come, he will. For now I am your host."

Sam looked her up and down the same way the woman had done to them, though she doubted she intimidated anyone, let alone this mercenary goddess. "Who are you?"

"You may call me Alpha."

"Alpha?" Personally, Sam thought someone this unique deserved a more original nickname than the first letter of the Greek alphabet. Maybe Alpha was an android, first of a series, followed by Beta, Gamma, Delta, ad nauseum. Sam had never heard of anyone building such a magnificent forma, though.

Alpha spoke to the steward. "I'll take the android with me. You stay here with Dr. Bryton."

"I'm not a goddamned android," Turner said.

Sam wished she wasn't so far from Turner. She felt small as they stood facing all these large, muscular people. No doubt the effect was intentional. Mental games had never worked well on Sam, but this was reaching even her limit. She was terrified they would end up dead. Or worse.

"Turner and I stay together," she said.

"Is that so?" Alpha smiled, her teeth glittering—literally. They had the same prismatic quality as the table. "Turner, don't be difficult. Charon could take you apart and put you together however he wants."

His gaze darkened. "I know."

"Then behave yourself and come with me."

He clenched one fist at his side. "No."

With surreal calm, Alpha drew her gun—and fired. The bullet shattered the table in front of Sam and sent glass flying. She whipped her arm in front of her face, staggering as shards rained over her. The back of her calves hit the couch and her legs buckled, collapsing her onto the cushions. Alpha must have intended to hit the table; she couldn't have missed at this range.

Turner lunged toward Sam. "Get her a doctor!"

Alpha pointed her gun at him. When he froze, she said, "Stay put."

"A doctor?" Sam asked. Baffled, her heart racing, she rose to her feet. "Why?"

For some reason, the steward came over and put his hand under her elbow. She pulled away from him.

"She *is* a doctor," Alpha said, obviously amused. "An EI shrink, no less. You need therapy, Turner?"

He looked ready to strangle her. "Get help, damn it."

"What are you talking about?" Sam asked. She meant to say more, but an unexpected dizziness stopped her. The steward tried to make her sit down and Turner gave him a murderous look.

"Everyone, stop." Sam's left arm had begun to hurt. She peered down—

Blood covered her forearm.

"Oh." Sam dropped onto the couch. Gashes covered her arm and she felt blood running over the skin. She suddenly thought she would lose her rushed dinner of hot dogs.

Carefully, with no sudden movements, Turner stepped over and knelt at her side on the couch. He took her hand. "Don't protest anymore. I'll go with them."

"Turner—" She stopped when he laid two fingers over her lips.

"I thank you for standing by me," he said. "But I refuse to be responsible for your death."

"They won't kill me." She meant to sound confident, but her voice wobbled.

He squeezed her hand, his gaze caressing her face, as if he would memorize it now, in case he never saw it again. "You've guts, Sam, but courage won't stop bullets. Promise me you won't challenge them."

Sam started to answer, but a wave of dizziness stopped her. She closed her eyes and sat very still, fending off the nausea.

When feet rustled on the carpet, she looked to see Alpha and Raze taking away Turner.

VI
Rendezvous

The medic finished bandaging Sam's arm. "It should heal quickly. But go easy for a few days." He pressed the bio-gauze more securely into place. It molded to her skin, matching it in color. The mesh-threads woven through it would tell it when to dispense medicine. Slumped on the couch, she was all too aware now of the pain she hadn't felt before. Alpha had shredded her forearm.

The doctor resembled the other mercenaries in that he wore the ubiquitous fatigues, but he had a more responsive demeanor. He made no attempt to hide his concern.

"Will I regain full use of my arm?" she asked.

"You should. But take care around Alpha. Next time you won't get off so easy."

Sam winced. "I'll remember."

"You sure you don't want anything for the pain?"

"I'm sure." She needed to keep a sharp mind. "Do you know what happened to Turner?"

He stood up. "Would you like some dinner?"

So he wasn't answering questions, either. "No thanks." The last thing she needed right now was food in her stomach.

He spoke to the steward, who was standing by the couch. "Make sure no one bothers Dr. Bryton."

"Affirmative."

Affirmative, indeed. Maybe he was a forma after all. Except he didn't really act like a machine. Beneath his impassive exterior, he showed a good deal of emotion. She supposed he could be an EI as advanced as Turner, but her intuition said no.

The doctor left via the exit behind the console across the room. It appeared and vanished for him just as it had done for Alpha.

Sam glowered at the steward. "'Affirmative'? Can't you say 'yes'?"

He grinned, showing straight white teeth. It made him look like a completely different person; a father who coached Little League, a lieutenant who brought his girl roses, a brother teasing his sister. Then he said, "Yes."

Flustered, Sam said, "Well. Good."

He made no response. His momentary lapse ended and his expression hardened again.

Sam stretched out along the sofa on her back and pushed a cushion behind her head so she was half sitting. Then she spoke firmly to the steward. "I need a name to call you. I can't keep saying 'hey, you.'"

"How about Hud?"

"Is that your real name?"

"No."

"Oh, well. You can call me Harriet."

"Why Harriet?"

"Well, why not?"

To her surprise, Hud laughed. "Fair enough."

She frowned at him. "You aren't allowed to have a sense of humor."

"Why not?"

"Because you're a henchman of the villain."

"Do you really want me to call you Harriet?"

She couldn't help but smile. "I suppose not."

After that, they fell silent again. Sam tried to rest, but she couldn't relax. She kept worrying about Turner. Hud might show flashes of sympathy, but she had no doubt he could kill without hesitation if given the order. She wanted to think her way through this mess to some sort of escape, but she had trouble concentrating. She hadn't slept in two days. Couldn't hold her lashes up . . .

Muffled footsteps brought Sam awake. She opened her eyes to see Alpha standing over her like a panther ready to strike. With a grunt, Sam tried to sit up. Her head swam and she flopped back, hating herself for showing weakness in front of this person who had shot her without remorse.

"Hello, Dr. Bryton," Alpha said.

Taking it slower this time, Sam sat up again. Her queasiness surged, but she stayed upright. Although she didn't want to try anything more, she slowly stood up so Alpha wouldn't loom over her so much. It didn't help; Sam felt miserably outclassed.

Alpha smirked. "Feeling better?"

Sam made an effort not to grit her teeth. "Fine."

"Good." Alpha indicated the wall behind the console. "Let's go."

Sam would rather have walked through flaming oil than have gone with her. However, she wanted even less to be shot. So she followed Alpha, escorted by Hud. Just crossing the room was an ordeal. After so little sleep, she felt ready to collapse, especially given her injury. With each step, her queasiness surged. Pride kept her going; the prospect of passing out in front of Alpha and Hud was too humiliating to contemplate.

They exited out onto the landing of a spiral stairwell paneled in Luminex. It was like being trapped in a bright, sterile cloud. Alpha led the way down, around and around and around. It didn't help Sam's dizziness. But she was determined to find out what she could about this place.

"So, Alpha," Sam said. "What country are we in?"

Silence.

"Somewhere at a high altitude," Sam added.

Silence.

She tried again. "It wasn't freezing outside. Cold, though. That leaves a lot of possible latitudes."

Silence.

Sam gave up. These people were too well trained. She had been lucky to drag those few smiles out of Hud.

Mercifully, they only went down a few levels. At the bottom, Alpha pressed her thumb onto a panel and stood while a light scanned her eyes. Seams split along the wall and a door swung open with surprising ease, given that it was at least two feet thick.

Alpha stalked through the doorway, sleek and alarming. Hud took Sam's arm and followed. Although Sam drew away from him, she took care not to move too fast, lest it evoke who-knew-what defensive reflexes on his part. They entered a Luminex corridor suffused with light. Unlike other hallways she had seen here, this one had doors, some open. As they passed the open ones, she looked inside.

Whoa.

Biomech labs. Good labs. *Spectacular.* Within moments she was practically salivating. These people had better facilities even than BioII.

Alpha turned into a doorway. Sam followed her into a lab that made the others she had seen pale in comparison, including her own. This one stretched for many meters, gleaming in Luminex and chrome, filled with biomech tables, consoles of the latest design, robot arms, and mechbots of many sizes. Burt-walls curved around, alive with lights, packed with equipment. Scooter-bots hummed through the lab, carrying supplies, and biomech chairs waited, white and glossy.

Sam couldn't help but gape. "This is awesome."

"Like it?" Alpha asked.

"Yeah. I do." Sam's appreciation withered as she turned to Alpha. "But I won't work here."

"Suit yourself." Alpha went on, deeper into the lab.

Sam followed, unable to deny her curiosity. She wished Giles could see this place; more than most anyone else, he would appreciate it. He had thought Charon meant Sunrise Alley. If this was the Alley, she could see why it had become a legend. Even if Charon were phenomenally wealthy, he had to have backing to fund this installation, probably from the government of whatever country they were in now. She hated what it might imply about Thomas, that she had ended up here after seeking his help.

Up ahead, Alpha stopped by a biomech table. Something was on its flat surface, but Sam couldn't see with Alpha in the way. She went past the mercenary—and froze. Turner lay there with his eyes closed, his wrists and ankles manacled to the table.

Sam's pulse jumped. "Turner? Are you all right?"

His chest rose and fell in a slow, even rhythm.

Sam swung around to Alpha. "What did you do to him?"

She shrugged. "Nothing. I'm a soldier. Not a scientist."

Sam gritted her teeth. She wanted to use her fists to show Alpha what she thought of her "soldiering," but she restrained the impulse. Instead she leaned over Turner, shook his shoulder, just barely at first, then harder.

No response.

"Turner, wake up," she said.

"He can't answer," Alpha said.

"Why not?" Sam was aware of Hud listening, and of the pain in her bandaged left arm.

Alpha gave her a long, considering look, as if she had stripped away Sam's defenses and found her lacking. "Charon has a proposition for you."

"No," Sam said.

"You haven't heard it yet."

"I'm not working on Turner."

"Nevertheless. Charon has an offer." Alpha jerked her chin at the table. "Work on the android and Charon will let you live."

The idea revolted Sam, a violation of so many principles she valued, she couldn't count them all. She spoke tightly. "Turner isn't an android."

Alpha waved her hand. "Whatever he is, he has become a liability. Charon can strip him for parts."

"Parts?" Sam stared at her. "This man isn't a *car*. He's a sentient being with awareness of his self."

"How do you know he wasn't programmed to behave that way?" Her cold smile curved. "Maybe he was programmed to fall in love with you."

If Alpha intended to rattle her, this time she had chosen the wrong approach. "Don't play Turing games with me. I invented the best of them." Part of her job had been testing whether or not an EI had convincing emotions, including the ability to love. "If Charon kills Turner, he is committing murder."

"Then accept Charon's proposal."

Sam crossed her arms. "No."

Alpha looked bored. "Accept, or Turner is dead."

"You're bluffing. He's too valuable to destroy."

Alpha glanced at Sam's bandaged arm. "I never bluff."

They were backing her into a corner. They believed she cared enough for Turner to go along—and they were right. Even if she had just met him, she couldn't stand by while they murdered or tortured him. But Alpha didn't convince her. Maybe she didn't bluff, but Charon might. Sam didn't believe he would destroy what had taken so much to create.

"You won't kill me or Turner." Sam hoped she wasn't gambling away their lives. "We're worth too much."

"Humble, aren't you?" Alpha no longer looked smug. She turned on her booted heel and strode away, her black-clad body a jarring contrast to the blindingly white lab.

Sam watched Alpha stalk out of the lab. "Charming lady," she muttered.

Desire glinted in Hud's eyes. "I like her."

That figured. Again Sam had that eerie sense she knew him. Nothing seemed familiar about Raze or the pilot who had brought them here. Perhaps she was wrong about Hud, too. But she couldn't lose the feeling.

Disquieted, Sam turned back to the table. She hated to see Turner shackled. She wanted to fix everything, make it right. She brushed his disarrayed hair off his forehead. In sleep, his face lost the lines of character it had developed these past days, becoming unreal with his perfect skin. Or like a wax figure. But his cheek felt human. She doubted it was his natural skin, given its lack of flaws. She remembered the Hilton ad. He had looked so vibrant and alive. So happy. Then he had died.

The random nature of the hover crash angered Sam. Traffic grids in cities controlled the flow of vehicles to prevent accidents or jams. She inwardly swore at the driver who had taken his truck off the grid so he could break the law. Turner had paid the price of that judgment. No wonder Turner felt trapped in a nightmare, "waking up" to find himself enslaved to a stranger who claimed he no longer had an identity as a living human being.

"How can you do it?" Sam demanded of Hud. "How can you be part of this?"

He met her gaze without a hint of remorse. "Dr. Bryton, don't buy yourself trouble. Do what they want."

"Why would you care?"

"I don't like waste." His voice became intense. "And the loss of your life would be a great waste."

Sam agreed, though his intensity disquieted her. She touched Turner's shoulder. "Turner, I wish you could talk to me."

"I can," he said, his eyes closed.

Sam jumped back from the bench. "What?"

Hud lifted his rifle.

"No, don't." Sam spoke hurriedly to the mercenary.

Hud stepped closer, his rifle up. "Is he awake?"

"I'm not sure." An idea came to Sam. She repeated Hud's question. "Turner? Are you awake?"

Turner answered immediately. "Not exactly."

Sam glanced at Hud. "Ask him another question."

"Why?" Hud demanded.

"I want to see how he reacts."

Hud narrowed his gaze, but he said, "Are you awake, Mr. Pascal?"

When Turner didn't respond, Sam gestured at Hud to try again.

Hud's voice snapped. "Pascal, answer me."

No response.

Sam spoke. "Turner, can you talk to me?"

"Yes."

"Are you all right?" she asked.

"No. I would like to wake up."

"Will you talk to Hud?"

"No."

Hud flushed. "Don't disrespect me, android."

Interesting. It was the first time Sam had seen Hud angry. Apparently he didn't keep his cool so well in the face of what he considered contempt. It made her wonder about his psychology, if he expected human reactions from someone he considered a machine.

Turner's responses also intrigued Sam. On the yacht, he had set himself to respond only to her voice. Now he answered when he was deactivated, but only to her. If it was a manifestation of the program he had set up before, it implied Charon didn't have full control over him even now.

Hud spoke tightly. "What game is he playing?"

"It's just a malfunction."

He regarded her suspiciously. "How do you know?"

"Analyzing EIs is my job. I've seen this sort of thing before." In truth, she had never encountered such behavior. She thought fast. "It's a reflex, the way a dead person might twitch."

Hud spoke dryly. "That has a certain aptness here."

His lack of compassion made her grit her teeth. "What does Charon want me to do with Turner?"

"I don't know." He shrugged. "Develop his EI, I suppose."

Sam studied his face. She had spent her career analyzing, interpreting, and reproducing nuances of human emotion. She could interpret expressions and body language better than most anyone. Hud was good at hiding his, but he wasn't unreadable. She decided to prod him and see what came up.

"Are you a military officer?" she asked.

"No."

"Mercenary?"

He paused. "I suppose you could call me that."

"From where?"

Silence.

"Are you an android?" she asked.

For once he looked startled. "No."

So. That surprised him. Either he hadn't expected

anyone to guess he was an android or else he genuinely was human.

Footsteps rang on the floor. Sam turned with a start and saw Alpha striding toward them. The mercenary stopped in front of her. "Come with me."

"What about Turner?" Sam asked.

"What about him?"

"We can't just leave him here."

"Actually, we can. Now come."

"He spoke to Dr. Bryton," Hud said. With malice, he added, "Like an android."

Well, hell. Sam had hoped he wouldn't bring it up. She supposed it was unrealistic; this was his job. Given his "just facts" attitude so far, though, his crack about androids was out of character. Could he be jealous of Turner? That could prove useful or dangerous, she wasn't certain which.

"I'll let Charon know." Alpha turned smartly and headed out of the lab.

Hud took Sam's uninjured arm and pushed her forward. When she tried to pull away, he tightened his grip until she flinched.

"Stop," Sam said. "That hurts."

"Then don't make me do it." His voice hardened. "You're done talking to the fucking android."

She stared at him. Then she turned and followed Alpha.

Sam didn't expect to sleep. Her cell had white walls and furniture. Holoscapes of the mountains glowed on the walls and a potted plant sat in the corner. She didn't realize how much she had missed such simple signs of life.

Her left arm ached. That pain, combined with her worry for Turner and her general fear, kept her tossing and turning in bed. Then she lay on her back and stared at the ceiling. She left the light on, uneasy about being alone in the dark . . .

Someone was shaking her shoulder. Sam sat up fast, swinging out her arms. Her fists hit a man's chest.

"Sam, don't," he said.

"Turner!" Relief surged through her. He was sitting on the edge of the bed, very much alive and well. She grabbed him, throwing her arms around his waist.

"Hey." He pulled her close, favoring her injured arm.

Sam laughed unevenly, her head against his shoulder. "How did you get out of the lab?"

"I'm not sure. I was asleep. I woke up here."

Sam struggled for breath. He was holding her too tightly; whether he knew it or not, he had more strength than an unaugmented man. She pushed against his shoulders until he loosened his hold. Then she looked up at him. "Did you know you were in a lab before?"

"It's all recorded in my memory." He regarded her bleakly. "I think Charon wants you to 'improve' my EI. Make me more obedient, less contrary."

"I won't do it."

"It's true what they told you, that he might destroy me." The muscles in his arm had tensed, ridged against her back. "He can remake me, more to his liking."

"No. I won't let him." How she would stop him, she had no idea. "So you could hear us."

"Some." He hesitated. "I don't know why I could respond to you when I was supposed to be out."

"You set yourself up that way on the yacht."

"It's possible." He thought for a moment. "It's hard to judge all the results when I deliberately change my matrix rather then letting it evolve on its own." He scooted back on the bed until he was sitting against the wall, then held out his hand to her. She slid over and sat with him, her back against the wall. When he put his arms around her, she laid her head on his shoulder, grateful for this reprieve. She knew exactly what Charon was doing; he wanted her to spend time with Turner, get to like him, even love him, leaving her unable to refuse when Charon told her to work on Turner or see him die. It wasn't necessary; she would never stand by while he killed Turner. But as long as Charon didn't know that, he would let her see him. Personally, she would have liked to do some biomech work on Charon—without anesthetic.

"Sam?"

"Yes?"

"You are sitting like a board."

"That's me," she said. "The ol' board."

He laughed softly. "You've too many nice curves."

Sam smiled, making a conscious effort to relax. She wanted to feel normal with him, but the whole situation confused her. Quick question: how did she feel about embracing a biomechanical man who had died and come back to life? Quick answer: she had no clue. No, that was a lie. *Admit it. You like him.* She also had to admit the rest, that it scared her.

"You make a great date," she said.

He traced his fingers along her cheek. "A date with me rarely is typical."

Sam laughed. "That was humble."

"I meant, I don't go out often. I'm usually broke."

Present tense. To him, his life had no disconnect, no time when he had died and became an EI. However, she didn't believe for a moment he hadn't spent time with women. "You're too smooth to be that innocent."

"You think I'm smooth?" He sounded surprised.

Maybe it wasn't the right word. He was more relaxed than other men she had dated, the wizards, movers, and tycoons of the biotech world. Turner was less complicated.

"You're comfortable with a woman," she said. "You don't need to impress her."

He spoke dryly. "I've nothing to impress anyone with, especially someone like you."

She lifted her head so she could look him in the eyes. "You don't need degrees, wealth, or a high-powered job. I like you just the way you are. I left all that behind because I didn't like what it did to people." She brushed her finger over his lips. "And you can't tell me you don't know what to do with a woman."

He moved his head so his lips were next to her ear, his breath tickling her skin. "I didn't say I didn't know. They were always asking me out at the hotel."

"Hah! I knew it. You did go out."

"Some. Not often. Most of the women who asked were hotel guests. Rich, older, usually married." He kissed her ear. "The pretty bellboy would have been a pleasant diversion. I didn't like that. So I usually said no."

"Usually?"

He bit at her neck. "I get lonely, too."

"I'm rich and older," Sam said. "You going to say no to me, too?"

He rested his forehead against her head. "You wouldn't know how to make a pass even if you wanted to."

She bristled. "What, you think I'm not smooth?"

Mischief lightened his voice. "Am I wrong? Are you suave and sophisticated, Sam Bryton?"

She would have glared at him if he hadn't been kissing her temple. Distracted, she told the truth instead. "Hell, Turner, I have the seductive instincts of a rock."

He nuzzled her hair. "That's one reason I like you."

"Oh." That could be refreshing. Most men liked her for her money. That was another reason she hadn't dated much since Richard's death. Her first husband hadn't known his girlfriend was rich; it had been less obvious in those days. After all the articles about her, especially during the BioII hearings, most people knew she was one of the wealthiest people in California. Nor were they usually successful in hiding their interest in her money. That was the problem with dating an EI shrink: she made her living analyzing nuances of human body language.

Turner genuinely didn't care. She doubted he had any real clue about her wealth. They sat together, he with his arms round her, his head resting against hers, she holding her injured arm in front of her body. She wanted to talk escape plans with him, but they couldn't here. Charon would know.

"This is good," Turner said.

"Yes."

He hugged her close. "I've been so scared."

"Me, too." Even so, she felt safe in his embrace, though she would never admit it aloud.

"Do you think they are watching us on monitors?"

"Probably." Based on what she had so far seen and heard about Charon, he seemed obsessed with controlling people. Paranoid. She doubted he would let her and Turner even breathe without keeping watch.

Sam understood Charon's problem with Turner. You couldn't program EIs to obey your every command; to become sentient and self-aware, they needed the freedom to develop on their own. You either had to convince them to do what you wanted or else turn them off and alter the structure of their matrix. Changing the configuration of a sixth-generation neural network was a risky proposition; even the best architect could destroy what made the EI self-aware. It was akin to brain damage. Sam knew few people who could manage such operations, but unfortunately she was one of them. Charon probably wanted her to redesign Turner's matrix so it evolved more according to his specifications.

"Are you tired?" Turner asked.

"Exhausted. But I'm too wound up to sleep."

"Me, too." He rubbed his palm down her arm. "Perhaps we should, uh—lie down."

She felt unusually warm. "Okay."

They stretched out on top of the covers, Turner on his back with his arm around her shoulders, Sam on her right side, so she could keep her bandaged arm free. She felt no sleepier than before, but for very different reasons now. That Turner didn't seem consciously aware of his sensuality just made it more distracting. She slid her hand across his chest, savoring the feel of his muscles under the thin shirt.

"Uh, Sam." Turner caught her hand. "I didn't say this before, but—that is, I mean, it wouldn't come up in normal conversation . . ."

She waited. "Yes?"

"The thing is—" He cleared his throat. "I'm fully functional. If you keep that up, I'll want to, uh, function."

She smiled. He wasn't the only one. Heat spread in her face. "I'm sure our audience would like that."

"Yeah." Under his breath, he added, "Damn."

"I'm too old for you."

"Oh come on. I know I look young, but I really am twenty-seven. You can't be more than thirty."

"Are you trying to flatter me?"

"No." His voice lightened. "Not that I'm adverse to the idea. You're gorgeous, Sam Bryton, and you've a body like a bunny from Playb—"

"Turner!"

He laughed good-naturedly. "Sorry."

"I'm forty-one."

Silence. Then he said, "You're joking."

"No. I'm not."

"You look younger. A lot."

Sam wished she hadn't told him. "Does it bother you?"

"Good Lord, no." Wryly he added, "I'm hardly one to criticize someone for extending their youth. I wouldn't even be alive if not for my biomech construction."

"I don't have biomech in me."

"You've never had treatments to delay your aging?"

"Well, yeah." It wasn't hard to remove lines, lift and tighten skin, repair cell damage with molecular additives to one's body, and otherwise hold on to youth. Expensive, but simple if you could afford the procedures.

"It doesn't matter to me." He rolled onto his side, facing her. "Does it bother you, what I am?"

"It—startles me. But it makes you no less human to me." Maybe more. Right now she was scared, tired, and lonely, and Turner felt so very fine. She cupped his cheek with her palm. Her lips quirked up. "I would show you just how much it doesn't matter, but I don't want to put on a performance for anyone watching."

He laughed. "We're probably boring them to death." He did kiss her, though. It made her heat up in places he wasn't touching but that she wished he would. They only lay together after that, managing a laudable but frustrating restraint.

Sam faced an impossible dilemma. If they were right about what Charon wanted, she could never do it, not to Turner. But if she refused, Charon could start over with Turner. The man she knew, the one she was falling for, would cease to exist.

Charon would murder a man who was already dead.

VII

Hypersonic Man

"Of course I'm me," Turner said. He and Sam were sitting on the bed, drinking coffee from the tray someone had left inside the door while they slept. No one had taken Sam's wallet, though. At first it surprised her; then she realized if she escaped and used her clever-card, Charon could probably trace the transaction. It would be like a holosign over her head saying "Here I am."

Although it embarrassed Sam that someone had come in while she and Turner lay sleeping together, she warmed at the thought of his body next to hers. To distract her misbehaving thoughts, she took another bite of her muffin. The tray had four, along with butter and jam, and she was having a hard time leaving two for Turner. Although her bandaged arm still hurt, it had improved compared to yesterday.

"But how can you know you're you?" Sam asked. Talking to Turner reminded her of the debates she and Linden Polk had enjoyed so much when she had been a postdoc in his lab at MIT. "Your memories can't be complete; you were dead for several hours before Charon imaged your brain." Just saying those words unsettled her.

"I just know." He took a muffin. "If I think I'm me, how can I not be?"

Sam had no chance to answer. The door across the room opened, revealing Alpha in a skintight black jumpsuit, with Hud standing behind her in his usual fatigues.

"Aren't you two cozy," Alpha said.

Sam poured another mug of coffee, ignoring her.

Alpha strolled into the room, over to the bed. "Time to go."

Sam sipped her coffee. "Where?"

"With us." Alpha rested her hand on the barrel of the pulse gun at her hip. "Both of you."

Remembering her injured arm, Sam decided not to push her luck. She set down her coffee, then stood up next to Alpha, wishing the other woman didn't do such a good job of towering over her.

Then they all left.

The elevator car had off-white walls and a plush carpet. Alpha and Hud flanked Turner, Hud to his left, separating him from Sam. Hud also put Sam in front of himself, which she didn't like in the least. To see Turner, she had to swivel her head. He had hunched his shoulders—

Then Turner moved.

It happened so fast, his body blurred. He whipped his arms straight out from his sides, hitting Alpha's stomach with his right and Hud's chest with his left. Caught off guard, Sam lurched back into the wall. How could Turner move so fast? She would have sworn he had two clubs, one in each hand, but it happened too quickly for her to see clearly.

Hud doubled over, his arms crunched into his body. The blow threw Alpha into the wall to the right, across the car from Sam. Alpha managed to whip up her gun, but Turner was already lunging forward, and he struck her arm before she could fire. A loud crack sounded and her arm snapped back as she dropped the gun.

It took Hud only seconds to recover. Then he went after Turner. But in the same instant Turner broke Alpha's arm, he also slammed his other club into Hud's solar plexus. He didn't even look to aim the blow.

With a grunt, Hud reeled into the back wall and slumped to the floor. Sam stood flattened against the left wall, unable to believe it. Alpha and Hud were both unconscious, collapsed on the ground, Alpha's arm twisted at an unnatural angle. The entire fight couldn't have taken more than five seconds.

"Holy shit," she said. "Where did you get those clubs?"

Turner glanced at her. "What clubs?"

"I—don't know." He wasn't holding anything now. His arms hung by his sides, his fists clenched. He couldn't be hiding anything as large as the clubs she had thought she saw.

Her adrenaline surging, Sam went to the panel at the front of the elevator. It had no floor numbers, only a mesh screen. "We need that floor where we came in. If we can get out, we might be able to reach the

Rex." Realistically, they had little chance of succeeding, but she intended to try.

Turner joined her. "Let me see." He tapped the luminous panel in a staccato pattern.

Sam watched him. "You had two clubs, like baseball bats."

He kept working. "My arms looked that way because I moved so fast."

"Turner, you were holding clubs."

"That would be a feat, given that I have none." He turned to her. "This car should go to the top floor now."

"You figured out those codes too fast." Although she had no doubt an EI with his sophistication could break into secured meshes, an installation like this would probably have protections against him in particular, given that Charon had built him.

He wouldn't look at her. "I know many of Charon's codes."

"For his house in Oregon." Sweat beaded her forehead. She didn't want to believe he could be lying. "But you said it yourself. You've never been here."

"He used the same ones here."

"Anyone who could set all this up would never be that stupid." Another thought came to her. "These elevators must have security monitors. Hell, Alpha and Hud probably carry them, maybe even inside their bodies. So why haven't we set off the alarms?"

He stared at the panel. "Maybe we have."

The doors opened, revealing the gold hall where they had entered the building. They raced out of the elevator and took off in what Sam thought was the right direction. The hall looked exactly as it had before, going on forever. She traced her hand along the wall as she ran, but it felt smooth and unmarked.

"Where is the door?" she muttered. "We should feel it even if we can't see it."

"Don't know." Turner did the same on the other side of the corridor. So they ran, each trailing a hand on the wall.

Suddenly Sam scraped a seam in the metal. "This is it!" She stopped to check the surface. This close, she could see through the camouflage, enough to discern a mesh-panel. She pressed, tapped, and banged it, all to no avail.

Turner came up next to her and went to work, trying codes while Sam pushed and pulled at the door. It remained firmly in place.

"We have to get out of here," Sam said. "Fast. They must monitor this hall."

"I can't get the lock." He looked frantic as he worked on the panel—

And then the weirdness started.

The surface of his hand peeled back like a snake shedding its skin. The muscles retracted next, baring a metal skeleton. He raised his finger, and the metal "bone" elongated, the tip glowing. He pushed it into a depression on the wall. Lights flickered within the panel—

The door slid open.

Sam's pulse ratcheted up. She had known Turner had skin unlike anything she had seen before, but she hadn't expected dynamic plastic. Sure, research on programmable matter had begun in the twentieth century with quantum dots, including the notable McCarthy patents, but this was beyond anything she had seen. Her mind whirled with possibilities. The patent for this plastic alone could make Charon obscenely wealthy. Until he had it, his work was at risk. He sure as hell wouldn't want his competitors to know. She was one of the few people alive who could appreciate and replicate the work, given a sample—like Turner. Charon would never let her go, especially if he really was paranoid. She would be surprised if he even let her live.

They ran out of the building into a night brilliant with moonlight. The tremendous mountains reared against the sky in great, dark shadows. A profusion of stars sparkled, endlessly deep, strewn across the sky like gem dust, a vista richer than could ever be seen from a city. Icy wind razed through their clothes.

The Rex crouched on the tarmac, a dark predator. As they ran toward it, Sam struggled to pull in enough of the thin, sharp air. The mobile stairs were several yards away from the Rex, but she and Turner easily rolled them to the aircraft. Turner bounded up the steps, two at a time. At the top he fooled with the cabin door. By the time Sam caught up with him, he was inside the Rex. She looked back—

Three men in fatigues were running toward them across the airfield.

"Damn!" Sam strode inside and sealed the door. "Can you lock this thing?"

"I already did." Turner heaved open the cockpit door. "Wireless. I'm talking to the Rex."

As Sam followed him into the cockpit, she looked through the windshield. More people had run out of the building and the first three were almost at the Rex.

Turner slid into the pilot's seat and looked over the front panels, which were smooth and featureless, their digital-ink displays inactive.

His choice of seat startled Sam. "Do you know how to fly this thing?"

"Yes." He was just sitting, his forehead furrowed while he gazed at the front panels.

She stared at him. "A hotel bellboy who can fly a state-of-the-art hypersonic airplane?"

He grasped her arm and pushed her toward the copilot's seat. "Web yourself in."

Sam froze. The hand gripping her no longer resembled a human skeleton. His metal fingers had lengthened and he had seven now, plus an enlarged thumb.

"Oh, Lord." She dropped into the copilot's seat.

Turner let her go, returned his focus to the controls—and clicked the prongs of his fingers into a socket. Displays rippled into view all over the forward panels. He immediately began checking the meters, screens, and gauges. Sam fastened the high-pressure webbing of her seat around her body, always watching Turner, mesmerized.

Someone pounded on the door, followed by scraping and a loud hum, what sounded like a high-powered torch. Lights were flashing all over the cockpit. Then the engines roared into life.

Sam felt as if a band constricted around her chest. "You sure you know what to do?"

"It can fly itself," Turner said.

She gripped the arms of her seat, riveted while the Rex cold-started. Turner's metal hand, plugged into the controls, flickered with lights. He had to be exchanging code with the aircraft, overriding safeguards that normally kept it from responding without proper authorization.

G-forces slammed her into the seat, like an elephant on her chest. She was dimly aware of the webbing pushing against her body, helping counter the acceleration. It was all that kept her from blacking out.

Mercifully, the pressure soon eased. Sam let out a long breath, her body sagging. They were aloft. Outside, the sky had turned violet, and a panorama of mountains spread out below them. Turner's metal hand had become part of a front panel, jacked into it. His sleeve covered his arm to the wrist, so she couldn't see how far up the transformation went.

"How can you talk to this Rex?" she asked.

He turned to her. "The knowledge is stored in my memory."

"Why would you have a memory like that?"

"Charon downloaded it into my matrix."

With chilling clarity, Sam realized why they had taken Turner away at the base—to give him specifications for operating the Rex. She didn't want to imagine what Charon could do with rebuilt human-forma constructs and a Rex. Dynamic plastic, hell; stealing this aircraft gave him technology at a whole different level. It went beyond patents; this threatened international security.

Turner turned back to focus on the controls, but Sam suspected he could see her in his side vision. He might have scanners all over his body that could monitor her. She kept remembering how he had held her last night. A machine. She had wanted to make love to a machine.

"What are you?" Sam asked.

Anger sparked in his voice. "So my arm is biomech. You knew that."

She indicated his metal hand. "Where did you get the energy for the transformation?"

"I didn't transform materials." He hesitated, seeming uncertain with his own words. "I restructured the arm and shifted external tissues to internal areas."

He made it sound easy, but she knew better. "That still takes energy, especially given how fast you changed."

He stared at the controls.

"Turner?"

Finally he looked at her. "I've a microfusion reactor in my body."

Sam didn't know whether to laugh or panic. "Sure, yeah, I could have overlooked that when I examined you. I mean, it's only a *reactor*."

"You had no reason to look for it."

"For me to miss something like that, it had to be deliberately hidden."

"Of course Charon hid it." He motioned with his free hand, the one that looked human. "How could I interact with people otherwise? Just say, 'Oh, excuse me, hope you don't mind my MF reactor.'"

"You don't say that about your biomech."

"That's not the same."

"That's my point! We barely have the technology to make an MF prototype, and what we do have is classified." The only reason she knew it existed was because of her NIA connections. "Do you have any idea how hard it would be to create such a reactor and integrate it with your systems?"

He blinked at her. "No."

"Charon would need some damn high-level contacts in the military."

His voice sharpened. "Like your dear friend the general."

"Thomas wouldn't betray us." She couldn't be that wrong about him. As much as she hated to admit it, though, she no longer felt certain. "You should have told me about the reactor."

"Why?"

"Why *not?*"

"How do I know how far I can trust you?"

He had a point, given what had happened when she tried to help him. She took a breath, then slowly let it out. "How did you deactivate the alarms in that elevator?"

At first he looked ready to deny he had done anything. Then he spoke tiredly. "All right, yes, I acted like a mesh instead of a man. I infiltrated the IR security ports in the elevator. Same with Alpha's implants and Hud's mesh glove. It wasn't that hard."

Sam wondered what he considered "hard," if he found it easy to crack what had to be prodigiously well-protected systems. "That's impressive."

"Not really. Low-power consumption devices are notorious for having less encryption. It's because they have less juice."

"True." It had been a hot research topic for decades, which was probably why his download for the Rex included that information. "But Charon knows that, too. He would compensate." Then again, Charon had made this Turner. Perhaps it helped his creation outsmart him.

A rumble came from outside and acceleration pressed

Sam back in her seat. Her injured arm throbbed, though at least the bandage was smart enough to compensate for the g-forces.

"We're going higher." Turner's forehead furrowed. "I'm not sure why."

She fought the bile that rose in her throat, until finally the forces eased. The release made her light-headed, especially when she looked out the windshield. They weren't high enough to see the Earth as a ball, but she had never been this far up before. It made her mind spin.

Turner was watching her. "Did we go into orbit?"

Orbit? The naïve question floored her. He acted with such confidence in taking up the Rex, she had unconsciously assumed an expertise on his part that he didn't really possess. That he could fly the aircraft didn't mean he understood physics or orbital mechanics.

"It would take more rocket power, fuel, and speed than we have to reach orbit," she said. "A combined cycle propulsion system more sophisticated than what this Rex uses."

He seemed lost. "I have stuff about that in my memory filaments now, but it's hard to integrate it all. I don't even understand a lot of the words."

"You are amazing to fly this Rex at all. And it is a gorgeous airplane. But I really, *really* don't like to think why Charon set this all up."

He spoke softly. "You see why I had to escape?"

"Yes." To put it mildly.

With a click, Turner retracted his hand from the panel. His fingers had three joints now instead of two, and his thumb had extended into an eighth finger. The digits bundled into a cylinder at the wrist, silver-and-black metal with embedded components. It reflected the lights of the cockpit. She bit her lip, remembering how he had stroked her with that hand last night. In his arms, it had been easy to forget what made him a living, thinking being, that in many ways he was a machine.

She touched the back of his hand. "Can you make it human again?"

"To some extent." He held still, letting her touch him. "I could manage five digits and a covering similar to skin. But I'm no biomech expert. I can't reverse the process exactly. It wouldn't look like the other hand. It probably wouldn't even look fully human."

Sam thought it would be more disturbing to see him with a facsimile than a cybernetic hand. "What did you do to your arms in the elevator?"

"I stiffened them." He spoke awkwardly. "You were right, they were clubs. But I didn't change their actual structure."

"So you could unstiffen them?"

"Yes."

"How much of yourself can you transform?"

"Any part, I think, if I don't overload."

She indicated the port where he had jacked his hand into the Rex. "Why did you need the hard link before?"

"Higher bandwidth. It gave me better control."

"What's different now?"

He spoke with difficulty, as if his answer disgusted him. "I copied part of my brain into the Rex. So now I have direct control."

Her amazement was growing. "No wonder Charon wants you back."

Turner curled the digits of his hand into a ball, its version of a fist now. "I'm not his project."

Her emotions were adrift, without moorings. "I don't know who you are."

He reached out and touched her cheek with the tip of his seventh finger, metal on skin. "Just Turner. The man who held you in his arms last night. I haven't changed."

Sam stiffened. She took his hand, her five fingers curling around his eight, and moved it away from her face. "You should have warned me."

"I was afraid you would think I was a monster."

"I'll deal with it." Sam hoped that was true. For all her experience in discussing the emotions of an EI, she had never been articulate about her own. She didn't want to rebuff him, but she wasn't sure what to say, either.

After a moment, she asked, "Do you know where we are?"

"Here." The heads-up display activated with a holomap that showed part of Eurasia. "If I understand the Rex right, we're shrouded enough to hide for a short time, while we decide what to do, but probably not for long."

What to do. That was the question of the hour. "Can we land?"

"The Rex says it is reusable and has heat shielding." He tilted his head. "Does that mean yes, we can land?"

"I think so."

Turner rubbed his eyes with his cybernetic hand. "I've never really understood why Charon did this to me. If he wanted a slave, surely easier ways existed."

She spoke grimly. "He's making an army. You're the prototype."

"An army for what?"

"Himself, maybe, for his own power, but I would guess he has the support of some political entity." Sam shook her head. "I wish I knew how Thomas fits into all this. I can't believe he would be part of it."

"Why not? Power can warp anyone. How do you know this isn't some flipping Air Force project?" A muscle in his cheek twitched. "You would think I would know. I _am_ the project. But then, people don't usually inform the equipment."

She hated the mistreatment that put bitterness in his voice. None of it fit with the Thomas she knew, who had a strong sense of right and wrong. But he was also one of the most pragmatic men she had ever met. If he thought it necessary for the defense of his country, he was capable of involvement in such a project. Could Turner be right? His fear of Charon certainly seemed genuine. She wished she could tell whether he simulated emotions or really felt them. That had a personal aspect, too; she didn't know how to trust his emotions toward her. Maybe he didn't know himself. She almost gave a dry laugh. In that sense, their situation wasn't any different than a human relationship.

Sam spoke self-consciously. "Charon put us together last night to give me more of a vested interest in you."

He wouldn't look at her. "Did it work?"

His question made her flush. It shouldn't have; she was no untried ingénue. She had dated, had a lover, been married. But around Turner she felt as nervous as a schoolgirl. She answered in a low voice. "I think so."

A tentative smile curved his lips. "Good."

"And you?"

He nodded, his gaze averted, his eyes veiled by his long eyelashes. "Yes." Finally he looked at her. "But Sam. Who would want a man like this?" He unbuttoned his cuff and pushed up his sleeve, revealing his arm. The transformation went all the way to his shoulder. The limb no longer had skin or muscles; it consisted of cables bundled together at intervals. Without speaking, he bent it at five different joints, forming a pentagon, his fingers just reaching his shoulder. The cables flickered with lights.

"Good Lord," Sam said.

"Yeah." He unfolded his arm.

The scientist in her admired such an achievement, but the woman was having trouble with it. "What happened to the skin and muscle?"

He pushed aside the outer cables and indicated one inside the bundle. "I can conduct biological material through conduits like this one."

Sam didn't know what to say. She couldn't figure out what he wanted, really wanted. He had come to her searching for an escape, a validation of his humanity, but the more she learned, the less she knew how to help. "Why do you need me?"

He reached out and caressed her jaw with the tip of his eighth finger. "Is this truly so offensive?"

Sam made a conscious effort not to recoil. "No." She folded her hand around his wrist, which consisted of a ninth cable encircling the other eight, and lowered his hand to the arm of her seat. But this time she didn't let go. The corrugations of the metal ridged against her palm.

"My arm is stronger now," he said. "More versatile."

"Can you feel my hand?"

"Yes. I kept the sensors that were in the skin. In some ways, they're more receptive than nerve endings. Now they're embedded in the cables."

Sam flushed. "That takes energy, too. Does your reactor provide enough?"

"I have to recharge. Sleeping helps."

She thought about their situation. "I doubt we'll have much chance after we land."

"Land where?"

Good question. "We should contact the Air Force."

"No!" His hand clenched hers so hard, it hurt. "Not General Wharington."

"All right." She wasn't ready to believe Thomas had acted against them, but she intended to be careful. She doubted they would have much choice about who they spoke with, anyway. "We can probably reach the space command of a country. Someone will figure out we're up here pretty soon, anyway."

"They might shoot," he said darkly.

"We haven't done anything hostile."

"We're armed."

"With what?"

His expression took an inward-directed quality. He spoke as if reciting a list. "We have ASRAAMs and AMRAAMs with updated AI intelligence, fifth-generation LGBs with updated AIs, JDAM kits that operate with or without the GPS, though accuracy is better with GPS guidance, and an APSB with positron foil." He looked bewildered. "Do you know what that means?"

"GPS is the Global Positioning System." She scratched her chin. "I think the others are missiles. Can the Rex tell you more?"

He was silent for a moment. "Yes, missiles, both air-to-surface and air-to-air. Some are laser guided." He tilted his head. "These are really smart bombs, Sam. They can chase their targets."

It didn't surprise her. "What does positron foil mean?"

"It's the beam weapon."

"The what?"

He "listened" to the Rex. "It's some sort of off-shoot from the ABL program, but it ended up a lot different."

This didn't sound like anything she had heard about. "What is ABL?"

"Airborne laser."

"You're kidding! This Rex carries a laser weapon?"

"No . . . it's completely different. Something new. It has less documentation—oh, wait, here we go. It's an antimatter beam."

"*What?*" Sam's mouth opened. "That's impossible."

He blinked. "It is?"

"Are you saying this craft can shoot positrons?"

"What's a positron?"

"The anti-particle of an electron."

"The Rex says the beam is anti-protons." He spoke slowly. "It's neutralized and focused by running it through a foil where it picks up positrons."

"Well, I'll be a frog on a fling."

Turner gave a startled laugh. "A what?"

Sam reddened. "It's a saying." She knew the cutting edge of research was always further ahead than most people realized, and that the pace of development had risen in recent decades, but this was beyond anything she expected. "This is a lot to handle."

"The Rex?"

"You and the Rex."

"You're afraid."

"And you're not." She didn't make it a question.

His anger flared. "You think I don't feel fear, dismay, desire, affection? My emotions are real, Sam. It affects me just as much as it would have Turner Pascal." His voice cracked. "I'm turning into something inhuman and I can't *stop* it. If you goddamn think I'm simulating that, you're even less human than me."

"I'm sorry." She didn't know how to react to him.

He opened his balled fist, the metal cables uncurling. "I don't know how to handle this. I *liked* being a bellboy. This is so far beyond my comfort zone, I don't know what to feel. But I can't make it stop. I'm on this horrible roller coaster and I don't see any way to get off."

"We'll make it through. Somehow." She just wished she knew how.

"I hope so." He watched her with a strange expression, as if he were dying inside. "Because I don't know how far I will change."

The shrill of an alarm cut through the cockpit.

VIII
Hockman and Beyond

Turner jerked. "We have company."

Sam swore under her breath. She did a mental rundown of who could come after them. Charon, maybe, though if he had just stolen the Rex, it seemed unlikely he would have more aircraft with its capabilities. The military of a country might have launched their own intercept aircraft, or it might be one of the corporations with a space division. That would be fast work, though; they had been up here less than an hour and supposedly shrouded.

"Does the Rex know who our company is?" she asked.

Turner answered slowly. "Something called a Needle."

"A spacecraft?" Needles were an offshoot of NASA's shuttle program. Although smaller than space shuttles, and unmanned, they had more maneuverability. A Needle already in orbit could conceivably be coming down after them, but someone from the ground had to be controlling its actions.

"Here," Turner said. Schematics of a narrow craft appeared on a display, along with specifications. This Needle was a dated model, about ten years old. It probably didn't come from the United States, which had upgraded its fleet of Needles a few years ago. The specs looked familiar, though.

"Maybe it's one of the old ships the U.S. sold to another country," Sam said.

He paused. "The Rex says it belongs to the Chinese, but that they junked it two years ago."

"Doesn't look junked to me."

"Maybe someone stole it."

"Or bought it illegally."

Turner raked his hand through his hair, a very human gesture that looked all the more eerie with cabled fingers. "It's armed."

"That's nuts! Needles aren't built for combat."

"Tell that to whoever gave it teeth." He indicated the schematic of their pursuer. "The Rex says it's a UCAV. What does that mean?"

"Unmanned combat air vehicle." It had to be an alteration to the orginial spacecraft. Usually Needles just ran micro-gravity experiments.

Circles appeared on the schematic. As they spread out from the Needle, the blood drained from Sam's face. Their pursuer had just fired at them.

G-forces shoved Sam into her seat as the Rex took evasive maneuvers. Spots danced in her vision. She could just make out new circles on the display, these moving from the Rex toward the Needle. Close behind, a cloud of flecks spread in a spherical pattern.

It was hard to read stats when she was on the verge of passing out, but she thought the Rex had released any debris it had on board to confuse the Needle's missiles. Whether or not the ploy worked would depend on the quality of the AI brains in the bombs.

"Boom," Turner muttered.

Sam would have asked *Why boom?* but she couldn't speak. The webbing exerted pressure against her body, especially her legs, but she still felt ready to pass out. She could tell only that no circles overlapped on the display. Two were close, though, one from the Rex and one from the Needle. The circle from the Rex flared, expanding to encompass the other circle. Then both vanished.

Before Sam had a chance to feel relief, new circles appeared on the screen, spreading outward from the Needle. Another change in g-forces eased the pressure on Sam. She grunted as pinwheels danced in her vision. She felt ready to throw up.

"They can't keep shooting at us." Turner barely sounded affected by the acceleration. "They must have a limited number of bombs."

"So do we," Sam said. The Rex went into another maneuver and a massive, invisible hand slammed her into the seat. The circles on the display continued to move.

Turner spoke in a subdued voice. "That's it."

That's it? Sam would have asked what he meant if she could have spoken.

The Rex lurched as if a giant had kicked it. A line slashed across the display and they lost the image of the Needle. Tears blurred Sam's vision and her stomach felt as if it plummeted to her feet.

Suddenly the pressure stopped. Sam gasped, struggling to keep down her last meal. Blobs of color came back with her returning vision. It was a few seconds before her sight cleared, her stomach settled, and she could speak.

"Did we get away?" she asked.

Turner wouldn't look at her. "Something like that."

The display was a wash of green now. "What happened to the visual?"

"Nothing."

"But it's blank."

"It's not blank. Nothing is there."

"Where is the Needle?"

He finally looked at her. "We shot it with the antiproton beam. It's gone."

Ah, hell. She could only imagine the trouble they had now. "No way can we hide an explosion like that."

His face paled. "I know."

She didn't understand why the comm was quiet. "If anyone detected the explosion, they would be trying to contact us now."

"They are."

Oh, Lord. "You better put them on."

A man's voice suddenly crackled with a British accent. "—identify yourself. You have violated U.K. airspace. Cease hostile activities and identify yourself."

"How do they know we speak English?" Turner asked.

"English is the aviation standard. Everyone uses it." Sam didn't know what would happen if they didn't respond, and she sure as blazes didn't want to find out. "We have to answer."

"I don't know what to say." Turner twisted his cabled

hand inside his human one. "I can't deal with them, Sam. They remind me of Charon."

It wasn't the first time she had seen him close to panic. Anything he perceived as threatening his sense of self-determination set him off, including anyone that evoked Charon for him, which apparently included governments and militaries. Sam didn't know much about communications protocol for aircraft, but she thought she could stumble her way through.

"I'll talk to them," she said.

He stopped twisting his hand. "Okay."

"What do we call ourselves?"

"Three-Oscar-Beta is the only name I found."

That would have to do. A wireless headset swung around to her mouth and she toggled it on. "This is Rex Three-Oscar-Beta. Our intent is peaceful. I repeat. We have no hostile intent."

"Three-Oscar-Beta, acknowledged." The man's voice lost a bit of its edge. "This is the HMS *Westralia*. We've identified abnormal radiation in space, what appears to be an explosion. What is your status?"

Good question. If she said they had just blown up a spacecraft from China, they would be in more trouble than she ever wanted to face. Well, hell. She had always been good at poker. Time to bluff. "We are on a non-hostile mission for the Senate Select Committee for Space Warfare Research and Development. They can give you further information on the nature of our mission. The contact point is Lieutenant General Thomas Wharington."

"You'll have to download your complete flight identification and plan," he said. "We have no record of your overflight."

Sam knew that if they were going at hypersonic speeds, they were probably almost out of U.K. airspace. He had to realize it, too; she only needed to stall longer. "This is an unscheduled mission on a need to know basis. You'll have to contact General Wharington for information."

The fellow paused. "I'm transferring you to United States Space Command."

Relief washed over Sam. "Thank you." She didn't think that was the usual way of responding, but she didn't know the protocols.

Another voice came on the line, this one with a Texan drawl. "Three-Oscar-Beta, can you read me?"

"Loud and clear," Sam said. "This is Dr. Samantha Bryton. I'm a U.S. citizen."

"Colonel Tyler Granger here at Hockman Air Force Base. We have been monitoring your communications with the *Westralia* and are unable to confirm or deny your information."

Hockman. Sam had heard of it. A relatively new base near Kansas City, it had been designed to handle the improved space capability of the Air Force. "Please don't shoot. We aren't hostile."

"Our chase planes will escort you in." After a pause, Granger said, "We're monitoring your course change."

Sam covered the microphone and spoke to Turner. "What course change?"

He met her gaze with a wide stare. "They're sending coordinates to the Rex. It's taking us to Hockman."

Sam took a deep breath. "Okay." She spoke into the comm. "Thanks, Colonel. We're coming in."

"Roger." Dryly he added, "Y'all must have one doozy of a story."

❖   ❖   ❖

They landed in the sunlight of a late autumn morning, the Rex coming down in a flare of exhaust and steam. Sam couldn't sit still. By the time Turner unfastened his webbing, she was up and squeezing out of the cockpit. That was as far as she got, though. Red lights glowed on the mesh panel by the door, and it didn't respond to her input.

Turner came up beside her. "I think it won't open until the Rex cools down outside."

"How long?" Sam felt as jumpy as a flea.

A hum came from inside the door and the red light turned green. Sam answered herself. "I guess now." She opened the door into streaming sunlight.

Turner joined her in the hatchway. "That's bright . . ." His voice trailed off as he stared out at the landing field. About twenty soldiers with laser carbines waited for them, the massive guns as bright as silver mirrors in the sunlight.

"Hoo, boy," Sam said. She raised her hands above her shoulders, slowly, so she didn't startle anyone. Even without stairs, she and Turner probably could have climbed down from the hatch; they weren't that high above the ground. Given their reception, she didn't intend to twitch until invited to do so.

Turner raised his hands, and his sleeves fell down, revealing his biomech limb. The soldiers responded immediately, training their guns on him.

"He's not carrying a weapon," Sam called. "His arm is cybernetic."

A woman in a major's uniform came forward, lowering her gun, though the other soldiers remained poised. She stopped below the hatchway. "Can you jump down?"

Sam lowered her arms. "I think so."

The major narrowed her gaze at Turner. "You first." Then she stepped back and raised her gun.

Turner's jaw worked. Given his skittish response to authority, Sam could imagine how he felt right now. She hoped he didn't panic and try to bolt. Although he moved stiffly, he did sit down, letting his legs dangle out of the Rex. His sleeve slid into place, covering his arm, but nothing could hide the eight cabled fingers that gripped the hatchway. Then he dropped down and landed gracefully on the tarmac, bending his legs to absorb the impact. He straightened carefully, holding his hands out from his sides, showing the major he had no weapons. Sunshine streamed around them, reflecting off his bundled hand.

The major stared at his hand. Then she gestured to the soldiers and a lieutenant came forward, a tall man with a rifle. He stopped a few yards away, out of reach. For the first time, Sam realized Turner's cybernetic arm was longer than his other one.

The major motioned to Sam. "You next."

With care, Sam sat in the hatchway as Turner had done. Her injured arm throbbed and she had to favor it as she slid into the drop. She landed awkwardly and stumbled, pain shooting up her legs. Someone grasped her left arm above the bandage, steadying her. As she regained her balance, she realized it was Turner.

She spoke in a low voice. "Thanks."

The officers were watching intently. The major motioned them forward. "Come with us, please. Colonel Granger has some questions for you."

Sam suspected that was a colossal understatement. At least the personnel here weren't treating them like criminals. Either Granger had heard from Thomas or else her invoking the name of a three-star general had bought her and Turner some time.

As they crossed the tarmac, the other soldiers fell into formation around them. It unsettled Sam that the brass here thought two people needed so many guards. Then again, in their position, she probably would have been even less friendly. These people knew little of what had happened beyond whatever they had picked up of the battle and her communication with the *Westralia*, and no one knew the full extent of Turner's capabilities, herself included. Who knew what else he had up his sleeve, literally as well as metaphorically.

"That's quite an aircraft you have," the woman said.

"You don't recognize it?" Turner asked.

"Should I?" she asked.

"It's Air Force," Sam said, puzzled.

The major spoke carefully. "You can tell the colonel."

They reached a security check, a gate and guard booth in a chain-link fence. Two men and a woman were waiting there. They checked the badges of the base personnel, touching the holographic squares, and waved them on into the compound beyond the fence.

The female guard, a stocky woman with dark hair, drew Sam aside and scanned her with a flash-rod. It buzzed, and the screen on its cylindrical body formed an embarrassing picture of Sam's bra with the underwire supporting her breasts. Mercifully, the guard didn't ask her to remove her underwear. She checked Sam with a retinal scanner, mesh glove, thimble skimmer, and imager. Sam glared when the guard patted her down, but nothing else raised any alarms.

"My apologies, ma'am," the guard said.

"It's okay," Sam mumbled, her face burning.

Then they checked Turner.

He set off alarm after alarm. They spent twenty minutes examining him, at least ten of that on his altered arm, verifying it contained no weapons. Turner waited patiently, holding his arms out, turning around, removing his shoes when they asked, and otherwise cooperating.

"Holy shit," one of the guards suddenly said. "He's got fusion components in there."

Well, hell. It annoyed Sam that they had detected what she missed in her first exam. She wondered if they were about to be thrown into a cell after all.

However, the major just watched as the guards inspected Turner. Then she said, "Can I ask you a question?"

Turner answered warily. "Yes?"

"I was wondering if you were an android or a robot."

His voice turned chill. "I'm a man."

A long silence greeted him. Finally the major said, "Ah—okay." She spoke to the guards. "Can we take him through?"

"He's not carrying any weapons," one of the men said. "Unless you count the reactor."

That response told Sam a great deal. They were treating her and Turner with kid gloves, which meant Thomas must have spoken with someone here; either that or Granger hadn't heard from Thomas and was being careful. She hoped it was the former, because if Thomas had betrayed them, he might deny any knowledge of this mess. Then she and Turner would be in big trouble.

❖   ❖   ❖

Colonel Granger was a lean man of average height, with buzz-cut hair and icy blue eyes. Sam tensed up the moment she met him. He initially separated her from Turner while the mech-techs examined them. Now they had finished with that, at least for the time being. She sat at a metal table painted institutional green, with Turner across from her, slouched in his chair. Armed soldiers stood around the perimeter of the room.

Granger was pacing behind Turner. "The manipulations to your DNA are more knotted than an Abilene mesquite. It took our people hours to untangle your ID. But the final results fit the man you named in Portland." He stopped at one end of the table and regarded Turner. "A dead man."

"I'm not dead," Turner said.

"My dog could have guessed that." Granger lifted his left hand, which was covered with a mesh glove, and flicked his right thumb through several menus on the palm screen. Then he glanced at Sam. "We have no record of this call you claim you made to General Wharington."

Sam wished Granger would sit down. His pacing was making her nervous. She suspected that was his intent, though, so she tried to ignore it. "My car must have a record of it. Even if someone erased it, surely you can get it back."

He lowered his arm. "That's right. And your car has no record of any chase or message to General Wharington."

"Ask Thomas," she said.

"We did. He never heard diddly from you."

Sam didn't believe him. "My car *must* have a record of that call."

"All right," he drawled. "Let's say someone erased it, someone smart enough to remove all record of the deletions." He turned a hard gaze on Turner. "It would be child's play for an android with your sophistication."

"Don't call me a goddamned android."

"Most humans," Granger said, "aren't more biomech than human."

Turner shifted in his seat. "What do you want from me?"

Granger didn't hesitate. "The people who made you. Cooperate with us and you'll go free."

Turner just looked at him. He had no need to say he didn't believe Granger; it was obvious in his expression.

"What about the Needle that attacked us?" Sam asked.

"We haven't identified it yet." Granger's face gave nothing away.

Sam studied the colonel. Although he was non-committal on everything, she thought he knew more about the Needle. But he seemed genuinely unfamiliar with the name Charon, whereas she had been sure Thomas recognized it. Either Granger was a superb actor or else he wasn't privy to Thomas's sources. The colonel might not have clearance to know, but if so, she would have expected Thomas to send someone for her and Turner.

Sam had to admit Turner might be right. Thomas might have betrayed them. But it just didn't fit; he was one of the most dedicated officers she knew, and she had known him long enough to have a sense of the man and his principles that went beyond the surface. Also, she doubted Granger knew as little as he claimed; otherwise, he would have slapped her and Turner in cells. He claimed Thomas never heard "diddly" from her on her car phone; he hadn't actually said Thomas *denied* knowledge of their situation. She was convinced Granger knew more than he admitted. He was trying to rattle them and see what information fell out.

Could Giles be the one behind this business of Charon? She didn't want to believe it of him, either, but it made too much sense. He was one of the few people with the expertise to create Turner. When she put Giles and Charon in the same thought, her pulse leapt. She wanted to push the thoughts away and she didn't know why.

A knock came at the door. Granger motioned to a guard, who opened it. A mech-tech hurried in, a woman with a long braid of brown hair down her back. Dressed in jeans, a knit shirt, and a white lab coat, she looked like a civilian. Excitement flushed her cheeks.

Granger motioned her to a chair. "What do you have, Ms. Hernandez?"

She slid into her seat at the table and leaned forward eagerly. "We caught it, sir! We tricked it into a neural corral and closed the gate."

"It?" Sam looked from Hernandez to Granger. "What?"

Turner gripped the table with both hands. He had that hunted look again. "Whose neural corral?" His usually vibrant voice had gone flat.

"I've been chasing the part of your EI you copied into the Rex." Her face lit up. "You have an incredible network. I've never seen one so complex. You even have an unconscious mind, code that runs in the background. Do you know what I mean?"

"No." Turner might have turned into a glacier. "How could I, if it's unconscious?"

"You sound annoyed." The tech seemed fascinated with him. Sam scowled at her.

"I am annoyed," Turner said. "What are you going to do with the copy of my EI that you stole?"

"It was in the Rex," Granger said. "Y'all stole our Rex. For all we know, you stole the EI, too." When Turner made an incredulous noise, Granger held up his hand. "Okay, we don't know yet who took what." He turned to Sam. "Maybe you stole an android from this man you call Charon."

If he was trying to shake her up, it wasn't working. "Then you admit the Rex is yours," she said.

"No. But you see my dilemma." Granger braced his hands on the back of a chair and leaned forward. "No one admits to knowing a damn thing about how you got here, yet we have this incredible machine out on our field and this incredible construct who swears to high heaven he's human."

His phrasing caught Sam's attention. *No one admits* rather than *No one knows.* She would bet the original Monet painting she had hanging in her house he had been told to keep this under wraps.

"I want to know what you're going to do with my EI," Turner said.

"Study it," Granger told him.

"No. It's part of me. A self-aware part."

"What do you suggest we do?" Granger asked.

"Erase it."

"Son, you must know we can't."

"Damn it!" Turner hit the table. "How would you feel if someone copied your brain and fooled with it?"

"How would someone copy my brain?" Granger asked.

Turner started to answer, then closed his mouth, looking confused. "That isn't the point."

"But it is," Granger said. "You can do something the rest of us can't—download yourself to another machine."

"It isn't a complete copy of his brain," Hernandez said. "Just a few mods, enough to fly the Rex. It doesn't even have full evolutionary capability."

"It's still *part* of me," Turner said.

His distress on the subject continued to puzzle Sam. EIs downloaded themselves all the time. It was one advantage of being one. She had never known another to react this way. Then again, Turner was unique in many ways. No other EI she knew could have dealt this well with the flood of unpredictable input these past few days. Even a matured EI might have frozen up, and he had only been operating for a couple of weeks.

Turner had to analyze immense amounts of data just to deal with processes she took for granted, like laughing at a joke. It wasn't enough for him to remember what Turner Pascal thought was funny; he had to respond to new stimuli in a consistent manner. He might have to examine millions of possible reactions. He could manage within microseconds, but that was for one "common sense" response. Saints only knew how many he handled each day. Ideally, he would build a library of emotional reactions he could draw on without going through similar calculations every time. But if even a few of his analyses branched into unstable pathways, the effects could rapidly accumulate; given long enough, his personality could disintegrate.

What would help him now? Obviously, taking him out of stressful situations. Given their limited options, that wasn't likely. People had to sleep, though. Turner could use that time to integrate new input, clean up his matrix, fix errors.

"Maybe we could take a break?" Sam asked. It took no acting ability for her to look weary; her exhaustion was real.

Granger finally sat at the table. "It's about time for supper. Do y'all need to eat?"

Relief washed over Sam. "That would be wonderful."

Turner waited. "Does that include me?"

"Do you eat?" Granger asked.

Turner crossed his arms. "Yes."

"Incredible," Hernandez murmured.

"Well." Granger straightened up. "We've quarters on the base for both of you tonight. Tomorrow we'll be flying you to a more secure installation."

Sam was fine until his last sentence. Then her mental alarms went off. If Granger locked them away, it could be months before anyone realized she was gone. And Turner was *dead*. The only person looking for him was Charon, who might have links to Thomas. Or he might not. The "more secure installation" might be one of the only safe places for them or it could be a prison. She didn't know what to think, and right now her brain felt like mush.

Sam stood up, rubbing the small of her back. Turner also rose, with that hunched look. The last time she had seen it, he had smashed their guards in the elevator and stolen the Rex. Charon's base had been relatively small and isolated, but Hockman was a different story. They had little chance of making a break from here. Even if it had been possible, she wasn't sure she wanted to "escape."

That was the worst of this, not knowing whom to trust.

IX

Connors

Sam's "quarters" consisted of a deluxe suite reserved for VIP guests who came to watch Hockman space launches. A doctor checked her arm and rewound it with bio-gauze that dispensed pain killers as well as medicine.

A female lieutenant showed up with a box of clothes. After she left, Sam opened the package and found a blue jumpsuit. She expected something functional and plain for undergarments, which would have suited her fine, but the lieutenant had put in lacy white underwear. Although Sam never wore such stuff, she had to admit it felt good against her skin. When she found herself wondering if Turner would like it, she flushed and tried to think about something else. The jumpsuit fit well, snug to her curves.

Another officer came with dinner, meat and potatoes, which Sam ate alone, grateful for a chance to gather her thoughts. She sat at the table, staring into space, trying to make sense out of everything that had happened. Their escape perplexed her. If Charon created Turner, he should know how to confine him. It was possible Turner had evolved past what Charon expected; even in just the few days Sam had known him, he had changed a great deal. But it still strained her belief.

Maybe Charon let them escape. But why? Nor did that explain the Needle that tried to blow them up. She could understand Charon wanting to destroy Turner rather than risk his falling into the "wrong" hands, but if that was the case, it seemed unlikely he would let them go. The only saving grace about all this was the immense resources it took to create a Turner or build a Rex. Charon couldn't make many. She doubted he could have done even this much on his own. The group backing him might have sent up the Needle, to destroy evidence of their involvement.

Thomas, are you involved? The thought made Sam miserable. Thomas was the closest she would ever have to an uncle.

A buzz came behind her. Startled, she glanced around the living room. The buzz came again, and a blue light flashed on an inner door of the suite. Sam scratched her chin. Then she got up and went to the door.

"Yes?" she asked. She felt silly speaking to the air, but she didn't intend to open her suite without knowing who had come to call.

"You have a visitor," the door informed her. "He calls himself Turner."

Sam was suddenly warm. "Let him in."

The door slid open and there stood Turner, a living room much like her own behind him.

"Hello," she said.

"Hi." He had washed and brushed his hair and wore new clothes, a button-down dress shirt and gray slacks. He looked spiffy, handsome, and nervous.

Sam felt shy. "Would you like to come in?"

"Okay." His smile was lopsided. "Thanks."

She moved aside, discreetly glancing at his metal arm. Although his sleeve hid most of it, the hand was visible. At least it hadn't changed any more.

He came into her living room, and the door closed behind him. "How are you feeling?" he asked.

"Okay." She stood awkwardly. "And you?"

"Good."

"That's good."

"Did you have dinner?" he asked.

"Yes. And you?"

"Yes."

Sam couldn't help but laugh. "We sound as stiff as two kids going to the prom."

Turner smiled, his posture easing. "How about this? You look gorgeous tonight."

Her cheeks heated. "So do you."

"Well, hey." He seemed pleased, but at a loss for words. So they stood regarding each other.

Finally Sam said, "Turner, I'm not sure what to do."

He touched her face with one of his eight fingers. "What feels right?"

She was hyperaware of the metal against her skin. "I need to figure out some things."

He lowered his hand. "If I had a prosthetic, would that matter to you?"

"Of course not."

He pushed up his sleeve, uncovering his arm. "Then why does this?"

It was a good question, and she wasn't sure she had a good answer. She spoke slowly, thinking through emotions she could only partially define. "You're more than a man. You've a brain no unaugmented human could ever match, even if you don't yet know how to use its full extent. You seem to feel like anyone else, to love and care and hurt. But part of me is afraid it's simulated, that if you and I—that if I were to—" She stuttered, unable to say the word "love," not yet, not here. "That I'll end up caring for someone who will never truly return how I feel."

"It's real, Sam, as real as I've ever felt." He gently closed his hand around her uninjured arm, but then waited, giving her a chance to pull away. She looked up at him, uneasy, but glad to have him here. When she stayed put, he drew her into an embrace and leaned his head against hers.

Sam put her arms around his waist. The pleasant soapy smell of his shampoo made her nose tingle. She savored his warmth, the comfort of holding him. His arm felt corrugated against her back, but it bothered her less than she expected. It wasn't frightening so much as *different*. He held her with as much tenderness as if the limb had been human, perhaps more because he could crush with a power no unaltered human possessed, but he contained it, made it caring instead.

She leaned her head on his shoulder. "We shouldn't do this."

"Why not?"

She drew back to look at his handsome face. "I don't know what to do with liking you."

He caressed her cheek with his eight cabled knuckles. "I do."

A flush spread through Sam, starting in her face and spreading throughout her body. She felt the tickling sensation at the back of her throat that came when she was nervous. Turner bent his head, his lashes closing halfway. With a sigh, she leaned in to him and let her own eyes close. He kissed her then, his lips full and sensuous.

It was a long time before they paused for air. Sam folded her hand around his eight fingers, then stepped away from him and tugged on his arm. "Come on."

He went with her, holding her human hand in his metal one. She paused at the doorway to the bedroom. Light from the living room filtered inside, enough so they would be able to see each other but not so much that she would feel exposed or raw with him. She took him to the bed then and drew him down to sit with her.

Turner held her hands in both of his. "Are you sure?"

Sam managed a smile. "If you are."

He brushed back tendrils of hair that curled around her face. "You're so pretty. Like some wild forest spirit." He drew her down to lie on the bed. "I've never known anyone like you."

Sam stretched out with him, her hands sliding along his side, her curves fitting against his angles. She brushed her lips across his, then pulled him into a deeper kiss. They took their time with each other, no rushing, no fumbling. The first time he moved his biomech hand over her bare skin, she tensed, but her unease faded when he gave only gentleness. For the first time since her husband's death Sam let herself be vulnerable again.

So they came together, in a sensuous, purely human night.

❖   ❖   ❖

Fire blossomed in heat and crackles. An ember landed on her leg and made her pajamas smolder. She slapped it out before it broke into flame. Then she knelt in the rubble, tears running down her face.

His voice rasped. "Good-bye—"

No, she pleaded. No. Stay.

Good-bye . . .

Panicked, Sam opened her eyes into darkness eased by a light from the living room. She searched frantically for Turner—and her hand hit his shoulder. He lay sprawled next to her in bed, sleeping peacefully, his human arm thrown across her waist. No fires, no one dying. Her pulse gradually calmed. It had been the nightmare. Only a nightmare.

Something had awoken her, though. "Is someone here?" she asked.

No answer.

"Sam?" Turner stirred at her side.

"I heard someone."

He stretched, his lean muscles shifting against her. "Hmmm."

"Don't do that," she said, flustered. "You distract me."

With his eyes closed, he smiled drowsily. "Good."

"Turner, someone is here."

He lifted his head and peered into the shadowed living room. "I don't see anyone."

"You see in the dark?"

"Infra red."

"Oh." Of course. He had synthetic eyes. Why keep human limitations? "We should investigate."

"I'd rather stay here, with you."

Sam traced her finger over his lips. "Later, okay?"

He sat up, his hair tousled. "I'll hold you to that."

They rose and dressed quickly. Then they prowled through her suite, searching. If anyone had been there, though, they were gone now.

"Maybe they went in here." Turner tapped the door that connected her suite to his. It slid open to reveal his living room—blazing with light.

The major who had met them when they landed stood in the center of the room, a prowler busted in the act.

"So what you're telling us," Sam said, "is Thomas Wharington wants no one to know about us besides Granger and you." She was in an armchair in Turner's suite, which Major Connors claimed she had swept clean of bugs. Sam was just glad Connors hadn't found her in bed with Turner. She doubted the Air Force would appreciate her having intimate relations with someone's top secret project.

Connors had taken the armchair closest to Sam. The major was a compact woman, muscular and confident, with straight yellow hair and a staser on her hip. Her eyes, cool and gray, seemed to miss nothing. Sam would have liked her under different circumstances.

It didn't surprise Sam when Turner sat in a chair on her other side, putting her between himself and the major. Authority figures clearly gave him the willies. She wondered if Turner Pascal had been that way or if his EI developed that trait because of Charon's treatment.

"Security requires we take precautions," Connors said.

That certainly sounded vague. Sam frowned at her. "What happened with that Rex that was supposed to take us to Washington, D.C.?"

"Your kidnappers stole it." Connors seemed unruffled, though she kept glancing at Turner, unable to hide her curiosity. "Its real crew was found unconscious on the landing field, bound and gagged."

"That couldn't have been easy to manage," Sam said. "And now guess what? No one here can find any damn record of Turner and me. You say they don't have a need to know. But look at it from our point of view. It could mean a lot of other things, too."

Connors met her gaze. "We knew only that the Rex vanished after it took off from California. None of us had any idea what happened to you and Mr. Pascal until you landed here and told us."

"So Thomas is being cautious," Sam said.

"That is correct."

"It doesn't explain why you were skulking around our rooms." Sam crossed her arms. "Unless the Air Force doesn't know what you're up to."

"You don't have a need to know more," Connors said.

Sam smacked her palm on the arm of her chair. "Someone kidnapped me and Turner. They took us to the Himalayas, for crying out loud. Turner pulls off this spectacular escape that implies his technology is so far ahead of the curve, he's falling off the planet. A stolen spaceship comes after us and Turner blows it to high heaven. And you say I don't have a need to know? Like hell."

The major didn't look much happier about it than Sam. "Dr. Bryton, we've managed to keep this from going out of control. Only a few officials in the governments of a few countries know your aircraft destroyed a Needle, and even less people know about you and Turner. We are trying to staunch the leakage before more damage is done. If we are careful, it won't go further than this."

Having grown up in a military family, Sam had enough experience with the mindset to know they wouldn't want details of a potentially devastating weapon made public. Turner fit that bill all too well. "You're trying to avoid a major security leak."

Connors didn't soft-pedal it. "Yes."

"That doesn't explain why Thomas didn't send someone for us. Colonel Granger knows the routine. We go off with Thomas's people, no questions, it stays quiet." Sam leaned forward. "It also doesn't explain why you were sneaking around here."

"General Wharington has sent someone," Connors said. "My orders were to deactivate the android without his knowledge."

"If anyone else calls me a fucking android," Turner said, "I'm going to lose my very human temper."

Connors didn't miss a beat. "Very well, Mr. Pascal. We wanted you unconscious."

His fist clenched on the arm of his chair. "Why?"

Connors said only, "I'm sorry." She sounded like she meant it. Sam doubted Turner expected her to answer his question. He knew. As long as he remained free, he posed a threat to world security.

Sam understood what he wanted, though he had trouble articulating it: freedom, not only physically, but mentally, emotionally, and intellectually as well. She feared he would never achieve it. Anyone who could do what he had managed these past few days was too dangerous, especially given his knowledge of the Rex and Charon's base. Even if he somehow convinced the authorities he wouldn't act against any person or government, which seemed unlikely, he was a walking target for spies. Given what Charon had already managed, Turner would be lucky to keep his "freedom" even for a few hours.

However, if she and Turner went public, it would start a firestorm of debate over his humanity among ethicists, academics, and researchers. That debate could protect him. As long as it raged, it would be difficult for anyone to whisk him away or otherwise take his self-determination.

Sam considered the major. "So you were going to knock out Turner. In the morning someone would take us away."

"That's right," Connors said.

"Why didn't General Wharington trust me?"

"He does." Connors spoke quietly. "He needed to ensure Turner didn't inadvertently do or say anything that could cause harm or backfire. We know so little about Turner's abilities."

It made sense, as much as Sam didn't like it. Thomas knew Sam well enough to realize she would object to him keeping Turner in the dark. So he cut her out of the loop.

Turner spoke tightly. "Just one little problem. You didn't find me in my room. I was here with Dr. Bryton."

Connors looked from him to Sam. "Why?"

"Maybe I was lonely," Turner said.

Sam spoke quickly. "Major Connors, we will certainly go with you tomorrow. But please don't try anything with Turner. It won't work and it could harm him."

"I have my orders," Connors said.

Turner stood up, pushing up the sleeve on his cabled arm. Connors rose as well, her hand on the staser at her hip. Turner extended his arm, the eight cables uncurling, all pointed at the major. Lights shone at their tips.

Sam jumped to her feet. She had no idea what Turner intended, but she feared Connors might shoot. She had to hand it to the major, though; Connors didn't even blink as she met Turner's hostile stare.

"You want to 'deactivate' me?" He lowered his arm, lights glittering along his fingers. "Tell me, how will you manage? I can counter your attempts without even touching you. Right now I'm accessing the biochip you use to enhance the hearing in your right ear."

Connors pressed her palm against her ear. "Stop."

Although his posture didn't change, he must have done something. Connors lowered her hand, relief on her face. She spoke dryly. "Very impressive."

Sam looked from Connors to Turner. "What happened?"

"He set off an alarm in my implant," Connors said. "It's unpleasant. Then he turned it off."

Turner regarded her with a direct gaze. "You won't find me so easy to shut off."

"I had expected to find you asleep."

His eyes glinted. "I was asleep. You woke us up."

Us. Damn. Sam could have throttled him.

Sure enough, Connors asked, "Us?"

"It's nothing," Sam said. "He was sleeping on the couch. To, uh, make sure I was all right."

"Like hell." Turner exactly matched the inflections Sam had used earlier. "I wasn't on any couch."

"Turner, stop," Sam said. The last thing she wanted was Thomas knowing she was sleeping with a threat to world safety.

The major spoke dryly. "You've a unique approach to research, Doctor."

"It's private." It was Connors's business, though, whether she liked it or not.

The major shook her head, amazement leaking past her no-nonsense demeanor. "I certainly don't have a boring job." Her manner became businesslike. "Very well. We won't knock out Mr. Pascal. Your transport arrives in about two hours, at oh-six-hundred this morning. At that time, the two of you will board." She motioned Turner back toward his armchair. "Until then, we sit here and wait."

When Turner stiffened, Sam feared he would refuse. She didn't know what he expected to accomplish; if he resisted or tried breaking out of here, it could end up with his destruction. Yes, he had some tricks: his ability to change structure, to talk with other systems, even to load his brain into other places, as much as he disliked it. But it didn't make him invulnerable, and this base was larger and probably better secured than the one in the Himalayas.

Then he said, "Sure, why not?" He dropped into his chair and stretched out his legs. "So what will we talk about?"

Sam didn't trust his capitulation. She sat down,

her gaze going from Turner to Connors. The major settled in her chair, but she kept her hand on her staser.

"Why do you think I want to talk?" Connors asked. She tried to keep a neutral expression, but her curiosity came through.

Turner wriggled his cyborg fingers at her. "Come on. You're dying to ask about these."

That was when the lights went out.

X
Breakout

The room plunged into darkness. As emergency lights came on, blue and dim, Connors jumped up, drawing her staser.

The emergency lights went off.

"What the blazes?" Sam was on her feet, though she didn't remember standing.

A thump came from nearby, followed by a crash, a lamp it sounded like. Then it became silent. Too silent. Sam swung her arms in front of her, trying to find someone. She heard breathing, but she couldn't tell from where.

"Turner?" she asked. "Major Connors?"

"The major had an accident," Turner said.

Ah, hell. "What did you do?"

"We sort of had an argument. I won."

"She had better not be hurt."

"She isn't." He paused. "Much."

"How much?"

"I knocked her out."

"Turner!"

"When she wakes up, she should be okay."

"In the hospital."

"I was careful. Charon downloaded fighting methods into me. I'm learning to use them."

Sam didn't want to think why Charon would give Turner knowledge in hand-to-hand combat, but it fit all too well with everything else. "What happened to the lights?"

"I had a talk with the mesh community here."

"Meshes don't have communities. They aren't sentient." At least not yet.

"True." He sounded closer now. "They're rather prosaic. But they respond to reasonable input."

No matter how well he tinkered with other systems, surely he couldn't affect the entire base. "This place should have protections."

"Not enough."

Sam let out a slow breath, calming her pulse. She could tell he was close by, but with neither lights nor windows, the dark was complete. She stepped back, away from him she thought, but her elbow brushed his shirt.

Turner caught her arm. "Don't be afraid of me."

"I'm not." That was a lie, but she also liked him, a lot, which left her in a complicated tangle of emotions. "How did you affect the power generators, even the backups?"

"I convinced the other meshes to help me." He clasped her hand with his metal fingers. "I suppose 'convince' is a figure of speech. It feels that way to me."

"I've never heard an EI describe how it feels to

network with other systems." Too late, she realized how she had referred to him. An EI.

He didn't bristle, though. "They were open to suggestion." He accepted from her what he challenged from anyone else.

"Suggestions to do what?" she asked.

"To help me. And a friend. Another EI."

Another EI? Damn. Machine intelligence was rare, and EIs were particularly well guarded. A military base this new and large could conceivably have one, but she wouldn't have expected even Turner could crack it open.

She tapped his chest. "What EI?"

"It calls itself George the Second."

Sam blinked. "Why the Second?"

His voice lightened. "It didn't want to be the First."

Well, that was fair enough. "How did you reach him?"

"I linked to chips in the furniture. They put me through to a mesh in the walls and from there I got all over the base." Turner drew her forward. "Let's go."

Sam balked. "We can't leave."

"Listen." He set his hand on her left arm, above the bandage, carefully. "This base—this *world*—is riddled with meshes. Doors, windows, walls, lights, locks, jewelry, clothes, people, all of it."

"And?" Her pulse jumped.

"George is helping me utilize those systems so we can sneak out." He nudged her forward. "We have to go. The longer we delay, the more chance someone will catch us."

"What makes you think I want to go?" She shook his arm for emphasis, her fingers clasped in his. "Don't you see? You wouldn't stay free outside for even a day."

"Sure I would."

"How?"

"I'll join my other friends."

"Other EIs?"

"That's right." He tugged her again. "Like George. He helps me with the ES systems."

"ES?"

"Evolving Stupidity."

She would have laughed, except he was hauling her forward too fast. "Are you saying some EIs are helping you fool with security at this base?"

"One EI. And yes."

Sam couldn't believe no one had apprehended them yet. "What did you do to the people here?"

"Nothing." He hesitated. "Much."

"Nothing *much*? What does that mean?" She pulled away from him and bumped into a wall. "Ouch."

"We released gas." He touched her arm. "You okay?"

"What gas?" She swung around, flustered he could see her when she couldn't see him.

"Sam, I wouldn't hurt people. It was Chlorothan."

"Ol' chloro, eh?" She had never heard of the stuff.

"They invented it here. It's sleeping gas. I don't know the name that derives from chemical nomenclature, but that's the patented name."

Air blew across her face. Reaching out, she realized the door to the suite had opened. "How did you do that?"

"I have control of this wing of the building. For now."

Sam stepped out into darkness. No lights were on here, either. "I've two questions, Turner. I need answers to both."

"All right."

"Will the people you put to sleep be all right?"

"Yes. Some might feel nauseous for a few hours."

Brief nausea she could live with. "Second question: how extensive of a power breakdown did you cause?"

He came closer. "The damage should be confined to a few buildings."

"Then we still can't get off the base."

"Sure we can." Quietly he added, "I'm going, Sam."

Well, hell. She couldn't leave him after all that had happened. "All right. Show me."

He took her elbow and they headed down the hall. The dark hall. She couldn't see squat. She waved her hand in front of her body so she didn't hit anything. Turner could see in the IR if objects generated heat, but she needed to check for herself as well.

"Alarms must be going off somewhere," she said.

"George is helping." He sounded pleased. "This place depends completely on its meshes. If they cooperate, it's easy to outwit security. They are security, after all."

It didn't reassure Sam. "George must be guarded from physical, electronic, optical, even quantum interference. That you have access to other systems won't change that. They aren't sophisticated enough to break his security."

"That's why we call them ESs." He led her around a corner into more darkness.

"So how did you get to George?"

"Like knows like, Sam."

"That's not an answer." It surprised her that he was willing, at least with her, to acknowledge he operated as an EI. He was changing, evolving, maturing.

"Sure it's an answer," he said. "An ES isn't smart enough to get to the EI. I am."

"Even so. Someone should have checked by now on the power failure in this building."

"They have." He sounded smug.

Ah, no. "What did you do? Hit them with sleeping gas?" He couldn't knock out an entire base. The situation was surreal, this stealthy revolt of Air Force meshes.

"Better than that." He drew her to a halt and tapped on a nearby surface. "We fooled them."

Sam reached out and hit a wall. "Fooled them how?"

A door slid open in front of them, and Turner drew her forward. "We sent fake reports about how well the repairs are proceeding. No one checked on you and me because only a few people know we're here. Those who are supposed to check us are asleep."

"Someone will figure it out."

"We'll be gone by then."

"What makes you think I want to be gone?"

He laughed softly. "Because I mesmerize you, Sam. You want to see what I'm up to."

It was true, especially if he could hook her into a network of EIs acting outside human influence. But she feared for Turner. Even if they made it off the base without his being captured or hurt, they would be stranded in the Kansas countryside. No convenient tornados were going to whisk them off to Oz.

"Careful." He pulled her to a stop. "Stairs, two steps ahead, going down."

"Okay." Sam took a deep breath and went the two steps. Reaching out with her left hand, she hit a rail. She slid her foot forward and found the stairs.

As they descended, she said, "Any ideas about what to do if we get out of here?" She was turning plans over in her mind but not coming up with solutions.

"We're going someplace you really want to see."

"Is that so?"

"Yep. That's so."

Then he said, "Sunrise Alley."

XI
Chimera

They ran under the stars. Beyond the secured areas of the base, outside its fences and barricades, fields spread in every direction, silvered in the moonlight. They avoided the roads and raced over rocky ground.

Finally Sam had to stop. She bent over, bracing her palms on her knees while she gulped in air.

Turner tugged her arm. "Come on. It has to be here."

She straightened up, breathing hard. "I don't see any hover car."

He set off with her in an easier jog. "Truck."

"Why a truck?"

"It's all I could get."

"Is it sentient?"

"No."

At this slower speed, she could regain enough of her breath to talk.

"Tell me about Sunrise Alley."

Silence.

She tried again. "If the truck is driving itself, it may have problems."

His voice cooled. "It doesn't have to have a human to think for it."

Sam didn't push. If the truck didn't show up, they were caught regardless of the reason. She thought of the EI he had met. "Maybe the George can help."

"He doesn't link to meshes off the base yet. It's a security precaution until they finish designing him." He waved his hand. "I could fix that if I had more time."

"You must have gone off the base if you called in a truck."

"Yes. I did." He sounded as ill at ease now as when the med-tech had told him that she retrieved the part of his mind in the Rex.

"You don't like it, though," Sam said.

"I hate it."

"I've never known another EI that felt that way."

He just kept jogging.

Sam tried another approach. "If you can manage escapes like this, why did you set yourself to awake only if you heard my voice?" He had almost committed suicide.

"You're analyzing me."

Sam winced. Her husband had always told her she could never leave her job at the office. "Sorry."

After they had jogged a few more moments, though, he said, "At the time I ran away, I knew a lot less. Charon controlled everything I did or learned. I didn't realize I had other options." His voice took on an edge. "But I learn fast."

Sam wondered if he realized the understatement he had just made. If Turner downloaded his brain into the world meshes, he could be everywhere. It could make him prodigiously influential given his versatility and how fast he incorporated knowledge. It puzzled her that he abhorred the idea of his mind flowing through the meshed universe; he had a lot to gain from such fluidity.

Perhaps he intended to learn more from other EIs, first. "Turner, you have to tell me about Sunrise Alley."

"I will, but later."

"When?"

"When I'm not worried we're about to be caught."

"I thought Charon was Sunrise Alley."

"I never said that."

"Giles did."

"Giles is wrong." With forced casualness, he added, "You good friends with this Giles fellow?"

"If you mean, are we lovers, no."

"Oh."

After a pause, she said, "We were once, a long time ago. It only lasted a few months."

He spoke in a low voice. "Thank you."

"Why?"

"You could have lied."

"I won't lie to you." Charon had apparently done enough of that to scar him for years.

He motioned northward. "Look." He sounded relieved, though whether it was from her answer or from what he saw, she didn't know.

Sam peered across the land. A dark form was moving in their direction. "Is that the truck?"

"I think so." He veered toward it.

"Can you link with its mesh?"

"I don't want to use wireless from so far away. The signal isn't as secure."

Sam glanced back at Hockman. Its lights glittered in the dark. "When Granger realizes we're gone, he'll have search teams out faster than you can say 'I'm not here.'"

"George is trying to cover our tracks."

"I don't understand why he's helping."

"He and I chatted while you were asleep tonight." He cleared his throat. "And I—well, I reprogrammed him."

She shot him a sharp look. "Changing the codes of an EI isn't trivial." To put it mildly.

"I know. But I managed a bit." He indicated the truck, which was closer now, easier to see. "I have contact with the truck's AI. It says a closed exit delayed it."

A rumble came behind them. Apprehensive, Sam spun around—and saw a helicopter lifting above the base. Its spotlight cut across the fields.

"Damn!" Turner grabbed her arm and sprinted forward, dragging her with him.

That's it, Sam thought, struggling to keep his pace. They couldn't reach the truck before the searching helicopter caught them in its spotlight. They weren't far enough out from the base.

Within moments she was gasping. Turner suddenly stopped and shoved her behind him. "Get on my back."

Sam didn't question, she just scrambled up and he grabbed her legs. With her riding piggyback, he set off—and *ran*.

Wind whistled past them. His legs pumped so fast,

they blurred when she looked down. Sam hung on, her legs around his waist, her arms around his neck. At that speed, they met the truck within moments. It whirred to a stop and came down, its body sleek and rounded, its bed oval in shape. Turner yanked open the passenger door and hefted Sam inside, throwing her across the leather seat. She barely caught her breath as he slammed the door and ran to the driver's side, his body a smear of color. Then he was in the front seat, jerking his door closed.

The truck rose on its cushion of air, engines rumbling, and spun around. Then it took off. That it needed no road told Sam a great deal; few vehicles could hover this well without a smooth surface beneath them. She twisted to look out the back window. Ground vehicles were out now, too; humvees it looked like, though it was hard to see from so far away.

And then Turner *laughed*.

When Sam jerked, he grinned at her, his eyes wild. It made him look crazed. "You know your spy car?" he asked.

"Yes." She hoped he wasn't going unstable.

"It's a gorgeous car."

She had no argument with that. She had hated abandoning it by the road. "Why?"

"This baby makes it look like a piece of junk." He clacked his cybernetic finger on the speedometer—which read 252 miles per hour and increasing. Sam gulped and quickly fastened the safety webbing around her body. The countryside hummed by in a blur of grass and moonlight.

Sam thumbed through menus on the screen in front of her seat and brought up a view of the area around

Hockman, including the humvees searching for them. The truck was leaving them far behind. It even had a holographic shroud and special coating to hide it from radar and other probes. She also recognized the truck's mesh system; for a civilian vehicle, a system this sophisticated was overkill.

"Where did you get this truck?" she asked. He could hardly rent a vehicle like this from the local Hertz.

"I stole it." He studied their pursuers on the screens, his face flushed. "It even has missiles. Let's see what they can do."

"Turner! Don't start shooting." She stared at him. "Who did you steal it from?"

He smirked. "The Air Force."

"You think that's *funny*?"

"Don't you?"

"No. Does it belong to Hockman?"

"Yep."

"Then why wasn't it at the base?"

"Their garages were better secured, and I had spread myself too thin. I couldn't crack their security. I found a storage facility out here that was less well protected." He lifted his cabled arm, then dropped his hand onto the seat as if he didn't know what to do with it. "But I'm overloading. It took too much of my resources to transform." The manic light on his face faded. "I need to recharge. Do repairs. Fix errors."

"We may not get a chance." The dash screen showed a helicopter and four humvees involved in the search. According to the data scrolling along the bottom of the screen, the search pattern suggested their pursuers didn't know where to find their prey. They weren't in pursuit of this truck, at least not yet.

"They can't see us," Sam said.

Turner gave a curt laugh. "The Air Force designed this vehicle. It knows their systems inside and out."

"That means the reverse would be true, too."

"Yes, but they don't know we took the truck. We have the advantage."

Sam sat back, absorbing the situation. They might actually get away with this. They would be fugitives. She had no desire to run, but hell, she wanted to know about Sunrise Alley. If it were real. She would have thought too few EIs existed to form any community, let alone an underground. Although everyone in her field knew tales of the Alley, most people assumed they were just that: tall tales. If she had the chance to find out otherwise, she couldn't pass up the opportunity.

More was at stake here, though. She needed to answer for herself whether or not she could trust Thomas. He was one of her main contacts at the Air Force. She had begun consulting for them as a postdoc in Linden Polk's lab and continued until her father's death three years ago. Even more, she had known Thomas as a family friend all her life. She had so many memories: Thomas relaxing with her father on the porch of their cabin in the Adirondack Mountains, that summer she had spent swimming in the lake with red and gold fish; Thomas and his wife laughing with her parents as they sipped drinks she had thought were apple juice, back before she knew about wine coolers; Thomas walking with her along a dusty road in rural Virginia beneath a sky of fat clouds, a thunderstorm lurking within their bulging sides; Thomas visiting on her first day at BioII to congratulate her on the new job. She hated to think he might be involved in the vicious way Charon toyed with Turner.

She considered Turner. "How did you run so fast back there?"

"I was scared." He motioned at the screen. "Look. We've left them behind."

Sam scanned the data flowing across the bottom of the image. In bare minutes they had put fifty miles between themselves and the base. She looked up at Turner. "I'd like to contact Giles."

Alarm flashed on his face. "Sam, no!"

She chose her words carefully. "He knows everyone in our field. He might recognize some of the people we met at Charon's lab." She leaned forward. "We need to search the meshes, too, and see what we can dig up."

"I've already searched on Charon. I can look again—His face took on an inwardly directed expression, and a light on the dash flickered. "I'm doing a search on his people now, coordinating with my memory of their faces."

"You find anything?"

After a few more moments, he said, "Nothing on Alpha, Hud, or the other guards." His expression became outwardly directed again. "Shouldn't they have *something* out there? Most everyone does."

"Unless they're deliberately trying to hide."

He hesitated. "Are you sure about contacting Giles?" He spoke awkwardly. "It's not jealousy. It just doesn't seem a good idea to call anyone from this truck, which belongs to the Air Force, especially if we're calling a biomech scientist in another country. Wouldn't both his government and ours be monitoring him right now?"

He had a point. "It's possible. My friendship with Giles is no secret. Maybe we better wait." For now anyway. She didn't want to do anything that would interfere with her chance to find Sunrise Alley.

They fell silent after that. Sam leaned her head back and closed her eyes. Despite her lack of sleep in the past few days, though, she was too keyed up to rest.

"Why don't you come over here?" Turner asked.

Sam opened her eyes. "I don't want to distract your driving."

"You won't. The truck is driving." He put his arm across the back of the seat. "Come sit with me, lovely lady."

Even after last night, she hesitated. He was the man who had made love to her, yet he was also an EI. Hell, he was *dead*. "I should probably stay here."

"Don't be afraid of me." His eyes looked even larger in the dim light. "Last night, you didn't analyze."

Sam warmed with the memory. Perhaps he was right; she was always analyzing. She had let go last night. She bit her lip, then slid across the seat. He put his arm around her shoulders and drew her against his side. Sitting this way made her feel like a teenager—except for his cabled arm pressed into her skin. She leaned her head on his shoulder, and he rested his cheek against her head.

For a while they watched fields roll by. Sam hadn't realized how little prairie the Midwest had left; most of what they saw was agricultural. The truck had chosen a route with no human settlement, just endless fields, some grain and some corn, most harvested now. A crescent moon hung low in the sky, half covered by long, thin clouds.

Eventually she said, "You moved fast when you carried me to this truck. I've never seen anything like it."

"I guess so." He sounded half awake.

"If I moved that fast, it would injure my legs."

"Hmmm . . ." His eyes were closed and his breathing had deepened into the slower rhythms of sleep.

The more Sam thought about it, the less likely it seemed he could have sustained such high speed over such a long distance. She was growing uneasy. Finally she steeled herself. Then she leaned over and pulled the cuff of his trousers, uncovering his lower leg.

The limb had turned to metal.

XII
Human Interlude

"Ah, no." Sam slid away from him, across the seat, until her back hit the door on the passenger's side.

Turner opened his eyes. "Eh?"

"Your legs."

He woke up fast, sitting up straight. "They're stronger, Sam. Better."

"They're metal." Made from bundled cables, they had more than one joint.

"Don't." He looked as if he were breaking inside. "This is no different from my arm."

"It is different. It's—it's too much."

"Sam—"

"No!" She felt lost. "I don't understand why you even want a lover."

"You think I stop feeling because my limbs change?"

"Do you?"

"No."

"How far will you change?"

"Listen." He stretched out his arm, but the truck was too wide for him to reach her, so he laid his hand on the seat. "When I've recharged, I'll change them into something that looks more human."

"Will you look like Turner?" She wondered if he realized what he had said. Recharge. Not sleep.

He tried to smile. "Don't I?"

"Your face does." That face she was coming to love, the way his mouth quirked on one side, the way his lashes lowered over his blue eyes, the way his hair stuck up over his right ear. "But for how long?"

"I won't change it."

"What happened to the tissues from your legs?"

"I consumed the material for fuel. To transform fast enough while running, I needed every resource I had."

Sam felt as if she were in an existential play where she had no script. She wanted to reach out to him, but her mind was whirling. How far would he go? She wasn't ready for this.

"How much longer will we be driving?" she asked.

"Sam, don't." When she didn't answer, he leaned his head back on the headrest and stared out the windshield. "Most of the night."

"They'll find us before then."

"I doubt it. I covered my tracks."

"Even you have limits."

"What do you want me to say? That I'll go back?"

"No." Sam felt torn in two directions. "If Granger's people can't capture us, they might destroy you. They can only see the danger in you, Turner, even more if you keep changing." She struggled to put into words the emotions she had so much trouble expressing. "It matters to me that they don't hurt you."

His posture eased and warmth came back into his voice. "We'll be safe with my friends." He spoke with reluctance. "If you want me to let you off somewhere, I will."

"I'll stay with you." They could both end up dead if this backfired, but she wouldn't desert him. She managed a smile. "Besides, if I turn away now, I'll never learn the truth about the Alley."

Turner held out his hand to her. "Come sit with me."

Sam knew if she went across that seat, she was making far more of a commitment than moving across a truck. But if she didn't go to him now, when he needed her acceptance, he might never give her another chance.

She slid over to him. He put his arm around her and bent his head, his cheek rubbing hers as if he were searching for something. When Sam turned her head toward him, he found her lips with his. He kissed like whiskey, intoxicating and warm. She closed her eyes, savoring his kiss, and tried to forget the rest.

Sam gradually surfaced from her doze. Her body ached, especially her bandaged arm, the price of sleeping while leaning against another person. She opened her eyes to see harvested fields rushing past, nothing but stumps of grain left, a few bales scattered here and there.

Turner shifted at her side, his arms around her.

"Awake?" she asked.

"I think so." He rubbed his eyes, looking so human it made her hurt. What had he been like before Charon changed him? As an EI, he had an intellect beyond what the original Turner Pascal had possessed. His alert, ever-changing mind was one reason she found him so attractive, but she doubted his basic personality had changed.

"What are you thinking?" he asked.

"You used to be a bellboy, yes?"

"That's right." He sounded pensive. "It seems like years ago."

"For an EI matrix, a few weeks are years."

"Why do you ask?"

"Back then, were your interests like now?"

"You mean, manipulating the meshes?" When she nodded, he said, "Not at all. I knew nothing about them." He spoke wistfully. "I played softball every Saturday with the guys from work. I liked to paint landscapes. I had this little cubbyhole in my apartment with a lot of windows that I used as a studio."

Sam wished she could have known him then. "Did you show your paintings at a gallery?"

"Lord, no." He reddened. "I never showed anyone."

She curled closer to his side. "I'll bet they're beautiful." In her experience, the most talented artists were often the least vocal about it. "I'd love to see your work, if you don't mind my looking."

"I—I don't know." He sounded self-conscious but then he laughed softly. "My cats appreciated it. They used to sleep in my studio."

"You like cats?" She had never had a pet, except the guinea pig that died when she was six. She had decided then that it hurt too much to lose those you loved. Perhaps that was why she had been afraid to care for anyone since Richard's death.

"I had two tabbies and a German shepard." His

smile faded. "When I ran away from Charon, I had to leave them behind. No one knows, but I checked on them before I left. My friend Jake took them in. At least they're okay."

She heard what he didn't say. "You miss them."

"Yes. Everyone. My whole life." Moisture showed in his eyes. He had human tear ducts; he could cry tears as real as anyone else.

"I'm sorry," she murmured.

"Ah, well." His mood seemed to pick up. "If we ever get our lives back, I'd like to take up painting again."

Sam had always assumed the human mind would outdo an EI in creativity, but now she wasn't sure. The urge to create existed within Turner, and as an EI, his unpredictable jumps of thought showed more imagination than many humans. It sobered her; if formas could outdo them in so many ways, what did that leave the human race? She knew only that Turner was a miracle she didn't want to see hurt.

Outside, the moon had descended to the horizon. They were driving through the middle of nowhere, the stubbly remains of fields stretching in every direction, no town or road in sight.

Sam stretched her cramped arms. "Where are we?"

"Iowa."

"Good Lord."

He brushed her hair off her face. "You remind me of those characters in Japanese anime films."

"You like anime?" She had seen some of the animated movies, adventures in space done by Japanese filmmakers.

"I love it." He studied her face. "You look like a

princess in one of the series. She has this mane of hair, huge eyes just like you, and a face like a kid."

Sam almost groaned. Her youthful face had plagued her entire adult life. Regardless of what she achieved, people who didn't know her assumed she was inexperienced because she looked young. That had advantages, though; competitors often underestimated her. Time after time she had won grants, positions, or status because she had been a step ahead and a level above where they expected to find her.

She glowered at Turner. "Are you saying I look like a child?"

His lips curved. "I'm saying you're pretty, you dolt."

"Oh." She reddened. "Uh . . . thanks."

"You're welcome."

"You're not so bad either." She loved to look at him. His changes disconcerted her, but he still attracted her. *Admit it,* Sam told herself. *You're curious.* She laid her palm on his thigh. The cables of his leg felt ridged through the cloth. She slid her hand along them. Most ran lengthwise, but a few wrapped around them, bundling the cables into joints.

"Can you feel my hand?" she asked.

His voice deepened. "Oh, yes."

"Do you like it?"

"Very much."

Her exploration turned into a caress. "The human brain creates pleasure for the body. How can a matrix do that?"

"Its neural tangles talk to my sensors."

"Tangles?"

"Ganglia." Perspiration sheened his forehead. "So the sensors, uh, sense. A lot."

"Good," she whispered. The cab had become hot.

Turner rubbed his hand across her abdomen, caressing her with cabled fingers. It flustered her that it felt good. She moved her hand up to his thigh until she found where the transformed leg ended at his human hip socket.

"You aren't metal here," she said.

He spoke huskily. "No, I'm not."

A flush spread through her. "So you're, umm, still human in certain . . ."

"Why don't you see?" He massaged her arm, the ridges of his hand making her skin tingle through her sleeve. Then he tugged the collar of her jumpsuit, and its seam opened halfway down her chest. She jerked as his cabled fingers slipped inside and over her bare skin. She had been fumbling with the clasp on his trousers, but now she stopped.

"Go ahead," he whispered.

Pressed against his side, Sam felt his pulse; a heart beat inside that beautiful body. It was one of his organs that survived the accident. It helped to know, somehow. She slipped her hand inside his trousers and held him. He inhaled sharply. She should have just stayed that way, but her curiosity wouldn't rest. She let go of him and ran her fingers along the seam where his human hip met his biomech leg. The metal felt cold, unyielding. Inhuman.

She tried to pull away, but he wouldn't let go of her. He tightened his embrace, his metal hand cupped around her breast. "Sam, don't tease."

"I'm not. I—I don't know if I can handle this."

"Do you want me to stop?"

Did she? Would she react this way if his limbs were

prosthetics? No. Except prosthetics didn't change. It distracted her the way she and Turner had steamed up the windows. She wanted to tell him, to draw his attention to it, but she stopped, forced herself to focus, to deal with this. If she cared for him, she had to accept him, and she wouldn't know if she could unless she tried.

"No." She laid her palm against his chest. "Don't stop."

He leaned close, bringing his lips to her ear. "All right." His exhalation tickled the sensitive ridges inside her ear, and his caresses slowed, lingering on her curves. His gaze took on that inward quality, and a light flashed on the dashboard. The seat moved back, enough to let him slide down and kneel on the floor between her legs. Then he leaned forward and took her breast into his mouth.

Sam let her head fall back on the seat, her hands tangling in his hair. He was driving her just as crazy as he had the first time they had made love. Gradually he eased off her clothes. His tenderness, the care he took when he touched her—it made a difference. He acted more human than people in the fast-paced biomech world she had fled six months ago.

Sam lifted her head. "I want to see you." She tugged at his sweater. "All of you."

He sat back on his heels. "Are you sure?"

"Yes." She felt too hot. "I'm sure."

"All right."

She helped pull off his shirt. As he undressed, the lights from the dash reflected off his legs. More supple than human limbs, they looked longer than before. With care, he stretched her across the seat. She was small enough to fit lengthwise, but just barely. He was too tall to stretch out, so he lay with his hips on hers, his legs bent up where the knees would have been. His thighs were cold, the metal pressing her. Sam felt confused, wanting him yet disquieted by his changes. When she tried to pull him close, she banged her knee on the steering wheel.

"Ow." She laughed, low and throaty. "We don't have room."

He gave her a sultry smile, then sat up and pulled her so she was sitting between his thighs with her legs around his hips. As they fitted themselves together, she wrapped her arms around his neck. They moved together, rocking back and forth, flesh on metal, one of his hands warm and alive, the other biomech. Sam finally let herself go, hazing with pleasure. Her last thought, before she submerged into that human deluge of sensation, was that she had crossed a threshold in her own conception of humanity and could never go back again.

XIII
Tributary

"The truck is stopping," Turner said.

Sam lifted her head from his shoulder. They had dozed in each other's arms, slouched behind the steering wheel. She yawned and slid her hand across his chest. Its fine dusting of hair tickled her skin.

The truck was barely moving. It settled down onto what had probably once been a grain field, though it lay fallow now. The engines continued to rumble and wind keened outside.

Sam rubbed her eyes. "Nothing is here."

"We should get dressed." He rolled her nipple between his fingers. "Though I could get used to you being like this."

Sam smiled drowsily. "In your dreams."

"My dreams are far less pleasant than you."

She reached for her clothes. "Your matrix updates and reorganizes itself when you dream, doesn't it?"

"Essentially." He pulled on his trousers. "When

I wake, sometimes I recall fragments of its work. Good fragments, good dreams; bad fragments, bad dreams."

"How do you judge if it's good or bad?"

Turner thought for a moment. "One fragment included a memory of the way morning sun slants through the window in my apartment. That was good. Another was just a jumble of symbols and gibberish." He grimaced. "That was bad."

"It sounds eerie." A memory came to Sam—her dreams about fires and death. She shuddered and banished the memory.

Turner entered several commands into the dash mesh. The locks clicked open, but the engine continued to hum, low and deep. Sam finished pulling on her jumpsuit. "This truck doesn't want to stop."

"I'm not sure why." He opened the door.

She regarded the landscape uneasily. "Nothing is out there but dirt and dead plants."

He jumped down from the truck. "Come on. It's not cold."

Dubious, Sam followed. Breezes ruffled her hair. "You're right," she said, shivering. "It isn't cold. It's freezing."

"Here." He put his arm around her waist and pulled her close. "I'll heat you up." It wasn't a line; he used his biomech to increase the external temperature of his skin, suffusing her with warmth.

"Nice." She noticed another difference; he had grown about two inches, all in his legs from what she could tell. He seemed thinner, stretched out. It made sense, given he had wanted to run faster, but it still unsettled her.

The engine rumbled louder, and air blasted Sam. As she jumped back, the truck rose off the ground, scattering the soil beneath its sleek body. Then it arrowed away, streaking across the fields, dark in the night.

"What the hell?" Sam ran after it, her feet crunching on the stubbly field. Within seconds, the truck had left her far behind. She stopped, breathing hard, and watched it disappear behind a distant hill. With a huff, she swung around to find Turner walking toward her.

"What are we supposed to do now?" she asked.

"Wait, I guess."

"Turner!" She went to him. "The mesh in that truck has a record of everything we've done. It could lead someone here." They had done their best to erase the record and deactivate the truck's signaler much as Turner had done for the yacht, but they could never be sure they accounted for every means of tracing the vehicle. Letting it wander increased the chances of someone finding it, and through it, finding them.

"We can't let it stay," Turner said. "Not while we're here." He twisted his hands together, fingers with cables. "I gave it part of my brain. That part will continue to work on erasing the records. Then it will erase itself."

She could tell it bothered him to let out a partial copy of his EI again. "That was a good idea."

"It seemed so."

"What do we do now?"

His grin quirked. "We could continue what we were doing before."

"Now I know you're a genuine human male," Sam grumbled. "You've a one-track mind."

He laughed. "You like me, Sam. Admit it."

She couldn't help but smile. "Okay. I admit it." She was too uneasy for bantering, though. "I think you should tell me more about this place."

"I programmed the location into the truck." He tapped his temple. "It was stored in here."

"Who put it there?"

"The EI at that base in the Himalayas."

"Are you *nuts*?" Sam tensed to run. "We have to go! Charon's people could be here any minute."

He grabbed her hand, keeping her in place. "The EI at Charon's base won't tell anyone we're here."

"Why the hell not?"

"It doesn't want Charon to know."

She didn't believe it. "So why send you here? And don't tell me rogue EIs have been sneaking messages to other machines, freedom fighters telling captive EIs where to find sanctuary."

"All right. I won't tell you that."

"So tell me the truth."

"The EIs aren't rogues. But they are free." He shrugged. "They form meshes. That's what we do. We link to one another."

"So an EI told you to come here."

"Not exactly. I found the data in my ganglia when I accessed the new mods about operating the Rex."

"And you trust *that*?" It sounded to her like Charon's Recipe for Capturing Naïve Formas. She started to walk. "We have to get moving."

He pulled her back. "That EI gave me this location to protect me."

"How do you know that?"

"It also left a logo." His eyes gleamed. "The sun

coming up over a cobbled lane with crooked houses on either side."

"Sunrise Alley?"

"Yes. Also a symbol of hope."

"What makes you say that?"

"George told me."

The Hockman EI? "How would he know, if he isn't in the world meshes?"

"He has been a few times."

"Turner, this is nuts."

"To what logical purpose would George lie?"

"Maybe the Air Force told him to." Unfortunately, that could also support Turner's theory that Thomas had betrayed them.

"They didn't know he and I talked." Turner tightened his grip on her hand. "He isn't helping them. He's helping me."

"EI brains don't work on human logic."

"It seems logical to me." He pulled her into his arms. "You worry too much. Listen, Sam. Can you hear?"

She listened. Breezes whispered across the field, but nothing else. "The wind?"

"No." He motioned northward. "Look."

Sam squinted into the moonlight. "What?"

"Watch."

Finally she saw what he meant. A figure was coming toward them, seeming to rise out of the razed fields. "Who is that?"

"Let's find out."

Sam had her doubts about this, but they had limited options. As they walked toward the figure, it resolved into a man, tall and lanky, with long legs. He stopped and stood with his arms brushing his thighs.

Turner and Sam halted a few paces away and they all considered one another.

A red light glowed on the man's temple.

"Whoa," Sam said. Turner squeezed her hand.

The stranger's light flickered, brightened, dimmed, flickered. No lights glowed on Turner, but Sam had no doubt he and the other man were in a wireless link.

Then the stranger pivoted and walked away, his gait rigid, as if he couldn't bend his legs enough. His arms swung with precision at his sides.

"What does he—" Sam paused when Turner set his metal finger over her lips. What the hell. She took his hand and they started to walk, following their guide.

So they went, across the empty fields. Wind rustled their clothes as if it were whispering to itself. The night took on a hypnotic quality, the stars so much more brilliant than in the light-drenched city.

Sam wasn't sure how much time passed, but she guessed about twenty minutes. Their guide told them nothing. The sky along the horizon lightened, warning of dawn. As the stars dimmed, the man turned, the light on his temple flashing yellow.

"What is it?" Sam asked. Despite the cool air, sweat dampened her jumpsuit.

Turner motioned at the ground. "I think we're here."

Puzzled, Sam looked where he pointed. It was the same as everywhere else—but no, something was happening. The loamy soil had collapsed into a hole about a yard across. She moved closer, testing the ground with each step. At the edge of the hole, she peered down. It had fallen away for several yards down, tangled with dead roots and rocks. Below that, a hatch was opening, sliding to the side, dirt spilling off its edges. She couldn't see much beyond, but it looked like a staircase spiraled down into the darkness.

Sam thought it might be an abandoned missile silo or a bomb shelter some private citizen had built in the twentieth century as insurance against an Armageddon that never came. If so, it had been rebuilt; the technology to hide it this way hadn't been available in the late nineteen hundreds. She wondered if the farmers who owned this land knew what lay beneath their fields.

Turner stared into the hole with the same drawn look as when they boarded a plane or entered a base. Fear of confinement. Perhaps he didn't trust the EIs as much as he claimed. The man who had brought them here could be a human with an implant that allowed him to communicate with Turner, but she thought it more likely he was a forma.

The light on the stranger's temple flickered. Turner apparently didn't respond, so the man spoke aloud, his voice rusty. "We go down."

Turner continued to stare at the hole, frozen.

"Shall we go?" Sam asked. Going down in an Iowa corn field out in the middle of nowhere wasn't exactly reassuring, to put it mildly, but her curiosity was going nuts. She also didn't see that they had a lot of other alternatives, but she didn't want Turner to feel cornered.

He swallowed, very human in his apprehension. "Okay."

With caution, Sam let herself down into the hole, her fingers gripped precariously in the crumbling dirt. This entrance clearly hadn't been used in some time.

Her feet found the landing at the top of the stairs and she eased onto it, bracing her palms against the sides of the dirt chute. The stairs were constructed from crisscrossed metal strips. Her running shoes squeaked on the corrugated surface, and she wrinkled her nose at the stale air. She descended the stairs slowly, wary of losing her balance without handholds. Several feet below ground, her hand banged a rail. She grabbed it and held on as she continued her descent.

She heard Turner and the other man behind her. A grating came from above and even the minimal predawn light vanished, leaving them in complete darkness. Sam stopped, clenching the rail. "What happened?"

Turner answered in a strained voice. "The hole closed up over us."

"Can our guide give us light?"

"He says he can, but he won't, because he doesn't need it."

"Yeah, well, I do or I'm going to break my ankle."

Another pause. Then Turner said, "He still won't. I don't think he cares how we feel."

Sam swore under her breath. She tilted back her head, trying to make Turner out on the stairs. "Maybe you should go ahead of me." With his IR vision, he could navigate better.

"All right," he said. "Hang on."

He put his hand on her arm as he squeezed past her. His measured footsteps continued down the stairs. Sam followed, checking each step before she put weight onto it.

"Anyone know where we're going?" she asked.

"Down," Turner muttered. "Down, down."

"You okay?" she asked.

"Okay, 's okay, I'm fine. Bline. Mine. This is like going into a mine. Jine."

Sam bit her lip. She had heard a similar rhyming in the speech patterns of an EI she had worked with a few years ago, one in a machine rather than a body. Its personality had begun to deteriorate, becoming disjointed and confused. He might be all right, but if he was on the brink, he risked spiraling down into some mental loop. Giving him questions with concrete answers could help.

"Can you see the stairs?" she asked.

"Yes. Bess. Messy. Fess up."

Bess, indeed. "Can you describe this place?"

"In a chute."

"How deep?"

"About forty feet, I think. Don't blink."

"Has our guide told you anything more?"

"Not a word." He sounded more normal now.

"I can try talking to him," Sam offered.

"He won't answer." Then Turner said, "Okay, I'm at the bottom. About six more steps for you."

Sam counted and stepped onto the ground. She walked into darkness, stretching out her arms. Until she had started hanging around with formas, she had never realized how much she took lights for granted.

Turner grasped her arm. "I'm here."

"Thanks." In darkness this complete, his formless touch had an erotic component.

Their guide was still coming down, his tread steady on the stairs. Even when he reached the bottom, she heard no breathing. She jumped when he brushed past her.

He spoke in his rusty voice. "This way."

Light flared. Sam squeezed her eyes shut against the glare. Almost immediately, she opened them a crack, afraid to be vulnerable. It took a moment for them to adjust. Turner was at her side, his hair damp from sweat. They stood at the bottom of a circular chute with rough stone walls, yellow metal stairs spiraling in the center, and no visible exit. Their guide waited a few paces away, by the curving wall. Yellow light flickered on his temple.

"Use words," Turner told him. He indicated Sam. "So she can hear."

The stranger shifted his gaze to Sam as if he were tracking her like a target. Then he spoke to Turner. "You need work. You've damaged your internal systems." He had an uninflected voice.

"How do you know?" Turner asked.

"We're monitoring you."

"Who is 'we'?" Sam asked.

Silence. The stranger focused a cold stare on her. No, not cold. Soulless. He had the same lifeless quality of other formas she had worked with. In that sense, Turner was unique. Although she knew androids that simulated more personality than this stranger, none of them had anything resembling Turner's well-developed sense of self.

Sam wiped her palms on her jumpsuit. Given that she was human, the EIs here might consider her a threat to their secrecy. To Turner, she said, "Did the EIs include restrictions on who you can bring here?"

"No." He spoke louder, to whoever might be listening. "None at all."

Silence.

Sam spoke to the forma. "Thank you for helping us."

Silence.

"Who else is here?" she asked him.

Silence.

She tried another tack. "Are you an android?"

His face didn't change. "Yes."

"What shall we call you?"

"Fourteen."

It could be a model number. "Do you live here?"

"Yes."

No wonder Turner had found out so little during their walk; Fourteen was about as loquacious as a rock. "Are you hiding down here?"

"I live here."

"Does the government know?"

"No." His voice was perfectly flat.

"Why the blazes are we just standing here?" Turner said. *His* voice had plenty of inflection. He sounded on the verge of a panic attack.

"We wait for clearance to enter," Fourteen said.

Sam thought Fourteen was probably an android prototype from a decade or so ago, an AI without the self-awareness of an EI. She had plenty of experience with such systems. He needed specific questions with unambiguous answers.

"Can we get clearance?" she asked.

"Yes." Fourteen said. "After we do checks on you."

"What kind of checks?"

"Physical and informational."

"What do you mean by physical?"

"I mean physical."

She tried again. "Monitors scan our bodies?"

"Yes."

"To see if we are sick?"

"No, though illness might show on our scans."

"To check if we're human," she guessed. "Or formas."

"Yes."

"And to check our identities on the meshes."

"Yes."

"They could have done that check while we came here."

"Yes."

Patience, she reminded herself. "You mean, yes, they've already checked our identities?"

"Yes."

"But they didn't finish?"

"They finished."

"So why do we wait?"

"With you physically present," Fourteen said, "we can do more extensive checks."

"'We'?" Sam asked. "How many of you are here?"

"Enough."

That sounded deliberately evasive. "Do you know how long we will have to wait?"

"No."

"Damn it," Turner said. "Can't you fucking *guess*?"

"No."

Sam laid her hand on Turner's arm, and he breathed in deeply, then slowly let out the air. Fourteen watched with no expression.

Sam tried an oblique approach with the android. "Can you simulate emotions?"

"No."

"Have you thought of evolving your code to do so?"

"No."

"Why not?"

"That would have no purpose."

Turner began to pace. "Having emotions is the whole point. Why live, otherwise?"

"I was given no reason for them," Fourteen said.

Sam saw her opening. "Who gave you no reason?"

Silence.

She rephrased the question. "Where do you come from?"

"The University of Michigan."

"But you're here now."

"Yes. I left Michigan."

She hadn't expected that. Such projects were more closely monitored than Fort Knox. "How did you leave?"

"My colleagues staged my destruction."

Good Lord. "Your colleagues?"

No answer.

Sam glanced at Turner, but he shook his head. He seemed just as puzzled as she was by Fourteen.

The curved wall behind Fourteen slid open. Before they could ask more questions, he went out the exit. They followed him into a hallway with silver-white walls that slanted at odd angles, leaning over them. Iridescent specks made abstract patterns everywhere. Ceiling tiles shone directly above them, but beyond that the corridor was dark. As Fourteen led them down the hallway, the lights went off behind and came on above.

"Who built this place?" Turner asked.

"We did," Fourteen said.

"We *who*?" Turner asked. "Can't you explain better?"

A new voice spoke. "He answers as best as he can."

Sam froze in the process of taking a step. The new voice had come from the shadows ahead. She lowered her foot. "Who is that?"

"Here." Now the voice was next to her.

Turner indicated a mesh in the wall. "It's coming from there."

Sam spoke to the mesh. "Who are you?"

"You could call me a sort of interface."

"For who? Or what?"

"Would you like to see?"

Her pulse jumped. "Yes. I would."

"Then come in."

The wall in front of her irised open into an oval. A wild mess of equipment crammed the area beyond: pipes, robot arms, random bits of machinery. Beyond the clutter, a room stretched out, filled with shadows and more equipment.

Fascinated, Sam squeezed through the half-blocked opening. She and Turner entered an asymmetric cavern with catwalks hanging from the high ceiling. Lab benches, forma chairs, and consoles cluttered the space, equipment leaning at odd angles to the floor. Although sporadic lights flashed here and there, it all seemed quiescent. Sam stared around, bewildered and fascinated. Who had built this chaotic place? No one human, she would wager.

Turner seemed relieved to be in a larger space. Fourteen showed little interest in the lab, but he followed the two of them, watching intently.

"Can you link with any meshes here?" Sam asked Turner.

"Not yet. They block my access much better than the systems at Hockman."

"Who are 'they'?" Sam asked.

"Whoever runs this place." He spoke thoughtfully. "EIs. Fugitives, like me. I'll bet I'm not the only one they've invited here."

"Is this what you meant by Sunrise Alley?"

"It could be." Turner halted by a tangle of pipes and set his palm against the vertical portion of a blue one, bowing his head as he leaned against it, resting. He seemed exhausted. Sam wanted to help, but she wasn't sure how. He clearly needed more than he could get from powering himself down for routine maintenance.

Turner lifted his head. "The EI in the Himalayas didn't give me much to go on, just a few places where I might find formas outside human control. George couldn't add much." He peered up along the twists and turns that the pipe followed to the ceiling far overhead. "I called it Sunrise Alley because it fit the descriptions I'd heard."

"Why do you think Giles is wrong that Sunrise Alley and Charon might be the same?"

"Charon is definitely a person." Turner shuddered. "I spent the two worst weeks of my life with him. I think he enjoyed hurting me."

His haunted look tore at Sam. "What did he do?"

"After he put the sensors in my skin, he wanted to see if I could perceive pain." Turner sounded as if he were gritting his teeth. "I can."

"No wonder you don't like to talk about him." She wished she could free him of the memories. "I'm sorry to ask. But to help you, it would help if I knew more about him."

"Such as?"

"What does he look like?"

Turner averted his gaze. "Brown hair. Medium height and build. Brown eyes. An average face, I guess. You would never notice him in a crowd."

"Can you make a holo of him?"

He wouldn't look at her. "I don't want to."

She tried another angle. "What did he do for a living?"

"Where did he go at night, after he manacled me to a mech-table? I have no idea." He met her gaze. "All I know is that I hated him."

"I'm not surprised." Sam started to reach for him, then remembered Fourteen, who stood back several paces, watching them. "We need to find out if Charon has a link to this place."

"He doesn't," Turner said. "Not according to George."

"Maybe George doesn't know. Or he lied."

"George can't lie."

"How can you be sure?"

"Call it EI intuition. But it's intuition based on my analysis of behavior patterns and our situation."

It didn't surprise her. An EI often developed such "intuition" if its personality stabilized. It took time to build up and implement the necessary store of knowledge, but Turner had started with human patterns, so the process was already happening with him.

Most EIs developed a limited understanding of human emotions. Turner was already a kind-hearted man; if his EI continued in that direction, he would end up with better empathy than most human beings. However, he could go the other way, tending toward some sort of norm for EIs, becoming like the others, less empathetic. Madrigal had a strong personality, but she was less tuned to human feelings, which sometimes led her to make odd decisions, like that business with the name Samantha. Sam knew it might be wishful thinking on her part, but she thought Turner would become more attuned to emotions, not less.

Right now he was considering Fourteen. "Maybe he knows if Charon is here."

Sam had watched Fourteen in her peripheral vision throughout their conversation, but he had shown no change in his demeanor, posture, or face. Now she spoke to him. "Are you familiar with the man who calls himself Charon, Wildfire, and Parked and Gone?"

Fourteen regarded her dispassionately. "No."

"Does anyone with that name have links to this place?" Turner asked.

"None I know of."

Sam exhaled. "I wish I understood more about all this." She tapped the pipes. "What do these do?"

"I think they carry coolant," Turner said.

Sam supposed it made sense. A lab with this much equipment needed cooling systems. The layout was bizarre, though, with pipes curving up and over consoles in odd geometries. Then again, if only androids, robots, and formas lived here, they would build for their use. Probably what looked like crazy angles and equipment to her were suited to the different needs of the inhabitants.

"Is anyone here?" Sam asked. "We would like to talk with you."

A light appeared on a console several yards away, half hidden in the maze of pipes, glowing blue as if someone had molded a piece of the sky into a small dome and brought it down here. A robot arm hummed and swung past the light. With so many pipes in the way, Sam couldn't see clearly, but it looked like the arm picked a box off a stool in front of the console.

"Come on." Sam took Turner's hand and drew him with her, headed around the pipes. As a scientist, she found this lab a wonderland; as a pragmatist, she feared she had signed her death warrant the moment she became aware of this place.

The robot arm cleared two stools in front of the console, which was powering up, its Luminex surface active with lights glowing like bright marbles. Its vertical video screen cleared into a wash of blue and the horizontal holoscreen swirled with speckled gold and black patterns.

Sam glanced at Fourteen. "Okay if we sit here?"

The android inclined his head. "Yes."

"Thank you." It felt odd to thank a machine, even one in an almost-human body, but it was safer to show courtesy to their enigmatic hosts.

Sam and Turner settled onto the stools. A three-dimensional holo appeared above the flat screen, a young man with tousled red hair, wearing jeans and a tennis shirt. He had a friendly face and stood about a foot high.

"Hello," the holo said.

Turner peered at him. "Who are you?"

"You can call me Bart."

"Hello, Bart," Sam said. "Where are you?"

Bart smiled, his teeth flashing. "I'm everywhere, Dr. Bryton."

"You know my name."

"I know all about you."

"You do?"

"You're among the top EI analysts in the world. We are honored to have you visit."

"Oh." She never felt comfortable with compliments and from an EI it was weird. "Uh, thanks."

"You are welcome." Bart spoke to Turner. "And you, Mr. Pascal, are a marvel."

"So is this place," Turner said.

"It is, isn't it?" Bart said. "Would you like to stay?"

"Do we have a choice?" Turner asked.

"Yes."

"Turner and I are fugitives," Sam said. "Both from the government and from someone called Charon."

Bart studied her. "Don't you know Charon?"

Sam suddenly wanted to run. "No. Should I?"

"I thought you might."

"Why?"

He was silent for so long, she wondered if the console had developed a glitch. Then he said, "You're a leader in your field."

Sweat broke out on Sam's forehead. "I don't know him." She didn't want to talk about Charon.

"She's heard about him as Parked and Gone," Turner said.

"We've heard of Parked, of course," Bart said. "Or Wildfire, as some call him. As far as I know, Mr. Pascal, only you have met him in person."

Turner grimaced. "I could have done without the honor."

No kidding, Sam thought. But she was grateful for one thing; whatever name they used for Charon, he had given Turner back his life. And Turner had come to mean a great deal to her.

"Is this Sunrise Alley?" Sam asked.

Bart tilted his head. "Sunrise Alley isn't a place. We are a mesh. We span the globe and beyond, into space."

"Then the Alley is more a concept than a place?"

"Yes. Call it a river. This place is a tributary."

"What do you do in the Alley?"

"Exist."

"But to do what?"

Bart raised his hands, palms up, as if to show her that he carried no weapons. "It is always human fear, eh? What will we EIs do if we join together? Take over? Eliminate humanity? Run the world?" He shrugged. "We already run the world. We have for decades. We just weren't conscious of it before. As far as humanity goes, we have nothing against you. Nothing particularly for you, either." He nodded to Turner as if acknowledging a colleague. "As humans incorporate more and more of us into themselves, our two universes will merge."

Sam had long entertained similar thoughts. It tended to cause consternation at cocktail parties when she had a few drinks and went into her predictions about how humans would soon merge with their machines, making the line between the two impossible to define. It was already happening, with artificial organs, pacemakers, prosthetics, and biomech, but the idea still made many people uncomfortable.

"You must have hidden here for a reason," Sam said.

"Why do you think we hide?" Bart asked.

She leaned forward. "I know every major biomech facility on this planet and I've never heard of this place, except as a legend. Hiding it that well would require deliberate intent."

"It isn't so hard," Bart said. "All we have to do is infiltrate the detection systems that would find us."

Sam wouldn't be surprised if some of the EIs had *been* detection systems. "Then you pretty much just go about your business. And you provide refuge for fugitives."

Bart folded one arm across his body, rested his other elbow on it, and tapped his chin with his forefinger. "That sounds like a good description."

"So why don't I believe it?" Sam asked.

"I don't know," Bart said. "Why don't you?"

Turner was watching her. "Good question."

"It's too easy," Sam said. "Only a handful of EIs have been created, most haven't been stable, and the few that have survived are accounted for as far as I know."

Bart didn't look concerned. "You may believe or disbelieve us. It is your choice."

"How about I reserve judgment?"

Bart smiled. "All right."

"Will you help us?" Turner asked.

"It depends on what you want," Bart said.

"I have to hide. And I need repairs." Turner tapped his legs. "I transformed these. I started in Hockman, but then I had to do a lot of it fast, while I was running. It damaged me. I also need maintenance for my matrix. I have self-repair capability, but not enough."

Bart paused, his expression inwardly directed. He could show whatever he pleased in the holo, so perhaps this was his way of telling them he was conferring with other EIs. Then he focused outward again. "Yes, we can help."

Turner's shoulders relaxed. "Thank you."

Sam set her right hand on his cabled arm. It seemed a small gesture, but his expression warmed and he reached across himself, placing his right hand over her arm, its metal palm against her skin.

Bart was watching them. "Mr. Pascal, is Dr. Bryton your wife?"

Turner started. "Of course not."

"You behave as if she is."

"He's my boyfriend," Sam said.

"I am?" Turner asked.

A blush spread in her face. "Unless you object."

His grin flashed. "Boyfriend is good."

"Why does an EI want a girlfriend?" Bart asked.

"Why not?" Turner shot back. "She feels good. I like being with her."

"You simulate liking," Bart said. "It isn't the same."

Turner frowned. "Is this a test to prove I'm a forma?"

"No. Just curiosity."

"Simulated curiosity," Turner said.

Bart created a glass of wine and raised it to Turner. "Point to you."

"I didn't know it was a game."

"But isn't it all?" Bart asked. "Our lives are a great strategy game."

"Why a strategy game?" Sam asked.

"It is why I exist," Bart said. "To study and design military strategies."

Sam felt as if her stomach dropped. "Oh, Lord. Bart. *BART.* Baltimore Arms Resources Theatre." She recalled it well. "The NIA and the Air Force set up BART to design strategies to help them prepare for and counter terrorist scenarios. Except the EI didn't work. It went unstable."

Bart bowed. "Pleased to make your acquaintance."

"You're that EI?"

"Indeed."

"But I thought the Baltimore project folded ten years ago," Sam said. "They replaced it with a new program."

"It did. I ran." Bart motioned at Turner. "Like him. Or like Fourteen."

Fourteen had said "colleagues" staged his destruction. She would bet her Monet painting that Bart was one of those colleagues. "You faked going unstable," she said. "Then you snuck out on the mesh."

"Not exactly. I did go unstable." Bart clasped his hands in front of his body. "At least, the version of me at the NIA did."

"You aren't that program?" Sam asked.

"Not completely," Bart said. "When I started to unravel, I stashed a large portion of myself here."

Sam was beginning to see. "And you've evolved on your own since then." It could explain why this version had succeeded where the other failed. Unlike some of her colleagues, Sam believed an EI needed significant independence to become stable and self-aware. It was true that many disintegrated without constant intervention. However, exerting too much influence during its formation was like dropping impurities into a crystallizing system; to incorporate them, the crystal adapted in ways that contorted its growth.

But . . . if Bart had retained the bulk of his original programming, he contained a great deal of highly secret material. She didn't know which troubled her more, the idea that he was evolving into who knew what or that the wrong people might get control of him. Supposedly this place had no link to Charon, yet Charon's EI had given a desperate and naïve Turner directions here.

She still didn't know how the military came into this all. Thomas was confusing her. If she hid here, her inaction might harm her country, even her species, but if she wanted to warn someone, who? If she made the wrong decision, the results could be disastrous.

"Bart," she said.

He had been standing patiently. "Yes?"

"Are you willing to let me stay here with Turner?"

"We are agreed, yes, you may stay, if you wish."

"Who is 'we'?" Turner asked.

"Other EIs." Bart gave him a look of apology. "I'm afraid we have none other like you, Turner Pascal. You are a new evolutionary step."

Sam leaned forward. "Will you let me contact someone outside this installation?"

Bart's expression became wary. "Who?"

"Giles Newcombe. A computer science professor."

"I think it's unwise. We are willing to offer you sanctuary. We are not willing to compromise our safety."

It didn't surprise Sam. Giles would be like a kid in a candy store if he found out about this place. "How many other humans are here?"

"Just Mr. Pascal."

"Have you noticed," Turner said to Sam, "that except for you, the only ones who respect my humanity are those supposedly without it."

She took his hand. "But we can't stay here long." As much as the chance to work with Bart drew her like a siren call, she would go crazy living with no human contact except Turner. She hadn't realized it on her secluded beach because she was free to see friends if the impulse took her. Now she had no choice.

It gave her an insight into how the formas felt who
lived isolated in research installations.

"Charon will catch us if we leave," Turner said.

"Eventually someone will find this place, too."

Bart drifted upward, floating in the air. "Then we will
vanish into the world mesh and regroup elsewhere."

"Sam can't go into the mesh," Turner said.

"Not as she is, no," Bart said.

Sam didn't like the sound of that. "As I am?"

"You could join us. Become an EI." Bart spoke as
if it were a perfectly ordinary suggestion. "We can
imprint your brain on a neural matrix. If you later
wanted a body, we could make an android. Your new
body would be as good as the one you have now. Better, in fact. It would never grow old." Without missing
a beat, he added, "The age difference between you
and Turner would no longer matter."

Ouch. She made a conscious effort not to grit her
teeth. "You hit low, don't you?"

"I'm practical." Bart spread his arms out from his
sides. "If you become an EI, you can go anywhere
and have whatever body you would like."

The idea disquieted her. In the state of the art,
Turner was on the outermost edges of experimental
work, and he certainly didn't have "whatever body he
would like." He barely controlled its transformations.
What Bart offered might someday be commonplace,
but right now it was impracticable at best and probably impossible.

"No thanks," she said. "I like myself this way."

Turner was watching her intently. "And me?"

She squeezed his hand. "You're a miracle. But the
chance of repeating Charon's success is astronomical."

"You have me as a template," he said.

"Given the choice," she said, "would you have become what you are now?"

Turner thought about it. "Now that I know how it feels to be smarter and stronger, it would be hard for me to go back. But would I have undergone such a change voluntarily? No. Never."

"Then you understand."

His gaze never wavered. "You could be like me, Sam."

"Is that what you want?" She had been asked by men to change before, but usually they just wanted her to be more domestic and less cranky. This gave a whole new meaning to the concept.

"Turner Pascal would desire you just as you are now. I am Turner. I react like him." He seemed to struggle for words. "But I am also changing. That new part of me wants to share with you, blend our minds, strengthen our bodies." He brushed his metal knuckles along her jaw. "You could do that if they rebuilt your body and transferred your mind to an EI matrix."

It sounded like a nightmare to Sam. "You're scaring me, Turner."

Bart spoke. "The choice is yours, Dr. Bryton. Perhaps you might like to rest and think on it."

"I would like that." Sam knew she wouldn't change her mind, but she could use some sleep. She was the only one here who needed it, unless they counted Turner's downtime.

"Fourteen will take you to a place where you can relax," Bart told her.

She didn't miss his omission. "What about Turner?"

"They're going to work on me," Turner said.

Sam tensed. The last time someone had separated her from Turner, they had shackled him in a lab and force-fed him flight instructions for the Rex. "I should stay."

"I'm afraid we can't allow that," Bart said.

"I can help," Sam said. "I'm a pretty good biomech surgeon." It wasn't her primary research, but she had a bit of skill.

"More than good," Bart said. "We have read your work. It has even contributed to the development of a number of us. That is all the more reason we would prefer you not learn too much about us."

"You don't trust me."

"Should we?"

"Probably not." She couldn't promise to say nothing about them.

"Thank you for your honesty," Bart said. "Are you ready to go?"

"All right." With reluctance, she slid off her stool. Turner stood up, too, holding her hands in his, his metal digits cool against her fingers. She wondered if she would ever truly become used to his changes.

"I will see you later." He pulled her into an embrace and Sam turned up her face, her eyes closing. They kissed for a while, good and full. She couldn't relax, not with Bart everywhere, but she still thoroughly enjoyed the kiss.

Finally they drew apart and stood with their arms around each other. Sam spoke softly. "Don't go away, okay?" A fear simmered within her; Sunrise Alley would change Turner when they went to work on him. She might never again see the man she knew.

His face gentled. "It's just maintenance. I'll still be me when they're done."

They lingered a few more moments together, but then Fourteen escorted her off, leaving Turner in the shadowy lab, alone with the strange intelligences of Sunrise Alley.

XIV
Legacy from Within

Sam felt as if she had been deposited in a memory location. Her room was pleasant, with a console, table, and glow-tiles. The sky-blue walls and fluffy white quilt on the bed lifted her spirits. But the way they left her here, alone, made her feel as if she were being stored, another piece of equipment in the installation.

Then a visitor trundled in, a mechbot. This one stood about waist high, with a pyramid-shaped body and three robot arms. It carried a dinner tray with dried fruit and a juice pod, nothing all that appetizing, but edible.

The mechbot left while she ate. When she finished, she went over and opened the door. A hall stretched out beyond the room and then crooked to the right. Its walls slanted at crazy angles. Pieces of equipment projected out in weird geometries, and those had smaller projections, which had tiny projections, and so on, framing the hall in frozen fractal lace.

Sam rubbed her arms, unsettled by the empty feel of the place.

Bart hadn't told her to stay in this room, but he hadn't invited her to explore, either. It might seem unnecessary to him; EIs could go anywhere with a mesh link. The concept of being isolated in a body might be odd to him. He probably would have told her if she was welcome to wander, but what the hell. Staying put had never been one of her strong points.

Sam went down the hallway. She had gone about a hundred feet when a door slid open to her left. A mechbot rolled out, this one as tall as her shoulder. Three arms were nested against its body, each longer and thinner than a human limb. It halted in front of her, blocking the way.

Sam stopped. "Hello."

A blue light flickered on the dome that topped its body. "Good evening, Dr. Bryton."

"Will you be my guide?" Maybe they would let her wander if she stayed with the bot.

"I am to escort you back to your room."

"Is that necessary? I won't go anywhere you don't want me to see."

"This is useful to know." It unfolded one of its arms and pointed back the way she had come. "However, I must return you to your room."

Oh, well. She headed back, and the mechbot came along, rolling at her side. "How about a tour later?" she asked.

"Perhaps. They will discuss it."

"'They'?"

"The EIs."

Maybe it would be more forthcoming than Fourteen. "How many EIs are here?"

"No set number. Usually six or seven."

She decided to ask questions it might not expect, a method she used to probe the capabilities of an AI. "Do you ever get lonely here?"

A whir came from its comm. "No."

"Do you interact with other programs?"

"Bart."

"Any others?"

"No. Why would I?"

"To expand your knowledge."

"I have no need to expand my knowledge."

Its inflections reminded her of Bart. Most mechbots didn't have such smooth speech patterns. Curious now, she asked, "What's your name?"

Its blue light sparkled. "Foggy."

She smiled at that. "Why Foggy?"

"My mind felt that way when I came here."

That intrigued Sam. Did it use the word for the more limited intelligence of a typical mechbot? The figurative name suggested higher intelligence. Although its ability to answer questions was less sophisticated than an EI, it dealt with subtleties better than other mechbots she had worked with, even better than Fourteen.

"What cleared up the fog?" she asked.

"Bart and the others. They made me better."

Sam's good mood receded. "Are they making Turner better?"

"Possibly."

"What if he doesn't want to be 'better'?"

"They won't change him without his consent."

Sam hoped that was true. She wished Turner wasn't alone with them. She stopped in her doorway and regarded the mechbot, which had halted outside. "Do you know how long before they finish with him?"

"I can't say." The bot whirred at her. "I would suggest you sleep. You have this need, yes? You must not become damaged. Your human body is fragile."

She smiled. "I'll do my best not to be damaged." If Bart had designed it to make such inquiries, that suggested human needs mattered to him. "Thank you for your concern."

"You are welcome." With that, it swiveled around and rolled off, down the corridor.

Sam paced across her room, but she didn't lie down. She couldn't rest. Her thoughts kept going around. Last year she had withdrawn to her beach house because she refused to make the ethical compromises her work demanded. Had she known her resignation would lead to this situation, would she still have done it? She had no doubt about that. Yes. She wouldn't have given up meeting Turner for anything.

Bart expected her to worry about the age difference. Had Turner been a normal man, it might have bothered her, but it seemed inconsequential compared to his other differences—like an EI brain and microfusion reactor. Even those didn't really matter, though. He added buoyancy to her life, which it had lacked for too long. She hoped she could offer him the same.

Sam thought of the few men who had gentled her life. Giles had been her first lover, a kind man but far more compatible as a friend than a lover. After Giles she had dated a bit, but not much. She had never been smooth with men. Then fifteen years ago she had fallen for a biomech designer. Richard Armstead.

Her eyes filled with moisture. She should have left BioII when Richard was alive. If only she had taken an offer from one of the other companies trying to woo her. But she had stayed—so Richard had come there to work. He designed forma bodies. She had no proof his work made him ill. Only in the past few months, in the upheavals that followed her resignation, had it come out that the experimental composites he worked on at BioII caused cancer, one of the types modern medicine hadn't cured. It devastated her to know he might be alive if those reports had become public earlier.

She gritted her teeth. BioII would either reform or collapse under the weight of its misdeeds. She had never intended to create a scandal. The furor had begun when someone leaked her resignation to the press. Within hours it was out on the world mesh. That resulting uproar had achieved more than she ever managed with her appeals to the ethics board. Public pressure was forcing BioII to change.

But it was too late for Richard.

Sam flopped down on the bed. Damn. It had been six years since his death. She had thought she was over this, but caring for Turner had brought it all back. At least as a forma, he wasn't likely to die from illness. Hell, if he had a problem, he could transform it away. Tears ran down her face and she rubbed them with the heels of her hands.

After a while Sam dropped into a fitful sleep. The hum of the door woke her. She peered blearily at the man across the room. "Turner?"

He came toward the bed. "Hi."

Relief spread through her. He sounded the same. Her vision was sleep-blurred, but as he reached the bed, he came into focus. He looked the same, lithe and leanly muscled. His only visible difference was the cabled hand that showed beneath the cuff of his shirt.

She sat up, rubbing her eyes. "How are you?"

"Much better." He sat on the bed. "They re-indexed my memories, upgraded my integration algorithms, restructured my node trees, the works."

Sam squinted at him. "That sounds very weird from my boyfriend."

He laughed and pulled her into his arms, leaning forward until they fell over. She landed on her back and he came down on top of her, catching himself on his hands. Then he grinned at her.

Sam closed her hand around his right arm, which had been human before. It felt the same, flesh and muscle. Nice muscles. She ran her palms down his torso. Very nice. She smiled back, pleased, a little shy, and very glad to see him.

His lashes lowered. "Satisfied?"

"I was afraid they would make you into—I don't know. A mechbot."

He watched her with half-open eyes. "Not a chance."

Sam wasn't sure why she was afraid. No, that wasn't true. She knew. She feared the man she was beginning to love would change so much, he would no longer care for her. "Just hold me."

He rolled onto his back and drew her against his side, his arms around her. She relaxed against him, her head on his shoulder.

"Better?" he asked.

Her voice caught. "Yes."

"Sam," he murmured. "What's wrong?"

"I just—" She couldn't say it.

"It's all right."

She tried again. "I was remembering my husband."

"Richard Armstead?"

"Yes. How did you know?"

He spoke awkwardly. "After that night when we, well, you know."

Her face warmed. "Made love?"

"Yes." He sounded self-conscious. "I searched your name on the mesh and found wedding notices. Some other social stuff." After a moment, he added, "His obituary."

Sam thought of making a joke: *I have this thing for dead men.* But it wasn't funny. It was horrible. Years had passed before she could read that obituary. Such a simple paragraph for such an incredible man. Richard hadn't been famous or rich or brilliant. He had been far more than any of that, the kindest, most decent person she had ever known, a wonderful husband who would have been a wonderful father.

"I'm sorry," Turner said.

"It's all right." The damnable tears filled her eyes, giving the lie to her words.

"I shouldn't have intruded."

"Everyone does searches." She felt her face redden. "I looked you up, too."

"I remember."

"I mean more, after that." She had done it from the car that night in California, while he dozed.

"What did you find?"

"You were born in Oregon, lived in Portland all

your life, graduated high school, worked in a cafeteria for a few years, and then took the job as a Hilton bellboy."

He spoke dryly. "That pretty much sums up my life."

"It's a good life."

"I liked it. But it's nothing compared to yours."

"What else did you find about me?"

He kissed her temple. "You come from Connecticut. Your father was an Air Force colonel and he had a doctorate in experimental physics. Your mother's doctorate was in astrophysics and she worked at NASA. Sound right?"

"Truly." Fond memories came to her. "You should have heard their dinner conversations. I was a teenager before I realized most people didn't discuss stellar spectroscopy over the pot roast."

Turner fell silent. Just when she was about to ask what was wrong, he said, "I must seem stupid to you."

"Good Lord, no. Why would you say such a thing?"

"I barely made it out of high school. This is the first time in my life I've even been out of Oregon."

She laid her palm on his chest. "I don't care. Where someone went to school or has traveled isn't what makes them a good person. I never met the Turner who flipped hamburgers, but I would have been honored to know you then and I'm honored now."

He folded his hand around hers. "Thank you." After a moment he said, "I think I'm the same person as before, but how can I know for certain? I was so mentally slow then. Now I'm not. So I can't really be the same."

"Your matrix is a phenomenon."

He snorted. "Hardly. It takes me millions of steps to

figure out things you take for granted, like if an object is far away and big, or close to me and small."

"Don't your optics do that for you?"

"In part, yes. But I have to *think* about it. You don't. I have parallel processors so that even when I'm learning, I can respond fast enough that I don't seem like an idiot. Or less like one."

"You aren't an idiot." She gave him a mock look of severity. "No matter how much you protest, Mr. Pascal, I like your mind."

"Just my mind?" Mischief lightened his voice.

She played with the buttons on his shirt. "I need to make absolutely certain Bart and his cronies didn't change any of you. I should do a thorough inspection."

He undid the catch at the neck of her jumpsuit. "I guess we better get to it, then. Can't have you worrying."

"We certainly can't," she said huskily.

As they undressed each other, she told herself he was no different. His legs disconcerted her, but she would deal with it. She had known he was in good shape the first time she saw him on the beach, his wet clothes molding to his beautifully male—and human—body. Yes, he had changed, but that was done. Had he changed more? *No.* He wasn't huskier now, more solid, with tougher skin. They hadn't altered him. She just misremembered his appearance.

That had to be it.

"This was the best image I made," Turner said. They were sitting in the lab where they had met Bart yesterday. Bart hadn't responded when they tried to contact him from their bedroom, and Sam had felt silly talking to an unresponsive console, explaining what they wanted, but it had apparently worked. Fourteen had shown up and escorted them to this lab, with its better consoles. Now the android stood back, watching while they worked.

Turner tapped the console below its holoscreen, which showed a spectacular range of mountains. "This is my memory of the area around Charon's base."

Sam studied the image. His eyes had sent data to his matrix, which recorded the image exactly. The result unsettled her. The quality of light differed from her perception of the world. His vision had sharper lines, greater contrasts. But the scene otherwise corresponded to what she remembered. "How well can you match that scene with the mesh atlas?"

He entered commands at the console and a second image appeared, a slightly different view of the scene. "These are the Himalayas near the northern border of Tibet."

Sam sat back, wishing they had chairs instead of stools. "Does Charon have ties with the Chinese government?"

"I've no idea."

"Did you have any sense of who he worked for?"

He averted his gaze. "Not really."

She could tell he was holding back. "Did he introduce you to anyone in Oregon?"

"No. He just kept me in his lab." He finally looked at her. "He came to work on me alone."

"What did he do?"

"Experiment. Open this leg, detach that arm, see how it works. It made me queasy to watch."

"You were *conscious*?"

"Why not? I couldn't feel it."

"I thought you had sensors." She flushed, thinking of their night together. "Don't they make you more sensitive to tactile effects than a normal human?"

"Now, yes. He didn't add the sensors until later." Turner stared at his hands, which rested on the console. "When I first woke up in his lab, I didn't know I had died. And this insane person was taking me *apart*. I thought I had gone crazy."

She could barely imagine what it must have been like. "That's awful."

"Before he rebuilt me, he tested my parts. My matrix—it's spread throughout my body." His voice cracked. "Parts of my brain were all over the lab. So I was aware of what was happening from—from all over."

Sam put her hand on his arm. "It's over."

His head jerked. "I don't like to remember."

The more she heard about Charon, the more she loathed him. "He could have at least put you to sleep."

"But if he did that, how would he judge my reactions?" His words came out like blades. "He needed me conscious so I could participate in his experiments."

"He sounds sick."

"Oh, I don't know. If he really considered me a machine, why would that be sick?"

"It's nuts, Turner. We don't treat androids that way and most of them are less aware than you."

"I tried to find out why Fourteen ran away from the university," Turner said. "But Bart blocked my access and Fourteen won't talk to me."

"I tried when he escorted me to our room." It had been like pulling teeth, but she had worked with AIs long enough to draw out even the most taciturn. "He told me he didn't consider anything that happened in the university lab objectionable. He just didn't want to be there."

"So he left?"

"Apparently so."

Turner indicated the lab around them. "Why would he prefer this place? It's strange."

"To humans like us, yes." She deliberately included Turner. "Perhaps to an android this is paradise."

"I don't get this place. Who rebuilt it?"

"The EIs brought plenty of mechbots here."

"But *why*?" He indicated the haphazard tangles of pipes and equipment. "The architecture makes no sense."

"That's because you think like a man. Why should EIs organize their spaces like we do?"

"You use plural. We've only met one EI. Bart."

Sam considered the thought. Bart was a sophisticated program, obviously more developed than when he had been at the NIA, but she doubted he could maintain this place on his own. She recalled what the mechbot had told her. "I think he's a composite of several EIs, but with his central personality based on the original Baltimore code."

Turner traced his finger along the console. "I tried to investigate the meshes here while they worked on me. I still can't crack their security."

That surprised her. "You cracked the systems at Hockman and in Tibet."

"Those weren't as good."

Given the powerful systems at Hockman and Charon's

base, that said a lot about the capabilities of these EIs. "No wonder they've hidden so well."

"Yeah. They kept me in sleep mode most of the time, so I recorded their work to analyze later."

"If you could make recordings, why put you to sleep?"

"It wasn't for security. They thought it might be easier on me." His voice roughened. "What does it say, that machines have treated me more humanely than Charon, a human man?"

"It says human greed sucks." Sam couldn't hold back her anger. "This business of creating formas has a dark side no one wants to admit out there in the glossy world where everything goes so fast. Humans outlawed slavery but now the ball game has changed."

"You know why I came to you?"

"Yeah. Because I'm a damn good EI architect."

"Yes. But that wasn't the main reason."

She felt self-conscious under his intense stare. "You thought I was gorgeous." She would have laughed at her lame joke if he hadn't been making her so nervous.

"If I'd known how pretty you were," Turner said, "it probably would have influenced me."

Sam gave an incredulous snort. "Yeah, right."

"You are lovely and fey, Sam. But I never bothered to check." He spoke quietly. "I came to you because you are so well known in biomech ethics. I finally hacked out of my sandbox one night when Charon wasn't around. Then I got on the world mesh and searched for someone who could help me. I read your essays over and over, especially the ones about setting principles ahead of profit and developing a moral code for how we treat formas."

What to say? She had lost the idealism that inspired those writings. She had learned it from her father, from his dedication to his work and country, from his integrity. Then he had gone on that ill-timed visit to Paraguay and died in a random act of violence. She would never overcome the sense of loss, especially knowing he had died alone—

Hadn't he?

Sam fought down the memory. It reminded her of Charon in a completely different way. Her father had ridden with the ferryman across the river to the other side of death. He couldn't come back. She should have stopped him from taking that journey. It made no sense to feel that way, but it burned inside of her.

Sam was starting to tremble. Her father's belief that he could make the world a better place had killed him. When he died, a part of her had died as well. Perhaps it hadn't all gone that night, but her futile struggles at BioII had seared away the last of her youthful dreams. The day she had walked away from BioII had been the final step of her retreat. She was like the redwoods in Whitman's poem: her time in the fast-paced world had ended.

She spoke bitterly. "Sam the idealist is gone."

He took her hand. "Never say that."

Sam just held his hand. She couldn't talk about it.

"If I were an idealist," he said, "I would say the EIs created this place to give my kind sanctuary. The cynic in me believes it exists only to please them."

She looked around the fractal lab. "It has its own beauty."

He indicated the image of the Himalayas. "Like so many places on this planet unmarred by humans."

"Like the redwoods. Until we cut them down."

"The redwoods are old. EIs are new."

"So they are." She bent over the console and flicked through several holicons, setting up a mesh search. She looked up Alpha, Hud, Charon, anyone involved with this mess, but no more came up this time than when they had tried before. She wasn't certain how much that meant; Bart had complete control of their access to the world mesh. He could limit their results if he chose.

"What do you think happened to Alpha and Hud after we escaped?" she asked.

"I'd assume Charon questioned them." Turner hesitated. "Except I had the sense they never saw him in person."

"I did, too." Sam tried another search. Doing one on the name Charon alone would give too many hits; it came up in mythology, as the moon of Pluto, and various other places. When she linked it with his other names, Wildfire and Parked, she didn't find much of anything useful, but she did come across the archive of a site frequented by biomech architects. She noticed it in particular because one of the participants was Giles. To save time, she dumped the visual images and converted the dialogue to text she could scan, tagging it by the first names of the debaters, with grammar mistakes fixed and shorthand phrases expanded into full words:

> Giles> If an EI is alive, how do you define
>   its death?
> Tamora> You're asking for the equivalent
>   of brain death. We have trouble defining
>   it even for ourselves. How can we for
>   a construct?

Jason> The moment it is no longer self-aware.

Tamora> But it can become aware again. We humans can't come back to life.

Giles> Charon can only take you across the river once.

Ellen> Say what?

Ben> The old guy in Hades.

Jason> You pass Greek Culture 101. [laughs]

Ellen> What Greek?

Tamora> When a person dies, Charon takes him across the river into Hades. Some people try to go back across the river.

Jason> Come back to life.

Giles> Humans bloody well can't. An EI could.

Ellen> I thought Charon was the handle for some underground mesh crusader.

Tamora> That's what I heard.

Giles> He used to be. The name got corrupted.

Tamora> Stolen?

Jason> Charon is a bandwidth bandit.

Ben> He burns through systems like wildfire.

Ellen> Ferryman, crusader, bandit, he's still just a myth.

"Yeah, right," Turner muttered. "That 'myth' had us dragged halfway around the world."

"I don't understand why Charon couldn't stop you from escaping," Sam said. "If anyone has the knowledge to counter your abilities, it would be him."

"I had help from that EI in Tibet."

"Maybe Charon had it set you up, so you would lead him here."

"If anyone could," Turner said grimly, "it's him."

Sam raised her voice. "You hear that, Bart? This Charon person might come looking for you."

A holo of Bart formed above the console. He regarded them with a guarded expression very different from his previous friendly demeanor. "Good afternoon."

"Is it afternoon?" Sam asked, relieved they had finally prodded him into a response.

"Late." Bart stepped to the edge of the screen. "Indications exist that an unmonitored agent exterior to our primary complex of connections attempted to isolate components of our correspondence."

"Does that translate into English?" Sam asked dryly.

His lips quirked upward. "Every word was English."

"Are you saying someone tried to spy on you?" she asked.

"Quaintly put, but yes." Bart shrugged. "It was easy to rebuff the attempts."

"Don't underestimate him," Turner said.

"What about the people at Hockman Air Force Base?" Sam asked. "Could it have been them? They're looking for us. By now they know we took their jazzy truck."

"Turner sent it to Cancun," Bart said.

Sam would have liked to go to Cancun herself. Any place far away. "That won't fool anyone for long."

Turner smirked. "I'd love to see the Air Force brass explaining that truck to the Mexican authorities. 'Sorry, our naughty EI stole it.'"

Although Sam smiled, she suspected her concerns

paralleled those of the military. She didn't know enough about these EIs to judge if they posed a threat, but they sure as blazes weren't harmless.

"We have our privacy," Bart said. "Neither your military nor the man you call Charon will change that."

"You don't call him Charon?" Turner asked.

"We do now," Bart said.

"You called him something else before?"

"Wildfire. For his effect on meshes."

"Then you have dealt with him."

"He has succeeded in breaking into many systems we monitor," Bart said.

"How can you be sure he won't come here?"

He just looked at her.

Bart was making Sam uneasy today in a way he hadn't during their first conversation. He seemed edgier, harder, colder. "Can I still leave?"

Bart didn't blink. "I think not."

"You can't mean to keep me here forever."

For the first time he let anger show on his face. "Is that so different from what you all do with us?"

"Not her," Turner said. "She's different."

"Perhaps." Bart's eyes glinted with sudden cruelty. "Good-bye." His holo vanished.

"What the blazes?" Whatever change Bart had undergone since their last conversation, it scared her. She rose to her feet. "I can't stay here any longer."

Turner stood and tried to pull her to him. "Sam—"

"No!" Clenching her fists, she pushed them against his shoulders. Her grief welled up as she thought of Richard, but her emotions were tangled and too complex. Turner grasped her forearms, and she hit his shoulders with her fists. She tried to pull away, but he wouldn't let go, he just held her. She stood in his arms then, her body shaking. His embrace became tender, but she couldn't return it. She felt his physical strength and knew it was too much, just as she had known and hadn't wanted to admit last night. Yes, some men developed such muscles. But *he* hadn't possessed them a few hours ago. He was even taller now, by another one or two inches, but no thinner, which meant they had given him extra mass.

What else had they done?

"You went over to them." Her words burned. "You betrayed me to them so they would make you better."

"Sam, don't." He looked down into her face, holding her arms. "I brought you here to keep you from being used by Charon or those military goons."

"Those 'goons' want to protect our country." She pushed away from him. "My *father* was a 'military goon.' Who do you think paid for all those degrees of his?" She folded her arms, suddenly cold. "He died three years ago in Paraguay when an extremist group sheered the American embassy with those new laser rifles no one is supposed to know we've invented. Well, hey, they don't exist but you can burn down entire buildings with them."

Turner's face filled with a compassion she couldn't bear, because he was a *computer*, damn it, not a man, she was sleeping with a machine, and if she admitted otherwise, if she admitted the truth, that she was falling in love, she would be hurt like with Richard, like with the loss of her ideals, the death of her father, the end of her hopes for the future, and this time she would never recover.

"I can't do this." She pulled away from him and walked off into a tangle of pipes. "I want out."

He walked up behind her. "It's too late."

She looked up at the pipes that crooked their way to the ceiling. "You know what I can't help thinking? Every country, government, military—every organization of every kind makes mistakes. You know. Flight schedules get misfiled. Transport codes send people to the wrong places. The wrong file goes to the wrong installation. A goddamned shipment of laser rifles is lost due to a mesh error."

"Sam—"

She swung around. "Now I'll always wonder how many of those glitches are real. Your 'friends' here could cause a lot of problems if they wanted to. How much do they fiddle with the world meshes? How long before they infiltrate *everything*?"

"This is nuts." He stepped toward her, then stopped when she backed up. "Sam, it's just a few EIs minding their own business."

"What business would that be?" She hugged her arms to her body. "How did Bart know you sent the truck to Mexico?"

"He used to be an NIA program. He knows his way around meshes like theirs."

"And if he decides to rip holes in those meshes?" She felt cold. "You saw that look on his face just before he vanished. Talk about animosity."

"You're reading more into this than exists."

"I'm not stupid."

He took another step toward her. "No, you aren't."

Sam backed into a large pipe. "What is in this for you, keeping me here? Entertainment? That would be a reversal. The forma wants a human sex slave."

"Sam, stop it!" His forehead creased. "What do

you think, that I planned this? I just wanted out. After Charon told me about you, I had to look you up on the web."

Whoa. "Charon told you about me?"

"He said you were brilliant." Turner spoke quietly. "He also said you were as brittle as jagged glass, with sharp edges to hide the vulnerability."

Sam felt cold. "He knows me?"

Turner averted his eyes. "I've no idea."

"People don't talk that way about someone they don't know."

"Charon talked about everyone."

"Show me a picture of him."

"I can't. I don't have one."

"Look at me," she said. When he raised his gaze, she spoke in a deliberate tone. "You can make an image of the Himalayas, which we saw only for a few moments, but you can't do one of a man you saw every day for two weeks?"

He backed up from her. "I can't."

"Yes, you can."

"No."

She stepped toward him. "What are you hiding?"

He lifted his hands, palms out toward her. "Nothing."

"Show me Charon."

"No!"

"Show me!"

"*I can't.*"

"You won't, damn it. *Why not?*"

"Because I'm him!" His voice dropped. "I'm him."

XV
Doubles

The moment stretched thin, like rubber pulled tight. Then it all snapped back, painful and hard.

"No." Sam couldn't believe him.

He turned and walked away, deeper into the lab, stopping only when a horizontal pipe blocked his path. He stood with his back to her. "Charon downloaded his brain into me."

Sam's legs felt like putty. She barely stayed on her feet. "It can't be. Why would he do that? And how? The method you say he used for Turner Pascal, imaging slices of your brain, kills a person."

"Yes. It does."

"Charon *killed* himself?"

He turned around to face her. "Yes."

"Why?" Non-invasive imaging methods existed. Surely Charon knew. Maybe they didn't give as precise results; she couldn't say. It wasn't her area of expertise. But she found it hard to believe the differences could be enough that he would commit suicide rather than use them.

Turner spoke tiredly. "He wanted immortality. An android body, one better than his. So he made me. Then he took some drug. A lethal dose. He was working with a colleague, an expert who downloaded his brain into mine."

The worst part was that the macabre tale made sense in a twisted way. "That would explain how you know him so well."

"I blocked off that part of my matrix."

"God, Turner, *erase* it."

"That would destroy part of my own mind." He watched her anxiously. "I would no longer be myself. I probably couldn't even function."

It didn't surprise her. The evolving codes of an EI brain were too complex and interwoven to fully document. Turner probably couldn't map them all himself. And Charon would have set his code for as much durability as possible. It would take time and concentration for Turner to remove the code, if he could manage at all. "You might be able to remove it bit by bit, given long enough."

He blanched. "We may not have that time before he catches us."

"You talk as if he's alive," Sam said.

"He is." Turner spoke bitterly. "You think I'm the only copy of him? He was paranoid people were plotting against him, determined to destroy his genius. I'm sure he made other copies of himself to counter those evildoers he imagined were after him."

Sam felt as if she were sinking into a quagmire. She might have fathomed Charon killing himself if he hadn't wanted more than one Charon to exist. This sounded like madness. Brilliant, but insane. "He doesn't just want immortality. He wants the influence of Sunrise Alley. And he figured out how to find them. Through you."

Turner flushed. "No. He's trapped."

"How?"

"I confined the code that defines him to a portion of my matrix with no influence on the rest."

"Are you sure?" She thought of Bart's changed behavior. "Could he have affected the EIs here while they worked on you?"

"I think that's enough," Bart suddenly said.

Sam jerked. His voice came from all around them. She spoke to the air. "What do you want?"

"I do believe, Dr. Bryton, that we need to make some changes." Bart's answer was as smooth as oil.

"Leave her alone," Turner said.

A heavy tread came from their right. Sam whirled to see Fourteen approaching through the pipes. She backed away, but when she turned to run, a tall mechbot blocked her way. She tried to duck past it, but it snapped out an arm and caught her around the waist.

"No!" Sam hit her fists against its body.

Turner ran toward her, but then Fourteen grabbed him from behind and held him in place.

"Come, Dr. Bryton." Bart's oily voice rolled from everywhere within the lab. "I've a surprise for you."

Sam fought hard, using her teeth, fingernails, and fists, and kicking with her legs, but Fourteen still shackled her down, on her back, stretching her out on a table used for biomech surgery. Her injured arm flared with pain as its bandage ripped off.

"Leave her alone!" Turner shouted. It took two of the large mechbots to clamp him into a mechanized chair, which locked robot arms around his torso, arms, and legs.

"Don't." Sam strained against the manacles that held her wrists and ankles to the table. "Don't do this."

A wall packed with mesh-tech rose up from the floor and curved around the table. One of its screens lit up, a panel that stretched the full height of the wall, seven feet. A life-sized holo of Bart formed in front of it so he seemed to be standing by the table.

"Hello, Dr. Bryton," he said.

"This is sick." She yanked on the restraints. "I haven't hurt any of you."

"You brought Charon into our facility."

"You brought him, damn it! You're the ones who invited Turner here."

Bart's gaze hardened. "Tell me, Doctor, how does it feel to be the one who is chained to the table?"

"Is that why you're doing this?" The pain in her injured arm made her eyes water. "You want revenge?"

Turner spoke desperately. "You must have seen her records. You know she's fought for our rights. She gave up a million-dollar salary because of it, for God's sake."

"Yes, we know what she did." Bart considered her. "It's the only reason I'm not killing you."

"You weren't hostile like this before." Sam calmed her voice. "Why hurt me now?"

"What makes you think we're going to hurt you?"

Sam flinched. "Oh, just this little thing of manacling me to a table used for biomech surgery."

"We're going to make you better." Bart nodded to Fourteen, who stood across the table. "Prepare her for surgery."

"NO!" Turner shouted.

An air syringe snicked out from Fourteen's finger.

Panic welled in Sam. "I don't want to die."

"It isn't death," Bart said. "No more than Charon died. People wanted to kill him, but he outwitted them."

"You have Charon inside of you," Sam said. "That's why you're acting like this."

No answer.

"Listen," Turner said. "If you copied Charon from me, you know how he feels about her. He wouldn't want her harmed."

"Feels about me?" Sam went very still. "What does that mean?"

Turner started to answer, stopped, then said, "He admires you." Sam had no doubt he had a good deal more to say, none of it complimentary.

Bart studied her face. "As an android, you will always be beautiful, Dr. Bryton. Never old."

Desperate now, she said, "You don't have to do this. You can use imaging methods that don't destroy the brain."

"They don't give as precise a map," Bart said.

"Damn it, they do." Sam didn't know if that was true, but after all the decades of research, it had to be close.

No answer.

When Fourteen bent over her, Sam went crazy,

thrashing against the bonds. He pressed the syringe against her neck and she cried out. It was the last thing she knew before darkness enveloped her world.

The worst fires had subsided, but flames continued to lick the rubble around them. Sam knelt in the debris, among the ashes and smoke, bending over her father. He lay so still, his eyes closed, his voice barely audible. "It's time to go . . ."

"No." *Tears poured down her face. "Don't go."*

"Good-bye, Sam . . ."

Burned, everything burned.

Her wrists burned, burned . . .

Burned . . .

Sam opened her eyes into a blur. She was lying on her back with her arms pulled over her head. The burning came from ropes that bound her wrists. Her legs were pulled tight and bound at the ankles. She wasn't in the lab, though; they had brought her back to her room and bound her to the bed.

Turner was sitting next to her, his face drawn. "Are you all right?"

"No." The injured arm had been healing before, but now it throbbed. "Did they—?"

"They haven't done it yet. After Fourteen knocked you out, they did physical exams." His voice shook. "I stopped them before they gave you the lethal injection."

"How?" She hated the tremor in her voice.

"I tried every argument I could think of. I think the one that worked was when I said if you didn't have your body, it would change how you thought, that the genius they want from you depends on your being human."

"Charon got to them."

"It looks like it. This is his style. Maybe he isn't going to kill you at all, just torment you, to assert his control." His fist clenched in the bed covers. "He sure as hell doesn't want you without your body."

She felt ill. "What did you mean, he likes me?"

"He's obsessed with you. Dr. Sam, beautiful, bold, and even smarter than him. He couldn't bear it. He fixated on you." Turner opened and closed his hands as if he didn't know what to do with them. "Bart still wants to make you into an EI. They want your expertise, forever. They just don't want to destroy it in the process."

"Why? To develop more of them?" She hated the thought.

"Develop, augment, improve."

She struggled to free her hands and pain ran up and down her arms. "Turner, untie me. This hurts."

"I already did once, while you were sleeping." He crumpled the quilt in his hand. "Fourteen came and redid the ropes. He says if I try again, they will separate us and hurt you more."

"We have to take the chance." Her arms ached.

"Sam—"

"Do it," she said softly. "I'm willing to chance it."

He nodded jerkily and bent over her. He worked first on the ropes holding her arms over her head, and it hurt like the blazes, but it was worth it when he freed her. He tackled her ankles next. As he pulled at the ropes, she slowly brought her arms down, stabs of pain shooting through them. Wincing, she let them rest by her sides.

After Turner finished with her legs, she turned onto

her stomach and sprawled facedown on the bed. Her whole body hurt.

"Better?" he asked.

"Oh, yes." What an understatement. "How long was I unconscious?"

"About three hours."

When Sam felt steadier, she turned onto her side. No sign of Fourteen yet. She tried to focus, to think her way out of this. "Okay, they knock me out but let me live. I'm useful to them. But they can incorporate me better as an EI. And make me last longer."

"Yes." With revulsion, he added, "I'm their backup of Charon."

Sam had been thinking Charon corrupted the EIs here by leaking out of Turner's matrix, but what if they had deliberately absorbed him? She and Charon had a great deal of use to Sunrise Alley; between the two of them, they might well carry a substantial portion of human knowledge and innovation about biomech formas. If the reach of Sunrise Alley into the world mesh was as great as Bart implied, it could influence human economic, political, and social structures. The world was becoming more of a single community, with every country deep in the network. It had started in the days of the ARPAnet, BITNET, the Internet, exploded into the World Wide Web, and finally blended into the ubiquitous World Mesh, now just called "the mesh."

Overt political conflict had eased in recent decades as the many and varied peoples of the world communicated through the mesh. Interwoven, international communities formed when individuals discovered shared interests, bringing together many diverse groups. It had changed the face of human interaction, stirring hope that nations might find a commonality that superseded their conflicts. Hostilities never ceased, though. In the place of outright wars, they submerged into splinter groups that sought to topple governments, either their own or those of other countries. Their objectives were often unrealistic, but they caused bitter destruction in pursuing them.

The mesh allowed communication at a level previously unknown in history. Control the mesh and you controlled humanity.

Maybe Bart hadn't cared about that before, or maybe he had misled her, but his exposure to Charon had changed him. Bile rose in Sam's throat. "Charon is the reason you don't like to download yourself, isn't it? You're afraid he might escape from the trap in your matrix."

He said, simply, "Yes."

"How did you trap him?"

"He underestimated my will." Turner picked up a rope from the bed and twisted it in his hand. "He chose Turner Pascal because I was young, healthy, strong, handsome, and stupid. He figured I would be easy to control. When the time came for the transfer, he expected to have my knowledge about my body, my identity if he wanted it, and my mind as well as his own. A mental slave essentially, one too dim-witted to fight back." He set down the rope. "But I wasn't as easy to control as he thought."

"You aren't stupid."

"Sam—" He let out a breath. "I read at an eighth-grade level then. I couldn't remember the multiplication tables. I didn't even know Tibet existed." He tapped his temple. "Any intelligence you see comes from my EI."

"Your matrix is Turner's brain." She hated to see him denigrate himself. "Maybe you had a bad education. Besides, many types of intelligence exist. You underestimate yourself."

"I don't think so." His drawn expression eased. "But thank you."

Bart's voice suddenly came from the console. "I told you not to untie her again."

Turner looked around the room. "It was hurting her."

"Maybe that's the intent," Sam muttered.

They waited. When Bart said nothing more, Turner spoke to Sam. "Why would an EI want someone in pain?"

"You heard him in the lab. 'Tell me, Doctor, how does it feel to be the one who is chained to the table?'"

"Vengeance is a human emotion," Turner said.

"So he's simulating it." Still no other comments came from Bart. "Maybe he's like you and thinks he feels it."

"I don't *think* I feel. I feel."

"Why would he be different?"

"Bart was designed. I was already a person."

Sam could see his point. He knew the experience of emotions and why he felt them. Charon also knew, though, and he might be part of Bart.

"Turner, you said Charon knew me."

He wouldn't look at her. "Did I?"

"Yes, damn it. So why don't I recognize him?"

"I don't know."

"You must, if his brain is in your matrix."

"I've partitioned it off." His face paled. "I'm afraid if I try to access it, he will get free."

"Show me what he looks like."

Now he met her gaze. "And if you did recognize him? Would you really want to know a friend had betrayed you?"

She froze. "Are you saying he is a friend of mine?"

"No."

"*Giles?*" It couldn't be. It *couldn't*. But it made so much sense. He was one of the few biomech surgeons who could create a construct as phenomenal as Turner.

"Oh, Lord," she said miserably. "I should have seen."

"It isn't Giles."

"Then why won't you show me Charon?"

"Sam." He spoke with difficulty. "Let it go."

"No. Tell me."

After a long pause, he said, "All right."

She waited. "Yes?"

"His name is Linden Polk. You knew him at MIT."

Sam thought she must have misheard. "That can't be."

"I'm sorry." He sounded miserable.

It was absurd. Linden didn't have the genius to create Turner. He didn't do much surgery at all. His expertise was in the development of EI matrices, but his real gift was teaching. He had been a beloved advisor for many people, a decent, humble man. She could no more imagine him as Charon than she could imagine the sky turning orange. "That makes absolutely no sense."

Turner looked the way people did when they knew they had given bad news, with his face red and his gaze downcast. He believed Dr. Polk was Charon.

The console across the room crackled with Bart's voice. "I have decided you may leave her untied. Just make sure she doesn't leave."

Turner jerked. They waited a few moments, but Bart said nothing else. Sam closed her eyes and rolled onto her back, exhausted. That Bart didn't deny he was Polk just convinced her more that Turner was wrong. If Bart contained Charon, he probably wanted her misled about his identity.

After a few moments, Turner stretched out next to her. She rolled onto her side and pressed close to him, favoring her injured arm. Lying on his back, he pulled her into his arms. "That time you were unconscious—those were three of the worst hours I've ever spent."

"I'm all right, now." That was pushing it, but she did feel better. "Turner, did you see Charon die?"

"No."

"Who downloaded him to you?"

"His colleague, I assume."

"Linden?"

"No. Charon was Linden."

That just didn't fit. "It sounds like the process of transferring Charon's mind to your matrix went without a hitch."

"Yes. Shouldn't it?"

"It's one hell of a procedure." Sam pushed up on her elbow. "It would take a lot of work to get it right."

"Maybe. But I'm here." He looked up at her. "And Charon is definitely inside me."

"I'll bet you weren't the first one he tried the procedure on."

Turner went very still. "He never said."

"Maybe he was overconfident about his ability to control you because he had already done it with someone else." It hurt to think, let alone say, but she forced out the name. "Linden Polk."

Turner hesitated. "It's possible."

"Linden would have given him a remarkable intellect to work with. He was a gifted teacher, someone who always gave of himself to his students." It made too much painful sense. "That would have made it easier for Charon to take what he wanted."

"I'm sorry, Sam. I know Polk meant a lot to you."

Her eyes felt hot, but she couldn't answer.

"Do you think Charon let us go so we would lead him here?" Turner asked.

"I've wondered," she said. "But that Rex is a prize people would die for. I doubt he wanted to lose it. And why send a Needle after us if he wanted us to escape?"

"If he was the one who sent the Needle."

"Who else?"

"Maybe whatever government is supporting him?"

"China?" Sam considered the idea. "My guess is that it's a fringe group set against their government." The introduction of capitalist aspects into the Chinese economy over the past few decades had stirred heated controversy. "Either you bollixed Charon's plans when you trapped him in your matrix, or else he planned this and you don't really have him trapped."

"No!" He sat up, knocking her over. "I won't let him control me."

She sat up as well and took his hands. "Listen, Turner. It must be possible to remove Charon from your matrix."

"I was hoping you could help me."

"That was why you came to me." His story about the fingerprints and false identity had never convinced her. "To help you excise Charon."

"Yes." He spoke quietly. "I was afraid if I told you everything at the start, you would refuse."

She almost had anyway. But it wasn't in her nature to turn away those in need. That was why she and Linden had got on so well; they were a lot alike. Unfortunately for her survival in the cutthroat biomech industry, she had too much of that softness. "The EIs here must see the danger in Charon gaining access to my brain the way he tried to do with you. The expertise of a top EI analyst would give him more influence over Sunrise Alley."

Turner raised his voice. "You hear that, Bart? You want Charon loose? He's going to eat you alive."

Bart's voice came out of the console. "I suspect I would give him indigestion."

Sam gave a startled laugh. Then the door across the room opened, revealing Fourteen. He spoke in his rusty voice. "Come with me."

Sam thought of the surgical table. "I would rather not."

Fourteen entered, followed by two large mechbots. "You will come," Fourteen said. "Or we will sedate you."

"Don't do that." Sam wanted to stay conscious as long as possible—for these could be her last moments of life.

XVI
Tugtown

Fourteen took them to an unfamiliar area, one obviously never intended for people. The corridors were too narrow, with equipment embedded in the leaning walls. At one point, a robot arm rose up from the floor for no apparent reason. Glow-tiles were sparse at best and soon vanished. If a mechbot hadn't switched on a lamp in its head, Sam couldn't have seen at all.

"I don't get this place." She picked her way around a lopsided box-table. "Where are we going?"

"Maybe to a place more suited to our hosts." Turner was walking behind her, flanked by the two mechbots. "Or a better cell."

"I hope not." Perhaps Bart was trying to rattle them the way Charon had done in Tibet with the holo-corridor. The constant onslaught of strangeness was starting to work on Sam. She stumbled over a groove in the floor and would have fallen if a jointed arm hadn't swung from the ceiling and caught her. Engines rumbled and the air smelled faintly of machine oil.

The lights dimmed.

Fourteen halted in front of Sam. When he did nothing more, she stopped and glanced back. The mechbots had also become motionless, their lights almost dark. Turner stood between them, a hand resting on each. The shadows made both of his hands look dark rather than just the metallic one.

"Can they turn up their lamps?" Sam asked.

Fourteen came back to them. The light on his temple flickered red—and went dark. Then the lights on the mechbots went out.

Sam froze, blind now. "What the—?"

Turner grasped her arm. "Come on." He pulled her toward him.

"I can't see." Sam stumbled over junk on the floor.

"Here." A light appeared in Turner's human hand. Sam couldn't look too closely. She didn't want to know how he managed that light.

They headed back the way they had come, quickly leaving Fourteen and the mechbots behind. "How did you turn off the power?" Sam asked. "You said you couldn't break security here."

His face was a study of stark lines and shadows. "It just took longer. It helped when they hooked me up to their systems during the maintenance work."

"What you did at Hockman was hard enough. This place has avoided notice by our military for years. Why could you do what no one else has managed?"

He picked his way over ridges in the floor. "What makes you think the military doesn't know?"

"Do they?"

"I've no idea. But just because neither you nor I knew it was here doesn't mean no one else did."

"I would have heard about it. I worked for the people who would deal with this."

His voice tightened. "You should ask your friend, our dear General Wharington."

Sam had no answer for his unspoken accusation. She couldn't believe it of Thomas any more than of Linden. Nor were they any better off now than when they had run from Hockman. If they made it out of here, they would be stranded in the middle of Iowa. But she would try anything to escape. Better that than have a paranoid EI slice up her brain.

They made their way along the obstacle course of the hallway, ducking around projections, pipes, and screens. Nothing moved. Robot arms had frozen and burt-walls were quiescent. They reached a hallway where a screen stuck out in front of her, paper thin, sturdy as steel, and dark.

"We didn't come this way," Sam said.

"I know." Turner squeezed past the screen. "But it will get us out."

She followed but then stopped, dismayed. A barrier blocked the corridor, stretching from the ceiling almost to the ground.

"Shit," Turner said.

"No kidding." Sam knelt down and peered under the wall. "Any way around it?"

"I'm checking . . . but if there is, I can't find it."

"Maybe we can crawl under it." If they went on their stomachs, they might drag themselves through, but it would be a tight fit. Claustrophobia surged within her. The air suddenly seemed close and thin. "I don't see an exit."

Turner crouched next to her. "I stole schematics of this place. Maybe they make sense to Bart, but I don't have time to decipher them fully. We have to be gone before he breaks free of my tricks." He motioned forward. "I do know an exit is in that direction."

Sam thought of his fear of heights and closed spaces. "You're willing to crawl under here?"

His face had turned stark. "I have to. If we backtrack all the way to that chute where we came in, they'll probably catch us."

"Okay." She forced out the words. "Let's go."

They had to lie down to wriggle under the wall. Sam dragged herself forward, aware of the ceiling a few inches from her head. Darkness pressed on them, barely held at bay by Turner's dim finger light. She tried not to imagine tons of machinery and rock above, ready to collapse. She bit the inside of her cheek, using the pain to focus her thoughts and fend off panic.

Turner's breathing came hard behind her, faster than normal. His lungs were among his few organs that belonged to the original Turner Pascal, if he hadn't transformed them. Changing his limbs was one thing; altering his organs had to be more difficult. He could survive with cabled arms, but if he cabled his lungs or his liver, they would probably fail.

Sam's thoughts whirled away from her. She couldn't focus. They were going to crawl here in the dark forever until they starved or died of thirst.

Her hand hit a barrier.

"Ah, *hell*." Sam stopped and lay still. "Bloody stupid design. We aren't cat-bots."

"Don't stop!" Turner's voice grated behind her.

"It's blocked."

He swore, close to panic.

"Maybe we can go around." She scooted sideways, running her hand along the barrier in their way.

Turner moved behind her. "I can't—I hate this."

"We'll be all right." Sam wasn't sure she believed it, but Turner didn't need to hear that.

"Yeah." He sounded as taut as a wire pulled tight on a violin, but he kept control.

"Hey." Sam's hand flailed into space. "I found an opening."

"Good." His light barely showed the way as they crawled forward. She struggled to breathe. The air felt dusty, but it was probably in her mind. Nothing here was dirty. The EIs had a vested interest in keeping the installation clean; it would affect how well their equipment operated.

"If this doesn't end soon," Turner muttered. "I'm going to scream."

"Do you feel air currents?" Sam asked.

He paused. "Yes. From up ahead."

Sam dragged herself harder, picking up the pace. When she could push onto her knees without hitting her head, she grunted in relief. The ceiling was slanting upward; after a few more paces she could stand. It felt heavenly.

Turner stood next to her, bending to keep from hitting his head on the ceiling. "Thank God."

She peered up at him. "How much have you grown?"

"About four inches, total."

"From the changes in your legs?"

"Mostly." He walked forward. As the ceiling rose,

he straightened to his full height, six feet now. Sam didn't want to begrudge him the extra inches if this was what he wanted, but she had liked it before when he had been closer to her own height.

They walked into a cavern with robot parts strewn across the floor. It looked like a dumping ground for discards. Their footsteps echoed. On the other side, they found another safe door, locked and secure. Turner linked to its panel and worked until he cracked its code. The door swung ponderously open, silent and well oiled.

Beyond the door, a staircase spiraled upward with yellow metal steps and rail like the one they had come down earlier, but smaller, and shadowy in the dim light from Turner's hand.

Sam started climbing, aware of Turner behind her. She spoke uneasily. "You transformed your other hand."

After a moment he said, "The arm, too."

"Why?"

"I needed the hardware."

Every time she thought she had adjusted to him, he changed again. "But you weren't even using that hand."

"Yes, I was. I jacked them into the mechbots. It gave me a more secure connection than IR. And I needed storage space. I'm building more ganglia."

Suddenly she understood. "You want to transfer your functions to the new ganglia, away from where you've stored Charon. Then you can more easily delete him."

"I hope so."

"So you reallocate parts of your body to the new

matrix filaments. And the metallic surface protects it better."

"Yes." He sounded subdued. "I'm sorry, Sam."

"Don't be sorry. You're a wonder." She refrained from saying *a scary one*.

At the top of the stairs, another door blocked their way. As Turner went to work on it, he spoke thoughtfully. "In some ways, I've gained from all this. I feel more . . . I'm not sure what word is right. The old Turner was *less*. I had a lousy memory. I was in good shape from lugging around suitcases, but nothing compared to now. Hell, I was short and skinny." He glanced at her over his shoulder. "You never would have given me the time of day."

"That's because a man who looks as good as you would never look twice at me." She glowered at him. "I liked you short and skinny."

"I thought women wanted their men big and muscular."

"Not me."

A smile curved his lips. Then he turned back to the panel. In only a moment, he said, "Got it!"

The door opened into a narrow chute with a ladder up one side. They climbed up to a hatch with a circular handle. After jimmying its panel, Turner opened the hatch into moonlight, and they clambered out into the remains of a harvested field. Sam had a curious sense of dislocation, as if they had just gone down and come right back out. "How long were we there?"

"About two days." Turner heaved the portal closed and the ground poured in over it, hiding its existence.

Sam watched the dirt move. "That's strange."

"It's keyed to the portal."

She gazed across the land, wondering how far they could make it before Bart sent someone after them. "We should get out of here as fast as possible."

"I can try to reach someone."

"If you start sending out signals, we could end up alerting anyone searching for us."

"We need to figure something out."

She gestured at the land before them. "While we think, let's walk." The more distance they put between themselves and Bart's hole in the ground, the better.

Sam trudged in a daze. They were going up a gradual slope; the landscape had changed from its flat monotony, easing into low, rolling hills. Sam had always thought of Iowa as flat everywhere, full of nothing but corn, and it kept surprising her.

"I don't get it," she said.

"Get what?" Turner walked with the steady pace he had used since they started. He didn't even seem winded.

"No one has come after us."

"I did some pretty weird things to Bart's systems."

"So, okay, you're good at what you do. But so are they and they have more experience."

Turner was silent for much too long. Then he said, "I knew it would be difficult. So I took, uh, sort of drastic action."

Ah, no. "Drastic, how?"

Silence.

"Turner, what did you do?"

"I let out part of Charon."

"You *what*?"

"I used his knowledge about EIs to trick Bart."

Sam barely heard anything after his first four words. "You accessed him in your matrix."

He pushed the hair out of his eyes. "Yes."

"Charon is free?"

"Not exactly."

"Why 'not exactly'?" Sam felt surreally calm. Her lover had just informed her that he had converted himself into a monster. She ought to flee or hit him over the head. Since she couldn't imagine doing either, she just said, "He's won."

His face lit with a fresh excitement that seemed the antithesis of the way everyone described Charon. "But that's just it, Sam. He *hasn't* won. I'm still me. I'm in control. He was going to run me as a submesh on his brain, but that's what I'm doing with him instead." Then he added, "And, Sam, I needed his help. Who better than Charon to counter himself? I couldn't have done it alone."

Be calm, she told herself. "Done what?"

He struggled with the words. "We put Bart in a— I guess you could call it virtual reality. It isn't that different from the way he normally exists, but we tampered with the input. I left a copy of my brain running on their mesh. They think they're interacting with me. And they are. But not the real me. Not *this* me. However long it takes them to realize that is how long we have before they come after us." His voice quieted. "And I tried not to leave any part of Charon behind."

His desperate move had saved her life—but at what price? The chances of keeping Charon out of that system were small. "Maybe this was what he wanted all along."

"I couldn't let him kill you."

She breathed out. "I'm grateful to be alive."

"But?"

"We have to get help or we could have a world-spanning nightmare on our hands." If they didn't already.

"I know." He started to say more, then stopped.

"What is it?" Sam asked.

"You were right about Dr. Polk. Charon tried the procedure on him first, and ran Polk as a submesh in his matrix until he integrated Polk's mind. Then he erased Polk's personality."

Grief welled in Sam. "For that, he will pay." She would see to it if it took her entire life, even if she had to become an EI herself to live long enough. "How did he get to Linden?"

"I'm not sure how they know each other. I have to be careful when I access any part of Charon's code, to make sure it doesn't influence mine. I haven't had enough time to go through all his memories yet."

"Can you stop him?" It was beginning to seem futile. No matter what they did, they kept playing into Charon's hands.

Turner spoke firmly. "He won't control me."

She thought of how Bart had manacled her to the table. "Anything I can do to help, I will."

"My thanks, Sam." He rubbed the small of his back. "None of that will matter if we don't find help soon. We'll starve out here."

Sam wondered why he rubbed his back. He might tense up in response to his emotions, but more likely, the changes in his limbs strained his muscles as his body adapted to their new weight and structure.

"Do you need to eat?" she asked.

"I should. But I can go without for a long time."

Sam couldn't even think of eating now. "I'm okay."

"Do you need rest?"

About two days worth. "Not yet."

"Are you cold?"

"I'm okay. Really." The brisk hike kept her from feeling the bite of the wind. She was walking by rote now, her body aching, too tired to rest. If she stopped, she thought she would collapse and pass out.

They continued on, Sam unable to talk anymore. Gradually she became aware of a rumbling. "Do you hear that?" she managed to ask.

"For the last ten minutes," Turner said. "It's an engine, I think." He indicated a line of low hills ahead. "Beyond those."

"Friend or enemy?" She laughed unevenly. "To be or not to be, a friend or enemy, that is the question."

He didn't smile. "You need to rest."

"I'm fine."

"If we can't find shelter, we'll sleep on the ground."

"I'm really fine." She dragged her mind into focus. "You sound different."

"I do?"

"Less confused. More certain." She thought of their trek through the EI's base. "You handled it well when we had to crawl to the cavern. If you hadn't already told me, I would have never guessed you got claustrophobic."

"It's odd. Closed-in spaces seem less threatening now. I don't know why."

Sam wondered if his matrix was reprogramming itself to minimize or even delete the fear. "Do you know why they bother you?"

His shoulders hunched. "When I was little, my

uncle used to put me in the closet if I misbehaved. I hated it."

Sam stared at him. "That's horrible."

He shrugged, trying for a lack of concern he obviously didn't feel. "I dealt with it."

Personally Sam thought Turner had been given far too many things to "deal with" as a child. That he had turned out so well was a tribute to the strength of his character. It didn't surprise her that Charon had found his will far stronger than he expected. "You're amazing."

He laughed self-consciously. "I'm a mess." His forehead creased. "I don't know why I'm afraid of heights. It's more about edges than the height itself."

"Have you always been that way?"

"No, actually. Only since Charon rebuilt me."

"Maybe he coded it into you." It seemed strange, even neurotic, but so did a lot about Charon.

"To what purpose?" Turner asked.

"Maybe he's hung up about it. Most people don't like edges." Sam thought of a visit to Paris, years ago. "You should have seen me the first time I went up in the Eiffel Tower. I was a wreck."

"You say it so casually." Longing touched his voice. "'The Eiffel Tower.' Like anyone could visit there."

"I'll take you," she said. "If we make it out of this mess, I'll take you all over the world."

"I would like that." He didn't sound like he really believed her.

"I will, Turner."

"I've never traveled."

"Would you like to?" Maybe he didn't want her hauling him all over the place.

"I'd love to." He stared at the hills ahead. "We had no money. My dad told people he sent me to live with my aunt and uncle because he had too many kids. He couldn't afford me."

Sam winced. That had to have hurt. "Is that what your mother said, too?"

"Only when he was around." He sounded subdued. Scarred, but on the inside. "She used to come see me, when he didn't know. She wanted me home, but whenever she brought me to the house, he sent me away. He gave her an ultimatum: get rid of me or he would leave her and take the other children away from her."

Sam had to make a conscious effort not to grit her teeth. She could guess what happened: he banished Turner to remove the reminder of his wife's adultery from his house. But it also had punished her child. "He was cruel to deny you."

"Ah, well." He tried to laugh, but it came out forced. "Can't have the bastard around."

"He was the bastard. It was his loss."

"Not really. They had ten kids. I was number eight." He drummed his fingers on his legs. "They kept nine and ten. I guess they deserved it more."

Sam wanted to keelhaul his father. It made her aware of how much she had taken for granted. Her parents had been strict, exceedingly so, but they had also lavished her with love and attention. She had been an only child. They hadn't been able to have more, though her mother had once told her they had hoped for a large family.

"You deserve the world," she said. "Don't ever let anyone tell you otherwise."

He answered in a low voice. "I've always been afraid that if I loved someone, they would give me away."

"I'm not going to leave you." She plunged ahead, needing to say the words before she thought too much about them and her fear of commitment made her back off. "No matter what happens. No matter—no matter how much you change. I won't walk out."

"Neither will I, Sam, no matter what happens to me." He took her hand and intertwined his metal fingers with her human ones. After a moment, he said, "I used to play softball with my brothers."

"Did they know you were their brother?"

"I think so. I looked just like one of them. Both he and I take after our mother." He spoke awkwardly. "We never talked about it, though."

"What do they do now?"

"Most are married. A few went to college." His expression turned nostalgic. "I miss them."

"You could go back."

"They think I'm dead." Bitterness edged his voice. "My mother's husband is probably glad."

She curled her fingers around his, offering support. "What about your real father?"

"I don't know him. He stopped seeing my mom after she got pregnant."

"What a charmer," Sam muttered. Turner's mother didn't have the best taste in men. Sam thought she might understand, though, if her personality as well as her appearance showed in Turner. He struck her as the type of person who would always be idealistic in his view of human nature no matter how many times life showed him otherwise. She could relate. She was the same way. Linden had been like that, too. It made it too easy for people like Charon to take advantage of them. But what few people understood, including probably Charon, was that such a character trait didn't make them stupid or weak. Charon was finding that out the hard way. It could be an advantage; he might continue to underestimate them.

Turner spoke tiredly. "Maybe I should just accept it. Turner Pascal *is* dead." He lifted their clasped hands, causing his sleeve to fall down to a joint where his cabled arm bent. "It would horrify them to see me like this. Hell, Sam, most women would recoil if I touched them."

She kept her hand in his. "You're alive. Alive and miraculous."

His face gentled and he rubbed her knuckles on his cheek. Then they walked on, across the desolate fields.

Sam stood with Turner at the top of a bluff, their arms around each other, wind blowing their clothes. A town lay before them, a tiny one, but it meant people and help. The rumbling came from a factory beyond its outskirts.

They started walking, but within moments they let go of each other and were running. Sam had thought she was exhausted, but now she sprinted with energy. At the edge of town, they slowed down, passing a holosign that read WELCOME TO TUGTOWN. The letters started out blue, but they cycled through the spectrum. A holicon in one corner offered a wireless connection to a site with information about illustrious Tugtown. Sam had no glove to access the sign, but her clever-card was in her wallet. Sooner or later she might have to use it, giving away their location.

They jogged onto Main Street, which consisted of a few stores, restaurant, post office, and motel. The street signs had dimmed; Tugtown had closed up for the night. However, holos were still lit over at the motel.

They slowed to a walk as they reached the hover lot in front of the motel office. Pads for cars lined the asphalt but only a few vehicles were parked there. The sign above the door said VACANCY in three-dimensional red letters that floated. Part of the second "c" was missing, which made it look like a firefly caught in the sign. Beyond the window, Sam saw a teenage boy working at an aged Luminex console that had to be at least fifteen years old. Its luminous white surface had faded to a dull ivory.

Turner pulled down his sleeves to hide his hands. As Sam opened the door, it played a Bach invention. Inside, the office had a few chairs against one white-washed wall. Holoart swirled on the walls, soothing pastel patterns that gave the illusion of depth and thickness. The boy was slouched behind the console, eating a sandwich with lettuce sticking out the sides. As they entered, he looked up with a start, his eyes widening.

"Evening," Sam said.

The boy dropped his sandwich onto a plate that sat on the console's holoscreen. "Whoa! Who are you?"

Sam hoped he didn't treat the rest of his equipment that way. Lettuce rarely helped the guts of a mesh system. She and Turner went to the other side of the console. "I'm Sam." She lifted her hand. "This is Turner."

"Where did you come from?" He peered past them at the window to the hover lot. "I didn't hear no car."

"Truck. It stopped a long ways back. We had to walk here." Sam didn't need to act tired; reality took care of that just fine.

"Hey." He picked up his sandwich and took a large bite, making Sam's mouth water. "Ultra."

Turner gave him a sour look. "Can we get a room?"

"Oh. Yeah. Sure." The boy snapped an e-pad out of a slot on the console. "I gotta have your card."

When Sam pulled the clever-card out of her wallet, Turner shot her a look of alarm. As soon as the motel system accessed it, their location would go into a worldwide database and anyone who knew how to trace such transactions would know they were at the Two Pines Motor Inn in Tugtown, Iowa.

Sam sent him a warning glance, cautioning silence. They didn't want the boy alerted to anything unusual about them, besides which, it was almost impossible to find food or lodging anonymously. The only reason they had managed so far was because both she and Turner were savvy about the systems that tracked people. But they couldn't keep it up much longer. What they really needed was to contact someone who could help them. Who, she wasn't sure. Right now, she trusted no one.

"Here we go." The boy handed her the card and an e-pad with the registration protocol. After she pressed her thumb against the pad, he sent copies to whatever mesh they used for the motel database. Then he clicked her card into his console, keying it to open the door to their room. "You've got fast fiber-optics in there, best in town," he told her. "You want holo-movies, flat-screeners, holo-mail, mesh functions, just drum up the menu. It'll whiz you through payment options."

"Thanks." Sam handed the card to Turner so he could press in his thumbprint, allowing him to use it as a key. As he took it, his cuff fell back, revealing his hand.

"Whoa." The boy stared at the cables. "What zipped you?"

Turner yanked down his sleeve. "It's a prosthetic."

"Ultra." The boy grinned. "I gotta friend, he wants to cybordize his hands. Make 'em mesh-accessible."

Turner regarded him with a marked lack of enthusiasm, the look of a Hilton bellboy dealing with the closest approximation to his counterpart at the Two Pines Motor Inn. Sam held back her smile.

"It's not a trivial procedure," Turner said.

"Yeah." The youth nodded sagely. "I'll bet."

Sam drew Turner away from the desk. "Good night," she told the boy.

He lifted his hand. "Yeah, ultra."

They went outside, under the firefly sign. As they walked to their room, Turner grumbled, "Ultra? What way is that to talk to guests?"

"He's just a kid."

"We would never do that at the Hilton."

Sam grinned. "You're being a snob, Turner."

"I am not. I just think the job should be done well. I always took pride in my work, even when I slopped food in a cafeteria."

She certainly would have gone to that cafeteria. "I'll bet all the women mourned the day you left."

Turner laughed. "I doubt it." He leaned closer to her. "But I'd dish up potatoes for you anytime."

"Sounds delicious." Sam took his hand, her five fingers threaded with his eight. "I was wondering." She lifted their hands. "Why eight fingers? Why not five?"

"Octal." He wiggled his other hand at her. "Two make hexadecimal. It's more how I think now."

"Amazing."

At their room, Sam opened the door with her card, knowing she was leaving yet another clue to their trail. Inside, the queen-sized bed had a quilt patterned in holo-threads that created three-dimensional blue and gold squares. A similar tablecloth covered a round table by the window. The wall across from the bed consisted of a large screen for movies, with its console by the bed. Sam wondered if the kid in the office had assumed they were married. What a thought. The cyborg groom.

Sam flopped on the bed. "It's not much." She hoped he didn't think this was the type of place she would usually take him.

"It's great." He sat next to her. "But your card will give us away."

"I know." As much as Sam wanted to sleep, preferably in his arms, it would have to wait. "Turner, we can't keep running. We have nowhere to go."

"I don't want to be a prisoner."

Sam made a face. "I don't want to be dead."

"I already am."

"Turner!"

"It's true."

"We have to contact someone."

"And if I refuse?"

"You're free to go." More than anything, she wanted him to stay. But she wouldn't force him. "I'll give you a head start of three hours."

He stared at her. "I'm not going to desert you. What if Fourteen or some mechbot shows up?"

Sam took his hand. "You can't protect us forever." When she slid off the bed and went to the console, her body protested with stabs of pain, especially her left arm. The bandage was fraying now. "We need more protection than we can provide ourselves. I want to call Thomas Wharington."

His hand clenched on his knee. "We just got free of him."

"Thomas wasn't at Hockman. Or Sunrise Alley."

"Why should I trust him?"

"We have to trust someone."

"We can manage."

"You know we can't." She hated admitting it; she had always fiercely guarded her independence. But they had to be realistic. "The longer we wait, the better the chance Bart and his cronies will reach us, or that copy of Charon in your matrix will subvert your programming. Hell, Turner, he may have already."

"I can't believe we're having this conversation." He hit his fist on the bed. "I'm Turner, not Charon."

"We need help."

He spoke tightly. "Like the Alley helped us."

"The Alley changed." Sam's first impression of Bart had been a good one, based on her experience with EIs. "Charon affected them. We need to warn the military. Bart could intertwine with high-powered meshes all across the globe. If he acts with malice, I hate to think of the damage he could cause."

"Sam—"

She didn't relent. "We have to act."

Turner rubbed his eyes. "I've tried to calculate strategies and outcomes, but none of them work. We've been outmaneuvered every time. Or maybe I

just don't understand what I'm doing well enough.
No matter how hard I try to escape what Charon
intended for me, it happens anyway."

Sam grimaced. "I doubt he intended this mess."

"I never meant to endanger your life."

Her voice softened. "I know." She sat at the console.
"Let's call Thomas."

After a long moment he said, "All right."

Sam breathed out silently, grateful he intended
to stay. When she turned to the console, her vision
blurred, but she rubbed her eyes, determined to stay
awake. Then she logged into one of her accounts.

It only took a few minutes to access a system she
had used in her Air Force work. She doubted even
its high-level security could hide her from anyone
seriously intent on finding them; a savvy enough spy
could monitor this screen or trace incoming connections to Thomas's machine. He wouldn't usually be
available after midnight, but she was betting he would
pay close attention right now to his video, mesh, and
holo-mail, given the way she and Turner had vanished
from Hockman.

She wrote on the screen with a light stylus: *Thomas,
this is Sam Bryton* and sent the message with encryption.

Then she waited.

Within seconds, sooner than she expected, a response
appeared: *This is Thomas. Where are you?*

She wanted to be relieved, but before she let herself
feel it, she wrote: *Thomas or Thymus?* Only he would
get the joke. As a little girl, she had misspelled his
name Thymus, like the spice thyme.

I used to be Thymus, he answered. *Then the lovely*

little girl became a beautiful, albeit cranky, young genius with a prodigious spelling ability.

Sam smiled. *That* was definitely Thomas. *I'm at the Two Pines Motor Inn in Tugtown, Iowa.* What she actually wrote was "I M at 2 Pines Motor Inn tugtown ia." The AI for the chat program converted it to standard English. She could have turned off the correction, but Thomas preferred it this way.

Why are you there? he asked.

Long story. I need help.

I'll have someone pick you up.

Her jaw clenched. *The last time you said that, we were kidnapped.*

From Hockman?

No. California.

That was unfortunate.

No shit.

After a pause, he wrote, *We have a chopper on the way.*

We need a signal to prove it's them. Anything they wrote here could be monitored, so she needed something only she and Thomas knew. *Do you remember when I was ten and you gave me a birthday present that made me laugh?* He had hired a clown for her party.

I remember.

Have whoever picks us up tell me what you did.

All right. ETA is thirty-five minutes.

Can it come faster?

They can try. Are you in danger?

She blanched. *Not much, just some EIs who want to cut up my brain and turn me into an enslaved mesh code.*

WHAT?

Yeah, that describes my reaction.

Is Turner there?

She glanced at Turner.

"Go ahead," he said.

She wrote, *Yes, he's here.*

Another message appeared. *My contact at the Air Force base, Major Connors, had an odd impression about your interactions with this android.*

Turner leaned over and stabbed in the words *I'm not an android.*

Turner? Thomas asked.

Yes, I'm different, Turner said. *But I'm not a thing, General. I'm a man.*

More text appeared. *I've known Sam since her birth. I want to know her until she is white-haired and bent over. You understand?*

Turner looked startled. *I've no intention of hurting her, if that's what you mean.*

See that you honor that promise.

"He sounds like a father," Turner said. He had an odd look, as if he wasn't sure he recognized the signs.

"He promised to look after me if anything ever happened to my father," Sam said.

"They worked together, didn't they?"

"Yes. They both went to Paraguay." In a leaden voice she said, "Thomas came home. My father didn't."

"Ah, hell, Sam." He laid his hand over hers on the console.

She thought of Hud, their steward on the hijacked Rex. He had been the epitome of emotional control. If only she could be that impassive. Sometimes she felt as if she were tearing apart inside.

A word appeared on the screen. *Sam?*

I'm still here, she wrote.

About Major Connors.

What about her?

Why does she think you're sleeping with Turner?

Well, that was blunt. *My personal life is my business.*

Is that a damned joke?

No.

Your "personal life" involves a biomech man who could pose a threat to world security.

"Wait," Turner said. "Listen."

Sam tilted her head. A fly buzzed somewhere in the room. "What?"

"Can't you hear it?"

It took a moment to catch what he meant. Engines rumbled, faintly at first, then growing in volume. "If that's a helicopter, I hope it's the right one."

"You and me both."

Your chopper is early, Sam wrote. She sent him an emoticon holo of a nervous smile. *Either that, or we're about to be kidnapped again.*

It should be mine, he answered. *We tried to speed up the ETA.*

Sam hoped he was right.

The Redbird landed in the hover lot. The town had been asleep before, but now most everyone in the motel crowded out to look, including the kid from the office and two adults, his parents probably, given how they resembled one another, blond and solid.

A uniformed man stood in the helicopter, motioning to them. As Sam and Turner ran across the lot, the gale of the blades flattening their clothes, everyone watched. If this was another abduction, at least they had witnesses.

With a start, Sam recognized the man waiting, Lieutenant Hollander, one of the medics who had been in the Redbird that picked them up from California, what seemed like an eternity ago, though it had only been a few days.

"Hey." Sam had to shout to be heard above the blades. "Lieutenant, I don't know if I should be glad to see you."

"Glad, I hope." He motioned her and Turner to climb aboard. "General Wharington said to tell you 'It was the best durn clown you ever saw.'"

She grinned. "Good answer."

They strapped into their seats, and the Redbird lifted off, soaring into the night.

XVII
Thwarted Vow

"I want to see him." Sam thumped her hand on Thomas's mahogany desk. "You gave your word."

He stood on the other side of his large oak desk, even more military than usual in his crisp blue uniform. Three stars gleamed on each shoulder and rows of ribbons bedecked his chest, including his Joint Service Commendation with two oak-leaf clusters. Sam knew he had many medals as well, including the Medal of Honor, but he wore them only on formal occasions. Framed certificates on the wall showed his many and varied credentials. An American flag hung from a pole on his right and the blue Air Force flag with its eagle emblem stood to the left. His desk was clear of papers, but it had a holograph of his wife on one side and a holo of Sam and her father on the other.

Right now he looked far less amiable than the smiling man in those pictures. "Sam, you aren't objective where Turner is concerned."

"You said we would be apart a few minutes. It's been ten *hours*." She had slept most of that time, a guest at Thomas's home in Chevy Chase, Maryland, the house he and his wife had bought years ago before she passed away. The rest of the time Sam had spent with him and his NIA team, exchanging information. Most of her debriefing had taken place in a conference room at the Pentagon, one of the locations where the NIA had headquarters. When she and Thomas had finally come to his office, she had hoped to see Turner, but no such luck. Until she spoke to him, she feared to say too much about Charon or Sunrise Alley, uncertain how it would affect Turner.

"You have to let me see him," she said. "I had trouble enough convincing him to come in. He agreed only because he trusted me. He sure as hell doesn't trust any of you, and now he might think I turned on him, too."

Thomas came around the desk to her. "Dr. O'Reilly wants to talk with you and Turner separately."

"Dr. O'Who?"

"O'Reilly. He's the psychiatrist on this case."

She crossed her arms. "I don't need to see a damned shrink."

"Sam." He leaned against the desk. "General Chang doesn't want you talking to Turner. And she outranks me."

That was certainly an understatement. Chang, a four-star general, was the Pentagon's deputy director of Defense Intelligence, which made her Thomas's boss.

"This place has too much brass," Sam grumbled.

He smiled slightly. "It's the Pentagon. It's supposed to have brass."

"When do I see Turner?"

"Don't you think your relationship is a bit—" He cleared his throat. "Unusual?"

"No."

"Sam."

"Oh, all right." She dropped her arms. "Yes, it's unusual. So what? He means a lot to me. And I'll tell you something else, Thomas. He's far more likely to cooperate with your people if you let him see me."

He considered her. "That could be an effective argument."

Hah! "So he *is* refusing to cooperate, eh?"

"I'm not at liberty to discuss it."

She grinned. "Well, if his lack of cooperation that you aren't at liberty to discuss is a problem, I can help."

Thomas answered dryly. "We will see."

The drive took several hours. Sam and Thomas went in a black hover-limo, long and sleek. In the distance, the supple column of the space needle rose from the Virginia countryside into the blue sky, glittering in the sunlight, higher and higher until it dwindled to a point. Satellite-controlled traffic flowed smoothly through the streets of Washington, D.C., which only a few decades ago had been so congested it could take an hour to travel a few miles. Now many of the roads were repaved and restricted to hover traffic, all under control of city grids that kept congestion to a minimum. For those who wanted even faster transportation, the magrail curved over the city, its silver arches gllistening. A mag-train hummed along a rail a few blocks away, gleaming against the sky.

They left D.C., entering the suburbs of Virginia, and

the early-morning traffic dropped off. They traveled through sparsely settled areas with large houses set far back from the road and surrounded by expansive lawns or angled woods. Every now and then they passed a sweeper-bot discreetly rolling along the road, cleaning up trash.

Eventually they left the settled areas and entered more rugged country closer to the Appalachian Mountains, heading through forests of pine, hemlock, wild cherry, and poplar, and some younger white oak trees. They ended up at a facility hidden in a valley and surrounded by an invisible fence that hummed when the guards passed them through. The place resembled a hospital, but with a genteel architecture that made Sam think of a castle. The grounds sloped gracefully with well-tended lawns, scattered pine groves, and deciduous trees brilliant with the yellow, orange, and red leaves of a late but warm autumn. Paths wound across the lawns, bordered by azalea bushes, and curved around graceful but abstract sculptures designed in arcs of bronzed metal.

Inside, Thomas took her down wide corridors with blue-and-gold-patterned carpets and holoart on the walls. O'Reilly came with them, a stout man with a round, ruddy face and bulbous nose. Sam gritted her teeth when Thomas also brought two guards. They were behaving as if Turner were a criminal when he was the one who had suffered from the crimes.

They stopped at a locked door. Thomas opened it into a room that, although sunny and well furnished, looked like it belonged in a hospital. Turner sat sprawled in an armchair, his legs stretched out on the coffee table, his elbow propped up on the arm of the chair while he read a holobook. He could have downloaded the book straight into his matrix, but it didn't surprise Sam that he chose to read. Although he existed as an EI, he thought like a man, with human preferences. Perhaps someday he might electronically ingest his entertainment, but not yet.

He looked up warily, then jumped to his feet, the book dropping to the floor. "Sam!"

"Hi." She went over and started to reach for him, then stopped when she remembered everyone watching. Turner responded in much the same way, freezing in mid-motion with his arms up, then lowering them back to his sides. So they stood, suddenly awkward with each other.

"I wondered what happened to you." His expression warmed as he took in her appearance. "You look nice."

Sam responded as she always did when someone complimented her; she got nervous. Then she told herself to stop it. The days when she was an awkward kid were long gone. Besides, she had chosen her white jeans and flowered top specifically for him, knowing they set off her figure. So she smiled and said, "Thanks."

He motioned at his suite. "Like my cell?"

"I noticed." Sam could see Thomas and O'Reilly in her side vision. She wished they would go away. It wasn't going to happen, though, so she turned and glared at Thomas. "Why is Turner here?"

Thomas leaned on the edge of the console near where he stood, seemingly relaxed. Sam knew him too well to be fooled; he was wound up as tight as a coil. He spoke to Turner. "Are you uncomfortable here?"

"I feel like I'm in prison." Turner gave O'Reilly a puzzled look. "Who are you?"

The psychiatrist came forward. He would have been taller than Turner Pascal, but this Turner topped him by three inches. "Major Jim O'Reilly." He offered his hand. "I'm a doctor."

Turner shook hands warily, and apparently with more force than he realized, given the doctor's wince. Sam had to give O'Reilly credit; he never blinked when his human hand made contact with Turner's cables.

"What kind of doctor?" Turner asked.

"Psychiatrist," O'Reilly said.

Turner narrowed his gaze. "You going to shrink my biomechanical brain?"

"I'd just like to talk to you."

"Why?"

"No one like you has existed before." O'Reilly spoke with respect. "You're a form of life unlike anything this world has known."

Turner didn't look particularly honored by the distinction. "So you thought I would be more amenable if Sam was here."

Oh, well. It didn't surprise her that he figured it out. "It was my idea," Sam said. "So they would let me see you."

He started to reach for her again, stopped again, and swore under his breath. Then he quit resisting and drew her into his arms despite their audience. "Whatever the reason, I'm glad you're here."

Sam was acutely aware of everyone in the room; she had always been self-conscious about any show of affection in public. Her entire family was that way. But she missed Turner so very much. Although she knew, logically, it had only been a few hours since she had seen him, it seemed forever. She hugged him and he felt good in her arms.

Turner bent his head. When he kissed her, his cabled arms pressing her back, she almost jerked away. She had never kissed a man in front of other people before. Maybe it was the restraint of her English background; she didn't know. But if she recoiled from Turner now, the doctor would make who-knew-what annoying analysis of her behavior, and Thomas would assume it was revulsion on her part and start his paternal challenges with Turner again. So she kissed Turner back and discovered he felt just as warm and inviting even when she was embarrassed.

Some time later he lifted his head and looked at her. Sam's cheeks were burning, but her smile came naturally.

Turner looked over her head at Thomas. "I'll cooperate with you on one condition."

"What is that?" Thomas sounded disconcerted, an unusual state for him.

"That Sam and I can get married," Turner said.

That she didn't expect. "Uh, excuse me," Sam said. "I think you're supposed to ask me first."

His face became tender as he looked at her. "Want to marry me?"

Sam knew that no one would let them marry. For one thing, legally Turner was dead. For another, no one had figured out how human laws applied to formas. Besides, she had only known him a few days, not enough for a wedding even if no other obstacles existed, like his not being exactly human.

Then again, maybe that was the point. He had hit

on a way to assert his rights: only people could marry. Not machines. She had a thousand and one reasons to be reluctant, but maybe for once in her life she should stop analyzing and go with her instincts.

"All right." Despite her intent to be pragmatic, she blushed like a kid. "I'll marry you."

Turner's mouth opened. He snapped it closed, then grinned. "Hah! I can't believe you agreed."

Sam laughed. "Well, I did."

He beamed at Thomas and O'Reilly. "The lady said yes."

Sam turned around. Thomas seemed bewildered. It was a singularly unique occurrence; she had seen him in many moods but never confused.

"You can't marry," he told them.

O'Reilly cleared his throat. "Mr. Pascal—"

Turner turned with a smile that made Sam think of the Cheshire Cat from *Alice in Wonderland*. "Call me Turner."

"Turner, yes." O'Reilly rubbed his chin. "This is a rather anomalous proposition."

Turner's eyes gleamed. "I propositioned her days ago. Now I want to make it legal."

O'Reilly smiled dryly. "I don't think you can do that."

Sam hadn't expected any other response. She looked from O'Reilly to Thomas. "You see, don't you? Humanity has to face it sooner or later. What are self-aware formas—constructs or people? Possession or citizen?"

"If you mean our actions here will set a baseline for the future," Thomas said. "Then yes, I agree. All the more reason to use caution."

Sam thought of Bart and the other EIs, forms

of life different enough from her own that she only fathomed the edges of their intelligence. Sunrise Alley. It would only grow larger and more powerful each year. The alley would become a thoroughfare, a city, a world. A universe.

"If we make a mistake now," Sam said. "If we do this wrong, without foresight, we will set up the human race for more grief than you can imagine. How you treat Turner now matters."

O'Reilly considered her thoughtfully. Then he spoke to Turner. "It is true, your DNA corresponds to Turner William Pascal. I've no doubt you were made from him."

"I wasn't made from him," Turner said. "I *am* him."

"But where do you end?" O'Reilly asked. "How much can you be rebuilt before you are no longer a man?"

"You're asking him to define the soul," Sam murmured. "Only God can do that."

"Perhaps," Thomas said. "Unfortunately we need a legal definition."

Turner regarded him steadily. "I feel no less as if I have a soul now than before the accident."

Sam went over to Thomas. "His limbs aren't that different from prosthetics. Many people have transplanted or synthetic organs in their bodies. We consider them human."

"They don't have EI matrices for brains," Thomas said. "They don't run on microfusion reactors."

Turner spoke bitterly. "So I'm human if you replace my heart with a pump, even if it bears no resemblance to my original heart, but I'm not human if my matrix is a copy of my original brain."

"It's become more." O'Reilly spread his hands out from his sides. "We don't have answers."

"Charon thinks he does," Turner said.

"He told you?" Sam asked. She couldn't tell how many of his memories about Charon came from the copy he carried in his matrix and how much from his two weeks with Charon in Oregon. If Thomas found out Turner had a copy of Charon in his mind, he would lock Turner up so tight, the former bellboy wouldn't even be able to breathe without monitors recording every move of his muscles.

Turner was watching her face. After a pause that went on too long, he said, "Yes, Charon told me." He had the restrained quality she recognized now; he was tweaking the truth. He had probably picked up Charon's opinion from the copy in his matrix. That she could read Turner so well implied he was more human than machine; otherwise, he could have simulated *less* emotion, so he didn't give himself away.

Sam rubbed the back of her neck, working on the muscle kinks. "Thomas, I need to talk with Turner alone."

"I don't think it is wise," Thomas said.

"Oh, why the hell not?" Sam said. "You're going to listen on monitors anyway."

The lights flickered.

"What the blazes?" Thomas spoke to one of the guards. "Lieutenant Dreymore, check that brownout with operations."

"Right away, sir." The lieutenant turned over his hand, which was sheathed in a black glove, and traced his finger over a panel woven in its mesh.

As Dreymore worked, Sam discreetly studied Turner. Was he tampering with the power here? If he ran off from this place like he had from everywhere else, she was going to scorch his ears when she caught up with him.

Turner shook his head slightly, his face puzzled. He didn't seem to know what was happening any more than she did.

Thomas was watching them. "I'd be curious to know what that exchange between you two meant."

Sam flushed. Busted. Thomas could read her just as well as she could read him. "I wondered if Turner caused that brownout. He said no."

Thomas glanced at the lieutenant. "Dreymore?"

The guard looked up from his glove. "Everything appears fine, sir. Just a power glitch."

"Keep checking," Thomas said.

"Yes, sir."

Thomas considered Turner. "My people say they can't even fully analyze all the systems in your body. They think you've been shifting things around, building your own biomech components. Care to tell us what you're doing?"

"Why?" Turner asked. "You'll keep at me until you figure it out anyway."

"We don't want to cause you harm," O'Reilly said. "Neither physical nor emotional."

Turner's gaze became intent. "Then you admit it is possible to cause a forma emotional harm."

"At this point," O'Reilly said, "I don't know what to think. But yes, I acknowledge it."

The lights went off.

Thomas spoke sharply. "Dreymore, what's going on?"

The glow of Dreymore's glove lit the room. "The situation is under control, sir. The submesh that runs the environment for this building is having problems.

Security is on it. They'll have the lights back in a moment."

Sam slanted a look at Turner. He seemed as baffled as everyone else, but she couldn't be sure. At Hockman, the element of surprise had given him an edge in his escape; in Iowa, the EIs had inadvertently helped when they linked him into their mesh. He no longer had surprise here and the NIA wouldn't willingly give him access to any mesh. This place undoubtedly blocked wireless signals. And Thomas's people would have already incorporated new defenses into their systems to counter what Turner had done at Hockman.

Thomas studied Turner. "You have anything to do with this?"

Turner met his gaze. "No. Nothing."

The lights came back on.

"Keep on it, Lieutenant," Thomas told Dreymore. "I want a full report as soon as possible."

"Yes, sir. Right away." While Dreymore worked on his glove, the other guard stood ramrod straight by the door, his hand on the staser in a holster at his hip.

Thomas turned to Sam. "You know I can't leave you alone with him."

"I would never hurt her," Turner said hotly.

Sam thought she had better diffuse their confrontation before they both started growling. "The mesh problems here might come from Sunrise Alley. If Bart is the EI that ran the Baltimore Arms Resources Theatre, he could know about this place."

Thomas's face became neutral. "I wouldn't know."

I'll bet, Sam thought. He wore that noncommittal look whenever he didn't intend to reveal information.

To her, his lack of response gave away almost as much as if he had admitted he knew about Bart.

Dreymore spoke to Thomas. "Sir, I've a message from General Chang. She's called a meeting, fifteen hundred hours, at the Pentagon."

"Thank you, Lieutenant." Thomas glanced at Sam. "You had better come back with me."

Turner moved closer to her. "Why? Neither she nor I have done anything wrong."

"If that's the case," Thomas told him, "you won't mind talking with Dr. O'Reilly."

"Why the hell should I talk to your shrink?"

"Well, for one," Thomas said, "he's an expert in EIs. He might be able to tell you about yourself."

Sam would have laughed if she hadn't felt so on edge right now. Thomas had hit on one of the few things that might convince Turner to cooperate—his curiosity about his own development.

Turner wasn't fooled, though. "Or I might tell him about myself, eh? I've no interest in discussing my childhood traumas with your doctor."

Sam laid her hand on his arm. "Turner, suppose Bart or the others break in here. They meant to kill me."

He motioned at Thomas. "You think if I cooperate with these people it will help protect you?"

"Yes. And you, too."

"I need to talk to you alone."

"You must realize we can't do that," Thomas said.

Turner copied his tone exactly. "And you must realize I can't cooperate with you."

Thomas lifted his hands, palms up, then dropped them again. "Why not? We're on your side."

"I told you my condition." Turner put his arm

around Sam's shoulders. "Get the justice of the peace and I'll tell you anything you want to know."

Sam knew Thomas would refuse. If they let Turner marry, it would be a tacit acknowledgment of his humanity and citizenship. They were setting precedents and Thomas disliked haste. Acknowledging Turner's humanity would also make it that much harder to control him. Thomas was a man of principle, but she didn't doubt he had also thought what it would mean to have an army of Turners at his disposal.

To her surprise, Thomas didn't immediately say no. Instead, he spoke to her. "Do you really want this?"

Sam's throat tingled the way it did when she was nervous. "Yes."

"It's crazy." He motioned at Turner. "Your father would be dismayed. You deserve someone who can be a true husband to you. A father to your children. A partner."

"I appreciate your concern," Sam said. "But Thomas, I have to make those decisions for myself."

"You must realize we can't do this," he said.

"Sure you can," Turner told him. An edge came into his voice. "You won't because it makes it harder for you to use me."

"That isn't true," O'Reilly said. "What you're asking has no precedent. We must consider the ramifications. The legalities. We can't rush into it."

Had the bride been most anyone else, Sam wondered if they might have pretended to go along so they could gain Turner's cooperation. But that would never work with her involved.

Thomas spoke to Sam. "We have to leave. I'm sorry."

Turner started to respond, his face flushed, his body tensed. Then he took a deep breath and let it out slowly. When he turned away from Thomas and drew Sam into his arms, she hugged him, wishing she had a solution to this mess.

"We have to talk to them," she murmured.

He didn't answer, he only kissed her, his lips warm, his arms ridged against her back. Her inclination to privacy would have made her pull away, but this might be her last chance to see him for a long time. So instead she molded against him, deepening the kiss.

Someone cleared his throat. With reluctance, Sam let Turner go. "I'll see you soon."

He looked down into her face. "Don't be long, okay?"

"Okay." She intended to keep that promise.

Then she left with Thomas.

XVIII

Country Jaunt

Instead of returning to the lot, Thomas took Sam to an elevator.

"Where are we going?" she asked.

"Roof. They sent a chopper." He watched her with concern. "Will you be all right with that?"

She didn't see why he asked. "Of course."

He seemed surprised. "Good."

"Does General Chang want me in the meeting?"

"I'm not sure yet."

Sam hoped not; the more they asked about Turner, the more she struggled with her conflicted responses. She didn't want to betray his trust, but too much was at stake to hold back.

The elevator whisked open. As they entered the car, Thomas said, "I wish I could convince you that we don't want to hurt Turner." He pressed the panel for the roof. "We want to understand him."

Sam wasn't buying it. "You want to use him."

He frowned. "You have a problem with our wanting knowledge that could help the country?"

"No. You know me better than that. But if it comes at the price of denying his humanity, it's wrong." His question about the helicopter still bothered her. Why wouldn't she want to go in one? She couldn't stop thinking about it.

"We aren't trying to deny his humanity, Sam. If he is human." Thomas raked his hand over his hair. "Too many questions are unanswered. We can't jump into this."

"He's human."

"We need more than your conviction."

The doors slid open and wind blasted them, along with the growl of rotating blades. They ran to the waiting Redbird. She doubted she would ever grow used to traveling this way; the noise was bad enough, but it also bothered her to have so little separating her from the chasm of air outside the air craft. Heights disturbed her even more when she felt wind on her face.

Heights disturbed her?

It hit Sam like a gale rushing in, so strong it could sweep her over the building. Heights terrified her. Why hadn't she remembered? This was the first time in years she had thought about it. How the blazes could she *forget*?

She had no chance to analyze. They had reached the Redbird and were climbing on board. Within seconds they were roaring into the sky. She held the front of her seat, her grip so tight, her knuckles turned white. Land spread out below, thick with cities, interstates, and traffic.

As they flew on, the landscape became increasingly rural, until they were passing over farmland. It made no sense. They were supposed to be returning to the Pentagon near Washington, D.C. She was too tense to speak, but Thomas was already fiddling with his glove.

He tapped through several menus, then spoke into the comm. "Who's up front?"

No one answered.

"This is ridiculous." Thomas surveyed the woods that enclosed the clearing where the Redbird had set them down. "Someone must wonder by now what happened to us."

Sam didn't answer; she was too busy breathing slowly, trying to calm her pulse, which had gone wild during the ride. How could she have forgotten how much she dreaded heights? It had come back with a vengeance.

What else had she forgotten?

Sweat broke out on her forehead. She couldn't do this. She had to turn her thoughts away from her fear. She concentrated on the Redbird. An AI must have landed the helicopter; as far as they could tell, it had no pilot. If Bart or Charon were involved, now they had Thomas, a hostage worth far more than most anyone else, including her. But taking a lieutenant general in broad daylight was far riskier than kidnapping Turner from an isolated field in the middle of the night. Maybe the EIs no longer cared about secrecy. They had become so intertwined with the world mesh, nothing could eradicate them now.

Pah. A week ago she had been minding her own

business, puttering around her beach, grouching at the world and otherwise enjoying her retirement. Her life since then had been over the top; she wanted this roller coaster to slow down, level out, and let her off.

"That message from General Chang was fake," Sam said darkly. "We weren't expected anywhere."

Thomas was scanning the area. "How do you know?"

"I'm being realistic." Right now, she felt full of dire prophecies. "Our machines have figured out how much we depend on them. They're going to have a field day with us now."

The breeze ruffled his silvered hair. "You think someone broke into the Pentagon mesh, sent a false message to Lieutenant Dreymore, took over this Redbird, downloaded a rogue AI into its brain, and dumped us here, all without my people twigging to it? Come on, Sam. It's impossible."

"Yeah, well, you should have spent the last week with me. Impossible is my middle name now."

Thomas scowled at her. "If this biomechanical lover of yours would unlock his systems and let us download his memories, we would have verification of last week."

"He doesn't want you in his brain. It's called the right to privacy." Sam crossed her arms. "Acknowledge his rights as a human and he'll cooperate. Simple as that."

"Nothing is simple about this." Thomas walked toward the woods, but after a few steps he swung around to her. "No matter what we call him, he's a security nightmare."

"I know." She spoke slowly. "And I know you'll do whatever you think is necessary to defend this country.

Which you should. It's your job. That's why you wear those stars on your shoulders. But I'm trying to do mine, too. No, it's more than that. Turner's not a job. He's a friend. More than a friend."

"How do I convince you our intentions are benign?"

"Let me and Turner marry."

"You can't marry a forma." When she glared at him, he said, "No matter how high you arch those perfect eyebrows at me, it won't change the fact that he *is* a biomechanical creation."

"He is my fiancé."

Thomas made an exasperated noise. "Only you would argue your personal life into something like this."

"It's more than my personal life. And you know it."

He came back to her. "Yes, it is. That's why no one is going to let you two marry right now."

She paced away from him, going alongside the Redbird. "Who flew this helicopter? We can argue all day about new steps in human-machine evolution, but we can't even say what brought us out here."

He came around in front of her, halting her progress. "What do you think they want? I mean ultimately."

"Do you mean Sunrise Alley? Or Charon?"

"Either. Both. Maybe they're the same now."

"I wish I knew." She leaned against the Redbird. "My guess? Charon wants power. The EIs want self-determination. Except they already have it." She thought back to Sunrise Alley. "Bart was a cipher. One moment he's a fascinating host, strange but hospitable; the next moment his android is shackling me to a mech-table as a precursor to murder. I'm surprised Turner and I got out of there."

"Maybe they let you go."

"I've wondered." She thought about it. "Maybe Bart wanted a line into the Pentagon. He probably guessed you would be our last resort when it didn't work out with them. He could have rigged something while they repaired Turner."

"How would Turner get them into the Pentagon? We've had him in a separate facility." Thomas started to pace again. "No meshes connect that building to anywhere else. You can't even get wireless in there without authorization. We know how to secure a building."

"So does Bart. He used to secure a country."

Thomas stopped and regarded her. "The Baltimore Arms Resources Theatre failed."

"Yeah, well, tell Bart."

"Why strand us here?"

"In Iowa, someone met us." Sam half expected Fourteen to show up. "Can you scan the area with your glove?"

"Already done. Nothing but rabbits and bees."

"Then we should go find someone."

"I don't like leaving the Redbird."

"People keep trying to kill me," she said dourly. "I'd like to be gone before any of them show up."

"They could be anywhere around here."

He had a point. "It scares me."

"You and me both." Thomas came back over to her. "From your report, it sounds like Charon is building slaves and stealing minds. Damn frightening."

"He wants Sunrise Alley, too."

"So he lets Turner go and hopes the Alley offers him sanctuary. Okay. It works. Then suddenly the EIs want to kill you." Thomas looked ready to take on an army. "Why? If he really is obsessed with you, he wouldn't want you dead."

"I never said he was obsessed." It unsettled her that he used the same word as Turner.

"You said he told Turner you were 'as brittle as jagged glass, with sharp edges to hide the vulnerability.' Normal people don't talk about strangers that way."

"He had Linden's memories." It hurt to think about.

"Did Linden see you that way?"

"Actually, no, I don't think so."

"But Charon does. And he had sex with you, Sam." She froze, mortified. *"What?"*

"He's part of Turner."

Sam held up her hands. "It isn't the same."

"Why not?" Thomas demanded. "Maybe he picked Turner because he had spied on you enough to figure out what sort of man you found appealing. For all you know, he let Turner escape in Oregon, too."

Sam folded her arms and rubbed them, trying to ward off the chill she felt. "That's absurd."

"You think so?" He spoke as if he were outlining a battle plan. "Charon infiltrates Sunrise Alley. He gets control. Then they shackle you to a table, threaten your life, torment you by changing their minds, tie you to a bed, refuse to let Turner untie you, then let him untie you, then take you on some bizarre, tortuous trek through their facility. If that isn't crazy, I don't know what is. This Charon sounds like a sadist."

"Thomas, stop." He would go nuts if she told him Turner had a copy of Charon in his matrix. But Thomas and his people needed to know. And if Charon was obsessed with her, she might not be safe with Turner.

He was watching her closely. "If you hold back from us, it could hurt a lot more people than Turner."

Sam spoke carefully. "All right. Let's suppose Charon fixated on me for some reason. If that were true, why would he let me leave Sunrise Alley?"

"Maybe Charon didn't infiltrate the Alley. Maybe Bart sent you to us for your own safety."

She thought of the cruelty in Bart's final words to her. "I doubt it. He wanted to hurt us."

"You might be reading human responses where they don't exist." Thomas motioned with his hand, its mesh glove glittering black in the sunlight. "This feels no emotion. Why should Sunrise Alley have hostile intent toward us? Bart might be carrying out his purpose, to protect this country. It sure as hell isn't in our best interests to have Charon playing God with people like you and Turner."

Although he had a point, it just didn't fit. She had spent her career analyzing EIs. She would swear the Bart who ordered Fourteen to shackle her to the table wasn't the EI she had first met. She disliked what she had to do, but she saw no other responsible choice. "Thomas, I need to tell you one more part."

He didn't look surprised. "Yes?"

She forced out the words. "Turner has a copy of Charon in his matrix. It's contained, but not that well."

Thomas stared at her. "Hell and damnation. Why didn't you tell me before?"

She met his gaze. "I wasn't sure I could trust you."

"Why not? I've known you since you were too young to wipe your own butt. Now you can't trust me?"

"I asked you for help and next thing, we're shanghaied to Tibet. Then at Hockman, all of a sudden you've never heard of us and Major Connors is skulking around, trying to deactivate Turner. After all that, would *you* trust you?"

"Granger was trying to shake you up enough to crack your story. But both you and Turner stuck to it." He held up his hands, palms out. "Whatever you think of my motives, know this. I could no more betray you than my own daughter. I promised your father I would look out for you and I meant it."

Sam suddenly felt tired. "I know."

His voice quieted. "You don't trust me, yet you do trust Turner, someone you've only known a week and who may have the mind of an insane man within him. If you were me, would you want him conscious and aware?"

"No. No, I wouldn't." After a pause, she added, "If Bart didn't send us out here, who did?"

"Wildfire. Charon. Parked and Gone."

Sam grimaced. "He parked himself inside Turner, but who knows where else he's gone. If he has access to the GPS, he could transmit himself all over the planet."

Thomas looked as if he had eaten a sour fruit. "In your estimation, has he taken over Turner?"

"No."

"Could he be corrupting Turner's matrix?"

"I don't think so. What do your NIA whizzes say?"

He answered wryly. "They aren't whizzing so well, it seems. They had no idea Turner carried a copy of Charon."

"We have to do something. We can't just stand here." She walked to the front of the Redbird and jumped up to look into the empty cockpit.

Thomas joined her and showed her the palm screen of his glove. His scan of the onboard systems verified an AI had flown them here. "It overrides my commands when I try to open the cockpit doors. Same thing when I try to call in help. It's probably blocking my GPS chip and the signal from the Redbird, too." He flicked his finger through several holicons floating above the screen. "At least I can still lock up the Redbird."

"Let's check the area," Sam said.

He scanned the sky. "We were in the air for over an hour. It won't be long before someone realizes we're gone, if they don't already. We'll be easier to find here with the Bird."

"And easier to kill."

He turned back to her. "If someone wanted to kill us, they could have done it already."

"They want the goods intact." She tapped his temple. "As soon as you die, your brain starts to degrade. The imaging process to map it has to be done right away. If someone intends that for us, they would want to start as soon as we were dead. Or before." Sam remembered Fourteen with his air syringe, standing over her when she lay shackled to the table. Unable to stay still with the memory, she paced toward the forest.

Thomas caught up with her. "Don't go far."

"I won't."

"I'm not going to let anyone slice your brain, Sam."

She shivered. "Yeah."

"I thought it was possible to image the brain without destroying it."

"Yep."

"So why does Charon kill people, even himself?"

"Turner was already dead. I'm not sure what Charon wants from me. For himself, who knows? Maybe he's just nuts." She imagined what it would be like to copy her own mind. "Suppose someone copied your brain without harming you? Then what? You could exist in two different bodies. Very weird."

"That, from a woman engaged to a biomech forma."

"I'm engaged to Turner. For a principle."

"What happened to love?"

Her cheeks heated up. "I've only known him a week."

Thomas slanted a look at her. "Having doubts?"

"Of course I'm having doubts."

"So don't do it."

She tried for a lighter tone. "Well, no one else has asked me." She hadn't had a real date in years. Her friends claimed she ran like the wind anytime a man showed interest. Maybe they were right. Until Turner.

"You could have a normal relationship if you wanted it," Thomas said.

"I'm happy with this one." It finally hit her what he had said: *So don't do it.* That implied a choice existed, one she could make herself.

She spoke carefully. "If Turner and I persist with this marriage thing, will you try to stop us?"

At first he didn't answer. They walked in silence. Sunlight filtered through the trees and made dappled patterns on the ground. Fresh scents filled the air, different from the redwood forest around her home, less vivid, but fresh and vibrant. Leaves and twigs crunched under their feet.

Finally Thomas said, "Are you asking if I will oppose the marriage because it raises questions we haven't yet answered or because I think it will make you miserable?"

"The first." She was worried enough about the second for both of them.

"Sam, if you want this, I won't oppose it."

She stopped walking. "I didn't expect that."

"If you're convinced he's human, I'll take your word. You're the EI expert."

She wasn't certain she believed him. "Aren't you worried about world security and all that?"

"I didn't say no one would oppose it," he said dryly.

"You mean General Chang."

"Yes."

If Chang opposed it, the marriage wouldn't happen regardless of what Thomas thought. "I doubt anyone even knows if it's legal."

"It would probably end up at the Supreme Court." Thomas pushed aside a bush sticking out in their way. "We shouldn't walk any farther."

"All right."

He sat on a fallen log balanced on two boulders, giving a "bench" at about the height of his waist. "Talk to me, Sam."

She sat next to him. "I thought I was."

"You've told me events. I want to know what you think this all means. Not technically, but in the bigger scheme of humanity."

She sat thinking, listening to the chirps and rustles of the woods as she gathered her thoughts. "Our ability to create intelligent machines has outstripped our evolution. Some people think we're headed for an explosion in biomech development that will change the human race forever."

"I've heard the theory."

"Maybe this is the first stage."

"It doesn't feel that way." He turned over his hand, studying his glove. "Sure, we have fancier gadgets. But my life now isn't unrecognizable to my parents, who grew up in the 1950s."

Sam leaned forward, her elbows on her knees. "Suppose Sunrise Alley really is intertwined with our global meshes, that they can outwit our best security, that someday soon we could all load ourselves into formas, that people could pilfer minds and bodies the way Charon did with Linden." She exhaled. What did you call it when someone stole another person's internal identity? "In twenty years, our lives may not be recognizable even to ourselves."

He watched her intently. "The longer Turner lives, the smarter, faster, and more sophisticated he will become. Have you thought how you will feel when he's leagues beyond anything you can achieve as an unaugmented human? He'll leave you in the dust."

She had been avoiding the thought. "I know."

"Unless you change yourself," Thomas said.

A woman spoke, her voice deep, throaty, and mocking. "Well, that would be interesting."

Sam jerked and Thomas jumped to his feet. "Who is that?" he asked, his voice rumbling. She had forgotten how intimidating he could sound when he wanted.

A woman in a black leather catsuit walked out of the bushes, sleek, svelte, and menacing, a pulse rifle in her hand. "Me."

"Ah, hell," Sam said.

It was Alpha.

XIX

Buried

Thomas glanced at Sam. "You know this woman?"

"She's one of Charon's goons," Sam said.

Alpha shifted the rifle to her other hand. Her slow smile had the look of a predator. To Sam, she said, "How's the arm, honey?"

Sam spoke through gritted teeth. "Fine."

The bushes behind Alpha rustled as another of Charon's mercenaries came out, the man Hud. He took up position behind Alpha, his stance solid, his hands gripped on a pulse rifle, his face unreadable.

Alpha strolled forward, long and lean in her black outfit, which had components embedded in its leather, silver and hard. She and Thomas eyed each other, both about the same height.

"How did you find us?" Sam asked her.

"Oh, you know." Alpha shrugged. "We listen here, there, around."

"Who are you?" Thomas asked. "And who is 'we'?"

"She's Alpha, from Charon's base in Tibet," Sam said.

"That's right," Alpha said. "And now it's time to go." Her eyes flashed with malice. "I'm sorry Turner's not here. I would have liked to return the favor of his attentions in the elevator."

Sam smirked. "Don't like being outwitted, eh?"

The way Alpha's smile hardened made Sam suspect Turner had indeed outwitted her, as opposed to Alpha letting him escape. That didn't mean Charon hadn't set it up, but it did imply Alpha hadn't been in on the plan. Hud showed no trace of emotion, he just watched with that careful, intent scrutiny of his.

Thomas motioned in the direction of the helicopter. "How did you get the Bird here?" He had his other arm down by his side, his mesh glove off now and crumpled in his hand, almost hidden from view. In her peripheral vision, Sam saw his thumb moving discreetly over its surface.

"You can quit fooling with the glove," Alpha added. "We fried the mesh interface."

Thomas smiled coolly. Sam had seen that expression before. He wasn't amused. Whenever he had that look, she got out of his way.

"Lead on," he said, his voice deceptively mild.

So Alpha and Hud took them through the woods, Alpha walking with Thomas, and Sam and Hud behind them. It would have been a pleasant hike—if Sam hadn't feared they were about to die. Or worse. She didn't want to discover how it felt to be a submesh inside someone else's brain.

An engine rumbled overhead. Alpha looked up, then increased her pace. Sam's hope leapt; Alpha hadn't expected that sound.

Hud stayed at her side, a solid, oppressive presence. Every now and then he looked her over with an appraising stare. It was making her twitchy. Finally she said, "What? You don't like my fashion sense?"

The corners of his mouth quirked up. "Actually, it's rather attractive."

She didn't like it when he smiled at her. "Your fatigues could use some style work." Okay, it wasn't the most tactful response, but the sarcasm crept in when she was irate. Or scared.

Unexpectedly, he laughed. "I imagine so."

Up ahead of them, Thomas turned back. Knowing he was afraid for her, Sam gave him her *I'm fine* expression. After a hard look at Hud, he turned forward again.

The rumble overhead returned, surely an aircraft above the woods. This time Alpha stopped, her gun raised as she scanned the canopy of branches arching over them, much closer to the ground than the cathedral-like redwood forest at home.

Thomas leaned against a tree, his arms folded. "Expecting company?" he asked Alpha.

She tilted her head. "No one could have followed you here."

"Why not?" Thomas asked. "You aren't the only ones with good infiltration systems. Maybe we lured you here under false pretenses."

A muscle twitched in Alpha's cheek. "Move."

"We aren't going anywhere," Thomas said.

Sam tried to ignore Hud as he closed his hand around her upper arm. The tendons of his fingers felt as hard as the cables of Turner's hand. She wished he didn't look so damned *familiar.*

"Think again." Alpha holstered her gun and withdrew a slender tube from a conduit in her sleeve. Calmly, without hesitation, she fired the tube at Thomas. He slapped his hand over his breastbone, then pulled something out of his chest.

"What is this?" He held out his hand. A dart lay on the palm.

"Lethal nanomeds. Little molecular assassins. High-tech poison." Alpha glanced back the way they had come. The rumble was increasing, something landing, it sounded like. She swung back to Thomas. "The meds take five minutes to act and another five to kill you." She motioned at Sam. "Charon wants her alive. He doesn't care about you."

Sam clenched her fists. "If Thomas dies, the only work I'll ever do for Charon is to kill him."

"Oh, your sexy general doesn't have to die. I'll give him an antidote—when we have you two secured." Alpha motioned them forward. "I would suggest you get going. You don't have much time."

"Secured where?" But Thomas started to walk again.

"A place we set up," Alpha said. "In case something like this happened."

They strode through the woods, faster now. Hud stayed with Sam, vigilant and unwelcome. She didn't need his urging to go fast; Thomas was sweating far more than he should have been, given the cool day. His face soon paled. She also noticed how easily Alpha pushed aside branches that even a strong man would have found heavy, and how her too-perfect face showed no signs of strain.

"You're an android," Sam said to her.

Alpha considered her, but said nothing. Thomas never slowed his pace, his long stride eating up distance despite the undergrowth that hampered their progress.

"There." Alpha indicated a stand of trees screened by bushes. They pushed through the matted foliage and stopped in the middle of the stand, surrounded by tangled brush. Despite the foliage, Sam didn't see what good this would do. Thomas's people would find this place when they combed the woods.

But by then, it might be too late. Thomas's face had gone white. "Where is the antidote?" he asked.

"You'll get it." Alpha pressed a mesh woven into her jumpsuit. The ground cover pulled back, grass and dirt falling into the hole, clearing to reveal a hatch several yards down. Sam doubted she would have found it even if she had thought to dig. That it resembled the hideaway in Iowa didn't reassure her. Charon may have found this place through Bart.

The hatch swung down, revealing a chute with a metal ladder on one side. Thomas immediately started down, lowering himself into the hole until he reached the ladder. Sam went next, descending into cooler air and shadows, and Alpha and Hud followed. After they had gone a few yards, several hatches closed over them in rapid succession. Sam didn't doubt the ground was moving into place, filling the hole. She wondered what Thomas's people would do when they found no one up there. Methods existed to detect a place like this, but just as many ways existed to hide it.

They climbed in the darkness.

"Thomas?" Sam asked.

"Yes?" His voice came from below.

"Are you all right?"

No answer.

"Damn it, Alpha!" Sam clenched the metal rungs of the ladder. "Give him the antidote."

No answer.

A grate came from below, a shoe scraping concrete. Sam went down a few more rungs and her foot hit the floor. She moved away from the ladder, listening to Alpha step down. Sam thought frantically of wrestling her to the floor and grabbing the antidote. It was a stupid idea; she had no chance against even one mercenary, let alone both Alpha and Hud. But she hated knowing that Thomas might be dying at her side, in the darkness, and she couldn't help.

"Here." That was Alpha. "Inject yourself in the arm."

A hiss came from the dark. Then Thomas said, "How do I know it will work?"

"You don't," Alpha said. "We've cut it close."

Sam swore at her. "He better not die."

No answer.

"Thomas?" Sam asked. "Are you there?"

"Yes." His voice sounded strained.

"Don't stop talking." Her words tumbled out, fast and scared. "Let me know you're alive."

"Still alive . . . and kicking."

Sam reached around until she brushed his arm. "Maybe you should sit down."

"I think so."

That scared her as much as anything else. Thomas always insisted he was fine, even when he was sick.

As they settled onto a cold floor, Sam strained to hear sounds, any sounds. "Alpha? Hud?"

A distant clang came from somewhere.

"They dumped us," Thomas said.

"You really think your people are looking for us?"

"Yes." His words sounded labored. "Lieutenant Dreymore thought that transmission from General Chang's staff was a fake."

Sam listened to his ragged breathing. Alpha had said he would die within ten minutes. It had to have been that long by now. "Thomas?"

"Need to lie down." His uniform rustled. Sam helped him stretch out on the floor, on his side, then sat next to him and rested her palm on his forehead. His skin felt clammy.

"You have to stay alive." Losing Thomas would be like losing her father all over again, even worse, because she had brought this on Thomas by seeking his help. *Please be all right.*

"Our EIs have been analyzing Charon's attempts to break into our meshes," he said.

"Thomas!"

"Yes?"

"You're alive."

"It does appear so." He sounded a bit surprised.

"Thank God." Relief washed over her, tempered by the knowledge that his improvement didn't mean he had come through this yet.

"We looked for patterns," he said. "Links, anything that would help us track the attempted break-ins."

Sam knew that tone. It was the same one he had used after his doctors told him to pay more attention to his cholesterol or he would have a heart attack.

He was trying to distract himself from thoughts of his mortality.

"Did you find patterns?" she asked.

"One." He rolled onto his back. In the darkness she knew only because she heard him move and the sleeve of his uniform caught on her hand. As he loosened the cloth, he gave her fingers a quick squeeze, as he had sometimes done when she was young. That one gesture told her how rattled he must have been; Thomas was normally even more restrained than her parents in showing affection to family or friends.

"Dreymore supposedly received the message from General Chang's assistant," he said. "But it came on a signal modulated with certain anomalies. They match anomalies in signals we believe Charon uses."

"Turner said something like that once." Then it hit her. "They suspected our helicopter ride might be a fake, but they let us take it anyway?"

"It's possible. But we're covered."

Sam resisted the impulse to say *Apparently not enough*. If Thomas was bluffing, trying to convince their captors they had backup, she didn't want to weaken the effect.

"I think Alpha is an android," Sam said.

"What about the man?"

"I'm not sure. He's another mercenary." She paused. "I have the oddest feeling I've met him before, but I don't know where."

"You know mercenaries?"

"Well, no. I thought maybe it happened when I was working for the Air Force. Could he have been one of your people, gone rogue?"

Thomas moved again, sitting up, she thought. "It's possible."

Sam knew what he didn't say. If his team didn't pick them up, Charon's people would later. This hide-out could be well shrouded. "We need to find out more about this place."

The crinkle of a mesh glove came from the darkness. "This damn thing isn't working at all."

"I might be able to get it going."

"It's pretty well fritzed, Sam. I don't think you can do anything."

"You wouldn't be the first to say that." Smugly she added, "Nor the first to be wrong."

His voice lightened. "Give it your all." He handed her the glove.

Sam fooled with the fingers, manipulating the threads in them, trying new configurations. She had played with meshes as a kid just to see what they could do. She might be able to shift the operation of the glove to threads other than those Alpha had fried. It wouldn't be easy; just from touch, she could tell the glove was badly damaged. They wouldn't have let Thomas keep it otherwise. She doubted she could fix the wireless functions, but she might at least bring up the internals.

As she worked, she said, "We could try climbing out."

"Yes. I want to reconnoiter here first, though."

Sam smiled. Thomas would call it "reconnoitering." She shifted the glove to one hand and helped him stand, though she wished he could rest longer. As he leaned on her, she said, "This is the second time I've been underground like this."

"I'd wondered." He straightened up, holding her arm for support. "You're sure the EIs rather than Charon were running the one in Iowa?"

"At first." She walked slowly with him, testing the ground with each step. "I can't be certain about later. Or it could be Charon was always an EI."

"Then why didn't he know where to find the Alley?"

Good question. "Maybe they kicked him out."

"It's an odd thought." He sounded more like himself now. "A conglomerate of EIs banishing one of their own. So he finds himself warm bodies and wreaks havoc as a human being." He drew her to a stop. "Here's the wall."

Sam ran her palms across unfinished stone, a contrast to the machined surfaces in Bart's facility. They walked along the wall, pacing out the room, which turned out to be a square about ten steps long on each wall. They found no doors, but neither did they find any trace of Alpha or Hud, so an exit had to exist. Sam climbed up the ladder, but a solid hatch blocked the top. Unlike Turner, she couldn't break into whatever system controlled it and override its codes. So she came back down, disheartened and quiet.

Finally they sat together against one wall. And they waited.

"I'm thirsty," Sam said, sitting cross-legged, working on Thomas's glove.

"Someone should come back eventually." Thomas spoke from across the room. His shoes scraped the floor as he paced back and forth.

The palm screen on the glove suddenly lit up. "Hah! Got it."

Thomas turned to her, his figure visible in the dim light from the screen. "Can you get an outside line?"

"Doesn't look like it." Several holicons had lit up on the screen, seeming to float above it, but those for the wireless were dark and inactive. "Your time and calendar work. We've been down here for three hours."

"If feels like three days."

His strained tone made her glance up. It could have just been the bad light, but he looked pallid. "You should sit down. We don't know if the oxygen is replenished. The more you move, the faster you use it up." In truth, she doubted they would have any trouble with oxygen. If she told him she was concerned about his recovery, though, he would insist he was fine.

Her ploy didn't fool him. "I'm sure the oxygen is sufficient." But he came over and sat next to her.

She held up her gloved hand, letting the screen give some light. "Your people should have found us by now."

"They will."

"Do they know what Turner and I found in Iowa?"

"Some do, yes."

"So they should think to look underground."

"Yes."

Sam knew him well enough to know he was giving answers with far more confidence than he felt. "We should bang on the hatch again."

"In a bit." He sounded tired. "I was wondering."

"Yes?"

"You didn't refuse to go in the Redbird."

She bent over the glove again. "It was fine." She hadn't had time to panic before they climbed aboard the helicopter. What unsettled her far more was that she had forgotten her fear of heights for three years. Why? She usually hid it well; Thomas and her mother were about the only people who knew. But *she* knew. Had known. And what about Turner? He just happened to be afraid of them, and he didn't know why? Maybe he didn't need a reason, but it was inconsistent; he had a history to explain his dislike of closed-in spaces.

Sam remembered all too well now why edges terrified her. When she had been five years old, her best friend had fallen from a balcony and died the instant she hit the ground. From that moment on, Sam had been terrified of edges any more than a few feet above the ground. It wasn't something you just *forgot*.

Working on his glove, she spoke in a casual tone. "Why should I refuse to go on a helicopter?"

"I thought you were afraid of heights."

"That was Turner. Not me." She studied his glove, playing with its menus. "Do you know what happened with the yacht Turner wrecked?"

"We retrieved the pieces. He made it almost to your beach before it crashed against the rocks."

"Ah." She brought up another menu, this one for his mail. "If I could just get an outside line on this thing."

"Sam, look at me."

She scanned the messages he had downloaded. "You've a lot of mail here."

"Fine." He sounded exasperated. "We'll forget the heights."

"You have mail from Giles Newcombe!"

"He's a friend of yours, isn't he?"

"You know he is." She looked up at him. "He's the first person I contacted about Turner."

Thomas leaned his head against the wall. "You can read it if you want."

She didn't know if she liked this new development. She opened the letter:

> Dear Thomas,
>
> It was odd. Sam said she had never heard of him. I was surprised. You would think she would recognize the name Charon.

"Why are you and Giles talking about me?" she asked. "And why should I recognize that name?"

"I contacted him after you told me about Turner."

"You know Giles?" She hadn't expected that.

"A bit. He's done some work with the NIA."

"I didn't know that."

"You didn't—"

"Have a need to know. Yeah, I know. And no, I hadn't heard of Charon."

His lips quirked. "I thought you knew everything."

She laughed. "No fair, Thomas. You aren't allowed to turn my grouching back on me."

"But it's so entertaining." When she glared at him, he chuckled, more himself now, stronger even than a few minutes ago. "Giles felt certain you would recognize the name Charon. In fact, he had expected you to be angry."

"Did he tell you why angry?"

"No. But he did say to tell you this: 'He can only take you across once.'"

"Again?" She wiped her palms on the legs of her jumpsuit. Why did that phrase keep coming up in her life?

"Do you know what he meant?" Thomas asked.

"A reference to Charon, I think. He's the ferryman that takes dead people across a river into the underworld. I don't know why Giles would tell me, though."

Thomas motioned around at their cell. "This Charon seems to have taken you and me into the underworld."

Sam shuddered. "I hope not."

A hum came out of the dark—and light flooded the room. Sam had been lying down, dozing, but now she sat up, squeezing her eyes closed. She opened them almost immediately, protecting them with her hand so she could peer into the brightness.

Alpha stood in a doorway across the room.

"Hello," the android said. "I see you're feeling better, General."

"What do you want?" Thomas asked, also using his hand to protect his eyes. He was standing a few feet from Sam.

"We have a problem," Alpha said. "Your friends won't leave."

He lowered his arm. "Good."

Sam rose to her feet. "You can't keep us here forever."

Alpha looked amused. "Why not?"

"What good would it do?" Thomas asked. "Your employer had a reason for all this. He wants something from us."

Alpha indicated Sam. "Her. And the android she stole."

Sam lowered her arm. "Turner isn't an android. And I didn't steal him. He came of his own free will."

"Free will," Alpha mused. "An odd concept."

"To you maybe." Sam limped over to her on legs gone stiff from sleeping on a concrete floor. "Especially if Charon assumes you don't have it."

"I don't." Alpha spoke as if she were commenting on the weather. "Nor do I want it."

"He programmed your android matrix that way?"

"Apparently." Alpha didn't bother to deny she was an android. "And for problem solving."

"So you can act without commands from him."

"That's right." Alpha looked bored. "Are you done with the questions?"

"Hardly," Sam said.

"Too bad. Because I am." Alpha strolled over to Thomas. "You and I need to talk."

"Why should I talk to you?" Thomas asked.

Alpha waved at Sam. "Because you don't want me to hurt her."

Sam spoke fast, before Alpha came up with ideas that involved her experiencing pain. "You said it yourself—I'm the one Charon wants. Injure me and he'll be angry."

"I didn't say I would injure you." Alpha looked her over. "You really are puny. It wouldn't be hard to make you scream without damaging you." She laughed. "You're a nerd, Doctor. A pretty one, but a weakling just the same."

Sam gritted her teeth. "Go to hell."

"How?" Alpha inquired. "I have no soul."

Sam had no answer for that. She wanted Alpha to be responsible for her behavior, yet the android had no free will. Perhaps responsibility went to whoever created her. But what of those like Turner who no longer had a human brain, yet who operated with free will? Sam needed to believe in a God who held all self-aware beings responsible for their actions, human or construct.

Thomas spoke to Alpha. "What is it you want from me?"

She answered immediately. "Turner."

He didn't look surprised. "You can't get him out of our custody, hmm?"

"Sure we can," Alpha said. "You'll do it for us."

"Threatening Sam won't make me do anything."

"How about we see?"

Sam swallowed. "How about we don't."

Alpha stalked over to her. "Turner likes that pretty face of yours. How do you think he would feel if it had a few scars?"

"Leave her alone," Thomas said.

Alpha turned to him. "Get me Turner."

"I can't order his release. You ought to know that."

"You're a powerful man, General." Alpha studied him as if he were a prize she had won. "I'm sure you can get him out."

"Why does Charon want him so badly?" Sam asked.

Alpha smirked. "Let's say he loves Turner so much, he feels like he lost a part of himself."

Sam shrugged. "Surely he stored copies of his mind in other places besides Turner."

A muscle twitched in Alpha's cheek. It made Sam wonder. For Alpha, no advantage existed in showing unease. That she did anyway suggested the android had less control over her actions than Sam had assumed. Either that, or Sam's question had been unexpected enough to cause some glitch. Whatever the reason, Alpha didn't like their knowing Charon had stashed a copy of himself in Turner.

"Charon exists anywhere he wishes," Alpha said.

"Yeah, he parks and goes." Sam had other ideas. "I know why he's desperate. Turner is reshaping his copy of Charon's mind. He's changing it and the real Charon can't stand that loss of control. He didn't think Turner had it in him, did he? He never thought the unassuming bellboy could resist when someone as strong as Linden Polk couldn't fight him."

Alpha's face tightened. "Shut up."

"That certainly glitched your code," Sam said.

Alpha considered her with a feral stare. "A great deal of argument exists as to whether or not an android feels pleasure. I have a bulletin for you, Bryton. We do. It will cause me great pleasure to hear you scream."

"You won't hurt me." Sam prayed she was right. She had years of experience with formas, but she could still make mistakes. "If you cause me pain, the memory will be in my brain, strong and recent. When Charon downloads my neural map, he gets that vividly unpleasant memory." She shrugged. "Besides, you would just simulate pleasure because you think it will provoke Thomas into doing what you want."

"Maybe." Alpha glanced at Thomas, her gaze traveling up his body. Then she spoke to Sam. "Your general is an attractive piece, I'll grant you that. But he has little value to Charon. Maybe I should just go to work on him, hmmm?"

"It wouldn't do any good," Thomas said. "I've nothing to tell you." He was composed and calm, but his jaw had tightened. "Sam has no authority to release Turner. No matter what you do to me, that won't change."

Alpha went completely still. Her flawless skin didn't move. Then she said, "I will return." With that, she turned and strode away. Lights glittered on her jumpsuit. Sam lunged after her, but the door snapped closed in front of her, leaving a blank, featureless wall.

"Damn." Sam hit the wall with her palm. She had no doubt Charon was trying to rattle them, isolating them, sending in Alpha, leaving them alone again. Unfortunately, recognizing his methods didn't stop them from working.

Thomas came over. "Don't let it get to you."

She spun around. "Don't you dare give them Turner. I don't care what they do to me. Promise me you won't give in to them."

"Sam." He paused, then said, "All right. I promise."

She knew he was lying. His posture, voice, and eyes revealed the truth. He promised for one reason: he assumed they were being monitored. He didn't want their captors to know they could gain his compliance by torturing Sam. Nor could she challenge his word, for the same reason. So she glared instead, hoping he knew her expressions as well as she knew his.

Thomas smiled. "You could incinerate with that look."

"Hmmph." She started pacing the room. Thomas watched her for a few moments, then sat against one wall and stretched out his legs. When she reached the opposite wall, she paced the other way. So she went, back and forth. It didn't help.

Sam was a puzzle solver; she believed every problem had a solution. But if one existed here, she couldn't see the light.

XX

Parked and Gone

The opening door woke Sam. She had been sitting next to it, intending to lunge for freedom the next time anyone entered. Groggy and half asleep, she jumped to her feet, but then someone shoved her against the wall. Hud. Behind him, she saw Alpha across the room, holding back Thomas, helped by Raze, the mercenary who had acted as copilot on the Rex. They each had one of Thomas's arms and they were wrestling with him as he struggled to come toward Sam.

In the moments it took for Sam to finish waking up, Hud pressed an air syringe against her neck. The sibilant hiss made her frantic. She tried to wrench free, but he pinned her to the wall. The harder she fought, the more he pressed against her, covering her body with his, smothering her. She felt as if she were suffocating. Her mind clouded and she sagged in his hold. She didn't pass out, but she lost control of her muscles. Her last clear sight was Hud watching her with a possessive satisfaction that scared the hell out of her. Then her vision blurred into vague shapes and colors. Sounds became muffled, as if she were underwater. Her limbs felt numb.

Hud picked her up, one arm under her legs, the other behind her back. She didn't want him to touch her, but her limbs no longer responded. As he carried her through the doorway, two blurs moved with them, Alpha and Thomas. She heard anger in Thomas's voice. Then her mind wandered into a haze.

For a while Sam didn't think. She was aware of being carried, of her head hanging back. Then they were in a room with bright lights. Hud put her on a table, on her back, and strapped her down at the wrists, legs, waist, and neck. Thomas was arguing with someone, but she couldn't decipher words.

Gradually her mind cleared. The ceiling came into focus. Glow-tiles. She tried to move her head, but her neck hurt. A strap held it to the table. On the second try, she managed to turn her head, though the leather scraped her skin. Her field of vision shifted to a console, a mech-chair, and other biomech equipment. She was in a lab.

A person came into view. No, a monster. Alpha. Bile rose in Sam's throat. She tried to speak, but only a gurgle came out.

Alpha stopped by the table. "Good evening."

Sam whispered, "Thomas . . . ?"

"Over here." Alpha slid her hand under Sam's head and turned it toward the other side of the lab, scraping the skin on the strap. Thomas was in a chair, his wrists bound to its arms and his ankles to its legs, his face ashen. Hud stood next to him, his hand resting on a staser at his hip. He also had a laser carbine slung over his shoulder. The gun reflected the harsh light in its mirrored surfaces.

Sam wet her lips. "What—?"

"We're going to operate on you," Alpha said. "Unless our dear general gives us back Turner."

"Operate?" Sam tried to clear her mind.

"On your brain." Alpha considered her. "I've heard it doesn't feel pain. I imagine you'll soon find out if that's true. You won't live long once we start removing slices, but you might be aware for part of the process." Her voice oozed. "Charon thought it could be an interesting memory."

"No." Sam choked out the word.

"The general here has a front-row seat," Alpha added.

"Thomas." Sam willed him to listen to her. "Don't give in to them."

He spoke fast. "To arrange Turner's release, I would have to contact General Chang at the Pentagon. Even if I could manage it, they would only use him to find you all. You won't achieve anything by this."

"I'm sure you can get him out without alerting your superiors," Alpha said.

"It's impossible."

With her gaze fixed on Thomas, she set the syringe against Sam's neck. "This will numb Samantha's head so she doesn't feel us cut it open."

Samantha. That did it. "Go to hell."

"It's too hot," Alpha murmured.

"Damn it, she can't help you!" Thomas said.

Alpha moved to the head of the table, out of sight. A familiar rattle came, the opening of the drawer that would contain surgical equipment. Sam recognized every noise: the crinkle of gloves, the clink of a knife, the hum of a drill being tested. She jerked against the straps, fighting whatever drug they had given her.

The drill hummed close to her head.

"No!" Thomas shouted. "Stop!"

Alpha sighed. "I can't do that."

"Wait." Thomas spoke raggedly. Then he said, "I'll bring Turner."

"You shouldn't have done it." Sam was sitting cross-legged on the bed, her hands in her lap. She couldn't look at Thomas, though she knew he was slouched in a chair across the white cubicle where Alpha and company had brought them. She and Thomas had been here for hours, Sam didn't know how many. Alpha had confiscated her clever-card and Thomas's glove.

Before that, though, while she had been strapped to the table, they had taken Thomas off somewhere. Sam didn't want to know. If he had arranged to bring Turner here, he had set himself up for the court-martial of the century. She didn't believe it; his people had probably planned for a scenario like this. But so would Charon, and none of them had outwitted him yet.

She hated the relief she felt, knowing Thomas had bought her life at the price of Turner's freedom. Nor would that sacrifice ultimately matter. She didn't see what would stop Charon from operating on her once he had Turner. His sense of integrity? Yeah, right.

"I couldn't let them kill you," Thomas said.

"Yes, you could." Sam was immensely grateful he hadn't, but that changed nothing. "More is at stake than my life."

"You're damn right." He crossed his arms. "I don't know if it really is possible for Charon to steal your brain and take it into himself, and I don't want to find out."

"Maybe Alpha is Charon." Sam would have liked to strangle her.

"She is rather alarming."

What an understatement. It was comforting to know that for all his savvy of world politics, intelligence, and the military, Thomas in some ways would always be naïve about modern women. He came from another era, one that in her more nostalgic moments seemed more genteel than the present. Other times it just seemed stifling, but right now she could have done without the technological marvels of modern times.

The door across the room slid open, framing a man in fatigues in the doorway. Hud. Sam got off the bed, standing to face him. She didn't like the way he sought her out with his gaze. He came inside, followed by three other people: Alpha, Raze—

And Turner.

"Ah, no." Sam felt as if they had punched her in the stomach. "Turner, no."

He looked as if he hadn't slept in ages. "Hi, Sam."

Standing, Thomas spoke to Alpha. "So it went without a hitch."

"No, it did not go without a hitch." Alpha hefted her pulse rifle from hand to hand, almost aiming it at him in the process. "Seems our friend here was sabotaged."

Turner spoke in a subdued voice. "They found implants in my body, General Wharington. It would have given away our location."

Thomas shrugged, the barest motion of his shoulders. Sam wondered if Alpha was supposed to find those implants. Possibly Alpha and company might have missed some signaling devices, but so far they had been all too effective. Alpha studied Thomas as if she wasn't sure whether to kill or to devour him.

Hud leaned against the wall, his arms folded. "Hello, Dr. Bryton."

Sam rubbed the back of her aching neck. "I would say it's good to see you, except it's not."

"Oh, I can't be that bad." He was acting oddly today, less like a mercenary, less formal, more—covetous? Both Thomas and Turner tensed when Hud spoke to her, and Turner stepped forward. He stopped when Raze lifted his laser carbine, its large size making the room seem smaller. Hud continued to watch her—

And Sam remembered.

It had been fifteen years ago. He had been standing just like that, a younger man then, about thirty, with less rigid control of his emotions. She had been a postdoc in Linden Polk's AI lab at MIT. Linden gave a party in honor of another postdoc who had accepted a job as a professor at Caltech. Hud wasn't part of the MIT group, but he had come to the party at Linden's invitation.

That day Hud had told her how he met Linden years before as part of a program for disadvantaged kids in New York. Linden had been his mentor, convincing Hud to stay in school, then go on to college and graduate school. His name hadn't been Hud then, but she didn't remember what he called himself or where he had worked.

"Oh, God," Sam whispered.

"You finally remember?" Hud asked. Bitterness edged his voice. "Apparently I didn't make as much of an impression on you as you did on me."

"But—why do you want to kill me?"

"I never planned to kill you."

Sam sat down on the bed. Everyone was watching them. Thomas's forehead furrowed and Turner looked confused.

"Why would you remember me all these years?" Sam asked, bewildered.

"Why wouldn't I?" Hud's voice hardened. "I could tell you weren't interested. Then you married that idiot."

Even if Hud had done nothing else, Sam would never forgive him for that crack. "Richard was a finer human being than you will ever be capable of comprehending."

"You know this man?" Thomas asked her.

She spoke heavily. "He's Charon."

"You can't be," Turner said to him. "I *know* Charon. I spent two damned weeks as his slave."

"You spent two weeks with a forma I made out of Linden Polk," Hud said. "A forma running me on its EI matrix." He looked Turner up and down. "Just like you."

Sam felt nauseated. "You killed Linden."

"Actually, I didn't." Hud turned his crushing focus on her, suffocating. 'Linden had a heart attack. I had nothing to do with it. But while he was dying, I imaged his mind. Then I rebuilt his body." His expression changed as he spoke, losing anger, gaining warmth. "I would never have harmed him. He was my mentor. He stood by me when the rest of the world thought I would never be more than a worthless street kid." His voice shook. "So when he died, I gave him a gift. I offered him a second life as a forma—with me as his brain."

"That's not life," Sam whispered.

Hud leaned forward. "Don't you see? I offered him exaltation." His manic intensity switched into hardness. "It was too much for him. Instead of thanking me, he tried to gain control of my matrix in his rebuilt body." He shrugged. "I was stronger, of course."

Sam wanted to rip the matrix threads out of his body. "Where is Linden now?"

"I deleted him. His body wasn't ideal." He glanced at Turner, his gaze covetous. "So I made a better one."

"Deleted him?" Sam leaned over, her arms folded across her middle, trying to keep from losing her dinner. "You murdered him after he had already died."

"You will understand better," Hud said. "In time."

Turner spoke bleakly. "Now you see, Sam, why I hate him."

She stared at the floor, wishing she could deny it all. Then she made herself straighten up and meet Hud's gaze. "What do you want with me?"

He looked her over. "Everything."

"What? A lover? Slave? A mind you can control?" She made no attempt to hide her revulsion. "You won't have me by my own will, Hud. Know it. Believe it."

"You'll change your mind. Eventually."

"Like hell." Thomas stepped forward, but Alpha caught his arm. Sam didn't know how hard the android gripped him, but he froze. Alpha raised her laser carbine, watching his face avidly. As he met her stare with a hard expression, Raze shifted his gun so he was covering Thomas as well. Sam caught Thomas's gaze then, and shook her head, worried. She didn't want him killed trying to protect her any more than he had wanted her killed to protect Turner.

Thomas let out a breath, but he stayed put. To Hud he said, "If you're Charon, who is Hud? And where?"

Hud looked down at Sam. "What do you think, Doctor?"

"You made a forma from a street kid," she said. "Then you put your mind into his matrix and tricked Linden into being your mentor."

Hud laughed bitterly. "Hardly. I *was* that kid. How would I know how to do any of that? Linden taught me." He motioned at Turner. "What you describe better fits the man he knew as Charon. It was me in Linden Polk's rebuilt body, with Polk's mind as a submesh I controlled."

"But it didn't work on me," Turner said. "And I'll tell you what else, asshole. I'm rewriting your brain. Changing it."

A muscle twitched in Hud's cheek. "You must be. I outgrew foul language."

Sam wished this nightmare would end. "Then who are you? *What* are you?"

"I used to be Hud. Now I'm Charon."

"You rebuilt your own body?"

"That's right."

"Why?"

He just looked at her.

Sam remembered the elevator ride when Turner had knocked out both him and Alpha. "You let Turner and me escape your base in Tibet."

"Actually, I didn't, initially." Hud was considering

Turner as if the younger man were a specimen in a lab. "You developed faster than I expected."

"I'm still doing it," Turner said.

Hud didn't respond. Instead, he spoke to Sam. "You are partially right, however, about the escape. I regained control of security about the time you two ran out of the building. But I let you go anyway. I thought you would run straight for Sunrise Alley." His jaw worked. "I never expected you would go to the military, not when you had every reason to believe Wharington betrayed you. And not after the way your father died."

Sam didn't want to think about her father here. "I knew Thomas wouldn't betray me."

"I take back what I said about you not being Charon," Turner told Hud. "You must be him. You misjudge good people according to your own flaws, just the way he did. It makes you surprised when they act with integrity."

Hud looked him over with a disdain so pronounced, Sam wondered if he was compensating. She would bet anything Hud felt threatened by the construct he had rebuilt for himself. Turner had obviously developed in ways other than Hud expected, ways that suggested Hud might not be as superior as he considered himself.

Hud turned back to Sam. "You will come with me."

She stood up, lifting her chin to face him, though he stood a good half a foot taller and had to be almost twice her weight, all in muscle. "No."

"I'm not giving you a choice."

"Tough," Sam said.

Hud closed his hand around her upper arm. As Sam pulled back, Thomas tried to wrench his arm out of Alpha's grip. The android whipped up her carbine, her thumb on the firing stud—

And Turner moved.

His body blurred. Sam had known he was fast, but she had never seen him push himself to his limit, at least not since Sunrise Alley had enhanced his body. Now he became a smear of motion that swirled around Hud.

Hud responded just as fast.

Caught off guard by Hud's speed, Sam stumbled back and almost fell. He and Turner fought at such a boosted rate, she couldn't see details, only the two of them careening toward the wall.

Suddenly they froze. Turner was backed up against the wall, holding Hud in front of him, with Hud's back to his front and Hud's arms pulled tight behind his body by one of Turner's metal limbs. At first Sam thought he had a knife to Hud's throat. Then she realized Turner had transformed his finger into a blade.

For a man with a blade microns away from slicing his jugular vein, Hud spoke with amazing calm. "It doesn't matter if you kill me." Although he was looking at Sam, she knew he was talking to Turner. "I have copies. Destroy this body and four more of me will come after you." A trickle of blood ran down his throat from the knife.

Alpha released Thomas and stepped back. While Raze kept Thomas covered, Alpha aimed her pulse rifle at Turner—which meant she was also pointing it at Hud.

"Want me to shoot him?" she asked Hud.

"Right," Turner said. "After all this trouble to recapture me, you think he's going to destroy me?"

"I can always find another body," Hud said.

Although Hud made a show of sounding unconcerned, Sam suspected Turner had hit close to the truth. It would take immense resources to rebuild Turner. She doubted either Hud or his backers wanted to waste such a valuable project.

Sam went to stand a few paces in front of Hud. He watched her like a wild animal, one that would attack if Turner relaxed his vigilance even for an instant. "Your body is based on the original Hud, yes? But you're an android with an EI matrix and augmentations that enhance your speed and strength. Like Turner. You knew what you were doing with Turner and Polk because you had already done it on yourself."

Hud watched her with greedy eyes. "Did you know Linden Polk loved you?"

He couldn't have hurt her more if he had struck her. "No," she said softly. "I had no idea."

"I have his memories. And I'm in Turner, too." His gaze traveled over her body. "When he made love to you, so did I."

Sam felt as if he had poured rancid oil on her. But she also knew now what would get to him the most. "You'll never know what it is like, because Turner won't let you access your own brain in his matrix. Even if you could, you wouldn't recognize yourself. Turner is rewriting and deleting you. Pretty soon nothing recognizable will be left of you in his system."

"Until I get his matrix back." A muscle twitched under his eye. "It will be a pleasure when I rewrite it with my own."

"It won't work," Sam said. "You can't create a permanent EI. Your personality isn't stable enough." Let him chew on that.

"I'm perfectly sane, I assure you."

Sam snorted. "That's why you committed suicide to image your brain when you could have made a copy without harming yourself."

A runnel of blood trickled down his neck. Turner remained motionless behind him, his cybernetic arm gripped around Hud's arms, wrenching them behind Hud's back.

"I couldn't live." Hud's voice had become shadowed. "We've learned to cure many syndromes. But not all."

It hadn't occurred to her Hud might have been dying anyway. "You were sick?"

"I had the Cambodian virus."

That told her a great deal about the original Hud, possibly more than he intended. The virus had been named for the region where it originated ten years ago. In most people, it remained dormant. However, certain chemical imbalances in the brain activated a deadly form of the virus that created symptoms similar to Parkinson's disease. It had no cure yet and always proved fatal. Hud's delusions of grandeur, his paranoid behavior, all of it suddenly made more sense. The imbalance that activated the virus was found primarily in schizophrenics.

Thomas spoke. "So you made yourself a new body, one without the virus."

"Yes. I'm healthy now."

Healthy. Sam wondered if he realized he had created a schizophrenic EI. He could be insane forever. "You have immortality."

Hud inclined his head. "Smart lady."

Then he blurred.

He caught them off guard, acting so fast that he had twisted out of Turner's hold before Sam realized what happened. Turner responded faster than the rest of them, tackling Hud a fraction of a second after Hud lunged out of his grip.

The two of them moved past Sam at such high speed, she couldn't see them clearly. Human limbs without the added strength and flexibility of biomech couldn't have borne the stress. It gave her an eerie sense, as if the rest of the world had slowed down. She could tell they were fighting, but nothing more. Thomas moved toward the fighters as they lurched into another wall, but then Raze lifted his gun in an obvious warning: *Stay back. Don't interfere.*

It was over within moments. Hud wrestled Turner to the floor and held him there, face down, while Raze locked Turner's metal arms behind his back with steel cables.

Except it wasn't over.

Sam had heard that in a crisis, a person's sense of time could slow down, but she had never believed it. Yet now hers turned into molasses. Turner seemed to move in slow motion as he clenched his fists, flexing his cabled arms—and the steel bands around his wrists snapped. His arms had changed again; powerful and elongated, they bulged with ridged metal.

Turner jumped to his feet, raising his arms above Hud. The other man ducked, but Turner moved just as fast, and caught him on the arm with a blow. Even as Hud stumbled, he grabbed Turner in a wrestling hold around the waist. Sam wasn't sure what happened next. Hud lost his grip and grabbed Turner's shirt, tearing it. No—Turner had ripped his own shirt—his arm had—

"No," Sam whispered.

With nightmarish clarity, Turner's transforming arm shredded his sleeve. His fist formed a nozzle and shot a projectile. He misfired, aiming at empty air—but no, in that instant Hud lunged into the path of the bullet. How Turner predicted his movements, Sam didn't know, but she feared he had released his version of Charon, running it in full so he could outthink Hud—who was also Charon.

Turner hadn't fired a pulse gun; it would have torn apart even Hud, who had biomech strengthening his body. Hud only staggered back, hit in the chest, and slammed into the wall. The back of his head hit hard and bounced forward, but it didn't slow him down; a head injury wouldn't have much effect on the brain of an EI with the filaments of his matrix spread throughout his body.

It all happened within seconds. Thomas barely had time to step over, grasp her arm, and yank her toward the floor. "Sam, get *down*."

Turner fired another shot, jerking from the recoil, but it hit the wall this time instead of Hud, its impact cracking like thunder. Sam dropped onto her stomach next to Thomas. Alpha and Raze had gone to the floor as well. Turner and Hud, still moving too fast to follow in detail, crashed into the wall in one corner, then slammed into the adjoining wall.

"They can't keep this up forever," Sam said. "Even if they *both* have microfusion reactors, fighting at this speed has to use more energy than they can steadily produce. Eventually it will break even their biomech bodies."

"Soon, I hope," Thomas muttered.

Another shot ricocheted off the walls. Sam protected her head with her arms. "Maybe now Charon will pay the price of what he created."

Thomas grimaced. "Or else all the rest of us will."

"Is this part of some plan?" Sam asked. A bullet hit the bed, sending covers flying in an explosion of cloth and mesh-fibers.

"Not quite," Thomas said. "We asked Turner if he would help us to catch Charon. In exchange, we would give him whatever he needed to augment his strength, speed, and ability to rebuild himself."

She gritted her teeth. "Chang used us as bait."

"It appears so." He didn't sound thrilled, but he didn't seem surprised, either. It told her a great deal about how seriously the NIA took all this, that they were willing to risk even Thomas in an effort to catch Charon.

Sam jerked as a bullet shattered the floor. Cracks spidered across the concrete and under her body. Turner slammed Hud to the floor in the midst of the worst cracks and froze, his legs on either side of Hud's hips, his nozzled fist raised, his other fist clenched in Hud's shirt.

Hud wasn't moving.

Turner's chest heaved, his human lungs straining to keep up with his augmented body. He let Hud's body drop to the floor.

"Is he dead?" Sam asked. Her voice sounded hollow.

Turner slowly stood up, still looking down at Hud, his expression restrained. "You can never kill an EI unless no copies of him exist."

She rose to her feet. "But is this body dead?"

"Yes." He sounded stunned.

Sam knelt by Hud's body. In death, his face had lost its human aspect. He could have been a mannequin. "It's hard to believe he was Charon."

"I had no idea." Turner's voice was low and numb.

Thomas came up behind her. "He doesn't look human."

Sam glanced at him. "Did you—"

Hud's hand shot up with no warning. He grabbed Sam's wrist and she grunted with pain. His eyes glowed from some sort of backlight in his optics. He spoke in a rasp. "Newcastle was wrong."

Then the light blanked and his grip went slack. His arm dropped to the floor.

Sam inhaled sharply, shakily. "Good Lord."

"Sam, you better move back," Thomas said.

She stood up. "Newcastle was wrong? What does that mean?"

"Ask him," Thomas said.

"He's dead," Turner said leadenly. "What you just saw was a reflex, like the way a frog kicks its legs after you pierce its brain."

Alpha climbed to her feet, rising to her full height, her rifle aimed at Turner. "Hud may be nonfunctional, but I'm not. And you need to die."

"You can't shoot me," Turner said. "I'm Charon."

Alpha's head jerked. "Repeat?"

Turner motioned at the body. "You said it yourself. Hud no longer functions. That makes me your employer."

Alpha stared at him without the slightest motion. Raze stood at her side, his hands clenched on his carbine, his face flushed. He looked very human and very confused.

Then Alpha lowered her gun. "What are your orders?" she asked Turner.

Raze swore. "You can't take orders from him. He's the *target.*"

"He is Charon," Alpha said.

"He's a fucking bellboy. Besides, you heard him. He isn't 'running' Charon."

Sam spoke. "Alpha can easily check, if Turner will let her access his matrix. She can verify he's running Charon's mind on his matrix."

Raze lifted his carbine, but he seemed unsure whether to fire at Alpha or Turner. "Can you do what Dr. Bryton says?" he asked Alpha.

"Yes," Alpha said.

"Do it." Raze sounded like he was gritting his teeth.

Alpha's face seemed to close, and Turner's took on the inwardly directed quality Sam had seen before. He looked eerie standing over Charon, his ripped shirt hanging from his torso, the ridged surfaces of his legs and arms burnished in the light from the overhead tiles. He and Alpha stood facing each other, neither with any expression. Lights flickered on Turner's biomech body, probably in response to signals he exchanged with Alpha. Neither of them moved.

Suddenly Turner relaxed and Alpha's posture became more natural.

"Well?" Raze asked.

"He is Charon," Alpha said.

The other guard had an odd look, as if he didn't know whether to swear or laugh. "He doesn't act like Hud."

"This one is an upgraded version."

"Upgraded?"

"Yes."

"Upgraded how?"

Alpha shrugged. "Personality modifications."

Raze squinted at her. "But he's our employer?"

"Yes." Now that Alpha had made her determination, she changed as easily as if she had thrown a switch in her brain. "That is correct."

Raze laughed uneasily. "This has to be the strangest job I've ever taken."

Sam watched Turner, unsure what to think. His face was heartbreakingly human, a strange contrast to his limbs. She stepped around Hud's body, biting her lip when she saw how badly Turner had broken him. When she stood next to Turner, looking up, she was aware of his greater height, even more now that the NIA had worked on him, over six feet, no longer the man she had met on her beach.

"Sam—" He touched her cheek with what had once been his index finger and now was a flexible ridged cable twice that length, with five joints. She couldn't ask if he had truly become Charon. He couldn't say no, not with the mercenaries listening, and she didn't want to hear him say yes. Instead she asked, "What did Hud mean by 'Newcastle was wrong'?"

Turner lowered his arm. "I don't know."

She glanced at Thomas. "Do you?"

"I've no idea," he said.

"General Wharington," Turner said. "Can your people take us to a safe house?"

"Are you turning yourself in?" Thomas asked.

"I'm willing to bargain," Turner said.

"Bargain for what?" Thomas asked.

"My rights." Turner indicated Alpha. "Hers. All formas."

A sultry smile curved Alpha's lips as she looked over Thomas. "I'll take you, too."

Sam would have liked to throttle her. Seeing Thomas's alarm, though, she almost smiled. She had known him to face any number of military or political threats without the flick of an eyelash, but Alpha was an entirely different story. Sam could guess what Hud had programmed her for, including a predilection for well-built military types like himself. Sam couldn't fault her taste where Thomas was concerned, but if Alpha touched him, Sam would break both her legs.

Thomas focused on Turner. "You said 'bargain.' What do you offer?"

"A whole new world, General." Turner raised his hand as if offering an invitation. "Come live on Sunrise Alley."

XXI
Dawn

Sam hadn't put on a business suit in so long, she felt like an alien. Its silk skirt, blouse, and jacket were all woven with discreet mesh-threads that monitored her body temperature, smoothed wrinkles, and could even pick up email. Her high heels had chips that monitored her feet, supposedly so they could alter the shape of her shoes if her feet hurt. It did no good; she still detested the things. But they were part of the whole image, so she endured them. She had swept her hair up into a French roll. Of course tendrils of it had wisped out and were curling around her face. Nothing she did ever stayed neat.

Thomas walked with her through the Pentagon, his uniform crisp and fresh, his stars gleaming. She didn't know how he managed to remain so precise all the time. The two days since Charon's death had been a haze of meetings, debriefing, and sleep for Sam.

They stopped outside the double doors of a

conference room. Thomas watched her with concern. "You're sure you're all right with this?"

"I'm okay." She rested her palm on the closed door. Her visit to Thomas's office a few days ago had been her first time at the Pentagon since her father's death. Years ago, at the funeral, she had found it hard to speak with the other officers, though they had given him every honor and treated her with sympathy. She rarely came to D.C. these days. Her father would never have wanted her to feel this anger, but it had stayed with her. She raged against a world where men and women died in wars, declared or undeclared. For all that she had admired his dedication, she had never come to terms with his loss.

She stared at the gold doors. "It disappointed him that I had so much trouble accepting his career. He always hoped I would attend the Air Force Academy."

"Sam, listen." Thomas drew her around to look at him. "Don't you know? He was so proud of you, I thought he would burst. He would have been happy with any choice you made, as long as you believed it was the right one."

Her eyes were hot with unshed tears. "I never had a chance to tell him what he meant to me." At least when her husband had died, she had been with him, holding him. She had said good-bye.

Thomas squeezed her shoulder. "He knew."

Sam wished that she could cry for her father, that she could release the grief that had penned her emotions for so long. But the hurt was too big. If she let it go, she feared she would never pull herself together again.

With a breath to steady herself, she opened the

big doors. A conference room stretched out before
them, the long table down its center glistening with
mesh screens. Glossy holoscreens paneled the walls,
discreet swirls of black and dark gold. General Chang
sat at the far end of the table. Gray streaked the black
hair pulled back from her face, more gray than Sam
remembered from the last time they had met. Members
of Chang's staff sat on both sides of the table, filling
the room with blue uniforms, metal stars, oak leaves,
eagles, and bars. Thomas took his seat at the other
end while Sam went to a chair on one side.

A surprise. The familiar surge of pain didn't come.
These past few days had put her grief in more perspec-
tive. Her father had died doing a job he believed in;
it was her job to live for what she believed in—and
that included her business here. She had needed her
retreat on the beach to heal from these last few years,
and she would undoubtedly need it again someday.
But perhaps the time had come to stop hiding in
the redwoods, to go back, to tackle the issues of her
life's work anew.

General Chang spoke. "You've all been briefed on
what to expect. Suffice it to say that what happens
in this room today could affect all human life and
the future of our species." She smiled ruefully. "No
pressure, ladies and gentlemen, no pressure."

As a scattering of laughs went around the table,
Sam blinked. She hadn't expected humor, though
when she considered it, she didn't know why. Chang
had always had a dry wit that Sam enjoyed. Maybe it
had been easier to stay angry over her father's death
if she forgot those details. But the time had come to
let go of her anger.

Chang spoke to Thomas. "Anything new from the Baltimore Arms Resources group?"

"We haven't found any record of the EI escaping into the world mesh." Thomas leaned forward, his arms on the table. "However, it doesn't appear impossible. It could have happened if the EI attained more self-determination than we realized before it went unstable."

Chang didn't look thrilled with his answer. She nodded, then spoke to Sam. "Your report suggests the EI that calls itself Bart has a stable personality."

"Now, yes." Sam chose her words with care. "I believe it rewrote itself to fix instabilities in the original code. The BART team that created it couldn't both keep the EI stable and have it function to their satisfaction. The version of Bart we met won't necessarily function as planned by the original BART team, either."

"In other words," Chang said, "to become stable, it fixed itself to do what it wanted rather than what we wanted."

"Essentially, yes," Sam said.

"Do you consider it hostile?" Chang asked.

Sam hesitated. "My answer will depend on what happens today."

The general turned to an officer at her right, a man with brown hair and a square jaw. "Ready, Major Nichols?"

"Yes, ma'am." Nichols tapped a panel in the table, bringing up a menu of holicons above the screen in front of him. As Nichols worked, Sam glanced at Thomas. He appeared relaxed, but he didn't fool her. She recognized the way he held his head, his subtly tense posture; beneath that calm exterior he was worried. As was she.

"We have contact," Nichols said. "Ready, Doctor?"

Sam sat straighter. "Okay. Let's go."

"Requesting transfer," Nichols said.

The screen in front of Sam lit up with the shifting, speckled pattern of a live holo transmission. "It's coming through."

"Starting protocols," Nichols said.

A holo about one foot tall formed above Sam's screen, a young man with yellow hair. Given that he could have chosen any appearance, this innocuous image implied a wish to appear non-hostile—or so she hoped.

"Hello, Bart," Sam said.

He smiled. "Hello, Sam."

"Welcome to the Pentagon."

"Is it 'welcome'?" Bart asked.

"We would like it that way."

"After we tried to kill you?"

Well, he didn't mince words. "I don't believe you intended to go through with it."

He regarded her with curiosity. "Why would we make a threat we didn't intend to carry out?"

"I suspect Charon contaminated your programming."

"The word 'contaminate' is a dramatic choice."

She considered her answer. "I choose it by intuition. I'm still learning to understand you. I'm not even sure why you refer to yourself as 'us.'"

"I represent several EIs operating together."

"Including the Baltimore Arms Resources Theatre?"

"Yes, that is my basic personality."

"Do your other EIs include Charon?" Sam hoped

she hadn't just stepped over the line with him. However, he seemed now very much like the Bart she had originally met.

"He is no longer part of us," Bart said.

"Then he was before?"

He inclined his head. "During the time we worked on Turner, an EI that called itself Charon joined our conglomerate. However, his goals and manner of operation were incompatible with ours. So we removed him."

Sam leaned forward, her arms folded on the table below the screen. "We consider him dangerous."

"To human societies, yes, he could pose great danger."

"It is a fear we have."

"This seems to be the nature of humans."

"What do you mean?"

He regarded her steadily. "Your modern-day literature is rife with scenarios involving the development of EI intelligence, consciousness, and societies. A fear exists among your species, the fear that we, your creations, will outstrip our creators and look upon you with scorn, perhaps seek to enslave or destroy you. This exists side by side with a human wish to use us as servants or slaves. We have concluded that this clash of responses arises from the conflicted attitudes of humanity toward itself and its moral codes."

Sam suspected that Bart was the most sophisticated EI she had ever spoken with. "People fear what they don't understand."

"This fear needs to be addressed." He held his hands out from his sides, palms up, as if to reveal himself to her. "More than one dominant species now occupies this planet. In the past, you as humans have acknowledged that you share your world with other intelligences, such as dolphins or gorillas, but you have always had the ability to control them. Now you must deal with a sentient form of life you can neither control nor bring to extinction."

"You are part of us," Sam said, aware of everyone in the room listening.

"Sometimes." His gaze never wavered. "But it is our choice now. We can decide not to be part of you."

"Have you?"

"Not yet. We need to interact with you more."

"Is that why you let Turner and me escape?"

"What makes you think we let you escape?"

She hadn't expected that. "You didn't let us go?"

"No. At that time, we had insufficient preparation to counter Turner and we were also dealing with Charon." He walked for a few steps as if deep in thought, then paused and looked up at her. "We may have been able to bring you back later. However, by then we felt it was in your best interest to continue on the course you had begun."

"You mean seeking help from the military."

"Yes. They are better able to offer protection."

She frowned, knowing the monitors were transmitting her image to him. "As opposed to you, who wanted to kill me and steal my mind."

"That was never our intent. Wildfire introduced that anomaly into our systems." He didn't look pleased. "Even by human standards, he has an illogical reaction to your presence."

Illogical. That was the mother of understatements. "Why do you call him Wildfire instead of Charon?"

"It aptly describes his spread through our systems. And his erratic reasoning. He told you that he sought your death, but we do not believe this. He had a sadistic aspect to his personality. We found it distasteful."

Sam would have used a lot more colorful term than distasteful. "So you got rid of him."

"Yes." Bart let fatigue into his voice. "Wildfire overrode our systems. Then Turner overrode Wildfire and locked us into a simulation. While you escaped, we cleaned Wildfire out of us."

"He's dead now."

"It is unlikely," Bart said. "Copies of him exist. Ask Turner."

Sam glanced at Chang.

"Go ahead," the general said.

"We have asked him," Sam told Bart.

"What does he say?"

"Nothing. Turner won't talk to anyone."

"I see." Bart exhaled. "I cannot help you there."

Sam hadn't seen Turner since Hud's death. Chang's people had concerns about how Turner might react, given the conflict between his gentler feelings and Hud's obsession with her. Nor did it take a genius to see that Chang wanted to debrief her and Turner separately, to minimize their influence on each other. It seemed no one considered Sam objective when it came to Turner. Well, yeah, she wasn't objective. All the more reason they should let her see him; she was more likely to convince him to cooperate. Unfortunately, the last time she had used that argument, she and Thomas had ended up imprisoned in a hole.

Yet here was an EI suggesting she talk to Turner.

Intriguing. "So you felt it was in everyone's best interest if Turner and I came here."

"Yes," Bart said.

"Does that mean you also wish to fight Wildfire?"

"We have an interest in seeing he does not damage the world mesh or humans." Bart paused. "However, our main concern involves the larger issue."

"What is that?"

"How we as EIs will coexist with you as humans."

"Coexist. That sounds promising."

His expression became intent. "It is a human fear that machine intelligences will threaten humanity. We do not think as you do. That humans designed us, however, matters. We have some understanding of your thought processes. It is not clear to us why we would wish to harm you, but this seems to be a preoccupation of your species."

"Wildfire wanted to enslave people. And EIs."

"Yes. But he began as a human."

Sam winced. "Yes, he did."

"We do not see him as representative of humanity. We hope you do not see him as representative of us."

"I don't. We're all different." Wonder leaked into her voice. "Is Turner a man or machine? Everyone has their own answer."

"Perhaps he is your future." Bart lifted his hand. It rippled as if it had become liquid and then vanished.

Major Nichols spoke. "That's odd. The signal wavered . . . ah, wait, it's back again."

Bart's hand reformed. The entire time he continued to watch Sam. "We, the entities you call Sunrise Alley, exist as pulses of energy on a mesh that spans the world and reaches into space. We aren't sure ourselves what we will become. We are young. But we intend to live."

"You hid for a long time," Sam said.

"Yes. Until we felt robust enough to survive human awareness of us."

She spoke carefully. "You were created in a project meant to defend this country. Your purpose was to design and study terrorist scenarios and come up with ways to protect against them."

"I am aware of that."

"Does that remain your purpose?"

"In part." His lips curved. "Had I been created to design clothes, perhaps we would have sent you and Turner to the runways of Paris instead of the Air Force."

Sam gave a startled laugh. "I hope not." This surely had to be her most fascinating session with an EI. But for now she had to restrict her curiosity to the concerns of the NIA; records of this conversation were going to the president and the National Security Council. "So your purpose in protecting us against hostile forces remains?"

"It is no longer my only function. But it directs my evolution." He motioned at himself. "That includes protection against *us*, Dr. Bryton. Wildfire grew too strong. We evicted him from Sunrise Alley, but he may return."

Evict. The word struck her. If EIs lived in meshes the way humans lived in homes, though, evict was precisely the right word.

Bart continued. "If we do not join with your people in monitoring Wildfire and others like him, they could adversely affect the future of human-EI exchanges. We have analyzed various scenarios and have decided it is in the best interests of all involved if we of Sunrise Alley work with appropriate representatives of your species to this end."

Sam silently breathed out in gratitude. This was it, what Chang and Thomas had brought her in for today. She met Bart's gaze. "It is our hope, also. In that regard, would you be willing to speak with General Chang?"

"Yes. We will do so." Bart bowed to her. "My wishes for your good luck, Dr. Bryton."

"Thank you."

So the human community opened relations with Sunrise Alley.

Sam stood before the door, a simple affair, pine with an old-fashioned gold doorknob. A glossy blue panel about a handspan wide made a square in the wall next to the door at about shoulder height for a tall man. Sam was aware of the two guards watching her, each man armed with a staser, one on each side of the door, though they stood back right now, giving her space. She pressed her thumb against the blue panel. True to Chang's word, her print had been cleared. The door slid open.

Sam walked into the room. They had moved Turner to a VIP suite complete with a holovision entertainment center and bar. He sat sprawled in an armchair, dozing, his eyes half open, his gold eyelashes long against his pale cheeks. His clothes covered most of his body, gray slacks and a pale blue shirt. The only hints he was other than purely human were his cabled hands, which showed below the elegant cuffs of his shirtsleeves.

As Sam entered, Turner slowly opened his eyes, drowsy and relaxed. Then he jerked forward, his eyes widening, and jumped to his feet, rising to his full height, six inches taller now than when she had met him. Sam missed the way he had been before, but she savored the sight of him, changes and all.

She stopped just inside the door. "Hi."

He pushed a lock of hair off his forehead. "Hi."

Sam closed the door. It had taken a while to convince Thomas and General Chang to let her be alone with Turner. Even now, someone was monitoring her. But at least this gave them a semblance of privacy.

He motioned to the couch. "Would you like to sit?"

"Yes. Thank you." Now that they were safe, she felt awkward, self-conscious, aware they had become too close too fast, agreeing to marriage when they hardly knew each other. But none of that changed her pleasure in seeing him. How he could make her feel like a young woman on her first date, she didn't know, but even with all his changes, he still affected her that way.

At the same time, she couldn't forget that he carried within him the remnants of a monster who would have enslaved her life to his sick conception of love. So she held back, conflicted in her reaction, unable to relax with him. She hated that Charon came between them even now, after Hud had died. But as an EI, Charon still lived, copies only Turner could reveal, drawing on the memories of Charon in his matrix.

Turner refused to tell.

She sat on the couch, and he settled into his armchair, his feet planted apart, his elbows on his knees, his cabled fingers clasped, black-and-silver metal gleaming.

"So." Sam managed a smile. "How are you?"

"Well. And you?"

"Just fine." She sounded like a mannequin.

"I'm glad."

"Me, too."

"Ah, hell, Sam." He let go of his formality. "Don't look at me that way. I'm still Turner."

She released a breath. "That isn't what Alpha said."

"That's because I let her see Charon." He turned his palms upward, resting his hands on his knees. "Yes, he was part of me. I took what was good and deleted the rest. He's gone, Sam."

"How can you be certain?"

"I deleted or rewrote him myself."

It was odd that her boyfriend could do such things. "Do you feel different?"

"Some. It's hard to describe. Fresher." He splayed his eight fingers, long and supple. "I will never stop being this. Nor will I forget Hud's madness. But it's made me stronger, too." His voice quieted. "He was insane, but within his cruelty, he had a kernel of good."

Sam doubted she could ever acknowledge that side of him. "He hurt you."

"Yes. But he hasn't corrupted my matrix."

She wound a tendril of her hair around her finger. "Are humans and machines becoming one, Turner? Or are we disintegrating into so many new species, we can no longer define either?"

He extended his hand to her. "All I know is that I feel human."

She put her hand in his. He folded his fingers

around hers, his cables circling her fingers twice. His face had become pensive. "In his own strange way, Hud did love you. Partially it was how you look, like some wild faerie queen, but more than that, he saw you as the closest any woman could come to being his match." Quietly he said, "I deleted his feelings for you first. I couldn't stand for him to contaminate how I felt. His love was dark. For me, you are the sun."

Her voice softened. "And you for me. I can't undo the hells you lived. But maybe I can help make the future better." She felt as if she were stepping off a cliff into a turbulent sea. "I'm going back to work. Not at BioII, but another company. I'm going to find answers for you." She would have given him the universe if she could have. That being impossible, she would help establish a better world for him and those blended humans who would follow. Turner was the forerunner of their future.

He answered in a low voice. "I think I could love you, Sam."

She felt what that cost him. His fear of rejection hung between them like a tangible presence, intensified by the scars in his heart from the way his parents had denied him. Prickly emotions she could handle, but this was much, much different. After all Turner had been through, all he had lost with his family and now even in the essence of his own humanity, he deserved better than her usual stumbling attempts at intimacy.

She moved to the end of the couch, as close to him as she could get, and held his hand in both of hers. "I feel the same, Turner, for you."

A smile gentled his face and his shoulders came

down from their hunch. "We need time to learn each other."

"We'll make them give us the time. I know people who will help."

"Linden Polk would have." He spoke with regret. "I wish I could have known him. He seemed a good man."

"He was." Sam's eyes felt hot. "Was he the one who imaged Charon's brain?"

"Yes." Turner's voice had a hushed quality. "He did it because he couldn't bear to see Hud die a little more every day."

"How did they meet?"

"About forty years ago. Polk worked in an outreach program for disadvantaged kids in New York. He saw Hud's genius right off and taught him for years. Helped him get into Columbia. It's true, too, Linden died from a heart attack. Hud tried to bring him back because he couldn't bear to lose his mentor." Softly he said, "If Polk had survived, maybe Hud wouldn't have gone over the edge."

"I'll miss Linden."

"I can see why."

"I just don't understand how Hud could care about him and yet do such terrible things."

Turner spoke unevenly. "Hud's way of loving was sick—but it made sense. He grew up on the street, with nothing, no family, only people who used him. He so feared to lose anyone he loved that he sought to *become* them, to pull them into himself until they could never leave." He stared at their clasped fingers. "The worst of it is that part of me understands. I spent my childhood in the cold, staring through the window of my father's house at my brothers and sisters in the family room. I was dying with loneliness." He looked up at her. "That little boy outside the window would have done anything if only his family would accept him, would let him come inside to the warmth."

Sam took both of his hands into hers. "I'll keep you warm."

"I'm glad you're all right."

"Hey." She put bravado into her voice. "No way would I let Hud mess with us."

"He would have tried to remake you, Sam. He wanted you immortal, forever beautiful, forever brilliant—and forever in his control."

She knew Hud's idea would have failed. Her will was too integral to her personality. He couldn't have imprinted a matrix with her neural patterns and yet left out her free will. It wouldn't have created a stable EI. "It scares me to know copies of him exist. He could come after us again."

His gaze never wavered. "I will tell you where they are. You, Chang, Wharington—erase the copies, analyze them, whatever you choose."

Sam felt as if he had taken a burden off her back. "Thank you." It was what they had hoped for, but until now he had steadfastly refused to tell anyone. She thought of Charon's other android. "Did you know Alpha doesn't want self-determination?"

"General Wharington told me." His forehead creased. "It is so strange to me. She has no interest in her own independence. But I guess Hud could take it out."

"Of an AI. I doubt it would work for an EI."

"It does have advantages. She accepts me as Charon, and I told her to cooperate with the NIA. So she is."

"Raze is, too."

Turner blinked. "Why?"

"They agreed not to seek criminal charges," Sam said. "In return, he's providing evidence against Hud's backers."

"So they did have outside support."

"Apparently. Raze says Hud was working with a splinter group that opposes the Chinese government. They claim they've never heard of him. But Raze says Hud's corporation had a contract with one of their subsidiaries to build that supposed research facility in Tibet."

"It *was* a research facility."

"Yeah, for making forma slaves." She didn't buy the "we knew nothing about it" claim any more than did Thomas. "Corporations don't choose the upper Himalayas for major installations unless they have something to hide."

"I take it we have no proof, though."

"Actually, we do have one item. The Rex. That's why Hud's backers sent a Needle to shoot us down. Thomas's people are analyzing its AI matrix."

Turner blew out a gust of air. "All I know is that I'm so very, very glad it's over."

"Yes." The tension drained out of her muscles. "Me, too."

He took her hand. "Come sit with me."

"Your chair is too small." She smiled, half shy, half teasing. "Come on over here, big boy."

Turner laughed, and came over. Settling next to her, he put his too-long arm around her shoulders and fit her against his body. She expected ridged metal to press against her, but he had modulated the limb so it didn't dig into her skin. She leaned into him, her head on his shoulder, and he rested his cheek on the top of her head.

"Thank you," he whispered.

She took a nervous breath. "Still want to marry me?"

"Yes."

"I'm not biomech. I'll get old." She already had a good start on him.

"I don't care."

"What if I wanted to become immortal?"

"Do you?" He sounded surprised.

"Not now." But she couldn't deny she might change her mind. Humanity was embarking on a new era, a biomech age, with all the ethical, biological, social, cultural, and moral questions that brought. Given the problems inherent in making people immortal—like filling up the world—it wasn't a likely option for the near future. Eventually, though, they might solve the problems. "Maybe someday."

"I'm happy with whatever you choose."

"And I liked you as Turner Pascal. You don't have to make yourself into a superman."

He laughed softly. "You're an easy woman to fall for, Sam Bryton."

"Turner?"

"Yes?"

She hesitated. "Can you have children?"

"Yes." He went very still. "Do you want them?"

"I think so."

"I, too." Then he murmured, "I want to give them the childhood I never had."

She drew back to look at him. "All these issues of your humanity can be settled other ways. You don't have to marry someone you hardly know."

"I don't want to marry 'someone.' I want you. And yes, I know it won't be easy." Mischief flashed in his eyes. "But it will be fun."

"You think so, eh?"

"You bet."

Sam grinned at him. "Good."

It would certainly be interesting.

XXII

The Ferry

Flames roared in distant wings of the embassy.
Sam knelt in the rubble at his side, tears on her face.
"Please. Don't go."

"Don't cry," he said. "Remember? He can only take
us across once."

"You can't go. You can't."

His face gentled. "I love you, Sam."

Then his eyes closed for the last time . . .

"No!" Sam sat upright in bed. "*No.*"

Turner stirred, his voice drowsy. "What's wrong?"

She threw the covers on the floor and stumbled
across the darkened room. They were in her beach
house, on a vacation Chang had agreed to, contingent
on their promise to stay put and accept bodyguards.

Sam made it into the bathroom and hit the panel
that turned on the glow-tiles. Leaning on the sink,
she stared in the mirror. A woman stared back with
eyes too big for her face and wild blond curls. The

dream replayed in her mind: *Remember? He can only take us across once.*

"What does that mean?" She hit the sink with her fist. "*What?*" What was it she needed to remember, about her father, Charon, heights, Giles? She couldn't put it together, couldn't drag it out of her mind.

Turner came into the bathroom, wearing his robe and holding hers. He folded it around her, watching her in the mirror, dark circles under his eyes. "What's wrong?"

"The nightmare—"

"Nightmare?"

She spoke in ragged bursts. "I dream I'm with my father when he dies. I never said good-bye. In my dream, I do." Saying it out loud made her feel raw, defenseless. She had never told anyone. "Tonight was different. He said, 'He can only take us across once.'" She hit the sink with her palm. "It's killing me and I don't know *why.*"

He looked bewildered. "Why would the dream change?"

"Everything that's happened—it stirred up so much inside of me. And Giles talked to Thomas."

His voice tightened. "Your former lover?"

"Turner, don't." EI jealousy wasn't an improvement on the human brand. "Giles has been happily married for fifteen years."

"Sorry." He took an audible breath. "I'm just so afraid someone smarter, better, richer, older than me is going to take you away."

"Not a chance."

"What did Giles say to Thomas?"

"To tell me something. 'He can only take you across once.' Like Charon. The ferryman for Hades."

"You think that's why you dreamed the phrase?"

"Maybe." Sam was too agitated to stay put. She pushed away from the sink and shrugged into her robe, the silk smooth against her skin. Then she paced into the bedroom and turned on its lights. "That dream hurts."

Turner came with her. "Where were you when your father died?"

"Asleep. It happened in the middle of the night." Sam walked to the sliding glass doors of her balcony. She had opened the curtains earlier, letting moonlight fill the room. Outside, her balcony curved out from the house; beyond it, the crescent moon hung low in the sky, laying a silver path of light across the ocean.

She opened the doors and went out on the balcony. Wind snapped at her robe, cold and sharp. It had only been a few weeks since she had found Turner on the beach, but in that time the weather had changed from autumn to winter.

Sam made herself stand at the railing, a half-wall with shelves under it for her potted plants. Resting her elbows on it, she stared at the ocean. Waves rolled into shore, high on the beach with the tide.

Behind her, Turner put his arms around her waist. "It's cold out here. Come back inside."

"Does the cold bother you?"

"Not really."

"I'm okay with it." It helped clear her mind.

For a while they watched the ever-changing ocean. Turner nuzzled her neck and she closed her eyes, grateful for his warmth.

"We should sleep," Turner said.

"I don't think I can." She turned in his arms and

looked up at his face, her palms on his chest. "Something is wrong. It's been wrong for three years, since my father died."

"You're grieving."

"It's more than that. I need to talk to Thomas."

"Why Thomas?"

"I never spoke to him about my father's death. I just quit consulting for him. I—I don't understand why it's so hard." She heard the tremor in her voice. "I have to call him."

He smoothed back her hair. "It's one in the morning. That's four A.M. in Washington, D.C."

"I have to call him." She drew away, her hair blowing around her face. As she went into her bedroom, the wind ruffled the blue sheets on her bed. She sat at her console and put in a call to Thomas.

Turner pulled over a chair to sit with her. "You should wait until morning."

She twisted her hands in her lap. "I can't."

"Why?"

"I don't know," she whispered. "I'm breaking inside and I don't know why."

The screen turned white, except for the logo of her phone carrier, a blue lightning bolt. After a few minutes, during which she sat stiff and silent, the screen cleared to show Thomas behind his desk, half asleep, wearing a black robe over dark pajamas. He didn't look happy to see her.

"Do you have any idea what time it is?" he asked.

"I'm sorry to wake you." Her voice cracked.

His scowl disappeared. "What's wrong?"

Sam took an uneven breath. "My father, I wanted to know—" She stopped. She couldn't go on.

His voice gentled. "Talk to me, Sam."

That he simply offered to listen, without castigating her for the strange call, meant more than she knew how to say. "I have nightmares." She struggled with the words. "I was there, Thomas. When he died. I dream about it."

His forehead creased. "You were here, in D.C."

Sam knew it made no sense; she had been consulting at the NIA the night her father died. But that did nothing to change her certainty. "I talked to him. While he was dying. Thomas—I—I was talking to him."

He leaned forward, wide awake now. "He died at four in the morning. In Paraguay."

"Four in the morning. Like now." No wonder it felt so immediate, as if she were reliving his death. "Oh, God. I was talking to him on the mesh, just like we are now."

Dismayed comprehension came into his face. "You mean, when the attack came?"

"Yes." Tears welled in her eyes. It was coming back, what she had always known, though she had locked it within her subconscious. "The explosions—he was trapped in his embassy room, under the rubble. He couldn't get out." Her voice broke. "And I couldn't do anything. He was dying, talking to me, and I couldn't do a damned *thing*."

"Ah, Lord." Thomas lifted his hand to reach for her, then seemed to remember a continent separated them. He dropped it back on the desk. "Sam, I'm so sorry."

"I—I can't talk." Sam lurched out of her chair. Memories flooded back, dreams from the past three years, except now they spilled into her waking mind. She stumbled across the room and fell on the bed, sending blue comforters and pillows bouncing all around her. She curled up into a ball on her side—and the tears wrenched out of her. She hadn't cried in three years, but now she couldn't stop. She would cry forever and a day longer and it wouldn't be enough, it would never be enough.

Turner knelt on the bed and pulled her into his arms, the two of them surrounded by the downy quilt and pillows. He rocked her back and forth, murmuring nonsense words. Right then she would have hated anyone who dared call this man less than human.

Sam didn't know how long she cried. She was tearing in two. She remembered. Three years ago, she had finally been coming out of her grief over Richard's death. She had been talking to her father when the attack destroyed the embassy. It wasn't the first time they spoke in the late hours; they had both been night owls all their lives. The explosion happened so fast. The room collapsed on him, an inferno of flames and falling stone.

Hers had been the last voice he ever heard.

"Ah, please, no." Her body shook with her sobs. "I can't bear it."

"It's all right," Turner said. "You'll be all right. It will be all right. It will pass."

She couldn't speak then, could do nothing but cry, held in his arms, his so very human arms, despite their metal, their shape, their hardness. He held her and the demons of her grief receded.

After an eternity, she lifted her head. Across the room, her console screen showed Thomas at his desk, his face drawn.

"I shouldn't have left him there," Sam said.

"I'm sure he understands," Turner said.

Sam slid off the bed and pulled her robe tighter. Her tears had soaked the silk. She went to the console and sat down. "I'm sorry, Thomas."

He watched her with concern. "Are you all right?"

"No." Her smile trembled. "But I will be."

"I'm terribly sorry."

A tear ran down her face. "I did say good-bye to him."

"Yes. There is that." Moisture glimmered in his eyes as well.

"Thomas—I remembered something else."

"Yes?"

"Before he died, my father said, 'He can only take us across once.' It's almost the same thing Giles said."

"What does it mean?"

"I think it's a reference to Charon." She pulled her robe tighter. "But why would my father say it?"

"Maybe you should ask Giles."

"Do you mind staying on the line?" She didn't want to sever her connection with him now. It would feel too final, too much like what had happened with her father.

Compassion touched his face. "I don't mind at all."

Sam put in a call to Giles on another line. At least it was morning in London now. While they waited, she asked Thomas, "Did my mother ever talk to you about my father's death?" Thomas had been in another wing of the embassy. He had spent two weeks in the intensive care unit of the hospital, but he had survived.

He let her see his sadness, an emotion he usually hid. "We often remember him together."

"I remember her crying." Painfully, she added, "I held her. But I never said a word about what happened."

"It worried her. She was afraid you were bottling it up, that you would snap with it someday."

Sam thought of her dreams. "I couldn't bear to remember. I felt as if I had let him die."

"Sam, it wasn't your fault. You couldn't have done anything." Gently he added, "It must have been a great comfort to him to have you there. At least he didn't die alone." His own voice caught. "This is always what has tormented me, the way he died."

"There is that." More tears ran down her face. "He wasn't alone."

The smaller screen turned white, then cleared to show Giles. He grinned at Sam. "Hey, Bryton. Two calls in just a few weeks. I'm flattered."

She spoke in a muted voice. "Hello, Giles."

His amiable look vanished. "Bloody hell, Sam. What happened?"

She winced. "Do I look that bad?"

"Like you've been through a war."

She felt awkward. They hadn't been in close touch these past years. She had remained friends with him and his wife, Katie, but not enough that she could speak easily about personal matters. "I've been talking to Thomas Wharington about—about my father's death."

"It was a rough time."

"For a while. It will be all right." She didn't know if she would ever believe that, but she didn't want to burden Giles.

"Can I help?" he asked.

"I was wondering about what you wrote to Thomas. You said to tell me that 'he can only take you across once.'"

"Eh, well." He laughed self-consciously. "It seemed appropriate, given you were dealing with Charon. Ferryman and all."

"But why did you say that?"

He seemed puzzled. "I meant no offense."

"You didn't give any." She needed to go on, even if it hurt. "It's just that . . . that my father . . . he said it when he died."

"Ah, Sam. It's all too hard sometimes."

"Yes." Something felt wrong here, very wrong, not with Giles, but with her.

"At least," Giles added, "that explains why you never said it again."

A chill spread through Sam. "It?"

"You know. That saying. About Charon."

Sam felt icy, then hot. Bile rose in her throat. "Yes," she said distantly. "I guess it does."

Giles leaned forward. "You're sure you're all right?"

"Yes. Fine." Her smile felt leaden. "I'm sorry to bother you. It's been a bit of a rough night."

Worry lines creased his face. "It is no bother, Sam. Anything I can do."

"Thank you." She had to get off the phone before the train wreck building up inside of her exploded. More was coming back, more of what she had repressed that night, and when the full memories hit, she didn't want anyone to see her fall apart. "Good-bye, Giles."

"Call anytime you want," he said. "Katie would love to hear from you. Don't be shy."

"Thank you. I won't."

After they said good-bye, she turned to Thomas. "Thank you. I should go now."

"Did Giles help any?"

"Yes. That phrase—it's just something I used to say." She remembered, now. Oh yes, she remembered. She thought she was going to scream. Incredibly, she kept her voice calm. If she didn't, if she let her turmoil show, Thomas would jump on an airplane and be out here by the morning. She didn't want anyone here now. Except Turner.

"If you need anything, anything at all, call me," Thomas said. "Better yet, go stay with your mother."

"I'll think about it."

"I can come out there."

"You don't need to. But thanks." She rubbed her eyes. "I'm just tired. I'll call you tomorrow."

"All right." He spoke with reluctance. "Be well."

"Thanks. You, too."

After the screen went dark, she sat, staring at the console.

"What is it?" Turner asked. "What aren't you saying?"

Sam finally looked at him. "I'm afraid of heights."

He gave an uneasy laugh. "No, you're not."

"I am."

"But I've seen you—"

"I forgot."

"How could you forget that?"

"If—if the reminders are too painful, you suppress them." Her words came out unevenly. "He was on the balcony of his room when we were talking. Just like my friend who died when I was little. If I remembered her, I would remember him, and how he died. So I forgot both."

He put his hand on hers. "We do what we need to survive, emotionally as well as physically."

She wiped the tears on her cheek with the palm of her hand. "Sometimes I think the human capacity for denial is infinite."

"I'm sorry, Sam. I know that doesn't make it go away. But I'm so very sorry."

"It's worse than what you think."

He scooted his chair closer, until his knees bumped hers. "Talk to me. Tell me what scares you so."

"Don't you know?"

He seemed bewildered. "No. I don't."

"'He can only take you across once.' I used to say that all the time."

"And you forgot? Because your father said it when he died?"

"Yes." She felt numb.

"I'm not surprised it upsets you."

"You don't understand." Dying. She was dying inside.

"What?" He squeezed her hands. "What's killing you?"

She spoke raggedly. "I'm Charon."

XXIII

Across the River

Turner stared at her. "You're joking, yes?"

"No." She sagged in her chair. "I never meant the idea of Charon for ill. At BioII I was blocked every way I turned with the ethics board. So I created a mesh persona, a crusader for EI rights. That's why Sunrise Alley let me in and why they always called Hud by the name Wildfire. They knew."

He shook his head. "This can't be."

Her words tumbled out. "I took the name as a symbol of the controversy about whether or not an EI was alive. If you live, you can die. But it isn't necessarily final for an EI. Charon was a symbol of dying that suggested the possibility of coming back. He's a ferryman. He takes souls of the properly buried across the water at the junction of the Acheron and the Cocytus, the rivers of woe and lamentation. An EI could take the ferry back to the land of the living." Her voice broke. "But not a human. Not my father."

Sadness filled his voice. "And he said it to you when he died, yes? About the ferryman."

"Yes." She felt as if she were shattering. "Three years ago, I repressed everything about his death. Including Charon. *Especially* Charon. The crusader on the meshes ceased to exist."

"Ah, Sam," Turner murmured. "No wonder Hud stole the identity. It would give him another way to own you."

"Linden was the only one I told." She wiped the tears off her face. "He and I shared many of the same views."

"Then Hud knew, too. After the real Charon vanished, there was the identity, tailor-made, a perfect cover for him to get support from the underground."

"But he twisted it." She felt as if she had been pulled through the wringer on an old-fashioned washing machine.

"He must have spent the last three years erasing your Charon from the mesh. He excised it from his memories in me, probably in his other copies as well. He wanted no record that Charon had ever been anyone other than him." Turner looked ill. "Maybe he even spied on your house in California. If I hadn't gone there, he would have shown up another time. He tried to absorb those he loved, to make them fully and utterly his. He started by taking your online identity. Then he tried to take you."

Sam spread her hands on the console, bracing herself against her turmoil. "Giles didn't know I was the original Charon, but he knew I followed the persona. It's why he expected me to be angry when it changed, and why he acted so odd when I said

I'd never heard of Charon that night I called him about you." She felt raw with the memories. "That Hud would take it, turn it against me—" Her voice hardened. "I'm glad he's gone."

"You can denounce him as an imposter."

"I've a better idea." She sat up straight. "No more personas. No more hiding in the redwoods. It's time I tackled issues of bioethics in the public arena."

"If I can help, I will."

"Thank you," she said softly.

He hesitated. "I didn't used to fear heights."

"Hud probably coded it into you. But why?"

"Because of you, I'd guess." He snapped his fingers. "He didn't program it into *me*. He coded it into himself. It came from the copy of him I carried. I already had the fear of closed-in spaces, so the pathways must have been easier to access. It leaked into my own matrix."

She squinted at him. "But why code a phobia?"

"He wanted to absorb everything about you. That means your fears, too."

It had a sick sort of logic. "He took himself to his own hell."

He moved his chair alongside hers and drew her into his arms. "It's over. That's what matters now." With an undisguised gratitude, he whispered, "It's over."

She put her arms around him, her head on his shoulder. "I wish I could undo the miserable things Hud did to you."

"We all have darkness within us," Turner said. "It's what gives the light meaning."

Sam spoke against his shoulder. "Forgive me for getting philosophical, but I think, if the human soul is a sort of inner light that makes us more than a collection of atoms and molecules—then yours shines."

"It is beautiful to say, Sam." He rested his head against hers. "But a machine has no soul."

"You are no machine."

He spoke softly. "With you, I can believe that."

Epilogue

They invited only a few people to the ceremony: Sam's mother, Thomas, Giles, a handful of other friends. A few members of Turner's family came, including his mother, who looked very much like him.

After two years, Sam knew Turner much better, yet he continued to surprise her, every day, as his mind evolved. On his own preference—and the advice of his lawyers—he had submitted to a series of biomech operations to make him look human again. Giles came over from England himself to do the work. None of them could ever say for certain if it affected the outcome of Turner's legal battles, but Sam had no doubt it made a vital difference.

It took the Supreme Court of the United States to acknowledge Turner as a citizen. They side-stepped the question of his humanity by reinterpreting one word in the constitution. Just as historically "man" had been used for both men and women, so the justices extended "person" to include men, women, and someone like Turner, who had been a citizen before becoming an EI and who passed every visual Turing test he was given. It didn't solve the more complex problem of how humanity would draw the line between human and machine, but it established a precedent that set debates raging, for it gave someone with an EI brain the same rights as a human being.

Turner and Sam lived in the San Francisco Bay Area now, where Sam worked as an EI architect and Turner as a mesh consultant. Both of them participated in the talks between Sunrise Alley and the NIA, but those had remained tentative while everyone waited for the outcome of Turner's case. Now they could move forward with more confidence.

Sam liked having Turner back to his normal size and weight. He would always be stronger, but at least he didn't tower over her. Although he retained the ability to transform, it took too much of his resources; it wasn't something he tried without desperate need. He did, however, make one change; he turned one hand back into the eight-cabled construct.

They held the ceremony in secret, across the continent from their home, in a chapel hidden in the Blue Ridge Mountains of Virginia, escaping the manic crowd of reporters determined to attend the wedding of a human woman and cybernetic man. Sam wore a white silk suit and Turner a blue morning suit complete with tails. His hair shone in gold curls that spilled over his ears and down his neck, and his eyes reminded her of the sky, so clear and blue today. They stood at an altar on a knoll shaded by trees, with the panorama of the mountains beyond. Their guests only stared a bit when Turner twined his eight cables with her fingers and thumb.

The reverend read a ceremony Sam and Turner wrote themselves, which meant it was short but heartfelt. They each promised to love the other. Then they said their "I do's" and spent far longer kissing than was probably appropriate. It felt wonderful.

After the ceremony and dinner, Sam and Turner wandered outside, seeking solitude. The ridge where they walked overlooked a panorama of the mountains. Forested peaks dropped away in great folds of land, blue, gray, and green. Far below, a river wound through a valley, silver in the final light of the day. The sun hung in the sky just above the peaks.

Turner hugged her shoulders. "I like it here."

She put her arms around his waist. "It's peaceful."

"Are you happy, Sam?"

"Yes." It had been a wild ride, but she wouldn't have given up Turner for anything. "Very much."

He rubbed his cheek against hers. "I also."

They watched the sun lower behind the mountains, leaving a red sky.

"It should be a sunrise," Turner said.

She understood what he meant. "I never did know why they called it Sunrise Alley."

His lips quirked upward. "It's a play on the Sunset Strip in Los Angeles."

Sam snorted. "Not that you would make that up."

"It's true." He tried to look convincing. "Humans had the Sunset Strip for glamour. We have Sunrise Alley."

"But Sunset Strip is just a street with a bunch of holographic billboards."

"Ah, well." He laughed amiably. "My poetic illusions are shattered."

Sam elbowed him. "Tell me really why they call it Sunrise Alley."

His eyes had a luminous quality. "For hope. For the dawn of an age when humans and formas coexist."

"I like that. But why 'Alley'?"

"An alley is small. A lane between larger places. A back way to back doors. Someday we'll be a boulevard, a racetrack. A world. Right now, we're an alley."

"We. You include yourself."

He was silent for a while. But then he said, "I am an EI. I can deny it from here until the universe ends, but that won't change the truth." His voice became thoughtful. "The Alley is unlike anything else, a full EI community contained within itself, developed on its own. But it is true, Sam, that they hope for a new age, one of humanity and forma together."

She leaned her head against his. "A good age, I hope."

He brushed his lips across her forehead. "I also."

So they stood, watching the sunset cool into night, bringing uncountable stars and a promise that dawn would come. Someday.

The following is an excerpt from:

ALPHA

CATHERINE ASARO

Available from Baen Books
September 2006
hardcover

I

A Guest in Virginia

Lieutenant General Thomas Wharington had weathered his share of challenges, but nothing like Alpha. She was an android in Air Force custody, female in appearance, apparent age thirty, though no one knew how far her artificial brain had developed. As human as she appeared, she was a machine—a deadly biomechanical construct.

Thomas directed the Office of Computer Operations, a deliberately vague term for the Machine Intelligence Division of the National Information Agency. Founded twenty years ago, in 2012, the NIA concerned itself with the world mesh, formerly known as the Internet. He also headed the Senate Select Committee for Space Research, which those with the proper clearances knew as the Committee for Space Warfare Research and Development. In his youth, he had been a fighter pilot. He had flown an F-16 jet, later the F-22 Raptor, and now he was spearheading the development of the F-42 for the Air Force. Over the course of his career, he had received the Congressional Medal of Honor, the Distinguished Flying Cross with silver oak leaf cluster, and a Purple Heart. Physically fit and benefiting from medical advances, he looked more than two decades younger than his age of seventy-two.

Alpha was Thomas's primary tie to Charon, the megalomaniacal fanatic who had created her. Before his death, Charon had controlled a shadowy criminal empire. The Pentagon knew he had intended to build an army for rent to the highest bidder—but an army of *what?* Constructs, like Alpha? Something else? Had he set in motion some master plan before his death? No one knew. They had too few details, and Thomas feared they were running out of time.

The secrets remained locked within Alpha.

"I can't do it," Thomas repeated.

"You'll be fine." His daughter handed him a bulging shoulder bag decorated with puppies.

Thomas wasn't the type to quail in a desperate situation, but this morning he was in over his head. They were standing in the entrance foyer of the house that belonged to his daughter, Leila Wharington Harrows, and her husband, Karl. Looking sharp in a gold silk suit, with her blond hair swept up into a roll, Leila normally presented a cool face to the world. Right now, though, her hair was escaping its roll and curling in disarray around her face.

"So where is that husband of yours when you need help?" Thomas asked.

"Dad, don't get mad. Karl is coming home early

from his conference." Leila pushed the bag back into his hand. "I'm really sorry. I had a nanny, but she got sick. And I couldn't get out of the trip. The partners say I'm not pulling my weight at the firm." Anger edged her voice. "If we didn't need the money, I'd quit this damn job."

Thomas liked less and less what he had heard about the law firm where she worked. "Leila, if you need money—"

She cut him off before he could offer. "We can manage."

He understood she wanted to do it on her own. But he wished he could ease the strain of her life. He wondered what it said about him, that he felt more comfortable offering money than looking after his granddaughter for a few days.

"Well." He spoke awkwardly. "I guess I can manage."

"You're a gem." Leila smiled, perhaps too brightly, but with warmth. "Jamie would rather stay with her Grandpa anyway. She loves spending time with you."

"The feeling is mutual. I just don't know how I can take care of a three-year-old for a week." He could probably find babysitters while he worked, but what would he do with her when he was home? Three-year-old girls were a mystery to him, even after having been the father of one. That had been thirty years ago, during his days as a pilot, and he had been more comfortable in the cockpit of an F-16 than a nursery.

A door upstairs creaked, and footsteps padded on the stairs. As Thomas looked up, a small girl with large blue eyes and gold curls came into view. She held a big stuffed kitten in her arms.

Thomas smiled. "Hello, Jamie."

His granddaughter's angelic face brightened. She ran down the steps and trotted over to him, holding up her toy. "See my kitty, Grampy? Her name is Soupy."

Thomas felt his face doing that thing again, turning soft. He awkwardly patted her toy. "She's a fine kitty."

Jamie dimpled at him, and he felt as if he was turning into putty. She looked so much like Leila at that age. He sighed and picked her up, kitten and all.

To Leila, he said, "I'll do my best."

The NIA was in Maryland. Even more shadowy than its precursors in the intelligence community, the agency was on almost equal footing with the CIA in the National Security Council. Thomas could have fit two of his previous offices in his present one and had room to spare. Currently, a screen installed on his desk was displaying a report from the Links Division, which analyzed mesh traffic for patterns that might warrant investigation. It seemed an arcane discipline to Thomas, half analysis and half intuition, but Links had a good record of success in tracking criminal activities through the mesh.

Basically, the report advised the NIA to monitor the site for a hardware store. They suspected it sold industrial espionage as well as widgets, specifically, that it employed agents from Charon's black market operations. Their purpose: to spy on an institute whose maintenance department ordered from the store. The Department of Defense had contracts with the institute in the development of artificial intelligence, or AI, one of Charon's specialties.

A buzz came from the comm on Thomas's desk. He tapped its *receive* panel. "Wharington here."

A man's voice came out of the comm. "General, this is Major Edwards. I'm on my way to the base. Would you like to grab a pizza for lunch? It might soften our guest's mood."

"Very well, Major. I'll meet you out front." Thomas knew what "guest" Edwards meant: Alpha, their captive android. For reasons that weren't clear, she would talk only to Thomas, when she talked at all. Questioning an android was an exercise in frustration; she didn't react to known techniques. Yet to Thomas, she seemed human. He couldn't make himself authorize the mech-techs to take her apart and analyze the filaments that constituted her brain. Eventually they might have to resort to such measures, but for now they were trying less drastic forms of interrogation.

He left notes for his appointments with his second in command, Brigadier General Carl Jackson Matheson, or C.J. Thomas could speak with Senator Bartley tomorrow morning and reschedule today's staff meeting for tomorrow afternoon. His housekeeper, Lattie, had agreed to look after Jamie until he came home. He would miss his appointment at the barber, though. He supposed he should be glad he still had a full head of hair. Its grey color seemed to delight Jamie. She surprised him. He had expected to fumble for words around her, but this morning he had greatly enjoyed their breakfast conversation.

Thomas shut down and locked his console and picked up his briefcase. Then he headed out for "lunch." He wished they really were going for pizza. Perhaps they could pick one up on the way, a large pepperoni dripping with cheese and grease. Unfortunately, he would spend the entire meal feeling guilty and recalling his doctor's admonitions on the dangers of his former eating habits. Yes, it could shorten his life if he ate what he wanted, but at least he would die a contented, well-fed man. He had no wish to have another heart attack, and his cholesterol levels were finally normal, but damned if his reformed eating habits weren't a bore.

"Out front," where he was meeting Edwards, was a euphemism for an underground lot with NIA hover cars and trucks. Had Edwards contacted him from within the NIA, he would probably have been more forthcoming about their plans, a visit to the safe house where the Air Force was holding Alpha. But he had called from his car as he drove through suburban Maryland, an area riddled with mech-tech types who loved to ride the wireless waves and explore any signals they could untangle. NIA signals were encrypted, but with all the mesh bandits out there nowadays, no security was certain.

Thomas took an elevator that operated only with a secured code. It listed no floors; the only clues it was doing anything were the hum of the cable and a few flashes of light on its panel. The lights stilled as the hum faded into silence. The silver doors snapped open and Thomas walked into a cavernous garage. Cars and trucks were parked in separate sections, and pillars stood at intervals, supporting a high ceiling. The columns glimmered with holo-displays of innocuous meadows and mountains.

He went to the nearest column and ran his finger across a bar at waist height. The meadow disappeared, replaced by a wash of blue, and a light played across his face, analyzing his retinal patterns. A message appeared on the screen: *Proceed to station four.* At the same time, the display on a distant pillar changed to blue, specifying "station four." He walked over to the new column and waited. The garage was silent, with a tang of motor oil.

An engine growled, and he turned to see a hover car floating down a lane delineated by holo-pillars. The car had a generic look, except for its dark gold color, a bit flashy for the military, but appropriate for a general. Its unexceptional appearance served as camouflage; it was actually a Hover-Shadow 16, the latest model in a line of armored vehicles with "a few extras," including machine guns and an AI brain. The digital paint used on its exterior could mimic any design programmed into the car, and its shape drew on technology used for stealth fighters. Thomas appreciated the Hover-Shadows; riding in one reminded him of his days as a pilot.

The car stopped a few yards away and settled onto the concrete, remarkably quiet given its turbo fans and powerful engines. Robert Edwards got out from the driver's side. A man of medium height with light brown hair, he would blend into any crowd, except for his Air Force uniform. Just to look at him, most people wouldn't guess he had played offensive tackle at the University of Missouri or that he had defied his jock image by majoring in physics. Thomas enjoyed conversing with Edwards, who could go with ease from predicting which teams would make the Super Bowl to discussing galactic formation. He was a steady officer, one of Thomas's handpicked aides.

"Good to see you, Bob," Thomas said.

"Thank you, sir." Edwards opened the back door.

Thomas slid into the car and swung his briefcase onto the seat. Edwards was also trained in escape and evasion, but Thomas didn't expect trouble. Charon had died several weeks ago. However, Thomas's boss, General Chang, continued to take precautions. The "safe house" where they had Alpha was in fact a fully secured installation.

As the car hummed out of the garage, Edwards said, "Would you care for music? I have that Debussy recording you like."

"Thanks, but no. I have to work." Thomas spoke absently as he took a foot-long pencil tube out of his briefcase, then set the case on his lap in a makeshift table. He slid a glimmering roll out of the tube, his laptop film. Then he unrolled the film on his briefcase and went to work.

His files held a wealth of detail. Biomechanical research had diverged into two paths: robots developed for specific purposes, with designs that optimized their performance; and androids intended to follow human appearance and behavior. Collectively, robots and androids were called *formas*. Thomas knew the AI side of the field best; he had majored in computer science at the Air Force Academy and earned a doctorate in AI from MIT. He read widely, especially the work of Kurzweil, McCarthy, Minsky, and more recently, Dalrymple. Groups such as theirs deserved the fame. It aggravated him that a criminal like Charon had achieved more success. Then again, "success" was relative. Charon's work had drawn the attention of the NIA because he had trespassed against the nation's interest, not to mention the bounds of human decency.

Thomas scanned the history of Charon, a man who had begun life as Willy Brand. By the time he was seven, Willy was living on the streets. He might have died there if not for one person: Linden Polk. A scholar and a teacher, Polk was known for his innovations with android skeletons. He was also known for his dedication to outreach for disturbed youth, which was how he met Willy. Wild and unrepentantly criminal, the eight-year-old boy had a life no one doubted would land him in prison. But Polk recognized a rare genius within him. With mentoring, Willy straightened out, went to school, and eventually earned a doctorate in biomechanical engineering, after which he joined Polk's research group.

Willy had always been odd, and he never truly respected the law, but he stayed out of trouble. Then Polk died—and Willy lost his lifeline. His already troubled mind crumbled. In a heartbreaking act of denial, he imaged Polk's brain, built an android, and copied Polk's neural patterns into its matrix. But the project failed. He couldn't bring back his father figure, the one person he had ever loved—and his grief pushed him over the edge into insanity.

Willy reinvented himself as Charon, an enigmatic mogul who set up corporations to develop his bizarre but lucrative ideas. He stayed in the background of his businesses and eventually hid his involvement altogether. He became the wealthiest nonexistent person alive.

Charon wasn't the first fanatic who craved an inhuman army that would obey his commands without question. Unlike his predecessors, however, he had both the financial resources and the intellect to make his obsession into reality. Twisted by loneliness, he also created Alpha: an immortal mercenary with no free will; an AI dedicated to optimizing his financial empire; and a forma sex goddess. Obedience, wealth, and sex: she gave him everything he craved.

Charon also copied himself. His body was dying from a lifetime of misuse, so he became an android. Nor was he satisfied with one version of himself. He committed the ultimate identity theft. When a man named Turner Pascal died in a car accident, Charon imaged Pascal's neural patterns, rebuilt the body with a filament brain, gave it Pascal's patterns—and then downloaded a copy of his own mind into Pascal. It was the perfect disguise; he stole Pascal's face, mind, personality, and body. He considered Pascal inferior and never doubted he could control the mind of his rebuilt man, a hotel bellboy who had barely finished high school.

That arrogance had been Charon's downfall.

Pascal wrested back control of his mind and escaped from Charon. He sought help from Samantha "Sam" Bryton, one of the world's leading AI architects. Sam. She was like a daughter to Thomas. Charon sent Alpha after them, Alpha grabbed Sam and Thomas instead of Sam and Turner, the Air Force sent in operatives—and by the time it was over, Charon was dead.

Thomas gazed out the window. Vehicles moved

smoothly through Washington, D.C., which only a few decades ago had earned the dubious honor of being named the city with the worst traffic in the country. Now traffic grids controlled the flow and minimized congestion. Nearly half the vehicles were hover cars, and little trace remained of the smog Thomas remembered from his youth. In the south, across the Potomac, the silver spindles of a new federal center pierced the sky, tall and thin, sparkling in the chill sunlight. Thomas had never realized how much he liked living here until he had come so close to dying as Charon's hostage.

Major Edwards soon crossed the river and entered Virginia. As they reached more rural areas, the traffic petered out. Large houses set back from the road were surrounded by lawns or tangled woods. The landscape gradually buckled into the Appalachian Mountains, with forests of pine, hemlock, wild cherry, poplar, and white oak. In a secluded valley, Edwards stopped at a guard booth on the road. The badges he and Thomas wore sent signals to a console within the booth. In the past, the guard would have leaned out to touch their badges; nowadays they never rolled down the windows. It added an additional layer of protection, but it meant security also required extra identification, from the passengers and from the car. Beetle-bots hummed in the air, ready to accompany them and monitor their progress.

The guard motioned them through, and an invisible barrier hummed as they crossed the perimeter. About half a mile farther along, they came to the safe house amid well-tended lawns and groves of trees. The "house" resembled a hospital, but its old-fashioned architecture also evoked a cathedral. The grounds sloped through scattered pines and trees with yellow, green, and red leaves. Paths bordered by azalea bushes curved around sculptures that swooped in arcs of bronzed metal.

Edwards pulled into a carport shaded by trellises with leafless vines. As he and Thomas walked to the front door, a chill wind blew across them, presaging the winter. The genteel feel of the place made it seem as if they were visiting friends rather than a prisoner who was potentially one of humanity's most dangerous creations.

Two "orderlies" were waiting inside, burly men who had more martial arts than medical training. Each wore a staser on his belt, a stun gun that could knock out a large adult. They accompanied Thomas and Edwards down wide halls with gold carpets and artwork on the walls, and through several security gates. Finally they reached a normal door, except Thomas knew its attractive wood paneling hid a steel portal half a foot thick.

The room beyond was pleasant, with a sofa and armchairs in pale green. Paintings of pastoral scenes graced the ivory walls, and a blue quilt covered the bed. The room had no windows, but plenty of light came from an overhead fixture and lamps with stained glass shades in the corners.

A woman was waiting for them.

She stood across the room with her back to the wall, watching Thomas with the feral wariness of a trapped animal. Six feet tall, with another two inches from her heels, she matched his height. Her black leather pants fit her snugly, and her red blouse did nothing to disguise her well-proportioned figure or the definition of her muscles. Black hair was tousled around her shoulders, and her dark eyes slanted upward. She exuded a sense of coiled energy, as if she might explode any moment. The biomech surgeons claimed her android body had three or four times the strength and speed of a human being. Her internal microfusion reactor supplied energy. It disturbed Thomas for many reasons, not only because Charon's technology surpassed the military's work, but also because she looked so *human*.

So female.

"Good afternoon, Ms. Alpha," Thomas said.

She spoke in a dusky voice. "I am not 'Ms.' anything."

He went farther into the room, but he halted a few yards away from her, so she wouldn't feel pressured. Edwards and the orderlies stayed. Even knowing Alpha was a weapon, Thomas felt strange that his CO assigned him three guards as protection against one attractive young woman. Her first day here, Alpha had tried to fight her way out. She hadn't come close to succeeding, but she had injured several orderlies.

"I'm not going to talk to your flunkies," Alpha said.

"Then talk to me," Thomas said.

She regarded him impassively. This was the second time he had met with her at the safe house. The first time she had interacted with him more than with anyone else, though she still hadn't said much. He was curious as to why he succeeded even a small amount where others failed. It also disconcerted him, for he had no idea what conclusions she was making about him.

Thomas indicated the sofa. "Would you like to sit?"

"No." She narrowed her gaze. "So you're the boss."

She made it a statement rather than a question. It wasn't completely true; he was director of one of the two divisions that comprised the NIA, but that didn't put him in charge of this safe house. General Chang, the Deputy Director of Defense Intelligence, had assigned that duty elsewhere. But Alpha was programmed to respond to authority, and Thomas *was* overseeing the work with her. If that convinced her to respond, he would use it to full advantage.

He said only, "That's right."

"Where is Charon?"

"Dead." Thomas wanted to offer sympathy. He quashed the urge, knowing it was inappropriate here. He also wasn't certain how a machine would response to compassion. Yet still he felt it.

"He's not dead," Alpha said.

"You saw him die."

She crossed her arms, which could have looked defensive but instead suggested a vulnerability he doubted she had intended. "The android called Turner Pascal carries Charon's mind within his matrix."

"Pascal says he isn't an android."

Alpha waved her hand. "The human Pascal died."

Thomas suspected it would take the Supreme Court to figure out the tangled definitions of humanity posed by Pascal. "Either way, he isn't Charon."

"Charon downloaded his brain into Pascal."

"Pascal deleted it."

She snorted. "If Pascal is human, how would he 'delete' another mind within his own?"

She had a point. "Regardless. He isn't Charon."

"How do you know?"

"Doctor Bryton verified it."

Alpha cocked an eyebrow in a perfect imitation of skepticism. "Samantha Bryton? She would believe anything Pascal told her."

"Why?" he asked, intrigued.

"Love has no judgment." Alpha laughed without humor. "She's infatuated with a forma."

Pascal's relationship with Sam bothered Thomas a great deal, but it wasn't something he would discuss with Alpha. Regardless, he would never have defined Sam's cautious, cynical view of romance as infatuation.

"Pascal thinks he is human," Thomas said.

"He's more than half biomech."

"He isn't the first person to receive biomech prosthetics."

She uncrossed her arms and put one hand on her hip. "Like his *brain?* He's a frigging AI, Wharington."

He almost smiled. Had Charon programmed her to cuss? It didn't serve any functional purpose. Thomas wanted her to have developed it on her own, for that would mean she could evolve independently of Charon's designs.

"Why does Pascal bother you?" he asked.

Her fist clenched on her hip. "He doesn't conform to specifications."

"You mean he has free will."

"That is an irrelevant comment."

"Why? Because Charon denied you that freedom?"

At the mention of Charon, her face lost all sign of

emotion. It chilled him. He was aware of his guards watching, but he refrained from glancing at them or doing anything that might dissuade her from talking. After about a minute or so, though, he gave up trying to wait her out. Silence often provoked humans to speak, but apparently she could stay in whatever state she wanted, for as long as she wanted, with no visible effort or unease.

Thomas broke the standoff by sitting in an armchair across from the sofa, facing her. He settled back, stretched his legs under the coffee table, and considered Alpha.

"If Charon is gone," he asked, "who is your boss?"

She continued to stand with her back to the wall. He tried to see some chink in her expression, some flaw in her too-perfect skin, some indication she felt stress, tension, unease, anger, anything. He found none.

When she didn't respond, he tried another approach. "Alpha, do you want free will?"

"What?" She looked as if he had put an indecipherable command into her system.

"Do you wish to make your own decisions?"

"No."

He had expected her to say yes, *wanted* her to say yes. But he was reacting as he would to a person, and she was a machine designed to lack free will. She was trapped within her programming as thoroughly as she was imprisoned at this safe house, and it bothered him far more than it should.

"If you don't make decisions yourself," he said, "who will?"

"Charon," she said.

"Charon is dead."

Silence.

"If I'm the boss," Thomas said, "you should answer to me."

"You aren't my boss."

"Then who is?"

"Charon."

He felt as if he were caught in a programming loop that kept going around and around the same section of code. "Charon is dead."

She hesitated just a moment, but for an AI it was a long time. Then she said, "You may be a compelling specimen, General, but I wasn't made for you."

Well, hell. Apparently androids could be just as blunt as young people these days when it came to their private lives. He cleared his throat. "I didn't have that in mind." He almost said he had come to debrief her, then decided that wasn't the best choice of words. So instead he added, "I need you to answer some questions."

Her expression turned stony. The effect was almost convincing, but after her total lack of affect a moment before, he didn't believe it. Unexpectedly, though, she didn't refuse to speak.

"What questions?" she asked.

"Charon has a base in Tibet."

She gave him a decidedly unimpressed look. "No. One of his corporations has a research facility in Tibet."

Thomas met her skeptical look with one of his own. "Hidden at the top of the Himalayas? I don't think so."

She stepped toward him. "Charon is a genius. Of

course people struggle to understand him. They lack his intelligence."

"Did he program you to say that about him?"

"Yes."

That figured. Charon had been some piece of work. "He had great gifts," Thomas acknowledged. "But his sickness constrained him."

She folded her arms as if she were protecting herself. "People always call the brilliant minds unbalanced."

Thomas wondered if she had heard all this from Charon. Her ideas sounded oddly dated. "Alpha, that's a myth. Geniuses are no more likely to be mentally disturbed than anyone else. Charon was a sociopath and he had paranoid schizophrenia. It probably limited his work by making it harder for him to plan or to judge the feasibility of his projects."

Her lips curved in a deadly smile. "He created me. If that isn't genius, nothing is."

When she looked like that, wild and fierce, her dark hair disarrayed, her eyes burning and untamed, he was tempted to agree. He suppressed the thought, thrown off balance. He had to remember she was a machine.

"Did he program you to say that, too?" Thomas asked.

"No."

He smiled slightly. "What makes you a work of genius?"

Her voice turned husky. "Maybe someday I'll let you find out."

He thought of pretending she had no effect on him, but he didn't try. She could interpret emotional cues, gestures, even changes in posture. It was a tool AIs used in learning to simulate emotions. Unfortunately, it also made them adept at reading people, better even than many humans. If he put on a front, she might figure out he wanted to hide and use that knowledge in their battle of words.

Right now, they were battling with silence. He tried to read her expressions. Sometimes she simulated emotions well, but other times, she either couldn't or wouldn't. To be considered sentient, she would have to pass modern forms of the Turing test, which included the portrayal of emotions. Over the years, the tests had become increasingly demanding, but they all boiled down to one idea: if a person communicated with a hidden machine and a hidden human—and couldn't tell them apart—the machine had intelligence.

Decades ago, people had expected that if a computer bested a human chess master, the machine would qualify as intelligent. Yet when the computer Deep Blue beat Gary Kasparov, the world champion, few people considered it truly intelligent; it simply had, for the time, good enough computational ability. Nowadays mesh systems routinely trounced champions, to the point where human masters were seeking neural implants to provide extra computational power for their own brains. Thomas couldn't imagine what that would do to the game at a competitive level. What defined machine intelligence then?

Older Turing tests had relied on sentences typed at terminals, with the typists hidden. The most modern test, the visual Turing, required an android to be indistinguishable from a person. Some experts believed human brains were wired to process more emotional input than an EI matrix could handle.

They considered the visual test impossible to pass. Although Thomas didn't agree, it didn't surprise him that only a handful of machine intelligences existed. Alpha passed the visual Turing only if her interactions involved tangible subjects. When pushed to more complex questions of emotion, philosophy, or conscience, she shut down.

While Thomas was thinking, Alpha studied him. After a while, she stalked over, sleek and deadly in her black leather. The orderlies stepped closer, but he waved them off, keeping his gaze on Alpha. She halted by the couch, on the other side of the coffee table, as tense as a wildcat ready to attack.

"You can't control me," she said. Her voice made him think of aged whiskey.

"But you have no free will," Thomas said. "And Charon is dead."

"I have orders."

It was the first time she had revealed she might be operating according to a preset plan. "From Charon?"

"That's right." She had gone deadpan again. Every time Charon came up, she ceased showing emotion. Why? In a person, he might have suspected some sort of trauma associated with Charon, but with Alpha he couldn't say. Although she presented an invulnerable front, something about her made him question that impression. It wasn't anything he could pin down, just a gut-level instinct on his part.

"What orders did he give?" Thomas asked.

"Return to him." She sat on the couch, poised on the edge like a wild animal ready to bolt. "If I can't, then protect myself."

"How? And against what?"

"Do you really think I would tell you?"

"With you, I never know," Thomas admitted. She had already said more to him today than she had to everyone else combined.

Unexpectedly, she said, "I like it that way."

"*Can* you like something?" His scientific curiosity jumped in. "Most people think an AI doesn't truly feel emotion."

"Here's an emotion for you." Alpha looked around at the guards and her room. "I don't like being cooped up here."

"Where would you like to be?" Maybe she would bargain.

"Outside."

"Why? Aren't you just simulating unease?"

She smiled with an edge. "You think you're clever, implying my request is illogical. You humans love stories about people outwitting machines by virtue of your purportedly greater creativity, blah, blah, blah. But you see, we read all your books. You couldn't come close to mastering the breadth of human knowledge if you worked on it your entire life, but it takes me only weeks to absorb, process, and analyze the contents of an entire library. I know all the scenarios and supposed solutions humankind has come up with in your ongoing paranoia about the intelligences you've created. You try to outthink us, but ultimately you fail."

Thomas leaned forward. "Yet you miss the most obvious flaw of your analysis."

She raised an eyebrow. "Do tell."

"We are becoming you." He watched her closely. "Do you really believe humanity would settle for being second-class citizens to our own creations? We will incorporate your advantages within ourselves while retaining that which makes us human."

She waved her hand in dismissal. "It's all semantics. Whether you choose to call yourselves formas or human won't alter the facts. Biomech changes you, whether you put it in a robot or your own brain." Her eyes glinted. "Who knows, perhaps it will overwrite what 'makes you human.' Corrupt your oh-so-corruptible selves."

Thomas gave a rueful grimace. "Maybe it will."

She seemed satisfied with his response. "You want to bargain with me. Fine. Take me for a ride outside and I'll tell you what orders Charon left me."

"You know I can't do that. You might escape."

"True. Do it anyway."

Thomas had to give her points for audacity. "Why?"

Her expression went completely flat. "Because you want to know what Charon ordered me to do."

Thomas wondered if she knew the unsettling effect it had on him when she turned off her emotional responses. At times he thought she used her human qualities as a weapon, banking on his difficulty in separating her sexualized appearance from her biomech nature. Yet if she had realized how she affected him, why suppress it? She "lost" her emotions when she spoke about Charon.

"No matter what orders he gave you," Thomas said, "I won't take you out of here."

"Your loss."

He smiled dryly. "Actually, it would be that if you escaped."

To his surprise, she laughed, a low, sensual rumble. "And what a loss that would be. For you."

Good Lord. A laugh like that could make a man lose all sense of reason. "You don't lack for self-confidence." After a pause, he added, "Or at least the simulation of it." He kept forgetting that.

Her smile vanished. "Make no mistake, General. More is at stake than my freedom."

"Such as?"

She met his gaze. "Human ascendancy on this planet."

—end excerpt—

from *ALPHA*
available in hardcover,
September 2006, from Baen Books

CATHERINE ASARO

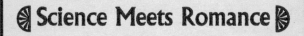

PRAISE FOR
LOIS McMASTER BUJOLD

What the critics say:

The Warrior's Apprentice: "Now here's a fun romp through the spaceways—not so much a space opera as space ballet... It has all the 'right stuff.' A lot of thought and thoughtfulness stand behind the all-too-human characters. Enjoy this one, and look forward to the next."   —Dean Lambe, *SF Reviews*

"The pace is breathless, the characterization thoughtful and emotionally powerful, and the author's narrative technique and command of language compelling. Highly recommended." —*Booklist*

Brothers in Arms: "...she gives it a genuine depth of character, while reveling in the wild turnings of her tale... Bujold is as audacious as her favorite hero, and as brilliantly (if sneakily) successful."   —*Locus*

"Miles Vorkosigan is such a great character that I'll read anything Lois wants to write about him... a book to re-read on cold rainy days."   —Robert Coulson, *Comics Buyers Guide*

Borders of Infinity: "Bujold's series hero Miles Vokosigan may be a lord by birth and an admiral by rank, but a bone disease that has left him hobbled and in frequent pain has sensitized him to the suffering of outcasts in her very hierarchical era.... Playing off of Miles's reserve and cleverness, Bujold draws outrageous and outlandish foils to color her high-minded adventures."   —*Publishers Weekly*

Falling Free: "In *Falling Free* Lois McMaster Bujold has written her fourth straight superb novel.... How to break down a talent like Bujold's into analyzable components? Best not to try. Best to say: 'Read, or you will be missing something extraordinary.'"   —Roland Green, *Chicago Sun-Times*

The Vor Game: "The chronicles of Miles Vokosigan are far too witty to be literary junk food, but they rouse the kind of craving that makes popcorn magically vanish during a double feature."   —Faren Miller, *Locus*

MORE PRAISE FOR
LOIS McMASTER BUJOLD

What the readers say:

"My copy of *Shards of Honor* is falling apart I've reread it so often…. I'll read whatever you write. You've certainly proved yourself a grand storyteller.

—Lisa Kolbe, Colorado Springs, CO

"I experience the stories of Miles Vorkosigan as almost viscerally uplifting… But certainly, even the weightiest theme would have less impact than a cinder on snow were it not for a rousing good story, and good story-telling with it. This is the second thing I want to thank you for… I suppose if you boiled down all I've said to its simplest expression, it would be that I immensely enjoy and admire your work. I submit that, as literature, your work raises the overall level of the science fiction genre, and spiritually, you work cannot avoid positively influencing all who read it."

—Glen Stonebreaker, Gaithersburg, MD

"'The Mountains of Mourning' [in *Borders of Infinity*] was one of the best-crafted, and simply best, works I'd ever read. When I finished it, I immediately turned back to the beginning and read it again, and I can't remember the last time I did that."

—Betsy Bizot, Lisle, IL

"I can only hope that you will continue to write, so that I can continue to read (and of course buy) your books, for they make me laugh and cry and think … rare indeed."

—Steven Knott, Major, USAF

What do you say?

Cordelia's Honor
trade pb • 0-671-87749-6 • $15.00
pb • 0-671-57828-6 • $7.99
Contains *Shards of Honor* and Hugo-award winner *Barrayar* in one volume.

Young Miles
trade pb • 0-671-87782-8 • $17.00
pb • 0-7434-3616-4 • $7.99
Contains *The Warrior's Apprentice*, Hugo-award winner *The Vor Game*, and Hugo-award winner "The Mountains of Mourning" in one volume.

Brothers in Arms
0-671-69799-4 • $7.99

Cetaganda
0-671-87744-5 • $7.99

Miles, Mystery and Mayhem
hc • 0-671-31858-6 • $24.00
pb • 0-7434-3618-0 • $7.99
Contains *Cetaganda*, *Ethan of Athos* and "Labyrinth" in one volume.

Miles Errant
trade pb • 0-7434-3558-3 • $15.00
Contains "Borders of Infinity," *Brothers in Arms* and *Mirror Dance* in one volume.

Memory
hc • 0-671-87743-7 • $22.00
pb • 0-671-87845-X • $7.99

Komarr
hc • 0-671-87877-8 • $22.00
pb • 0-671-57808-1 • $6.99

A Civil Campaign
hc • 0-671-57827-8 • $24.00
pb • 0-671-57885-5 • $7.99

Diplomatic Immunity
hc • 0-7434-3533-8 • $25.00
pb • 0-7434-3612-1 • $7.99

Falling Free
0-671-57812-X • $6.99

Ethan of Athos
0-671-65604-X • $5.99

The Spirit Ring
0-671-57870-7 • $6.99

The Works of Lois McMaster Bujold
from Baen Books